To Karma

What Goes Around Comes Around

Murder on Monarch Mountain: A Miner's Mystery

By

Pam Carothers

Catronaut Books
Buena Vista, Colorado

Credits

Cover & Title Page:

Modified version of: Currier & Ives, Gold Mining in California, from Library of Congress Prints and Photographs Division Washington, D.C. https://www.loc.gov/pictures/item/2001700204/

Back Cover:

Modified version of: Crystal Goodman, A Downtown Mural, from Library of Congress Prints and Photographs Division Washington, D.C. https://www.loc.gov/pictures/item/2014631397/

Modified version of: Carol M. Highsmith, Stagecoach, from Library of Congress Prints and Photographs Division Washington, D.C. https://www.loc.gov/pictures/item/2015632280/

About the Author Page:

Author's picture taken by Joshua Baker, Monarch Images Makers, PO Box 114 Poncha Springs, CO 81242, info@viewmyimages.com

Publisher's Data

Carothers, Pam
Murder on Monarch Mountain: A Miner's Mystery

Library of Congress Control Number: 2024925887
ISBN Number: 978-0-9893522-9-1

Printed in the U.S.A.

Acknowledgements

Throughout the story are characters from the history books, ones that I created, and members of the community, past and present. It is this last group that I would like to acknowledge, as they made it possible for this story to be told.

First, I want to thank the administration and staff at Monarch Mountain (23-24 Season) for their support, even letting me use their names as part of the story. Thanks also to Josh Baker, Monarch Images Makers, for taking the author's picture. I would especially like to thank Dan Bender, who helped me early on with the history of the Monarch Ski Area and connected me with Duane Vandenbusche, a retired Professor of History at Western State College who shared his book, *Images of America: Around Monarch Pass*, along with Brad Acres's *Monarch Ski Area: The Untold History*. I would like to thank both authors for their assistance.

I want to thank the following for giving me permission to use their names in my story. The two USFS Salida District Rangers do work in the positions named. Dan R is a local radio announcer on Hippie Radio.

I would also like to give a special thanks to the following for sharing their family histories. Craig Cardwell's granddad, Grady Cardwell, did encounter resistance when he staked his claims on Antero Mountain, but it was at a later date. Misti Cureton's and Doug Douglas's ancestor,

Peter Giebfried, owned a ranch at Clear Creek during the time of the story. Randy Loback's family ran a bakery in Buena Vista, but they came later. Len Chamberlain grew up in Wyoming on land that was part of the Oregon Trail. He shared how human bones were found by his dad using metal rods.

I would also like to thank Lindsey Lighthizer, owner of the Black Burro Bikes, for allowing me to use one of her burro stories. Mary Margaret is a local favorite in the pack burro races and has won the World Championship and the Triple Crown multiple times.

Thanks, too, to Jeff McGuinness and Kathi Perry at Aspen Leaf Printing & Office Supply and to Bob Dorenfeld for their help in setting up and printing files.

Though we live in a small town, the Buena Vista Public Library is a treasure. I am grateful for the helpful, friendly staff and outstanding facilities, which were instrumental in getting this book to print.

Finally, I would like to thank Jean Gabardi for her help with the editing. Her insights into storytelling were greatly appreciated.

Thanks to all. I hope you enjoy your story.

Murder on Monarch Mountain: A Miner's Mystery

A Lessons in a Story Book
From

Catronaut Books

Other Lessons In A Story Books
You Will Enjoy

The Last Launch: Liftoff
The Last Launch: The Mission
*Hiking Colorado: A Story and Pictorial Journal
of Hiking in the Colorado Rockies*
Full Moon Rising: The Coffin Point Mystery
The Ghost of Beaufort
The Young Firefighter: A Prairie Dog's Story
A Bike for Betsy

Contact Information
thelastlaunch@hotmail.com

PROLOGUE

arkness. All consuming. Cool, dry. The earthy odor permeated her senses. It was overwhelming. Why she wasn't scared, she did not know. She only knew that she had to find her way through the gloomy haze. Someone was near, trying to communicate; of that, she was sure. She navigated through—a tunnel, she assumed. Suddenly, a small light appeared in the far distance. She worked her way toward the beam. A ray of hope? The answer? To what? She got nearer, and the light was brighter. Almost there—

April abruptly woke up. It was still dark. The clock showed that it was only 3 a.m. "The light. I never saw that before." She drifted back to sleep.

When April woke again, she remembered the recurring dream that left her wanting to know more. It didn't leave her sweating and frightened, not as a nightmare would, but seemed to draw her into another world, another time. She sat up and petted her 19-year-old gray-and-white cat, Winston, who was stretched out on her bed.

"I haven't had *that* dream in a long time. It's funny how coming home brought it back."

April was visiting her family in Colorado while on her winter break. She had received a degree in geology from Montana State University, and she had stayed in Bozeman to finish her postgraduate work. When she came down for breakfast, her parents were waiting.

"Happy Birthday!"

Her dad presented her with a unique gift—a cedar box with native art carvings. "The box has been in the family for many years. It's given to the eldest on their 25th birthday. Since you're our one and only, it's yours."

April took the present. "It's beautiful!"

Her dad saw her puzzled look. "The Lakota Indians gave it to your ancestor, Lucky Doyle, when he was in the Black Hills."

April scanned the patterns that covered the sides of the intricate woodwork. "Why haven't I seen this before?"

"You have. You were too young to remember. It's very valuable, so we keep it in the safe." Her mom watched as she opened the top. "As you can see, the images on the inside are lined with silver and gold. They got the gold from the hillsides, but the silver probably came from melted-down coins."

"They tell a story. Let me explain." Her dad pointed to the pictures and told their meanings. "You start here. Do you see the pile of rocks? Shows the discovery of the gold. Then here, they use it in their pottery. The next set shows how strangers came, dug up the valuable ore, and destroyed the land. A battle ensued, and some were killed. In this last picture, they hide their cache and warn to keep its secret."

April's mom summarized the art's meaning. "They used the metals in their crafts, but after the 49ers came, they heard the stories and knew they had to protect their sacred grounds, so they decided to conceal the whereabouts of the gold."

"That's what happened. Once Custer verified that gold was in the Black Hills, their land was taken—land they had to fight for after being displaced from their original territory. There was already a lot of unrest back then. The coming of the emigrants only aggravated the situation, even united some tribes that were enemies. So why would they befriend my kin? And how'd he get this?"

Her dad retold what he remembered. "Your great-great-great-grandfather, Lucky Doyle, had been traveling all over the West, going from one mining camp to the next or just drifting and picking up work. He was in the Black Hills when Red Cloud's War was going on. I was told that he saved the life of a Lakota Sioux medicine woman, and in the process, he was bitten by a rattlesnake. He was brought to her village, and she cared for him. Some of their people knew our language, so he was able to communicate with them. While in their camp, he warned them of the coming of his people and the impending trouble. They already knew this, but his words showed his sincerity. They could see that he intended them no harm."

"He also helped when there was a ruckus with a small group of miners. In the ensuing battle, one of the miners aimed his rifle at their chief. Lucky shot and killed him. Before he left, the chief gave him the box. Your dad's father told us there was a special trinket inside. It had high-quality gems encased in a molded nugget of *pure gold.* I'm sure the piece was something else and worth quite a bit, but I doubt it was *pure* gold. I'd read that early attempts to use its pure form in coins failed because, under pressure, the coins lost their shape, and their printed surface got distorted. If heavily packed, they'd clumped together, so they were made into an alloy of gold and silver, or some other metal, to make the gold harder."

"My dad only repeated the story that was passed down to him. Maybe it wasn't 100% gold, but I'm sure it was up there. They must have known how to fit the gems into the soft piece so they'd stay in place. I was told it had green, red, and orange crystals and stones interwoven throughout the piece."

"The green was probably hiddenite, a type of spodumene; the red, garnet; and the orange, an agate," April guessed, remembering her geology. "These are found in the Black Hills."

"I knew we weren't wasting money on your education. Your geology classes have paid off," her mom joked.

"They must have *really* trusted...my *Greats Granddad* Lucky." April shortened the title, and all agreed it was an easier way to address their ancestor. "The nugget itself would've drawn a lot of attention, and with the adornments, it must have been quite a sight."

"They knew he wouldn't reveal the source of the gift. He'd already proven himself," her dad affirmed.

"So, what happened to the gold piece?" April didn't remember hearing about the nugget.

Her dad frowned. "Its whereabouts went to

the grave with your Greats Granddad Lucky. No one knows what happened to him. He just disappeared."

"I think I remember the story, but it's been a while," April admitted. "Can you tell it to me again?"

"We know that, in 1877, he was grubstaking. He was to check out a mine up the mountain and never came back. If he was murdered, no one knew where or by whom."

"We were told that he was happy at home and would never have deserted his family, so, most likely, it was foul play," her mom added. "People were crawling through every nook and cranny of the mountains then, and lawlessness was commonplace. Anyone could have been a suspect."

"Towns had to be incorporated or officially recognized before organized law enforcement was established. Lucky disappeared before the Monarch Mine existed, so most of this area had yet to be on the map," her dad told her. "Even Salida. The town wasn't established until 1880."

"When telling the story—for fun—we'd say that Lucky could have grubstaked Nicholas Creede. He was prospecting in the area at the time, and he did have partners. I'm not implying that Creede was the murderer, but before or after a meeting, something could've happened …while Lucky was on the road."

"Creede?" April had heard his name before. "Didn't he discover the Monarch Mine?"

"Yeah. From which the camp was eventually named…all the surrounding area, as well. Could have been Doyle's Mine, Doyle's Pass, Doyle's

Mountain, and even Doyle's Ski Resort," her dad laughed. "Has a nice ring, huh?"

"*Whatever*," April smirked. "So, why did he choose Monarch as the mine's name?"

"Your mother asked the same question. She even wrote a paper on the subject. I remember her talking about it when we first met."

"It was only for a high school class, but I tried to find an answer. I was stumped, so I proposed two theories of my own. The first one was based on something I'd read. He was a loner and used the term 'merry monarch' when describing himself once. Maybe he saw that he had the potential to be rich and could be the ruler of his destiny, and this first important discovery reflected that idea."

April was intrigued. "And the second theory?"

"He was a soldier who protected the railroad workers from Indian attacks, and Pawnee Scouts served under his command. They were just as eager to fight their common enemy—the Sioux. Creede learned their language and, most likely, their customs. The Pawnee respect all things of the earth, and Creede could have shared this belief. I read that he loved the prairie and the mountains. He was described as nature-loving. When he found such a rich rock and thought about what it implied, a monarch butterfly could have flown by. It was July. Wildflowers would have been displaying colors of their own."

"Makes sense," April confirmed, "but did they call butterflies monarchs back then?"

"Yes. Monarch was one of the common names that had been given to that butterfly by the early European settlers. They thought they were regal because of their striking colors. Though other names had also been used, that one stuck."

April wanted to read the report. "Do you still have the paper?"

"I wish I did, but no. I threw away the hard copy...all my floppy disks, for that matter. Technology had advanced so much, and I had other interests."

"You mean Dad!" April laughed. "Back to the trinket." She peered into the empty interior. "No clues? Any speculations?"

"Lucky had joked about it being his *lucky charm*, so it's likely he had it with him. If he *was* waylaid, the jewel was probably stolen," her dad surmised. "After that, who knows? It could've been broken up, and each gem sold separately, making it untraceable."

April reflected on her ancestor's story. "Lucky seemed to have lived a *charmed* life. He was *definitely* an interesting character."

"He was. Lucky's luck may have run out, but not before he had established our family line and settled in such a great location. Salida is a wonderful place to live." Her dad reached for the box. "Want me to put it back in the safe?"

April handed it over. "Please."

Her mother went to get some food from the refrigerator. "I've got fresh biscuits. If you want, I can also whip up bacon and eggs."

"Perfect. Thanks."

"So, April, what plans do you have for today?" her dad asked after looking out the window.

"I'm going skiing. I thought Judy might want to come, but she has a meeting she couldn't miss. We're getting together for an early supper, though."

"I heard Monarch had six inches of fresh snow last night. Looks like it's still snowing up there too. Should be a good powder day. Wish I could go with you, but I've got to get to work. See you later tonight. Happy Birthday!" Her dad gave her a hug before he left.

"Thanks again for the lovely heirloom!" April noted the time. "I need to get ready, too. I'll be back in a gif. The bacon sure smells delicious." April went to change into her skiwear.

After she left, her mom added the eggs to the pan, then went to turn up the radio. She caught the weather forecast. When April came back, she shared what she had heard over the breakfast table.

"Looks like we'll get more snow down here today. Dan R, on the Hippie, said another four inches...in Salida...more in the mountains. You should also expect high wind gusts."

"He's usually right. Thanks for the wonderful breakfast. I need to load the car, then get going. I should be back around one...one-thirty at the latest." April saw her mom's worried look. "I'll be careful," she promised before leaving.

There had been a lot of snowfall in the last few days. Even though the ski areas and the road crews monitored the weather situation, avalanches and blizzard conditions could cause havoc without warning. The mountains always had the last say.

The weather in Salida was twenty degrees. April expected colder temperatures at the resort. The strong wind shook her car as she headed toward Maysville. Once she reached the town of

Garfield, flakes were visible. In the short time that it took to reach the ski resort's parking lot, the snowfall had thickened and formed a white coat on the highway.

She recognized Pat, one of the Base Area Services workers, who was parking cars. His bright orange vest was dimmed by the falling snow. He directed her to a parking spot in the lower lot. She put on her boots and grabbed her skis. A skinner was already coming down the Gunbarrel run. I bet you've been here since daylight, April thought as she watched the skier maneuver around the etched moguls that had formed because others continuously followed the same path, causing the curves to deepen and the bumps to form.

She was carrying her skis across the lot when she saw a familiar face. "Hello, Mark."

"Hey. How's it going?"

"Must be working tickets today."

"Yeah. Filling in for a co-worker."

They reached the stairs that led to the lodge and the ski area. "Follow you up. I'm headed to Java for a quick cup of coffee before I hit the slopes." After they made the climb, April veered toward a nearby ski rack. "See you."

"Alright. I'll holler at you later." Mark turned left and headed to the lodge.

The coffee shop was busy, but when April reached the counter, Sydney, the barista, had her drink ready. "Monarch Mocha," she said and handed April the hot brew.

"It amazes me how you can remember what people order." April reached into her pocket to get her stashed cash.

"Repetition." Sydney replied as she took the payment.

"Well, if I were in your place, I would still struggle. Everyone looks different with their headwear on."

"I guess I've been doing it long enough," Sydney admitted.

April added some money to the tip jar. "Why you deserve *this*."

"Thanks." Sydney watched as Shayna, the Gunbarrel Supervisor, wrestled with the sliding door that closed off the Gunbarrel Grill area. She was coming out to bring food.

"Let me get that for you," April offered when she noticed that the door refused to budge.

Shayna was carrying a pan full of breakfast burritos, and it hindered her ability to tug the gate open. "Got it," she replied without looking to see who was offering help. After they got the door open, Shayna looked up. "Oh, April. Didn't know that was you. Thanks." They went to the coffee shop.

"How've you been?" April asked.

"Another day in paradise." Shayna placed the food into the warmer behind the counter.

"Isn't it always?" Matt, the Food and Beverage Manager had just come around the corner and had caught the tail end of their conversation. "Hey, April. A great day to be out."

"A bluebird day," April said with sarcasm. "Looks like you're busy already. I saw a delivery truck unloading as I came in."

"On my way down now. All good?" Matt asked his employees. When they gave a thumbs-up, he went to check on the delivery.

"I've got to run, too. Nice seeing you both." April nodded to Sydney. "Thank you."

She took the steaming brew to the lounge and sat in one of the leather chairs that faced the slopes. As she drank her coffee, she watched the lift operators, called lifties, as they prepared for the day. April recognized Helena and Dezmon. They were setting out barriers to separate the approach lanes for the Tumbelina Lift. Their coats were already covered with snow. Jacob, a young ski instructor that April knew, walked past the window.

Jack, the Senior Director of Guest Services, came into the lounge. "Good morning," he said when he saw April.

April turned away from the wintry scene. "Hey, Jack. How're you doing?"

"Great! We're getting lots of good powder. Should be fun out there."

"My kind of weather." April held up her cup. "Just need to get fueled first."

"I understand. Well, enjoy your day!" Jack headed toward his office.

"I will." April finished her drink. She saw the chairs of the lifts move, so she put her cup into the trash can, collected her skis and poles, and headed down the hill. When she reached the Garfield lift, she saw an old friend standing in line. "Hello, David."

"Hey, April. I see you're back in town. Got my nephew, Trent, with me today. Notice his Team Monarch jacket?"

"Your uncle and I were on the team many years ago, but David was a better competitor than I was."

"I was older, and you were new. In time, you held your own." David followed Trent to the red "load here" line.

"Nice seeing you...and meeting *you*, Trent," April got out before they were swept up the hill.

"Hi, April. How's it going?" the lift attendant asked when she approached the freshly swept red line.

"Hey, Tristan. Fine, thank you. Surprised you recognized me with all the headgear. How's your day going so far?" April sat in the revolving chair. It whisked her away before she could hear his answer.

April got off the lift. David and Trent had already disappeared. She skied down a blue intermediate run, Romp, then followed the cat track to the top of Sidewinder, a green beginner slope that was groomed. It was her favorite warm-up run. She wanted to get her leg muscles ready for the harder terrain ahead.

"The snow's great!" she heard someone say.

April slowly made her way down, carving out wide S-turns that formed a pattern like ribbon candy. She wanted to extend the time on this easier run. I love the feel of the powder under my skis and the sound that's made when I glide over the snowy surface, she thought as other skiers zoomed past her.

By the time she approached the lift for the second time, a line had formed, but the pace was steady. The lifts at Monarch had recently been upgraded with RFID technology. April wore her Season Pass in a pocket on her jacket's sleeve. When she got to the gate, the scanner detected the valid ticket and quickly opened. An older gentleman came up beside her. They moved forward until it was time to board.

"Having a good day?"

"Every day up here is a good day. The natural powder's so much better, not like what you get with the man-made stuff."

"I agree. That's one of the pros of skiing here." The cable carried them up the slope. "I'm headed to Tango, so I'll go left when we get off. How about you?"

"I'm sticking to the greens and blues. Think I'll head to Liberty. At eighty, you've got to be careful."

"Well, you sure don't look that old," April said before it was time to dismount.

April watched as the man gracefully skied ahead of her and hoped that she would be as conditioned when she reached his age. She saw the sign that announced her run and easily went down the black slope, zigzagging left and right to capture the moguls that had started to form.

Once downhill, April was ready for the more challenging runs that were across the mountain. She took the same chairlift so she could catch Sleepy Hollow, a fun green that led to Pinball, a short black that would get her to Panorama, a lift in the middle of the resort. Several harder blacks, or difficult runs, could be accessed from this lift. It didn't take long to reach the loading zone, and with only one other skier waiting for the ride up, she didn't have to wait in line.

April decided to take some turns on Mirage, a groomed black run. The gusty wind blew her chair sideways, and the snow fell around her in circular swirls, so she pulled up her buff to protect the small portion of her face that was still exposed. She knew her layers of clothing would keep her core warm. She also had hand and foot warmers in her gloves and boots.

The run brought her back to the Panorama lift. April felt she was ready for more challenging opportunities, so when she was brought back up to the top, she went to the right until she saw the sign for High Anxiety. She made the leap of faith over the edge and ripped down the steep slope. She saw a young snowboarder ahead of her fall. When he stood up, he was covered in snow. He looked like a snowman.

April went to offer aid. "Are you *all right*?"

The boarder brushed away the powder. "Still learning. First time on this particular black. It's a bit harder than I expected. I'll get down, but it won't be pretty."

"Glad you weren't hurt. Can I *help*?"

"Thanks, but I'm fine." The boy looked at his board. "Thought I had this mastered. Have yet to fall when getting off the lifts, *at least*."

"Don't be discouraged. The soft powder can be deceptive. You can't tell what's underneath it, and *that* can throw you off."

"You seem to know your stuff."

"Grew up here. Been doing this for quite a while...since I was *five*. My mom taught me."

"Skiing must run in your family."

"Many generations. My great-great-granddad skied around these parts before Monarch was even built."

"You're lucky. I'm from the Springs, so I don't get out as much as I'd like. I started boarding a year ago, and I'm just now getting it down."

"Takes a lot of practice...and patience."

"So I've learned. I'm definitely not ready for the big leagues. Did you enter the contest they were having today? I heard it was some local racing event."

"The Town Challenge? No. I used to compete ...when I was younger. I'm not very competitive anymore." April remembered her conversation with David. "I was on Team Monarch when I was a kid. But now, skiing is a recreational pastime. I'm what I call a *fading* ski bum."

"It's *sick* just being on the mountain. Well, thanks for stopping, but I shouldn't hold you up any longer."

"No problem. Enjoy the day!"

"I'll let you go first."

April knew that he wanted to have an open slope. "At least the snow has stopped for now. Should be easier to see ahead. Nice talking with you."

The conditions are perfect, April thought as she sailed over the snow. Time was slipping by, so she made her way to the Breezeway lift. She used the momentum gained from the steeper terrain to keep her speed so she wouldn't have to use her poles when passing the flatter area at the base of the Panorama Lift. She glided past the towers and headed to the lower part of the mountain, where the other lift started.

"Hello, Jeremy," April said when she saw the liftie shoveling snow.

"Hi, April. Which run are you headed for?"

The chair rounded the pulley, and she got on.

"Upper Hall's Alley," she got out before she was taken up the slope.

Since the run ran under the lift, April was able to see its condition as she was pulled to the top of the hill. Because she usually worked her way to Geno's Meadows, a black that ran through the trees, she wasn't too concerned with the lower, blue section of the run and was glad to see moguls had started in the tougher, upper section. She got off the lift and started down the slope. The riders on the lift above her watched as she zoomed down and around the fluffy moguls that parted like cotton candy when she skied across their tops.

"They will be less forgiving this spring," April mumbled. She remembered a time when she misjudged a turn and plowed into the side of an icy mound. She thought her skis would split when the tough mogul didn't give.

"April!" someone shouted. By the time she looked up, the caller had been carried too far along for her to see who it was.

"Have a good run?" Jeremy asked when April returned for a second ride up the lift.

"It was great. The snow's so soft and smooth. Now it's time for Mirkwood."

Jeremy bumped the chair, or held it briefly, so it wouldn't hit April before she was safely seated. "Have fun!"

Only experienced skiers or snowboarders went to Mirkwood, the backcountry section of the resort. April was ready for the challenge of this extreme terrain. As she neared the top of the lift, a gust of wind blew her chair out to the side. I bet Breezeway will be closed soon. At least I'll get up before then. She decided to do the Orcs run in case the weather got ugly.

April got off the lift and skied to the base of the hill that led up to Mirkwood. She took off her skis for the twenty-minute walk up to the towering archway. She was the only one at the top of the basin. By the time she had her skis back on, the clouds had dropped and were releasing a thick blanket of snow that was whirling around with the wind.

"Oz!" she exclaimed. She enjoyed the cold, blustery conditions that, for most, would be too harsh to endure. As she made her way to the start of the run, the wind suddenly picked up, and the blizzard drastically decreased visibility. April followed the ridge. "I know the start of Orcs is free of trees. It's just, I'm not sure how far I need to go," she voiced as the wind howled.

April was caught in a whiteout. Thinking that she had made it to the run, she started down the slope. She hit an unexpected bump, a deeply carved mogul that was hidden by the thickening powder, which caused her to glide out of control. She fell to keep from hitting an oncoming tree. The maneuver caused her to roll head over heels and to slide headfirst down the steep grade. Her skis popped off, but they followed her path. She stopped at the edge of a group of trees.

"I'm good!" she instinctively confirmed as she popped up from the snow. April looked around but was unclear about her surroundings. She adjusted her goggles, which had loosened during the spill. "Huh. Must not have gone far enough. Maybe I'm near Mirkwood Trees or Staircase," she said in reference to two runs that veered off into the woods. The wind blew harder. "The gusts are *really* crazy." She put on her skis. "This doesn't look right," she told the ghostly face that had formed on a mound of snow that was perched on a pine branch. "I know I'll find a way out if I keep going down, though." April slowly moved through the trees. A large pile of rocks loomed ahead, so she stopped. I hope I haven't cliffed out. Maybe I should walk around and see if this is the best way to go. After she released her second binding and started to move forward, a strong gust of wind blew, pushed her onto a large tree, and pinned her against its trunk.

April's impact was the final straw for the old pine that had already been leaning downhill. It gave. As the fierce wind continued to push, the heavy evergreen took a couple of smaller ones down with it. The conglomerate mass made a mangled mess.

Who...osh. Cr...rack. The falling tree did make a sound in the forest.

April heard the eerie, ghostlike noise above the roar of the wind and tried to move, but as the tree fell, its roots popped out, pulling rocks and other debris in its wake. The unstable ground caused April to flounder, so she knelt down and fought to keep her balance. When the trembling finally stopped, she tried to stand, but she lost her footing and slipped.

"Arrgh!" April gasped as she fell backward into a newly exposed cavity of an old miner's dig. A tree well, she thought before falling into the abyss.

She hit flat on her back, and when her head came to rest, it struck the side of a rock. She felt something touch her, but before she could scream, she lost consciousness. April was not alone. She had fallen on top of the sprawled extension of an old pile of bones—an ancient skeleton. When she landed, its left arm rose up, and the hand fell on her hip. It embraced her, as if to keep her safe.

PART ONE

The Way West

1859

CHAPTER 1

"It's an itch I can't scratch. Come west with me Sam," Lucky pleaded with his older brother for the umpteenth time.

"Ya know I've yet ta make up my mind. I'll give ya my answer, Lucky Doyle, when I know myself. Now leave it be!"

Lucky knew his older brother was serious when he heard him use his full name. He knew to drop the subject. No, now's not the time to push him, Lucky realized. But soon.

Though Sam was the elder of the two, it was his younger brother who often pulled the strings. Lucky was curious and outgoing, an Irish charmer who got himself into, and just as quickly, out of, many a fix. His name was a testament to the Irish luck that had brought him into the world. His early arrival caused complications. When he was born, he didn't cry or show any sign of life.

"He's too tiny." The doctor wrapped the baby and placed him inside a bassinet that sat on the table. "I'm afraid the wee one didn't—" He was interrupted by a soft cry.

"Look!" The newborn's father saw his son, who had been lying so still, stir. "He's movin'!"

The bystanders were in tears, first of sorrow, then of joy.

"Well, I'll be! I didn't think he'd made it. You

sure got *lucky* with that little *fighter*."

His dad gently picked up his gurgling boy and repeated the doctor's sentiment. "We are *lucky*." He handed the cooing bundle to his mom.

She stared into his baby blue eyes. "Lucky! That's what we'll call him."

What the small child lacked in stature, he made up for in spirit. His inquisitive nature often got him into sticky situations. Someone usually had to come to his rescue.

"Ya wild, freckle-faced redhead!" his mom would yell after she had gotten him out of one predicament or another. One day, she saw him by the fence with his finger in a knothole. "Ya stuck again?" On another occasion, she found him in the cellar, and he couldn't get back up the stairs. "Ya need someone ta come git ya?"

Lucky would climb up trees, only to find that he couldn't get down. "Ya was lucky I was here ta help this time, but one of these days—" His dad abruptly stopped, hoping his words wouldn't ring true. He continued to reprimand the rambunctious child. "Someone won't always be thar ta rescue ya."

Years later, when they were at the dinner table, Sam decided to expose his brother's latest ruse. "Whar'd ya git tha rockin' horse?"

"Ya know. You was thar."

"Well then, how 'bout lettin' *us* know?" his dad probed.

Lucky recalled how easily he made the swap. His face beamed with pride. "Traded for it."

"What'd ya *trade* this time?" his mom asked.

"Gave Stevie all my marbles." Lucky hung his head. He knew what was coming.

"Did he believe they had *magical qualities*?" Before Lucky could respond, he added his usual reply. "Give it back." He inwardly laughed at his son's persuasive powers. "You could talk a leprechaun into givin' away his pot of gold." He knew his son could trick most people out of their possessions.

Sam snickered as Lucky was scolded. He had heard it all before.

"But..." Lucky pouted.

"Ya heard yar Papa!" His mother's tone left no doubt that the discussion was over.

"Ya should've listened ta me," Sam chirped. "*Told ya.*"

Lucky sneered. "I'd never git anywhere if'n I followed yar advice. Yar too practical."

Lucky knew his older brother well. Sam was realistic. He took after his sensible, sweet-faced mother. Both possessed a homey demeanor. His hair was red, not fiery like his brother's, but more subdued and leaned toward blonde. His cherubic face had a smooth complexion. He had a calm, soft-spoken manner until he got mad or passionate about something; then, like a volcano, he'd erupt and show an inner strength that was as tough as a polecat. He rarely got into trouble, but when he did, his little brother was usually involved.

❦ ◆ ❦ ◆ ❦

The 1850s were nearing their end. As Lucky waited for Sam to make his decision, others had already been on the move, paving the way to the goldfields. The financial panic of 1857, along with the growing population in the East, left many uncertain about their future, so they joined the crowd and went to find "new digs" of their own.

The migration had started slowly. The early travelers were explorers, missionaries, farmers, trappers, and miners. They used horses, mules, burros, oxen, and wagons to get across the country. Many even walked. The emigrants came to farm, to sell goods, to prospect, or to get away. Some were drifters, moving with the flow. They headed to the new lands, ones that offered wealth or solitude. Most sought to reach the Far West, but many stopped short and started their new lives far from their original destinations. A good number had to turn back and return to their homes, discouraged and broken.

The first travelers faced many hardships. Routes were often sketchy. Animals were lost. Diseases and other maladies took many lives. Disturbing behaviors surfaced. As the stories circulated, the risks became known, but many made it to the end, and their adversity turned into achievement. Families wrote back, telling about the rich soils and the unlimited business opportunities. The promise of a prosperous life was procured, and dreams were fulfilled, so the expeditions continued, and the idea of Manifest Destiny prevailed.

Western ranges were the targets of this mass movement. The sweeping prairies, plains, and mountains, once open to all, were being claimed and plotted. Who really owned the land would be extensively debated and would forever remain the subject of much controversy.

The indigenous people would be the most

affected by this new crusade. They had created territories of their own and fought to keep them. They had learned how to survive in the harsh conditions that changed with the seasons and had lived in harmony with their environment for many generations. When the early explorers came, the groups traded with each other and shared their respective knowledge, but this peaceful exchange would not last. The gradual influx of newcomers dramatically changed when one word echoed across the nation and altered the West forever.

CHAPTER 2

Gold!

Four letters. A shiny metal. On the Periodic Table, it is written as Au, aurum—the Latin term for gold. The element is naturally colored yellow and can be found in its native state unattached to other minerals. It is soft and malleable, so it can easily be made into coins or jewelry. This rare, unique mineral, soon to be found in quantity, would bring out the best and the worst in mankind.

The great gold rush started with a find in California. The year was 1848. A small nugget was found by a man named Marshall, a sawmill builder. The location was at the base of the Sierra Nevada Mountains, near Coloma, where the South Fork of the American River flowed. It did not take long for the news to spread, and by 1849, the rush was underway. The gold, seemingly plentiful in the rivers, was easy to extract. The 49ers, as the wave of prospectors migrating west were called, left their farms, homes, and sweethearts. Many never returned.

Within years, as the gold was sought and claimed, the initial hotbeds started to peter out, but the fever continued as other, more prosperous strikes popped up and kept the movement alive.

"Gold at yar fingertips. Come with me Sam,"

Lucky pleaded again. He had just read another account of the golden riches within reach for any adventurer. "Tha wagon in tha accompanyin' picture is speakin' ta us—Pikes Peak or Bust!"

"What makes ya believe such writin's?" Sam countered. "If'n it's too good ta be true…"

"I know," Lucky agreed. "But it's like…it's sort of a message…that it's *time* ta go."

"An' git away from all this potato plantin' ya love so much, I gather."

"No…well…*yeah*…ta do somethin' *different* with our lives…not ta be rooted…"

"Like tha potatoes?" Sam finished Lucky's thought.

"Yeah. So, what do ya say? Shall we start an adventure of our own?"

Before Sam could answer, their folks walked into the room.

"Just *what* are you boys up to?" their mother asked as she entered the parlor. "Ya look like you've had yar hand in tha cookie jar."

"More like bears caught in tha cropper." Their dad grabbed the newspaper from Lucky.

Sam was caught off guard. "Mum. Papa." He looked at Lucky.

"Just hype. Sure has taken over reasonable thought," their father scoffed after seeing the headline that had drawn Lucky's attention.

Neither of us wants to say that we believe the propaganda, well, halfway, Lucky thought, but we want to chase after gold too, he affirmed before speaking aloud. "*Know* what yar thinkin', but thars some truth ta tha stories. Take Mr. Ryan. He was able ta buy a proper farm with tha money he brought back."

"One of tha few. Don't forget 'bout Mr. Moore. He's yet ta return," his dad retorted.

"More left thar homes deserted an' thar crops partially planted. Sure, they left in good faith, but when they did come back, they were worse off," his mom reminded him.

"They were tryin' ta make thar livin' situation better," Lucky said in their defense.

Their mother pointed out more drawbacks to the rush. "Accordin' ta what I've been readin', many have succumbed ta tha elements, or ta some disease, or ta tha violence in tha lawless minin' camps."

"I agree. Tha stories either romanticize or expose tha ugliness brought on by tha greed. It's hard ta know tha truth. But me an' Sam were of tha mind...we thought that...well, we may wanna see which of 'em stories are true," Lucky stammered.

Sam quickly countered. "Hold on! I didn't say I *would*!"

Lucky looked at his older brother. "You didn't say *no*!"

"Whoa! Now wait." Their mother was taken off guard by this revelation. "Just w*here* is this goin'?"

"If'n we went, we'd be different. We're young. We don't have tha same attachments," Lucky justified. "Nor as much ta lose."

"Before this conversation goes further," their dad interjected, "we all need ta think rationally."

Lucky quickly continued. "We're old enough ta go out on our own. Ya still have Connor an' Jacob ta help out with tha farm...an' Jamie ta help 'round tha house. It's not big enough for all of us, anyway. If'n we go...there'll be more for everyone."

"Now, ya hold it right there," their mom cut in. "If'n ya boys want more room, we can add ta tha back. An' there's always been plenty for everyone."

"That's *not* what I meant." Lucky hated that he made his mom feel guilty because of their living situation. He tried to explain. "It's just... I've had this itch ta see other places. I want ta do somethin' different with my life. Not sure farmin' is for me."

"No one wants ya ta stay if'n ya have a mind ta do somethin' else," his dad assured him. "I've known 'bout yar wanderin' ways, boy." He looked at his other son. "Do ya wanna go as well?" Sam hesitated. "Now don't let yar little brother talk ya into somethin' ya don't wanna do."

"Reckon I've a wanderin' mind sometimes too," Sam admitted. "Never thought it'd be this soon, but if'n Lucky's ready ta move on, then I reckon I'll go with 'im."

Lucky was so happy to hear his brother's response that he rushed to his side to show a united front. He knew that when their parents saw this bond, they would have to accept the inevitable—their oldest boys were leaving the family homestead, possibly never to return. The thought made Lucky sad, but the euphoria of the moment brought excitement, too.

The expressions on his sons' faces said it all. "Now, don't git cocky!"

His words broke in on Lucky's thoughts. "Ya mean?"

Their dad relented. "Yeah. Yar 16, an' Sam's just shy of 18. Reckon yar old enough ta make up yar own minds. Just know, tha journey will be dangerous. You'll need ta take heed an' watch yarselves every minute."

Their mother gave a shrug of resignation. "An' never feel that ya can't come back. This will *always* be yar home."

The brothers cheered when they got their parents' approval. They embraced and jumped up and down with bliss. Sam's foot caught on the leg of a chair, and he lost his balance. The boys fell to the floor, laughing with joy.

CHAPTER 3

They started out like many of the others of the time, eager and full of hope. Their parents made sure they had enough supplies and money for the start of their journey. Before Lucky and Sam mounted their horses, their mom handed each of them a Double Eagle gold coin.

"Put 'em inside yar shirts...in tha hidden pocket I stitched for ya." She gave her boys a last hug. "Thar not for wastin'. Use 'em only if'n thars an emergency."

"Thanks, Mum." They were both near tears. Leaving was harder than they thought.

The two older brothers gave their younger siblings a hug. "Love ya!" they echoed.

"Take good care of tha place," Sam said to Connor. "An' don't tease yar lil sister," he told Jacob, then he smiled at Jamie.

"Yar ta have money waitin' for ya when ya git ta Independence," their dad told them. "I'll git tha draft wired today."

"Don't go flashin' yar money 'round, once ya git it," their mom warned.

"We'll hide it too," Sam assured her.

"Look after Bullet an' Lindy. Thar good horses an' should git ya far." Their dad gave them a hug, then they said their final farewells.

"Californ-i-a or *bust!*" Lucky whooped after

they were out of sight of their home. He had adapted his own version of the "Pikes Peak or Bust" cry that had made the headlines after gold was discovered in the Kansas Territory the previous year. Sam joined in the hollering.

The boys had little trouble as they worked their way west. They rode until they reached St. Joseph, Missouri, where they got passage on a riverboat that was headed to Independence. This was the stopping point for many, who would then join a wagon train. From here, travelers would have to traverse a large section of unorganized territory, the Great American Desert. This land was a wide, open expanse full of danger. The region would later become the states of Nebraska, Colorado, Wyoming, and Kansas, but in 1859, it was a harsh, barren barrier—Indian Territory—that had to be crossed to reach the rich lands of the "Far West."

"We're *here*. Independence!" Lucky whistled with excitement as they debarked from the boat.

"Never seen such activity." Sam tied his horse to the hitching post that was in front of the bank. He followed Lucky inside.

After they got their money, they went to get their horses. Before they untied them, a gust of wind blew sand in their faces. Sam spat out the dirt. "Feels like we're in a *dust devil*."

Lindy whinnied her agreement.

"Just need somethin' ta wash tha grit outta our throats, is all," Lucky observed. "Ya see tha swingin' doors? Let's head that way."

They led their horses to the nearest trough and let them drink. Then, they tied them up to the railing in front of the watering hole. They entered the noisy saloon and pushed their way through the crowd to the counter. Elk antlers hung on each side of an ornately framed mirror that reflected the madness inside the building. The room rang with the loud talk of gold. One spot opened at the congested bar, giving Sam access to the busy barkeep.

The bartender took his order and placed two beers on the counter. "Three bits each."

Normally, establishments charged one bit, 12.5 cents, or two bits, 25 cents, per drink, but beer prices had escalated once the business owners realized that they could take advantage of the multitudes migrating west.

Sam sneered at the bartender as he handed over his coins. "Have ya noticed that tha prices *rise* as ya go *west*?" he asked loud enough for those around him to hear.

Lucky responded in an equally loud voice. "Yeah. Everyone's got tha *fever*, an' it's not just 'bout findin' *gold*. It's out 'n' out robbery tha way tha *merchants* are overchargin'."

Though the bartender ignored the remarks, the man beside Sam loudly agreed. "Hear, hear!" He raised his glass. Others in the bar joined in the toast. The man turned to face Sam. "For all tha price raisin', they *still* serve us warm beer."

"They need ta keep it in tha cellar longer."

"Need men like ya ta be shopkeepers."

"Would give proper service if'n I did."

"Whar ya comin' from?" Lucky asked.

"Californie. Ya think price gougin' is bad here, just wait. It's rampant thar, too. Ta me, it's stealin'. May be called by a different name, but it's *stealin'* just tha same."

Sam looked at Lucky. "Gonna cut inta tha amount of supplies we're ta have as we work our way 'cross tha continent. If'n I ever run a shop, I'd not take advantage like that an' mark tha prices up so."

Lucky saw men vacating a table. "Join us?" he asked the stranger as he grabbed Sam's arm and pulled him away from the bar.

"Reckon I could sit a spell."

After they sat down, Sam started to question the prospector. "Did ya *find* any gold?" He was anxious to hear from an experienced miner.

"Sum, but 'twas tough goin'. Had ta push my way just ta git onta tha river. Then held my own, 'cause if given tha chance, sumun woulda pushed me outta my place. Panned from sunup ta sundown, then froze ta keep my spot durin' tha night. Tha riverbed usually got panned out after a few days. I could only stand it for that long, anyways, then we'd move on ta another spot an' try again."

"How'd ya know *where* ta go?" Lucky had no concept of the spatial distribution of the gold.

"Most couldn't hide thar excitement, an' thar shoutin' told tha story. Rumors often proved ta be true. Just had ta follow tha mass migration of miners."

"What was it like...tha pannin'?" Sam didn't know what to expect.

"Tha bendin' an' stoopin' hurt my back an' knees. My hands an' feet were wet an' cold... an' tha naggin' hunger...couldn't leave ta git ta my horse. Hardest work I ever done."

"Heard they found more'n just dust when

pannin' on tha rivers. Are thar nuggets for tha takin' too?" Lucky hoped the stories were true.

"Only if yar first ta tha find. If ya git sum, ya had ta watch yarself...have yar pistol ready. Didn't trust tha man next ta me not ta take it away...at any cost. Too many were slippery snakes ready ta strike. Kept my pouch inside my shirt tha whole time."

Lucky and Sam instinctively put their hands over the stitched pockets their mom had sewn inside their own shirts. They gave each other brotherly looks.

"Whar ya goin' next?" Lucky asked.

"Home. I've had enough." The miner thought about the family he had left behind. "Farmin's not so bad...compared ta what happened out thar. Barely scraped enough ta live on, let alone ta bring back ta my family." He lied to downplay the amount of gold concealed in his clothing. He had been one of the first to arrive at several goldfields. He had done well.

Sam finished his drink. "We're still eager ta give it a try. Any advice?"

"Yar 'bout ta be tested. Gittin' thar is gonna be tough, an' tha terrain is gonna be rough. Beware of tha bandits. They'll steal an' kill with even more tenacity than tha Indians." He looked at the young, innocent-looking boys. "Join up with others. Makes ya less of a target. Maybe ya should hook up with a wagon train. Then, you'll have sumun 'round ta help ya out."

"Thanks for tha heads-up. We'll be expectin' tha worst an' hopin' for less. We're ready ta face what comes our way with our eyes open," Lucky assured the man.

"Yar young'uns...know thars no changin' yar minds, but I've *got* ta say it. Go back ta whar ya come from. An' if ya don't...*watch yar backs.* I was waylaid once. Lucky ta have escaped with my life. Didn't even have anythin' worth stealin' then. They don't care. Theys sees ya, an' wants what ya got."

The prospector's words left the young boys more circumspect in their expectations. They left the establishment and found a place to order food. While there, they found out what they already knew—the gold in the streams was quickly getting depleted, but new finds were still being reported.

"Talked with some fellows who'd just come from Coloma," Sam stated after they left the diner. "Most of tha panners have moved on. Still wanna head out thar?"

"No need ta decide just yet."

"Yeah. Why don't we figure our way outta here, first? We can hear what others have ta say, then make a decision 'long tha way."

"Have my heart set on goin' ta California. I'd like ta see whar it all began."

"That prospector was right. We know nothin' of what's ahead, an' it'd be foolish ta travel alone from here."

"Kinda feel like we'd be sittin' ducks. We wouldn't know if'n tha Indians were peaceful or at war, either."

The boys were contemplating their next move when they saw a man set up a table in front of a mercantile store. He posted a crudely written sign.

Lucky could barely discern the words "Men

Wanted" in the chicken scratch. "Let's see what that's all 'bout."

When they arrived, a man, sitting on a stool, rose and offered his hand. He had a friendly grin. "Howdy fellas. Name's Tincup. Be needin' help for our wagon train. We're takin' tha Oregon Trail ta tha Willamette Valley. Leavin' in 'bout a week. Interested?"

They took in the character before them. He had gray-spotted whiskers that ran down to the middle of his chest. Only a few teeth were visible when he smiled. He was a stocky, older man, and when he stood up, he was taller than he appeared. He wore clothes that made him look like a cowboy ready to call steps for a square dance.

"Maybe. What would we do?" Lucky replied.

Tincup explained the operation of a wagon train and the work needed to keep it rolling. "Ya probably heard 'bout tha difficulties tha past trains had. Don't need ta worry so much now. Tha route's improved...well-used. Tha wagon master has experience. He's taken other trains 'cross...done so many times."

Sam looked at his brother and shrugged his shoulders. "How 'bout *Indians*?"

"I'll be up front with ya, boy. Thars been *sum* trouble...more'n we've had in tha past, but tha forts have been fortified ta help with uprisin's."

"Reckon we can't blame 'em for wantin' ta hang onto thar way of livin'," Sam noted.

"Tha country's growin'. Not sure what's tha best way ta share it. We're changin' tha rules on 'em."

"An' it's all happenin' so fast." Lucky knew

it wasn't looking good for the native people who originally settled in the West.

"We can only hope thars a *fair* solution in tha end," Tincup confessed. "Tha western part of tha country won't stay wild much longer. Newer an' easier trails have been blazed, an' tha covered wagons have been improved. With each successful crossin', tha cry ta "go west" is heard by both men an' women alike."

The explorers who made this journey were called argonauts, overland travelers, emigrants, pioneers, and sodbusters. They knew the risks, but they were willing to take them. Regrettably, the settlers, in their passing, wiped out the wildlife and trampled the water holes. They introduced new and deadly diseases. At first, the changes happened slowly, but as the flood of emigrants prevailed, the situation only got worse.

This mass movement created hardships for the Indians, as they were called, and changed their way of living. The prairies, plains, and mountains that had been under their domain were starting to be ruled by a new master, one who sought to take at any cost, one who wanted to conquer the land and to make it yield to their will. War, as a defense, was inevitable and ultimately futile.

After taking time to reflect, Tincup continued. "*Sure*, it's *still* a tough go...will be, all 'long tha way...'til we git ta tha end. Somethin' ya wanta take on?"

Lucky was about to give a response, but he was distracted. The door of the saloon swung open, and a man was thrown out. He fell onto the street with a loud thud and lay sprawled out on the dusty surface. A carriage rounded the corner and headed for the ousted drunk. The driver tried to slow his horses, but they were coming upon the man too quickly.

Lucky waved his hands and ran ahead of the team. "Whoa!" he yelled, hoping the wagon would veer off in a different direction.

CHAPTER 4

While Lucky was diverting the wagon, Sam headed toward the limp body. He grabbed the man's leather boot and pulled him away just as the stampeding horses sped by.

"That was *close*," Lucky huffed when he met up with Sam.

"Ya slowed tha team enough ta give me tha time I needed."

"Always said we make a *good team*."

The befuddled man groaned and started to move. "What happened?"

"Ya *'bout* got run over. My brother dragged ya outta tha way." Lucky picked up the man's hat and handed it to him.

"Don't remember bein' out on tha ground. How'd I git here?"

"You was thrown from tha saloon." Sam tried to lighten the mood. "Seems ya *displeased* someone in thar."

The man rubbed his forehead. "Oh yeah. An ol' fur trapper I used ta hang with. He's meaner than a bear. Reckon I oughta *thank ya* fer helpin'. Name's Argent." He slowly got up and offered an unsteady hand for Sam to shake. "Ever needin' *anythin'*, I'd be obliged ta help ya out." He put on his hat, then weaved his way down the street.

The boys went back to Tincup's table. "Yar

quickness saved ol' Argent. He's been throwin' 'round some gold dust...musta struck it big, but he drank up most of what he had. Be tha end of 'im yet."

"Reckon he's meant ta live another day." Lucky untied his bandana and wiped his brow. "We're interested in workin' for ya, but got a few more questions. How big's yar train, an' what *particular* job did ya have in mind for us?"

"We got 30 wagons, which means we'll have just over a hundred emigrants in our care... plus tha crew. You'll wear many hats, but you'll mainly help with tha stock, load supplies, help tha teamsters, an' do whatever else comes up. You'll git standard pay, an' if'n ya make it tha *whole* way, we'll give ya a *bonus*."

Lucky got the nod from Sam. "Ya got yarself two new hands. I'm Lucky, an' he's my brother, Sam."

The wagon master had watched the heroic rescue through the store window. He paid his bill, then came out to meet the boys. He was a tall, middle-aged man. His face, wrinkled beyond his years, sported a clean-shaven mustache and goatee. His salt-and-pepper hair was thinning but still showed under his broad-rimmed hat. He wore an air of authority—one that was earned, not brought on by wealth.

He introduced himself to the boys. "Call me Banks. Are you interested in joining up?"

"Yes sir. We're good at huntin'...an' we'd be useful...helpin' anyway we can," Sam boasted.

"Have you worked with cattle or sheep? We're needing someone who can handle stock."

"We're diggers. Come from a potato farm, but

we're quick learners." Lucky bragged. "We're pretty good riders too."

Banks wanted to see how committed the boys were. "Why do you want to go west?"

Sam looked at Lucky. The ball was in his court for this answer. Would they be taken in if they were just driftless prospectors looking for gold? he wondered.

"Like tha others on yar train, we're seekin' a new life. Our family farm can only support so many. We wouldn't mind tryin' our hand at a number of jobs, not excludin' prospectin'."

Sam tried to diffuse Lucky's last words. "We heard thar were lots of opportunities out west, an' we wanted ta find out for ourselves."

Banks could see that they were young and strong. They were eager for adventure but, at the same time, unaware of what lay ahead. He knew they didn't have the experience he was looking for, but they had qualities he favored.

"It's going to be a hard crossing. Though the Kansas Territory was mapped in '54, the region's still a wasteland...up to the Rocky Mountains. As hard as that passage is, the real test will come later. We'll have to cross two deserts, then get over the Sierra Mountains. By then, every man and beast will have reached their limit and will still be called upon to find their last ounce of strength. If they *still* have the *will* to go on... then, and maybe then, will we reach the end."

"Yes sir. We didn't expect it ta be easy," Sam said after hearing the dark report.

"Why workin' for ya makes sense ta us," Lucky reassured him. "We'd already decided not ta go it alone."

"Saw what you did for that man in the street. Took courage. What I look for in a man. You're *just* boys...but you're *hired*," Banks decided. "What provisions did you bring with you?"

"Just what we have on our horses. Will we need a wagon?" Lucky was relieved that their passage was set.

"I'll keep you busy on your horses. You can store your stuff with mine."

"When do we start?" Sam asked.

"We'll be getting supplies tomorrow morning. Meet Tincup at the mercantile...the one down the street...at nine?" Banks looked at Tincup for confirmation.

"Yes sir." Tincup pointed to an old, weathered wagon. "That's our setup in front of tha store by tha dressmaker's shop. As you can see, it's been 'round tha block a time or two, but we've got a strong team ta keep it movin'."

"See ya tomorrow mornin'. Come on, Sam, let's git tha horses bed an' fed, then we can git a room for tha night."

"Did ya try ta scare tha boys off, tellin' 'em 'bout how tha trip *used* ta be?" Tincup asked Banks after the boys had left. "Ya know it's not as bad...just different now."

"Yeah, but they're young. They need to be prepared. The trip's *still* tough, even with the changes. You never know what we'll be facing. Anything can happen on any given day. You know that."

Lucky and Sam arrived at the appointed spot the following morning. Tincup was not in sight. They saw another man waiting by the wagon.

"Y'all must be tha new hands Banks was

tellin' me 'bout. Call me Davis. I'm tha train's scout."

"Sam, an' he's my brother, Lucky."

"Ya work with a wagon train afore?"

"No. We're lookin' forward ta tha challenge, though," Lucky answered.

"You'll find *that* early enough," Davis smiled, and then he headed down the road.

Tincup came up carrying two bags of flour. "See ya met Davis. He's Banks's right-hand man. Both are good, honest men. Thar tough. Banks fought in tha Mexican-American War... was a ranking officer. He graduated from West Point, but he never mentions nothin' 'bout 'em days. Prefers not ta use titles. Follow me. Ya can git tha cornmeal an' salt I just put on top of our stuff. It's by tha door, on tha left."

After carrying potatoes, apples, candles, lard, and some dried fruit, Sam wondered what he would need. "How 'bout Lucky an' me? Should we be gittin' food of our own?"

"Add what ya want; elsewise, ya git what I fix. I'll be cookin' for ya."

Lucky added a bag of coffee to the wagon. "Will we need anythin' other than for eatin'?"

"Yar wearin' tha right clothes. Are ya ready for tha rain? An' tha cold? You'll curse tha heat most of tha time, an' then you'll wish ya had it bottled up when tha temps drop as we cross tha mountains."

"We're set," Lucky confirmed. "Whar do we store our stuff?"

"Put yar extra gear in here. You'll share space with tha other hands."

After the supplies were loaded, the boys tied

their horses to the back of the wagon and sat up front with Tincup. As they rode back to the camp, he told them more about the trip.

"Tha emigrants'll be responsible for thar own oxen...no mules or horses allowed for pullin' tha loads. Banks requires an extra pair that'll travel behind thar wagon. He only takes prairie schooners usin' two yokes of oxen an' carryin' no more'n 1500 pounds of weight."

"Why not tha Conestoga?" Lucky asked. "I heard they are good, sturdy wagons."

"Thar too heavy, an' tha pullin' takes too much outta tha stock. Banks has learned what works best an' what ta avoid."

"Will thar be others, just ridin', like us?" Sam wondered.

"Only tha cowhands. Course, Banks an' Davis will ride. Most of tha emigrants will be walkin', but sum brought horses too. Wears tha team out, if'n everyone rides in tha wagons. They'll need ta keep thar oxen's strength up, as sum won't be able ta go on, no matter what...why tha extra team." Tincup sadly remembered the bones and carcasses he had passed along the way on previous trips.

Banks came to meet them when they arrived at the camp. "All the shopping done?"

"Yep. Have lunch ready in 'bout an hour." Tincup knew Banks would want to know the time so he could tell the hired hands. They were always ready for a hot meal.

Banks called the boys over. "I want you to go and mind the herd. We won't be needing them at first...game will be plentiful. You'll hunt for our meat 'til we're ready to use the beeves."

Lucky shifted his hat. "Fair enough."

"Each wagon is responsible to take care of their own, but you'll see who the greenhorns are. They'll fall behind and hold us up if we don't help them out."

"We'll help as you see fit," Sam confirmed.

"Off you go then. Kolt'll be waiting."

Kolt saw the boys riding his way and waited for them to join him by the herd. "Y'all be tha *green* cowboys?"

"Know ya seasoned wranglers are leery of us *tenderfoots*," Lucky defensively started, knowing what the man was thinking. "But we *are* good at followin' orders an' wanna do ya right."

"Heard yar *farmers*. Done any herdin'?" Kolt asked in such a way that the boys had to retort.

"Seen how *ornery* field cows can be." Sam wanted to show he wasn't intimidated.

"You'll see a lot *more*." Kolt was not amused. "Follow me." He galloped toward the remuda.

The boys looked at each other and grinned, then brought up the rear.

Kolt waited until they regrouped. "You'll help with tha horses too. Tha days'll be long an' hot, hotter than ya ever felt afore. You'll need ta rotate yar own horses...so they don't git wore out. Thar as valuable as tha herd."

"How often will we need ta exchange 'em?" Lucky hesitantly asked. Kolt's authoritative air had a way of making him feel his age.

"You'll know. Don't wait 'til yar horse is spent. Tell someun 'fore ya pull out ta make tha switch. Tha herd's small an' follows with tha train, so it should be a quick turnaround."

Lucky wanted to show they were ready for

the challenge. "When's our first shift?"

"Ya each'll be out tonight. Keep a watch for Indians. They can be real sneaky, especially 'round tha horses. Bandits too. An' look for wolves. Sometimes mountain lions will show up, as well. The animals usually make sounds ta warn ya. A tied horse is just 'bout helpless against predators. Keepin' tha animals safe is yar job." Kolt spoke with a more civilized tone. "Got any questions?"

"Let ya know as they 'rise," Sam replied.

The preparation time sped by. The wagons were almost ready to start the journey. Banks knew the anxious pioneers would have fully stocked wagons. He had already told them that the oxen, though strong, would have a hard time pulling heavy loads. Even so, he knew he would have to visit each family and point out what had to be discarded.

"You won't need that iron stove," Banks told Jon Baker.

Nancy, his wife, protested. "But we'll need it when we open our eatin' place."

Banks stood his ground. "It's too heavy. Will slow your team down...*sap* their strength." He looked at the pots and pans that were strewn along the inside of the wagon.

Jon saw Banks scan his wares. "We'll be *needin'* those, too."

"Nope. You'll be overweight if you try to carry that stuff. It has to go. *All of it*," Banks ordered. "Table and chairs, too!"

The Bakers made a show of removing the items, but when the wagon master was out of sight, they disregarded his advice and quickly hauled the valuable items back inside their wagon. Some of the other emigrants had also ignored his suggestions. Parting with family heirlooms proved to be too hard.

The following morning, when the caravan was ready to roll, the wagons carried ornate dressers, wooden clocks, musical instruments, and other luxuries. Later, when the going got tough, these treasures would be reluctantly discarded, but not before the settlers had a chance to see others that had already been claimed by the Oregon Trail.

A few days into the journey, Lucky rode up to relieve Sam of the drag position on the cattle drive. "How ya doin'?"

"You'd think I'd git used ta this," he moaned as he shifted in his seat. Saddle soreness was setting in again. The long hours of riding had that effect on him.

"Ya just need *more paddin'* down thar," Lucky joked. Sam was still lean and lanky. He had yet to gain the muscular strength that would come with age.

"An' this…*dust*," Sam groaned from under his kerchief. "Someone needs ta teach tha beeves how ta walk without *scuffin'* up tha ground." The dust was bothering him more than sitting on the horse's back.

"Ya want my bandana?"

"Nah. You'll be needin' it soon."

"On a *high note*, Bixby's wheel was fixed. Banks was pretty mad when he saw thar load. Had 'em leave some of thar stuff behind."

"Bettin' thar was a decorative rockin' chair."

"An' one of 'em fancy clocks. Thar'll be more

stuff left by tha road, as tha way gits rough.”

“Otherwise, things are goin’ better than I expected. We’ve had no major mishaps.”

“Don’t *jinx* us. Tha prairie’s providin’ us well. ’Tis just mid-May, an’ tha grass is still plentiful. Even tha flowers seem ta be welcomin’. Spirits are high. Tha only problem has been saddle soreness like ya got, an’ muscles adjustin’ ta tha long days of walkin’.”

“And a few with tha Prairie Madness. Tha *endless openness*…has gotten ta me too. Gives me a funny feelin’. Can’t explain it. It’s like I’m bein’ smothered, as if tha sky’s pressin’ in on me.”

“Ya just need a change of scenery. We’ll be crossing tha Big Blue River within tha hour. That should offer ya somethin’ different.”

“It’s not what’s on tha ground, but what’s above tha horizon. I feel like I can’t git a proper breath, though I’m breathin’ fine.”

“It’s tha dust, most likely. *It’ll pass.*” Lucky tried to console his brother. He didn’t know how to help, so he turned the conversation back to the river. “Haven’t had rain in a while, so not expectin’ any trouble with tha crossin’. Be a chance for tha teamsters ta prove they can handle thar wagons in deep water, too.”

“Reckon we’ll…” Sam stopped. He gave Lucky a questioning look. “Was that a gunshot?”

CHAPTER 5

Lucky turned and rode toward camp. After he got off his horse, Tincup came up and told him the news.

"Mrs. Covey's been shot. She'd been wantin' ta turn 'round…said she'd had enough. They thought she was bein' more reasonable, but she became hysterical. She got thar gun…ta make 'im listen. Mr. Covey tried ta take it away, an' in tha shuffle, it discharged." Tincup's head slumped as he relayed the events.

"How's she doin'?"

"Doesn't look too good. Banks's lookin' after tha missus now. Thar were witnesses, so we know it was an accident."

"Prairie madness." Lucky hoped that Sam's despair wasn't as deep or as disturbing. "Sorry ta hear."

Mrs. Covey was still holdin' her own when the wagon train lined up the next morning.

"Think she has a chance?" Davis asked. "It's awfully rock-strewn along this portion of tha trail."

"Hard to say. She's still unconscious. The Coveys want to go on, though." Banks looked at Tincup. "Let's get rolling."

"Hyah." Tincup got his team moving. The other wagons followed his lead.

It wasn't long before the train stopped. Mrs.

Covey had succumbed to her wound, so they gave her a quick burial. When they were on the road again, the sun had climbed higher in the sky and the cool of the morning was lost. The wind kicked up the dust that rose with each step and roll of the wagon wheels. The pioneers didn't have long to dwell on this first fatality, as the frontier forced them to focus on getting through another day.

A few days later, as they were sitting around the campfire, Banks gave a progress report. "So far, the wagons are holding up, and the teams are getting stronger. We're averaging close to 15 miles a day. Barring any unforeseen problems or delays, we're on schedule."

Davis knew some of the reasons why they were doing so well. "We haven't had any rain or windstorms ta slow us down."

Tincup didn't want to spoil the mood, but he had noticed that the clouds had started to move in. "Tha weather's changin'. Can't see but a portion of tha stars now."

Banks looked at the sky. "At least we're days from the next river crossing."

"Tha rain may be a welcome relief from tha heat." Sam had his prairie fever under control, but the underlying feeling that the world was closing in had not left.

"Reckon so." Tincup agreed. "We're due for a pleasin' summer shower."

The heavy pelts of rain came later when the night was well underway. The pioneers sought shelter in the confined spaces of their wagons, but the continuous drenching saturated their protective canvases, and the water found them in there, too. To some, the drip-drop sounded like a baby's lullaby and lulled them to sleep, but for others, it rang louder than a school bell, calling them in from recess.

By morning, the pouring rain had turned into a drizzle. When the emigrants stepped out of their wagons, they were welcomed by a ground that had turned into a muddy platform. Though the temperature was above freezing, the cold, damp air made everyone miserable. Their rain gear offered some defense, but the water seeped in through the exposed openings. No one was disappointed when the word came that the train would move out soon. The activity gave them a chance to focus on other things.

Banks was issuing orders as soon as there was light. "Tincup, serve jerky and last night's biscuits for breakfast. Lucky, Sam, go down the line and tell everyone we're getting ready to pull out. Kolt, get the guys and prepare the herd."

Tincup walked up to Banks and offered him a biscuit. "Are ya worried 'bout tha wet an' tha cold?"

"Has a way of making itself known."

The caravan made slow progress. The lead wagons churned up the loose, wet soil. Those passing later had to ride through the muddy ooze or find a new path. Several were delayed when their wheels got stuck, but the hardy men pushed and pulled until the oxen got their wagons rolling again. Usually, only the drivers, small children, and the frail were allowed to ride, but the weather was taking its toll. The wagoners took on those wanting to escape the rain's assault, but it was at the expense of the tired beasts that had struggles of their own.

As the morning wore on, signs of fatigue began to show. Spotting the best course was iffy, with the water covering up much of the trail. The train had to wait when one of the wagons hit a boulder and cracked its wheel. Since it was still raining, Banks decided to make this their midday stop.

Lunch breaks were necessary for wagon trains. Since most of the travelers walked, they needed the nourishment. The animals were fed and rested as well. Sometimes, hot meals were prepared using the fuel collected along the way, and on the prairie, this meant picking up buffalo chips. Even wet, these patties were too important to ignore.

When Lucky was relieved from his duty with the cattle, he came into camp for a hot meal. The rain had stopped, and though the sun was trying to peek out from the clouds, he was still damp and cold. "Ohh yeah!" he exclaimed when Tincup handed him a hot brew of coffee, the preferred drink on the trail.

Lucky took a couple of sips from the tin cup. "Not tastin' like tar...*yet.*"

"Yar jokin's not warranted. Ya know it's tha minerals in tha water that make it bitter."

"So, I've been told. Tha stronger tha coffee, tha higher tha alkaline level."

"Tha next time ya got a complaint, take it up with tha *water fairy*." Tincup's reply left Lucky unsure if he was serious or not.

"Better be careful. He may *tar an' feather* ya," Davis joked. "Hear *chicken's* for dinner."

"Lucky, sit here." Banks patted the top of a

barrel that was placed by the fire. "Want to have a serious talk if you boys are done with all your funning."

"Glad to. I'm chilled ta tha bones." Lucky took in the heat from the fire. "Hope ta see tha sun soon."

"Be a few hours the way things look." Banks got to the news at hand. "Had to call on the Prestons. Their boy's been sickly. He stayed in the wagon yesterday and all morning. Too soon to tell, but he may be showing signs of cholera."

Just saying the name caused panic. Cholera was one of the leading causes of death for the pioneers. The germ was very contagious, and its source was often unknown. It usually came from bad water and was spread by unsanitary practices. By the time symptoms appeared, the tainted watering hole would have been left far behind.

"With this damp, cold weather…" Banks got a chill, thinking of the worst.

"Tha Prestons had a few of us over for dinner tha other night," Lucky informed him.

"Let's not put tha cart afore tha horse," Davis advised. "No need ta worry, 'til we know one way or tha other."

"You're right. Before I make assumptions, I'm going to check on the boy again." When Banks returned, he confirmed it was cholera. "I had them move their wagon to the back. Lucky, tell everyone at that dinner to watch for symptoms and to stay to themselves. We'll camp here for the night. That should give us time to know the extent of the outbreak…and time to dry out, too." He downed the rest of his coffee, then he went to talk to the other families.

The next morning they buried the Preston boy. His dad had become delirious overnight and had been put to bed, unaware of his son's death. Katie Preston couldn't confirm if she was sick or overcome with grief from the loss of her son. Sally, their other child, seemed to be asymptomatic.

Three others from the Preston dinner party were confined to their wagons with symptoms. Sam, though feeling some nausea, didn't have further discomfort. He felt he could carry out his duties and stayed with the herd. Lucky, on the other hand, had already vomited several times. He had a fever and diarrhea, so the Prestons offered to let him have a bed in their wagon where Sally could watch both him and her father while her mother drove the team.

Before they left, Sam rode up beside Sally. "Make 'em drink water every hour or so, even if they don't want it. Heard somewhere that that was important."

CHAPTER 6

By the end of the week, the disease had stopped spreading. Two emigrants had succumbed and were buried. The others slowly recovered, Lucky and Mr. Preston included.

"No new cases have been reported in the last few days. The outbreak is over," Banks reported as they left Mr. Humphrey's burial service and headed for Mr. Pope's tribute.

"Mrs. Pope feels that her son's able ta drive thar team. They'll stay with tha train for now," Davis told Banks. "Mr. Murphy said his son, Sean, would drive for tha Humphreys."

"Good. I've seen the boy hanging around their wagon. I suspect Sean's fond of their oldest. Getting those kids together is a good thing for both of their families."

The emigrants took off the following morning with heavy hearts. They had known about the risks, but death had reached out again, and its dark, somber shadow weighed heavily upon them.

"Welcome back, cowboy!" Sam yelled when Lucky rode up a few days later to help with the herd.

"Lost a few pounds, an' I'll need ta git some of my energy back; otherwise, I'm healthy as a horse. Did anythin' *happen* while I was out?" Lucky had heard rumors. He waited to hear what his brother had to say.

Sam was evasive. "No, nothin'."

Lucky could see that Sam was not going to give anything away. He was told that Sam had spent a lot of time helping Sally care for the cholera patients. They had gotten close. Many in the camp had noticed their growing affection, and rumors had started. Lucky knew his brother was too shy to talk about his feelings, so he thought he would be more direct.

"Heard you an' Sally made *quite* tha pair, tendin' ta us sickly ones."

Sam's face turned red. "*Know* what yar a hintin' at...she's a fine girl."

"Ya nothin' more ta add?"

"She's a *real* fine girl!" Sam rode off, leaving Lucky to draw his own conclusions.

❦◆❦◆❦

"I talked with Davis afore he took off ta scout today," Sam told Lucky a few weeks later. They were at the remuda getting the horses settled before eating lunch. "He said we'll have a good valley ta bed tha beef tonight. May be tha last of tha good grass for a while."

"Then on ta tha river crossin'. We'll be leavin' tha prairie behind. Ya still feel funny bein' out here?"

"Kinda went away," Sam just realized.

Lucky laughed. "Reckon ya had somethin' else, or should I say *someone* else, ta focus on."

Davis came back with his report on the North Platte River. He dismounted and let the boys tend to his horse. "Storms upriver have caused tha water level ta rise."

Lucky detected a note of concern in Davis's

59

voice. "Expectin' trouble if'n tha flow's up?"

"Could be a problem."

They would reach the river crossing, an area that would later become Casper, Wyoming, the following day. Ferries were operating, but the high water had caused them to shut down until conditions improved. The delay was creating a backlog, as travelers on both sides of the river came to make the traverse.

"Tha ferry's down," Davis told Banks when he reached the wagons. "Should be runnin' in a day or so. Thars quite a gatherin' already."

Banks scowled. "Reckon we'll have to see what we're facing when we get there."

The sun was shining, and the sky was clear when the wagon train started out the next day. The pioneers hoped that the good weather would hold so they could get the dangerous crossing behind them.

"I'll git tha wagons circled," Davis announced when they arrived at the banks of the mighty waterway. "Tha water's still up."

"Tha gnats are up, *too*." Tincup swatted at a critter that had lodged in the fold of his neck.

"These bloodsuckers are worse than skeeters. 'Tween tha two, I'm lookin' like I got tha measles," Lucky brooded.

"We've all been amply nipped. Some just wear it better," Banks boasted, because he didn't swell from their bites.

"Bitten or *smitten*?" Lucky teased Sam, who just rolled his eyes and rode away.

"I'll hold a camp-wide meeting…about one o'clock," Banks decided. "That should be enough time for everyone to get settled and to tend to their animals."

The pioneers gathered around the lead wagon and waited for instructions about the upcoming crossing. There was a tone of anxiety in their conversations. The roaring sound of the river warned of the danger. Tincup held a pot and hammered it with his serving spoon. He waited for the noise to echo through the crowd. "Pipe down!"

Banks waited until it was quiet. "Listen up. We've made it to this milestone, and you should congratulate yourselves. You've done well. Now you'll face something new. I'm not going to lie. The crossing is going to be a challenge. The river's always tricky, but the storms have made it riskier. Besides worrying about the water, there will be sandbars and quicksand to get around. That being said, we expect the river to settle enough to make the crossing tomorrow."

Davis took over. "If'n we use tha ferry, we'd have ta wait our turn. Thar several wagon trains ahead of us, some much larger than ours."

"We have access to rafts. A party ahead has offered to sell us theirs...keeps us from waiting for the ferry. It'll save you some money, too." Banks explained further. "Most use them to carry their wagons while their animals swim across. If that's what you decide to do, we can start with our animals, then get to the wagons when the rafts are available."

"But tha choice is yars ta make. We'll abide by yar decision. Once we git 'cross, tha trail follows tha North Platte. It's tougher...not as flat. Expect ta have ups an' downs...all while gainin' elevation. Thar will be times when tha goin' will be a challenge." Davis quickly added, "But don't worry, we'll git ya through."

"Thars a small tradin' station near tha ferry that's sellin' supplies. If'n ya decide ta clean yar clothes, watch tha currents. They can pull more'n yar clothes down," Tincup warned.

Banks ended the meeting. "It's going to be a hard day tomorrow. Get your wagons ready."

"Should we scout tha river now, so we'll be ready for tha crossin'?" Lucky asked.

"Not yet. Don't wanta put tha cart afore tha horse," Davis advised. "Tha river may change overnight, or tha group may take tha ferry, or others may git ta our spot first."

"Yar right. Better ta wait," Lucky realized.

When morning arrived, the river was full of activity. Several wagon trains were already on the move, and the ferry had its first load in transit. Banks had his crew gather by the fire so he could give instructions.

"They voted in favor of buying Bond's rafts. He's already started. They were in the water once it was light. You can see why." They viewed the long line of wagons and animals ready to cross. "We should have them by late morning. That's Bond standing over there." Banks pointed to a middle-aged man giving orders to a teamster who was struggling.

Davis saw that a large part of the river was clear of traffic above Bond's train. "I'll go an' find a good crossin' ta git tha stock across."

"Start with the cattle. Follow with the oxen, then the horses. You should have most of them across by the time we get the rafts. I'll get an update from Bond." Banks went to talk to the other wagon master.

Davis scouted the unpredictable river and made a preliminary crossing. His return proved to be equally suitable, but he knew that his traverse on horseback was only a trial. The true test would come with the continuous travel of man and beast. He went to get the herd.

"Over here!" Davis called. "Bring 'em on."

The cowhands were ready and slowly led the cattle toward the water. The lead cow bellowed a reluctant cry before walking into the muddy water. With a little help from Lucky, he took a few guarded steps, and then he plunged into the swollen river. The other bovines followed. Once they got into the deeper section, the current pushed them downriver, but they were strong enough to keep a forward motion. When the cattle reached the other shore, the cowboys took them away to a grassy meadow. A few of the hands stayed behind to watch the herd while the rest of the men went back to bring the oxen across.

"Tha current's strong, but tha cows were only carried a few yards down," Davis told Lucky. "Just need tha bottom ta hold up."

"Ready ta start tha teams?" Sam shouted from the bank. "I've got tha first group of oxen here. Just waitin' for yar signal."

"Git 'em movin'," Davis yelled back, then he addressed Lucky. "Keep an eye on tha riverbed. If'n it gits loose, move 'em further down. Once ya git 'em all across, come an' help with tha wagons."

The morning went much as expected. Sam and Lucky had made several trips across the river with the oxen before the Bond rafts were released to Banks. The wagons lined up, and one by one, they were pulled up the ramp onto the waiting rafts. After the men secured the wheels, the women and children came aboard. They used ropes attached to the banks on each side of the river to pull the boats across.

Progress was slow. By early afternoon, the wind had picked up, creating gusts that kicked up the already active river. Most of the oxen had completed the traverse, but less than half of the wagons had made it across.

Lucky noticed that some of the oxen were struggling. "Bennet, watch out!"

His warning came too late—the bottom let loose. Three of the oxen lost their footing and were at the mercy of the water. The two men who were guiding them across followed in their wake. The fast-moving current pushed the group downstream toward the rafts. The men jumped off their horses and tried to make it on their own. Though one and all desperately swam toward the shore, only the horses made it to safety.

Lucky frantically yelled a warning to the rafts downstream. "Incomin'!"

CHAPTER 7

Two of the struggling oxen headed toward a sandbar that was near the shoreline. Though the first one gained the surface, his victory was short-lived. The sand gave away, and his weight pulled him down into the bottomless pit. The helpless animal sank until he was lost from sight. When the other ox reached the same bar, he was too exhausted to fight, and the quicksand won again.

One of the wayward men drifted behind the two oxen. Seeing their plight, he swam until he found a current that pushed him in a different direction, toward the towrope used by the boats. He grabbed it and pulled his way to shore. The other man and the third ox came straight at the rafts. Banks yelled, but his warning was in vain.

Jon Baker, in his haste to get started that morning, had not loaded his wagon properly. The uneven weight had shifted even more as he bounced along the rocky road that led to the river. When his wagon was loaded onto the raft, the heavier side faced downstream, causing the raft to lean. As he struggled to secure the wheels to the platform, a strong gust of wind blew, causing the canvas to act like a sail. At that moment, the ox hit. The combined forces pushed the schooner overboard. Jon's arm got caught in the spokes of the wheel, and he was pulled into the water. Upon contact, the wagon broke apart, exposing its contents. The swift-moving water swept Jon and his possessions away. By the time his body was dislodged from the wreckage, water had filled his lungs.

Tincup was helping Jon when the raft was hit, but he had managed to stay on board. He knew the man was in trouble, so he dove into the river and swam downstream to search for the teamster.

Nancy Baker was waiting on the shore with their young ones. Time moved in slow motion as she watched the scene unfold. She instinctively reached for her children and pulled them close to her.

After the collision, the wayward ox managed to get to land—alone.

"Take over!" Lucky yelled to Sam. He raced downstream, following Bennet's trail.

"Too late," Tincup said when Lucky appeared by his side. "Found Jon after he was swept into tha pool over thar." He pointed to a spot where the water veered away from the main stream. "His body was limp, so I drug 'im ta shore. Thar was nothin' more I could do for 'im."

"I'll go an' see 'bout Bennet. He was swept away, too." Lucky didn't have to go far. He saw the man lodged amongst some branches that were stuck in the sandy bottom. His contorted body left no doubt that he was dead. Lucky hurried to fetch him anyway.

Lucky returned to the wagon train with the second corpse. After consoling his wife and son, he went to get a cup of coffee. "Bennet's with his family."

"Tha rest of tha wagons an' tha remainin' livestock made it without any trouble," Tincup offered in consolation.

"Glad ta hear it."

Banks addressed the crowd sitting around the fire. "A sad chain of events, made worse because Jon's wagon was filled with stuff that should have been left in Independence."

Davis shook his head. "Saw a fancy stove an' enough cookware ta *feed an army* fall out."

"I *specifically* pointed those items out...told him they would make his load too heavy, so he had to leave them behind. The furniture, too." Banks sighed. "*Why* didn't he listen?"

"I watched 'im unload 'em. He musta put 'em back." Davis tried to console the leader. "If'n orders aren't followed, then it's on 'em, not you ...whatever happens."

Tincup tried to be optimistic. "At least sum of thar items were saved, an' one loose ox made it out."

Banks had led all kinds of trips across the country. He never liked losing anyone in his charge, especially if it was unnecessary. After they performed the memorial services, he called another camp-wide meeting.

"Not to speak ill of the dead or to place blame, but the Baker incident *could* have been avoided. Their wagon was overloaded, and this extra weight contributed to its capsizing. Items I said to leave in Independence were seen in the river. I *specifically* went to each of you and told you what *had* to be left behind," Banks narrated with frustration. "Seems some did *not* heed my advice."

Davis took over the lecture. "As we git closer ta tha mountains, tha goin' gits rougher. Yar teams have gotten ya this far, but what's ahead will test 'em...*wear 'em out*. Some of yar spares have already succumbed. As y'all were told afore ya joined up, thar'll be stretches whar food an' water'll be scarce. You'll need ta ration. Tha heat'll be even more oppressive...*brutal*. Yar animals'll be taxed ta thar limits, an' death *will* be likely. We've been through this afore an' know what's best. Y'all must trust our judgment, or ya *won't* make it, an' ya may take *others down* with ya, too."

"If you didn't leave the items I pointed out to you in Independence, then you must discard them...*now!*" Banks emphasized. "I'm not going to go wagon to wagon again. It's on each of you to do the right thing. What you decide is between you and your *conscience!*"

"If'n these *nonessentials* are somethin' ya think you'll need later, you'll just have ta buy 'em once ya git ta yar stoppin' point." Davis strongly orated a final warning. "For now, yar *possessions* are yar *curse!*"

Before they left the campsite the next day, an assortment of decorative items—dressers, tables, chairs, and picture frames—was left on the trail. A beautifully inscribed needlepoint, surrounded by a lavishly carved wooden frame, was left leaning against a shiny chamber pot. The words reflected the mood of the emigrants, who were still grasping the ideal of beauty in simplicity and how it was a necessary reality of wagon living.

"I know what you're thinkin'," Mrs. Pope said to her son after they read the message. He was looking at the clock left inside their wagon. "'Twas given ta me by yar Pa. I just *can't bear* ta part with it now that he's gone."

"That's OK Mom," Dusty replied. "I've seen others with more'n they need, too. They can't let 'em go, either."

"Sad," Lucky said as he rode past some of the debris that had been dumped. "Heirlooms that can't be replaced."

Sam tried to look on the bright side. "It's easier on tha teams, though."

As they rode on, they met up with Banks. He was conversing with Hank, Bennet's son.

"You think you can handle them?" Banks had the young boy hitch the wagon and drive around. He wanted to make sure that Hank could control the team.

"Yes, sir!" Hank, exhibiting the pioneer spirit, was too proud to admit otherwise. "Ya sure tha Bakers don't wanna keep thar animals? They may need 'em down tha way." He knew that the Baker's wagon had been broken beyond repair and that Mr. Baker had drowned along with his dad, but he didn't want to be a charity case.

"Nancy and her children are riding with the Lobacks so they won't need them. You lost both pairs of your oxen, so it would only be right to let you have them."

"We could pay her after we git ta Oregon."

"No need for that. She was happy to help."

Hank gratefully accepted. "Reckon it'll be OK then. Thanks ta all of ya fer helpin' us out."

"Now that *that's* settled, I want you to ride the lead today so I can watch you. We'll get going as soon as you're in place."

Banks rode toward the front of the train. Sam and Lucky caught up with the wagon master. "Hank'll do just fine. He's a strong lad." Lucky saw a bit of himself in the boy.

Sam thought about the implications of the disastrous river crossing. "Tha Lobacks were kind ta take in Nancy an' her children."

"It's just tha two of 'em, an' since most of tha Baker's belongin's was lost ta tha river, thar won't be much ta take in," Lucky noted.

"It's a good match," Banks verified. "They're both interested in cooking. The Lobacks want to start a bakery, and Mrs. Baker can help them when they get established. May not be as she planned, but it's an amiable solution."

"They were already comparin' thar recipes," Lucky shared. "They had me over ta see whose cornmeal pancakes tasted tha best."

After crossing the Platte, the wagon train entered the dry, barren land of the High Plains. The trail led them uphill to a tableland. They spent a couple of days traversing across the treeless terrain, then they descended into Ash Hollow, a valley that offered shade and cool water. From here, they followed the banks of the river. Nights grew colder as they slowly ascended and made their way to the Laramie Mountains. They passed the familiar beacons, Courthouse and Jail Rocks, extraordinary clay formations, rising above them like stoic giants. Then they came upon Chimney Rock, with its peaked spire reaching to the sky, and, finally, Scotts Bluff.

"Fort Laramie is only a couple of days from here," Davis noted as they admired the famous landmark. "Named after a fur trader, Hiram Scott. Tha stories of his death vary. Some say he was left by tha river because he was ailin' an' tha party had ta go on. Others claim that his bones were found nearer ta tha bluffs."

"Any foul play?" Lucky liked a good mystery.

"No one knows tha real accountin's or tha whys. Just know that he wasn't able ta go on," Davis replied. "Heard he was sick or injured, maybe from fightin' Indians. He may have told his companions ta leave 'im, or they may have had to, ta survive themselves."

"Ya never know when tha truth gits mangled with all tha *tall tales*," Lucky deduced.

"Like that fish ya caught last year. I was thar. It was *this* big." Sam spread his hands to show a medium-sized catch. "But accordin' ta you, it was *this* long." He spread his hands to double the length.

"Well, it makes tha tellin' better. Don't ya agree?" Lucky asked Bullet, his horse.

As the wagons headed west, the emigrants faced a barren land that was an endless series of uphill and downhill traverses.

"Doesn't do any good ta reach a high point," Sam said after a grueling day of riding.

"Why?" Lucky asked.

"Only means another one will be loomin' ahead on tha horizon."

Tackling each onslaught of rises and descents presented problems of their own. Some were steeper than others. Multiple techniques were used to pull up or slow down the wagons to keep them under control.

"Yar favorite view," Lucky said to Sam after they had reached the top of another crest. "Tha next rise doesn't look ta be as far off as tha last one, though."

"Should be able ta git up an' down without tha wagons needin' assistance."

"Won't know 'til we git closer. Looks can be deceivin' from a distance."

"Yar right. Wishful thinkin'." Sam grinned, then raced off to keep a stray cow in line.

When they reached the summit of the rising land, they gasped when they saw the downhill traverse.

Sam scowled. "Steep. Tha uphill approach was smooth, but it's a different story on this side. Ya called it right."

Lucky moaned. "Unfortunately."

The herd crawled down the treacherous slope. After they were settled in the valley below, the boys went to help with the wagons, which were being lowered down the gravelly slope using a pulley system that Banks had rigged together. The oxen had been removed and were already being led down one by one.

"Sam, check the rope that's tied to the rock pile. I want to make sure it's not fraying," Banks ordered as they started to lower another wagon down the hill.

Lucky saw the rope jerk. "Hold it!"

Mr. Murphy's wagon had abruptly stopped.

Lucky went down to investigate. The rope that was attached to the front end of the vehicle was tangled, so he proceeded to sort out the knotted mass. The delay gave Mr. Orr, the next to go down, time to remove some of his heavy items. He decided to leave his anvil. As he was getting the bulky tool out of his wagon, he lost his grip. The anvil slipped out of his hands, hit a rock, and then bounced down the slope toward Lucky.

"Watch out!"

CHAPTER 8

Lucky looked up. The falling debris stung his face. His eyes closed tight, but not before he saw a dark mass coming at him. Before he could react, the beak of the anvil smacked his shoulder. He lost his footing and tumbled down the slope. When he stopped, he was too shaken up to do anything but lie there and gather his wits.

Sam raced down the hill. "You're conscious," he noted with relief. "Don't move 'til I've had a chance ta look ya over."

Lucky tried to sit up, but when he moved his arm, a severe pain stopped him.

Sam heard him moan. "Whar ya hit?"

"My shoulder."

Sam ripped open Lucky's shirt and instantly saw the problem—a dislocated shoulder. "Hold on." He jerked Lucky's arm and got the joint in place.

Lucky yelled. When the worst of the pain subsided, he scolded his brother. "Ya could have *warned* me!"

"I kinda did, but I didn't want ya ta tense up."

"Yeah! Well...it worked!"

"Ya got a nasty bruise. Ready ta git up?" Sam helped Lucky rise.

"Tha legs are holdin' up." Lucky slowly got on his feet. "Should be able ta walk."

Mr. Preston rode up from the bottom of the hill. "Saw ya fall. Ya OK, son?"

"Seems so."

"Hand me yar kerchief." Sam tied Lucky's bandana to his. He slipped the hastily made sling over his brother. "Ya ready for this?" Lucky gave the go-ahead. He saw the pain that was obvious on his brother's face when his arm was moved into place. "Can ya ride?"

"Be easier than walkin', I reckon."

Sam helped Lucky get his foot in the stirrup, and with Mr. Preston's help, he was heaved up on the horse. Lucky groaned, then he took a few deep breaths and assured them that he was ready to ride.

Banks had untangled the rope, and when it was clear below, the schooner was lowered down the slope. The last one made the steep descent by sunset. The following morning, the wagon train was ready to roll.

The pioneers faced new trials with each passing week. Windstorms caused delays. Stock dropped. Wagons broke down. Most of their troubles needed only minor attention, but some demanded more. A few took this as a sign and dropped out, while others made do and stayed with the train.

The importance of Banks's earlier warning had finally sunk in, and by this time, even some inconsequential items, including excess food, had been discarded. The pioneers continued to follow the established, rutted trail, which by now had become void of vegetation and strewn with litter. Come what may, the tired animals kept moving, usually encouraged by the crack of a whip, so the wagons rolled on, and somehow, the people managed to follow.

Banks was sitting around the fire with the crew awaiting supper. "I've noticed that some are using their cornmeal. I wonder if they're getting low on eggs and bacon."

Tincup saw Lucky's bewildered look. "Tha cornmeal keeps tha bacon from spoilin' an' tha eggs from crackin'. They wait 'til thar gone afore eatin' it."

"Should be a supply station soon," Banks pointed out.

"It's not like tha old days when ya had ta make yar food an' water last. Thar were only a few stops then. By this stretch, most were short of food, an' water was scarce," Tincup recalled. "Have ta say, though, this did prepare us for tha hard times ahead when we'd face our *real* challenge, gittin' ta tha Sierras."

"We made it through...never had it as bad as some of the other trains." Banks was thankful they escaped what others had faced.

"Ya thinkin' 'bout tha Donner expedition?" Tincup asked.

"I reckon their tragedy was one of the worst. They did *many* things wrong...so, so many," Banks acknowledged.

"What happened?" Lucky asked.

Tincup had a funny look on his face.

Lucky stood up and got more coffee. "Well, ya piqued my curiosity. Don't leave me hangin'."

Tincup yielded. "All right. I reckon ya should hear 'bout 'em, but it's not a pleasant story. It happened back in '46. Not as many trains had done tha trip, an' they were lookin' for better routes ta git ta Oregon an' California. Tha way was rough. Two families, tha Donners an' tha Reeds, had decided ta make tha journey. They were well ta do an' had overloaded wagons. They started late in tha season an' tried ta make up time by takin' a shorter trail outta Fort Bridger...usin' tha Hastin's Cutoff. Tha route was supposed ta save 'em time, but it was new an' untested."

"A few weeks earlier, Hasting had taken the route coming eastward. He arrived at the fort and convinced a wagon train to follow him back, using his newly discovered path," Banks filled in. "But the trail hadn't really been used, so they didn't have any clear markings or ruts to follow like we have now."

"Problem was, Hastin' came with mules. Tha trail hadn't been tested for wagons. His group had a hard time gittin' through tha narrow passageways...had ta hack through a lot of brush an' find new routes, which slowed 'em down," Tincup explained. "They barely survived an' just beat tha winter snows."

"No one knew about their struggles and delays. When others reached the fort, the Donner's train being one of them, they were told about the expedition. Remember, it was already late summer, and those at the fort still had a hard journey ahead. They had to cross the Wasatch Mountains and the Salt Lake Basin before reaching the base of the Sierra Mountains. So the cutoff seemed like a good alternative, and the Donners and some others decided to give it a try."

Banks had paused, so Tincup continued with the story. "Like Hastin's group ahead of 'em, they had ta cut an' clear tha trails, an' thar progress was slow. What tha mountain didn't take, tha desert did. Many lost thar animals, abandoned thar wagons, an' ran low on food an' water. They were on foot an' had little in tha way of provisions. As ya can imagine, sum started ta lag behind, an' tha groups started ta split up. They still had tha Sierra Mountains ahead of 'em, an' it was late October. Tha first group made it as far as Truckee Lake, but thar attempts ta git over tha final summit, Truckee Pass, failed. Tha winter storms had started, an' tha snow was too deep ta go on, so they regrouped at tha lake an' built shelters. Tha others were 'bout five miles behind 'em, at Alder Creek. They, too, had hunkered down."

"Reed had gone ahead to get help. He did make it to the other side, but the rescue team was stopped by heavy snows on the west side of the pass. Help was a long time in coming. Their food supply was getting low. They hadn't tied down their stock, so many wandered off and died. Some tried to hunt, but game was scarce. Even with rationing, the food supply eventually ran out."

"Afore things were at thar worst, a group left an' tried ta git help. They got over tha pass, but tha blizzards slowed 'em on tha descent. They, too, ran outta food an' started ta die off. Then...those still alive were really put ta tha test." Tincup told the gruesome part of the tale. "Tha dead were cut an' eaten."

"This did save some, and they were able to

get help," Banks emphasized. "Renewed efforts were made to get over the pass. When the first rescue party made it to the lake, there were survivors, but many had also died. They were eaten...and not by wolves. Eventually, both groups were reached, but all weren't able to leave at once, and snowstorms caused even more delays. Once again, as the provisions ran out, the dead became sources of food. In their defense, they only ate those who had already died."

"Except tha two Indian Scouts. They were reportedly killed afore they died. Hunger can be a strong drivin' force," Tincup reasoned. "Tha survivors were finally taken ta Sutter's Fort. Now tha pass is called Donner Pass, an' tha lake has been named Donner Lake."

"Seems when things go wrong, it's 'cause of a series of events...*bad* choices," Lucky noted. If'n they'd left earlier or taken tha known route."

"Why I try to do it right the *first time*," Banks confessed. "You learn from your own mistakes as well as those of others."

"Enough talkin' of such *unpleasantness*." Tincup got up and stirred the stew. "Be nearin' tha Sweetwater River soon."

"Be a blessed break from *this*." Banks spat out the bitter coffee. "Be glad to get fresh water again."

Tincup recalled how sweet the water tasted. "Tha Sweetwater does live up ta its *name*."

Davis had just returned from a scouting trip and heard Tincup's response. "What name?"

"Sweetwater," Tincup repeated.

"Which one?" Davis teased.

Tincup smirked. "Tha *one* we're comin' up on, which has water *just* as tasty as tha *one* we crossed back east a ways."

"Tha water *is* sweet," Davis finally admitted.

"Did you notice the dust behind us while you were out?" Banks asked when the banter was put to rest.

When Davis replied, his tone became more serious. "Saw tha disturbance from tha ridge. Too far ta see what's causin' it. I haven't heard 'bout any Indian uprisin's 'round here...most likely *bandits*. Coulda waited for us ta be on our own."

"They're staying behind, but I doubt we'll lose them. Like you said, we're now out of sight of other parties," Banks confirmed. "We'll keep an extra watch 'til they make their move. Lucky, you and Sam can patrol the wagons. Leave it to you to decide which shift you'll cover."

"Yes sir. I'll go an' tell 'im now." Lucky went to find his brother. He knew he would be near the Preston's wagon. Sam was spending more and more time with Sally.

"Lookin' for Sam?" Mrs. Preston asked when Lucky approached. "Thar over *thar*."

Sam saw Lucky coming. "Hello little brother."

"Evenin'. Sorry ta interrupt, but Banks wants us ta help with tha watch tonight." Lucky didn't give an explanation because he didn't want to alarm Sally. "I'll take tha first shift, so ya don't have ta leave right away. Come by, say, 'round two?"

"OK." Though Sam's voice was calm, he gave Lucky a suspicious look.

"Don't worry. I won't keep him. I'll make sure

he gits some rest afore he has ta perform his duty," Sally assured Lucky.

Sam relieved his brother at one o'clock.

Lucky yawned. "You're an hour early."

"Couldn't sleep. Knew somethin' was up."

"Yep. May have some bandits followin' us."

"Thought it might be trouble like that. You can go an' git some rest now."

"Just finished walkin' tha perimeter. Got my blood pumpin'. I don't seem ta be so sleepy now. I'll stay with ya a while."

"Fine with me."

The two boys sat under the night sky, not having a need to talk. After a while, Lucky told Sam about the Donner Party. After he finished the story, they sat there, contemplating what trials awaited them. When Lucky finally fell asleep, Sam covered him with a blanket and went on patrol.

The next day, silhouetted in the light of the rising sun, the dust cloud showed its menacing force. Ten men on horseback emerged from the horizon. They went for the herd.

The cowboys saw the bandits. "Hyah, Hep, Yah," they yelled to drive the cows away from the upcoming assault.

The wagon train was moving in single-file formation. Banks rode up beside Tincup, who was driving the lead wagon, and pointed to the eastern threat. "Bandits. Circle back up!"

The pioneers had prepared for this scenario. They formed a tight band, keeping their oxen hitched; then they grabbed their weapons and got ready to defend the train.

Banks joined Tincup "Get ready for a fight."

Davis took off to help with the affront on the cattle. He arrived just as the bandits started to fire. One of the cows went down. The hands fired back while trying to keep the herd intact. A gunfight ensued. Sam was hit, but he managed to stay on his horse.

Lucky saw his brother struggle. "Sam!"

Davis and a few of the men from the camp had ridden up to Lucky. "Go ta 'im. We'll help with tha herd." He took his team to thwart off the thieves.

"You alright?" Lucky asked when he reached his brother.

Sam gave a thumbs-up. "Just grazed me. Look!" He motioned toward the horizon.

Another group of bandits had materialized and was heading toward the wagons. Lucky turned, ready to ride out and help, but when he saw Davis and his men race back to the train, he decided to stay with the herd.

When Davis rode inside the group of wagons, he heard Banks issuing orders. "Tighten up. Get your family under cover. Have your rifles ready."

"Here they come!" Davis shouted as he got into position and started firing. "Don't let 'em git through!"

The battle began. Banks heard a shot strike the wood on the wagon wheel that was his cover, so he jumped behind a water cask. When he rose to fire back, he saw a new and imminent danger. He ran up and down, frantically waving. "Turn the herd!"

The cattle came straight for the wagons. With all the gunfire, they were stampeding out of control.

The noise made by the running beasts muted Banks's words, but Lucky saw the situation and, with the other cowboys, worked to get the herd to change direction. Their efforts paid off, and most of the animals turned, but three of the bandits had split a few of the cows away from the main group. They chased them toward the barricade, causing the oxen of the Martinez's wagon to panic and pull away. A large gap opened, and the unwanted party entered the inner circle.

Banks took out the first bandit who rode through. One of the emigrants got the second outlaw, but not before he got a shot off. The man's wife lay lifeless beside him. The third, being outnumbered, hightailed it out of the ring of fire and, with the remaining band of thieves, headed back the way they came.

Since the herd was scattered, Sam and some of the other cowboys followed the rustlers. They didn't want to catch them; instead, they chased after the raiders to show their force and to scare them away for good.

Lucky was riding fast to stay with the herd. While the size had been reduced since the start of the trip, the beeves were still hard to manage, and he needed to stay in control.

"Hang with me. Don't panic," he urged his horse after he saw one of the bandits get bucked and trampled in the skirmish.

Bullet held his ground. The race continued as the bandits kept following and firing. When they turned to make their escape, Lucky went after them. One of the rustlers got off a last shot. The slug grazed Lucky's temple, causing him

to flinch and lose control. He flew off his horse
and hit the ground. Bullet, realizing that his
rider had fallen, returned to retrieve him, but
Lucky just lay there. The impact had caused
him to black out.

CHAPTER 9

"**G**ot 'em," Kolt inwardly cheered. He had taken care of a bandit who was after the herd. He knew it was hopeless to round up the cattle and had seen the others chase the rest of the rustlers away, so he decided to return to camp. On his way back, he spotted Lucky. He got off his horse and knelt over the inert body.

"Lucky. Can ya hear me?"

When there was no response, he pulled off his bandana and wiped the blood flowing down the wounded boy's face. He saw where the bullet had scraped his forehead. Another gash behind his head told where he had hit a rock when he fell. Kolt wrapped the red-stained rag around the oozing cuts.

"Yar still breathin'. Ya just have ta hang in thar 'til I git ya movin' again." He tended to the wounds of the young boy who had proven his worth and had become his friend.

Though the emigrants held their own, three had died from gunfire. After they dressed their wounds and buried the dead, the pioneers spent the rest of the day cleaning up the mess that was left behind.

Sam had been out all morning chasing the bandits. When they were no longer in sight, he returned to the train. Banks was heating coffee over the fire. "Have ya seen Lucky?"

"Not since he turned the herd. He wasn't with you?"

"No."

"Did you chase the rustlers far enough away to keep them from coming back?"

"Thar gone, except for thar dead, an' tha buzzards are takin' care of 'em. They did take some of tha meat from tha cow they kilt afore they skedaddled, though."

"Thought that's what the scavengers were after." Banks stared at the circling birds that filled the sky. "Two of a kind."

"I'm goin' ta look for Lucky." Though Sam was tired from riding hard all morning, he went to search for his brother.

Kolt was tending to Lucky when Sam rode up. "Found 'im here. Musta fallen off 'is horse after bein' shot. Looks like he hit 'is head when he went down. Bullet's been by 'is side tha whole time."

"How bad is it?"

"Don't rightly know. He just opened 'is eyes afore ya rode up."

Sam inspected the wounds, then he looked into his brother's eyes. "Lucky? Lucky, how do ya feel? Ya OK to ride?"

Lucky was still in a daze. He could only stare at his brother. His brain wasn't ready to form words yet, let alone sentences. He moved his hand to his head and touched the bandana that crudely covered the cuts. It caused him to wince. "Ouch."

"Stay an' rest. I'll git somethin' ta git ya back ta camp." Sam tried to lighten the mood. "Hey, yar usin' up all yar luck. Save some for when we start our gold minin'."

The words did bring a smile, though it looked more like a grimace, Sam thought as he rode away. He returned with a stretcher, a blanket stretched over a spokeless wheel, and dragged his brother back to camp. The rough ride caused Lucky to pass out again. Sally had offered to take care of Lucky, so they put him inside her family's wagon.

"Can't *thank* ya enough. Be back ta check on 'im after I've a chance ta git some sleep." Sam gave Sally's hand a loving squeeze before leaving. After a restless few hours, he went back to check on Lucky. "How's he doin'?"

"He ate a little but he's sleepin' now." Sally opened the canvas cover that acted as a door to let him see his brother.

"Looks *peaceful*. Reckon that's a good sign."

"Banks said we're gonna stay here tomorrow, so he'll have a full day ta recuperate, but, more importantly, it'll give him a chance ta rest afore gittin' bounced around."

"That's probably for tha best. I heard some moanin' when we drug 'im in. Tha rest will do 'im good."

"You *too*! Did ya git *any* sleep?"

"Think I tossed an' turned more'n I slept," Sam admitted. "I saw a lot of canvas patchin' an' wheel replacin' goin' on. How'd yar rig hold out? Do ya need help with repairs?"

"We were blessed. Dad only had ta replace one spoke that was weakened when it was hit. Tha slug was still embedded."

"Whar are yar parents *now*?" Sam asked with a mischievous look in his eye.

"Thar helpin' ta organize…services will be held this evenin' for Mrs. Langley, Mr. Fisher, an' Mr. Hightower"

"It never gits easier, does it? I'm sorry for thar families…it'll be a hard thing for 'em ta bear."

Sally remembered her brother, who had died from cholera. "I know." She turned her focus to the present. "You've blood on yar sleeve. Let me have a look at it."

"I forgot I was hit. Reckon I've been thinkin' 'bout other things." Sam unbuttoned his shirt and let Sally clean his wound. "Were thar other cowpokes hit?"

"None that I'm aware of." Sally put a bandage around his arm.

Sam grinned when Sally finished. "What would tha Doyles do *without you*?" He closed his shirt and scanned the area. Since no one was in sight, he pulled Sally close to him and gave her a quick kiss.

"I should be *mad* at you…but I'm *not*."

"I need ta git goin'." Sam reluctantly broke the embrace. "Gotta git ta tha herd."

When Sam saw Lucky the following day, he was sitting up and drinking coffee.

"Sally serve ya breakfast in bed?"

"She *sure* did!" Lucky couldn't resist teasing Sam. "I think I could git used ta this. She'll make *someone* a wonderful wife."

"That *someone* will be *me*!" Sam smiled at his brother. "Yar jokin' tells me yar back ta yar ol' self. Wanted ta check on ya afore I go on watch. Stay an' git some rest."

"Not goin' *anywhere*."

"Make sure ya don't! Ya need ta heal."

Despite his injury, Lucky had slept soundly through the night. He was feeling restless and wanted to get back to work, but his aching head told him otherwise.

Elijah came to visit Lucky later that day. "Amazing how much damage those bullets did to my wagon. Been working all morning fixing things up."

"Best it was yar wagon an' not *you*. Any sign of tha bandits returnin'?"

"Not even to get their dead. The buzzards are having a *real* feast. They've been fighting for the pickings. Reminds me of the gulls following the fishing boats back home."

Elijah Coffin was the nephew of a wealthy plantation owner in coastal South Carolina. Like Sam and Lucky, he came from a large family, and he, too, felt that his destiny lay west. When they first met, he took an instant liking to the Doyle brothers.

"Haven't you heard their squawking all day?"

"No. Reckon I'm sleepin' more'n I thought. Is anyone gonna give 'em villains a proper burial?"

"Banks has a few out digging holes. Bet their lot's gone. I saw another train coming up from behind. After they pass, we'll be following them for a while."

"Safety in numbers, as they say. I doubt tha rustlers'll give us any more trouble."

❊✦❊✦❊

It was July 4, 1859. Like others before them, the Banks's wagon train had reached a familiar landmark—Independence Rock. They were not alone. The wagon train that was ahead of them had already set up camp. A couple of others weren't far behind.

"We'll stop at the *Rock* for the night," Banks told Davis before they left that morning. "We'll get there early enough to get in a good rest. I'll get the boys to cut out the best beef, and we'll have a *real* celebration!"

"I think that's what tha doctor ordered."

Independence Rock was more than a big rock formation. Names and dates were etched on its surface, telling who had made it thus far. After the pioneers had secured their wagons, they went to check out the inscriptions. Some went to see if they could find the names of friends or family who had already taken the journey. Others just wanted to find out what the markings had to say.

"Let's see if'n Travis left word somewhere," Mrs. Preston said to her husband. They were strolling along the base of the outcropping with Sally, Sam, and Lucky.

"Our neighbor left a couple of years ago," Mr. Preston explained. "He should've come this way, but thar are so many names it would be hard ta find his, even if he did make it here."

"Why don't we leave ours, too?" Lucky got out his knife and carved his name and the date on the granite surface. He handed his brother his knife. "Here Sam. Write yars above mine."

When Sam finished, he passed the knife to Sally. "Yar next."

She put her name above his. In the space between the two, she drew a heart. "There. Now our love is *set in stone*," she proclaimed as they admired their work.

"I think it needs ta be *sealed with a kiss*."

Sam embraced Sally, and they showed the love they felt for each other.

Mrs. Preston smiled at the youngsters. "I hate ta *spoil* this moment, but we'd better git back. I have a cake ta make."

Mr. Preston reached for his wife's hand. "Let tha kids have thar *moment*."

"Ya feelin' *frisky*, too?"

Mr. Preston looked at his wife and gave her a sly smile. "May be a *late* night."

Lucky was oblivious to all the love in the air. "Skinner's gonna call for tha dancin'. He'll keep things lively. I'm sure Banks'll let us start later tomorrow."

"It did take me by surprise when he told of his plans," Sam admitted. "I wasn't aware tha fourth was today. Time has little meanin' out here."

"An' *time's* awastin'. Come!" Mrs. Preston led them back to camp.

The feast provided a much-needed respite from the mundane menu they had on the trail. Beans and biscuits were still served, but when added to the fresh, roasted meat, they tasted different, somehow better.

Sam stood. "I'm still hungry. I'm gonna git a second helpin'."

"Save room for dessert. Mrs. Loback's made a delicious lookin' apple pie, an' Mom's cake should rival tha others," Sally bragged.

"No need ta worry. Sam has a bottomless pit," Lucky informed Sally.

"Reckon tha same could be said of you, too."

Mrs. Preston laughed at the boy's bantering. "Eat up. Ya both still got a lot of growin' yet."

The weary road travelers had devoured the food in less time than it took to prepare the meal. Lucky volunteered to help Tincup clean up while Skinner rounded up the band and started the after-dinner festivities. They played a jovial tune as a warm-up before the square dancing began.

Sam saw Sally stomping her foot to the beat. "I'd ask ya ta dance, but I don't know how."

"Come. I'll show ya." Sally grabbed his hand and led him to the dance floor.

At first, Sam was all feet, but with Sally's careful counsel, he held his own. Lucky took a few turns with her on the dance floor after he had finished washing the dishes. Thanks to her guidance, he was slowly figuring it out, but he decided he would rather play cards. Tincup had recently taught him some games, including poker.

"Our group plays a friendly round, but when ya sit at a table elsewhere, ya need ta know tha tricks tha swindlers use. Let me show ya." Tincup slowly dealt off the bottom of the pack. "Tha hands are quicker than tha eye, but if'n ya know what yar lookin' for, ya can spot tha cheaters." He showed Lucky a few other ways the gamblers kept the cards in their favor.

"Yar a regular card shark!" Lucky exclaimed. "Not sure I wanna play with ya. I won't know when yar slippin' one over on me."

"Wouldn't cheat a friend, but I'll do a few tricks, ta keep ya quick with tha eyes," Tincup confessed. "Only way ta make sure ya know tha game's on tha up an' up."

"You'll make a gambler outta me yet!" Lucky

joked. "One day, I'll surprise ya with a few tricks of my own."

"We got a real surprise comin' up tha trail," Tincup announced unexpectedly.

"Well, don't leave me hangin'."

"This time, I ain't tellin'. You'll just have ta wait an' see!"

They celebrated well into the night. Banks had already given instructions regarding their late departure. It was up to each of them, but he had advised against having a hot breakfast if they chose to get up late. Most of the families decided to sleep in and to eat leftovers.

Even with the extra time to sleep in, Tincup struggled to get breakfast out on time. He barely had the coffee ready when the cowboys came into camp. They grumbled when he passed out the stale biscuits.

"Hardtack is all?" Lucky's face showed he wanted more.

Tincup handed him some jerky.

"Only thin' hot this mornin' is tha coffee," Kolt grumbled. He preferred a cooked meal.

Tincup had had enough. "Ya heard Banks. Now fill yar cup an' *git!*" Tincup raised his foot and booted the man away.

CHAPTER 10

The wagons plunged forward, closing the distance between them and the mountains that were looming over the horizon. After a few days of peaceful riding, the caravan reached another amazing landmark.

"We'll be at tha Ice Springs within tha hour," Davis informed Banks when he came to make his scouting report. "Thar are places that have been ruined, makin' much of it a mushy mire. Need ta keep tha animals clear of tha spots that have been overrun. Saw buzzards picking at the bones of a new carcass…must have strayed an' got stuck, *permanently*." He turned up his nose to indicate the rank smell that accompanied the decaying animal.

"Making more of the water putrid. Soon, none will be fit for drinking. I remember how the place used to be." Change was inevitable, Banks knew, but he didn't have to like it.

"Yeah. Still seems unreal…how tha ice stays thar an' tha water's so pure an' sweet tastin'. Such a luxury after drinkin' tha alkali stuff that most of tha waterin' holes offer up ta here."

"It won't be long before the place becomes a swampland, or worse, completely dried up."

"Turnin' into a graveyard. Too many comin' through now. Tha ground's just not holdin' up."

"The peat grass is dying…can't handle all the

trampling, and without its protection, the water below won't stay frozen."

"It'll be a real disappointment for those comin' later."

The wagon train stopped at the ice preserve for the night. As predicted, the treasured spot would soon be completely destroyed, but until then, the thirsty pioneers, in the middle of the hot summer, would have access to ice and the pure-tasting water the slough provided.

"Follow me. This is tha surprise I was talkin' 'bout a few days earlier." Tincup took Lucky through the marsh. They had to bypass a large section of mushy terrain. "Watch whar I go." Tincup seemed to know where not to step. They stopped. "Put yar hand down here."

"Freezin'!" Lucky was surprised to find ice below the ground when it was so hot outside.

"Call this tha Ice Slough. Used ta be tha best stop on tha whole trail, but ya can see what's happenin'. Still sum good spots left, though." Tincup pulled his knife from his pocket. He used it like a pick and broke small pieces off the underlying block. He handed them to Lucky.

Lucky rolled the frozen liquid around his tongue. He relished the cold, natural taste of the melting ice. "Priceless. Right now, this find's *better* than a gold strike."

"Come on, let's git sumthin' that'll really cut this stuff up." Tincup led the way back out of the maze.

When they reached camp, Banks was talking to a crowd. "Try not to disturb the ground. And don't cut the surface grass if you can avoid it.

Any disturbance will have an effect, so let's try not to do more damage than what's been done already."

Sally followed Sam across the slough. "It feels like tha ground's gonna *give*."

"Tha surface does rock ya as ya walk." Sam found a fresh patch of peat. He got out his knife. As he moved the tufted plants away, the cold water that sat above the ice soaked his sleeve. He reached down and chipped at the frozen layer beneath. "*Cold!*" He took his hand out. "Too thick for this." He put his knife back into his pocket. "Tha ice is well-preserved."

"I'll git something," Sally offered. She came back with Lucky, who was holding a hammer and wedge.

The cool, tasty ice was a refreshing respite after weeks of drinking hot, sun-baked, alkali water. The tense atmosphere, created from the weeks of hardship, melted away like the ice that filled their drinks. Spirits were lifted.

Lucky took a big gulp from his drink. "Brain freeze! Haven't had that in a *long time*."

Tincup shook his hand. "My fingers are still tinglin' after gittin' so cold. Kinda weird ta think 'bout, but I reckon someone could git frostbite in this heat."

Though their troubles had been forgotten for a time, the break of day brought the pioneers back to reality and their usual routine, but the lightness lingered with the morning mist, and they tackled their chores with renewed energy. They knew they had an easy day ahead and would reach another huge milestone—the crossing of the Continental Divide.

Lucky couldn't believe they had reached the high point. "This is *it*? South Pass?"

Davis laughed at his reaction. "Told ya it wouldn't be what ya'd expect."

Lucky scanned the grassy openness that marked the crossing of the Rocky Mountains. "Rather have this, though. It's a nice respite afore we start goin' down."

"The Oregon Buttes." Banks showed Sam the flat-topped formation. "We'll be camping soon ...at Pacific Springs, about four miles further down. We're now leaving the Nebraska Territory behind us and are crossing into the Oregon Country."

Sam had night duty and was slowly circling the herd. Lucky joined him. "We'll have ta decide which way ta go soon."

"I know." Sam was torn. He was going to share his life with Sally; he was sure of it, but he wasn't ready to leave his brother, not yet. "I'm goin' *with ya*."

"Ya *sure*? I know how important Sally is ta ya. I can go it alone if'n ya decide ta stay on with her family."

The next night, Sam and Sally talked about their future. "I want ya ta go with yar brother," Sally emphasized. "Ya both need ta git this *fever* outta yar systems. Then, when yar ready, you can come ta me."

Sam sighed. "I'll think 'bout ya every day."

When two prospectors joined the train for a few days, their stories gave a positive slant to the mining craze. Their enthusiasm affected many on the train, including Lucky and Sam.

After the miners took off, Lucky approached

Banks. "We told ya 'bout our wantin' ta try our luck prospectin'. Well...we kinda thought 'bout headin' ta California soon. That is, if'n yar OK ta let us go."

"The herd's been thinned out enough, so I reckon I could release you of your obligations." Banks couldn't leave it at that. He gave advice against the pursuit and ended by saying that he understood. "Heck, after hearing those men go on..." He hesitated. Though the talk of gold had an effect on him, too, he knew he had other responsibilities. "Of course, the decision's yours to make."

"We'll let ya know when we reach tha cutoff."

"We should be there in a few days."

For Sam, the time flew. He spent most of his time with Sally. Lucky learned to play cards like a professional gambler. Tincup felt that he had prepared the boy well.

When they reached the popular split in the trail, Lucky went to find Banks. He was with Davis. "What did you boys decide? On with us or to Fort Bridger?"

"With Sam sweet on Sally, we'll go on with ya a bit longer."

"Tha farthest ya should go is ta tha cutoff near Fort Hall." Davis hated to see the boys go, but he understood.

"I'll let Sam know."

"We'll have work for you until you split off. For now, you can get the wagons going to Fort Bridger to pull off over there." Banks pointed to an area of the heavily used trail that was well marked with wheel tracks. "And if some want to say their farewells, tell them to do so now."

"Yes, sir!" Lucky was relieved. He realized he wasn't ready to leave.

Banks turned his attention to Davis. "After they've said their goodbyes, pass the word that we'll go on a few more miles before we set up camp for the night."

"Yes, sir." Davis went to carry out his orders.

Banks was alone. He sat on his horse and reflected on the journey that had brought him to this point. He thought of the young boys and envied their brotherly bond, one he never shared with his older sibling. At least they'll have each other when they go it alone, he thought. A call brought him out of his reverie. He went to see the wagons off.

PART TWO

Parting of Ways

1859-1863

CHAPTER 11

Even though the main train was headed to Oregon, some of the pioneers had decided to veer off and head to Fort Bridger. The Murphys had originally planned to settle near the fort. Their oldest son was a lieutenant serving at the military post. The Humphreys had decided to go with them. The Lobacks, after hearing the prospectors talk about the growing towns around Denver, thought they'd take the cutoff and head to the Kansas Territory.

"Tha area should be ripe for establishin' a bakery," Mr. Loback told Lucky. "We'll take tha Cherokee Trail an' go east, then head south ta tha goldfields. We'll keep droppin' down 'til we find tha right spot."

"Ya boys stay out of trouble." Mrs. Baker had grown quite fond of Lucky, who had regularly stopped by to check in on her family. "Made this cake for ya." She handed him a parcel wrapped in cloth. "I added some fruit that I got at tha last supply station."

"Wow! Thank ya." Lucky favored sweets, and this was a treat. He passed the cake on to Sam so he could give each of her children a hug, then he helped them onto Mr. Loback's wagon. "Be missin' ya. Take care, now." The sound of a gold town was as tempting as getting another taste of their delicious food. "I just might git out yar way."

"Can't thank ya enough for gittin' us this far," Mrs. Baker said when Banks rode up to see them off.

"You should have no trouble from here. The Lobacks will take good care of you."

Final farewells were said to the Murphys and the Humphreys, then the teamsters got their oxen moving and the wagons headed to the fort.

Lucky watched as they rolled away. "Feels like losin' family."

Sam knew what he meant. "A trip like this brings people together in much tha same way."

The main wagon train spent the next five days traversing a dry tableland. The gravelly terrain was barren and devoid of grass, so the dust that was kicked up only thickened in the air. Even the alkali lakes were dry. The sun burned each day without mercy. To avoid the afternoon heat, they traveled by night into the early morning and stopped to rest during the middle of the day. The extra water Banks had them carry was enough to get them across the desert, but the warm fluid did not quench their insatiable thirsts. It only removed the layer of dust that had coated their throats.

"Haven't even seen a snake," Sam noted as they followed the seemingly endless terrain.

"Bullet likes tha sound of that. I think he's perked up. Seems tha herd is movin' faster, too. Must be gittin' near tha Green River. Funny how tha animals can smell tha water."

"Be glad ta git outta this graveyard." Sam felt a chill. He had passed another white carcass of an ox that had literally been worked to death.

"Eerie, tha way tha bones stand out in tha moonlight." Lucky shivered. "We musta passed hundreds of these poor, dead beasts."

"How long do ya think it takes ta bleach 'em so white?"

"Don't rightly know."

"Banks had us ready. At least we haven't lost any of ours on this stretch. Surely, we're close enough for all ta make it now."

Davis rode up. "Be at tha Green River in less than an hour."

Lucky rubbed Bullet. "Or sooner, tha way tha animals are gettin' thar second wind. I can tell they've picked up thar pace."

Davis confirmed their earlier thoughts. "They can smell it."

"Just talkin' 'bout that. But have ta say, I'm with 'em. Once we git thar, I'll be ready for a washin'." Sam coughed. "Seems tha dust has worked its way inside of me, too."

The relief offered by the waters of the Green River was a welcomed break from the grueling traverse. After following the waterway for a week, they reached Soda Springs. Some of the pioneers used the naturally carbonated water to make bread, as its bubbly nature helped to make it rise. Others made tasty lemonade or spirits with the unique liquid.

Tincup built a fire and started a pot of stew. He used the soda water to make the broth, then he poured the extra in his cup.

Lucky came to relax by the fire. "A watched pot never boils."

"I'm not in a hurry." Tincup leaned against a boulder and took a swig of the sparkling brew.

"Tastes like beer!"

"Only 'cause ya haven't had tha taste of it for so long."

"I'll make tha comparison when we reach tha Fort on Saturday."

"An' yar first one's on me."

The aroma from the cooking food brought more people to the fire ring. Tincup removed the simmering stew and replaced it with a pot for brewing coffee.

"You sure it's ready?" Banks asked when Tincup handed him his serving. "The vegetables still have color."

"An' are crunchy," Kolt observed.

Lucky slowly chewed so he could savor the meal. "Tastes better, somehow."

"Tha stew's been cookin' over tha fire long enough." Tincup tasted a sample. "Must be from tha soda water."

Banks looked around. "Where's Sam?"

"Guess. Now that we're nearin' tha partin' point, he's been spendin' all his free time with Sally." Lucky laughed. "Believe tha boy's been *bit*...first time too."

Tincup got up and added more stew to his plate. "Thar both decent people. Would be a good match if'n they do decide ta hitch up."

"I'll take her as an in-law. I can see why he's so smitten. If'n I were in his shoes, I'd dread tha partin' too."

"When we get to the fort, stock up on things, like extra canteens for water storage, and if you can get them, some fresh horses. If none are available, give yours a break and fatten them up," Banks advised. "They're already tired, and you'll need them to be in good shape to get you to California."

"OK, Papa," Lucky teased. "Seriously, though, we appreciate all you've done for us." He looked at everyone sitting around the fire. "We were green, an' ya taught us well."

Kolt raised his cup. "Ya proved yarselves."

"Thanks for coverin' our food an' upkeep thus far. We appreciate all tha advice you've given...you've been our teachers." Lucky knew he would miss this group of friends.

It was getting late. Everyone had retired for the night except Lucky. Sam came to set up his bedding and found his brother sitting by the fire. When Lucky saw him, he tossed on another log.

"How's Sally?"

"She's doin' fine. What ya been up to?"

"Been sittin' here with tha gang. They gave some helpful suggestions afore we head out."

"Did they say anythin' 'bout a fresh change of clothes? I don't think ya can wash tha *smell* outta yars."

CHAPTER 12

Visions of fresh food, warm baths, and cool drinks floated in the emigrants' minds as they made their way to Fort Hall. When they saw its outline ahead, they cheered. Everyone was ready for the downtime after another long stretch of dodging dust.

The boys' first stop was the livery. It was located at the far end of the compound.

"'Too many like ya passin' through.'" Sam repeated the stableman's explanation for not having horses for sale. "Kinda glad, though."

"Hate ta part with Bullet, anyway. He's got me this far. I'll git 'im some good grain, an' he'll do me right."

"Yeah. Same with Lindy. Kinda wanted ta keep her, too."

"We'll stay on 'til thar well rested."

"Gonna git new duds. I've got my first...well... an *official* date with Sally tonight."

"Reckon we'll need ta git ya all cleaned up. Can't have ya courtin' unless yar lookin' like a *proper* Doyle."

"I see a sign that says Bath an' Shave. Even has *hot* water!"

Lucky brought up the subject once again. "Ya sure yar not wantin' ta stay with tha train an' Sally?" They were soaking in wooden tubs filled with soapy water. "Ya know, yar free ta go yar own way."

"No. *No*," Sam repeated to emphasize his point. "I've talked with Sally. We both agreed. I need ta go with ya. It's *my* dream too. We've arranged ta keep in touch, an' when tha time is right, I'll be gittin' back to her."

Two days later, Banks was getting his wagon train ready for departure.

"Ya go a few miles west, then make yar cut at tha Raft River," Davis instructed before he left. "Can't miss it. Tha trail's well-worn now."

"Expect the start to be rocky and arid. Land's nothing but sagebrush and greasewood," Banks informed them. "Takes you to the first drainage of the Great Basin. It'll be a dry and hot 50 miles …without water holes. Make sure your horses are ready, and you stock up on water."

Lucky shook Banks's hand. "Wanna thank ya for lettin' us come 'long."

"Felt like ya were our papa, a watchin' over us an' all," Sam added.

"You're fine boys…make your pa *proud*. Was glad to have your help. You worked hard, so I feel you earned *this*." Banks handed each of the boys an envelope. "Though you're not going all the way with us, I felt you were entitled to some of the bonus. Hide it inside your clothes. It can be your emergency money. You never know what may happen."

Sam laughed. "I take that back. You were like our *mum*. She said tha same thing when we left home." He explained about the hidden pocket in their shirts and the Double Eagle coins.

"Didn't expect ya ta add this. Don't know what ta say." Lucky blushed. "Thanks!"

"We'll remember what ya said earlier, and take heed," Sam assured everyone before they parted.

"Wagons...ho!" Banks yelled as he raised his hand and waved his outfit onward.

The two boys stayed and watched as the wagon train moved away. When the Prestons passed, Sam got off his horse, and Sally ran up to him. They embraced for a moment before he gave her a final kiss. As Sally walked back to her wagon, she turned multiple times to get one last look at Sam.

Lucky could see the torment on his older brother's face. "Gonna be OK?"

Sam tried to hide his tears. He could barely speak. "Will be."

CHAPTER 13

"**P**annin' for gold in California is a *fool's errand*." Lucky summarized the sentiment of the weary prospectors who were still hanging around the fort. "No one's bein' encouragin'."

They stopped at the bar one last time before leaving the garrison. The stories were the same.

"I've seen 'em take a whole hillside down by sprayin' water from a nozzle. Call it hydraulic minin'," one prospector told them.

His partner was just as discouraging. "Or thar drillin' deep shafts into tha earth ta git at tha gold pockets. Tried workin' in one of 'em holes...didn't last...tha dark made me feel all closed in....'fraid of bein' buried alive!"

"Gotta have special machinery ta git it out. Who has tha money for *that*?" Sam sneered as they took the turnoff that led to California.

"Tha miners workin' their way back ta tha East are just expressin' thar frustration," Lucky justified. "Reckon we won't know what we'll face, 'til we git thar."

"We got tha Great Basin ta cross, then we gotta git over tha Sierra Nevada range," Sam reminded him. "No need ta git ourselves in a tizzy 'bout tha gold just yet."

"Yar right. First things first. Yar soundin' like Davis." Lucky wiped his forehead and shifted his hat. The sun was already high in the sky, and its radiating heat, pushed around by the wind, made him feel like he was inside a large convection stove.

"Let's camp 'long tha river. We can start in tha cool of tha mornin'."

"Enjoy tha calm afore tha storm, ya mean."

It was another clear, cloudless start to the day. The boys mounted their horses, ready to begin the next phase of their journey. After they left the comforts of the Raft River, they faced the sun-baked lands of the Great Salt Lake Basin, a drainage of the Great Basin.

"Tha City of Rocks!" Sam cheered as they passed through a valley of boulders and pillars.

"A milestone down, but ahead is tha sandy, salty desert of tha Humboldt River drainage." Lucky dreaded the traverse.

"Least thars no wagons ta slow us down."

"Only tha ones we pass. Likely ta see plenty of bullwhackers driving thar freights. With tha dry terrain, bet we'll see more usin' oxen."

"Yar right. Here's one comin' up tha trail, usin' those Texas longhorns. I bet some'll take our mail. So, what are we complainin' 'bout?"

"Just weeks of travelin' through sultry land. 'Like bein' in a big, hot cauldron whar all tha water is sucked through tha bottom of tha pot.' Tincup's description of tha Humboldt River section."

"Tha river's an ooze-filled waterway barely fit for drinkin', an' tha other water sources are likely ta be mudflats or dry. Davis's words."

Those following the California Trail had to cross hundreds of miles of the Great Basin, a dry, arid region between the Wasatch and the

Sierra Nevada Mountains. The large system is made up of smaller basins, and none of their waters drain into the ocean. The mountains that surround these unique watersheds trap the heat inside, keeping the sands salty, dusty, and clay-baked. Water, when available, is hot and alkaline.

"Can see why Kolt kept sayin' Tha Barren instead of Tha Basin," Sam groaned.

"Tincup told me that tha Humboldt River ends when we reach tha sink, a place where it'll disappear into the ground. Reckon we'll see a pool when we git thar."

"Since tha river's water is all we got for a while, we should think of it as a *treasure*." Sam was trying to be optimistic.

"Yar right. Tha water'll be hot an' tasteless. Lucky turned up his nose. "A real *jewel*."

"All jokin' aside, it's just tha two of us now, an' this section's gonna be our test. Just glad ta know you'll have my back."

"Right back at ya. No worries. We got this."

⚜✦⚜✦⚜

"Yar eyes burnin'?" Sam asked Lucky after another day of riding.

"Tha dust must be doin' it."

"My skin's stingin' too...even what's covered over. Can't wait ta git through this."

"Should be out soon."

"Tha farther 'long we go, tha worse tha water tastes. *Humbug*. See why tha river's called this too," Lucky spewed.

"Not just that, seems each day is just as blah as tha last. Tha days are just *humbug*!"

Lucky sensed a strange tone in Sam's voice.

"Ya gittin' tha same funny feelin' ya had when we crossed tha prairie?"

"Nah. Reckon I beat it back thar."

"Ya must be missin' Sally, then."

"Yeah. Be a while afore we'll be near enough ta town ta git an answer ta my last letter."

"Least ya got one ta her on that stage we passed. Lookin' on tha bright side, we should reach tha Sink an' be outta this tomorrow."

"Yeah. Not expectin' much of a lake, but it'll be another milestone ta pass."

"Then we've tha last desert section ta cross. It's just September. At this pace, we should git over tha Sierra Mountains afore tha snows hit. Kinda lookin' forward ta tha cold again."

When they reached the meadow that marked the end of the dreary river, they realized they would be sharing the marshes of the Humboldt Sink with others. Some Indians, Paiutes they later found out, and two wagon trains had also stopped. A small trading post had been built to accommodate the crowd.

"Ya be needin' someun ta git ya over tha mountains?" one man asked Lucky and Sam as they walked amongst the crowd. "Know all tha waterin' spots."

"Ya wantin' ta hire a guide?" another man asked them after they rejected the first offer.

The boys waved the hawkers off and walked toward a big white tent that was covered in dust. Inside, there was a makeshift store selling supplies. In the corner, a few tables were set up, and men were playing cards.

"Whar ya headed?" the clerk asked when Sam paid for some coffee and beans.

"California. Which route would ya suggest?"

The man studied the boy in front of him. "Ya goin' ta pan? Gold's been gone thar fer a while now...leastwise, tha easy pickin's. Heard of a strike in tha Kansas Territory, though. Other side of tha Rockies...back tha way ya come."

"We've got our mind set on prospectin' in California, anyways," Sam assured the man.

"Waste of time." The man shook his head. "But if'n yar mind's set, when ya git outta here, you'll see whar tha trail forks. Go right fer tha Truckee an' left ta take tha Carson. Both will take ya 'cross tha desert ta tha mountains."

"Much obliged." Sam knew that they would take the Carson Route. The trail wasn't as steep. He waited for Lucky to make his purchase, and then they left the crowded store.

Lucky had heard Sam's conversation with the clerk. "He thinks we're crazy, but we *have* ta go whar tha rush started."

"Yeah," Sam agreed. He was just as anxious to see where it all began. "Maybe we'll surprise ourselves an' make a strike."

The boys settled for the night, away from the scurry of the other visitors. As they lay under the stars, a strange brightness caused them to wake up and open their eyes.

CHAPTER 14

Streaks of light flittered above them and fanned into flares of flamingo-colored light.

"Lucky, you awake?" Sam asked when he first noticed the unusual, ribboned rays.

Lucky had just opened his eyes when he heard Sam's voice. "Think tha sky's tryin' ta tell us somethin'?"

"Let's make a wish, if'n it were."

"Know what ya wished for."

"Likewise."

"No need ta jinx ourselves by tellin', though."

The boys watched in silence. After about five minutes, the auroral display was over, and the stars once again dominated the night sky.

Lucky broke the spell. "Reckon that's tha end of it. That was cool."

"But a bit scary."

A strong solar flare caused the great aurora that was seen around the world. Later called the Carrington Event, it's still the most intense storm of its kind on record. The stellar display peaked on the first and second of September and caused telegraph lines to fail across America. In the East, the vibrant red sky mimicked the color of the rising sun, causing birds to chirp. Some who were awakened by the light started to get ready for work until they noticed that dawn was still hours away.

When the boys woke again, it was daylight. Sam faced the barren landscape. "Welcome ta tha Forty Mile Desert."

"Didn't we just finish tha Fifty Mile one? They sure look tha same. No shade, lots of wind, silty dirt, an' more creosote. Another dream world. What else could we ask for?"

"Stronger alkali water?" Sam spat. More lightheartedly, he added, "Starry skies?"

"Yeah! Another light show like last night."

"It looks like we'll have company 'long tha way." Sam saw a muleskinner crack his whip to keep his animals moving. He had also spotted a wagon train far ahead.

By 1859, other users had made travel on the wagon roads less lonely. Though the Pony Express had yet to start, freight companies were busy transporting the mail, tools, food, and a host of other supplies to the settlements, trading posts, and military fortresses that had sprung up along the way. The once deserted paths were quickly becoming established roadways.

They stopped to rest during the heat of the day. "Kinda liked it when we were lone ducks. Less dust bein' kicked up." Sam's skin did not like the caustic coating that once again had saturated his clothing.

"I agree. Tha wind doesn't help, nor does tha dry heat. Can kinda grate on yar nerves. I'll be glad when we git through this section. If'n we travel longer tonight, we may git ta tha Carson River tomorrow."

"Let's ride 'til tha horses tell us otherwise. We'll have ta watch once they smell tha water. We don't want 'em ta wear themselves out."

"Tha night air'll be cooler." Lucky looked at the clear sky. "Nice ta git a break from this heat."

"Won't be much of a moon tonight. That may be a problem."

They didn't have to worry. Abandoned items left along the trail by travelers ahead of them had already been set on fire. The path was also lined with dead beasts that had long ago succumbed to the harsh elements. The boys followed the gruesome trail. The light of the improvised torches lit the way.

"Seems others had tha same thought," Lucky observed. "Have ya noticed tha way tha light from tha fires makes tha oxen's eyes glare at us...or was that a mule?"

"Hard ta tell. Think it was a horse."

"How come thar eyes are glitterin'?"

"Must be filled with salt."

"Tha carcasses seem ta be movin' too."

"Maggots, most likely."

⁂

After days of riding in the desolate land, the boys reached a section of the traverse where the sand was deep and formed dunes. Bones were strewn in all directions.

"Feels like a graveyard," Lucky whispered.

"It is. Tha sand's sapped tha life outta 'em."

"Wonder what else is buried here?"

They came upon a man who was walking, his horse trailing behind. He was holding two long knives, one in each hand. He held them parallel to the ground as if he had dowsing rods and was looking for water.

"Anythin' we can do ta help?" Lucky asked when they caught up to the stranger.

The man continued to walk past the decaying carcasses. "Not unless you find my wife."

Sam gave Lucky a questioning look. "Don't see anyone else."

"I had to leave her out here. She was buried somewhere in the sand. These rods will tell me where."

The boys tried to get the man to sit down and have a drink. They thought he was delirious.

"Can't. Gotta focus...feel the rods."

"Isn't that how ta find *water*?" Sam asked.

"*Bones*, too," the man shot back.

Sam stated the obvious. "Ya can see 'em. Thar *all around* ya. Yar *steppin'* on some."

"They're not *human!*"

Lucky knew the man was getting annoyed. "It's just, we don't understand."

The stranger took a few more steps, then he abruptly stopped. His hands crossed in front of his body. "*Male.*" He stooped down and swept away the sand until he uncovered a corpse. It was a man.

"Reckon I've *seen it all!*" Lucky proclaimed. "How will ya know if'n it's yar wife?"

"The rods will turn outwards if the bones are those of a woman."

The diviner stood and continued with his search. The boys tried to help, but the man was intent on finding his wife, so they decided to let him be.

"I hope ya find her," Sam said before they rode off.

"Don't know if'n he's plumb crazy or has some *special* powers."

"With this heat, maybe a little of both." Sam

noticed Lindy's labored steps. "Why is thar just as much sand 'long tha trail as was at tha spot whar tha man was buried? Ya'd think, with all tha passin', some of it would git pushed away."

"Tha wind blows it 'round. What makes tha dunes. At least it's loose. Accordin' ta Tincup's report, thar should be 'bout six miles of this, then we'll be at tha river."

After a few miles, they stopped to give their horses a rest. Lucky poured some water into his hand for Bullet. The horse licked his palm dry, so Lucky continued the process until the last of his water was gone. "Tha river better be a few miles more."

Sam gave Lindy another lick. "I saved a swig for each of us."

"Should git thar by lunch. Bullet an' Lindy can git a good rest then." Lucky patted his horse. "Good boy. Yar doin' great."

Sam also gave his horse a rubbing. "Yeah. Lindy's been a good steed."

Lucky mounted Bullet. "Thar both holdin' up just fine."

"I agree. Helps that we've taken such good care of 'em."

The foursome continued to trudge through the seemingly endless sand dunes. The heat of the day increased with each mile, but the smell of the river kept the horses moving, and the thought of fresh water lifted the boys' spirits.

"What tha...?" Lucky questioned when they finally reached their destination, and he saw the trees that grew along the riverbank.

CHAPTER 15

Clothes were strewn across every available branch. Tents lined the waterway. People were sitting around their campfires.

Sam took in the view. "Reckon this is why they call it Ragtown."

They passed the camp and followed the river. "Whoa, boy." Lucky had to fight Bullet's drive toward the sweet-smelling water. "We want ya ta git a clean drink." Lucky found an open spot away from the established sites.

As the horses drank the fresh water, the boys filled their water pouches.

"Gittin' mighty ripe smellin'." Lucky snorted, then threw his canteen on the bank and jumped into the cool water of the Carson River.

"Wa...hoo!" Sam followed his brother and made a big splash.

They kept their clothes on so they could clean all at once. After they freshened up, they hung their wet clothes on the trees and headed to the small outpost that was selling supplies.

"Whar ya headed?" a man asked the boys as they waited in line to pay for their goods.

"Goin' ta Placerville," Lucky answered.

"I'm headin' in that direction as well. Been restin' here a few days afore goin' on. Tha desert really takes it outta ya, an' thars still more of it ahead."

"Reckon I'm gittin' use ta tha badlands," though I'm thankful for places like this. My horse likes 'em too," Sam joked.

"Yar horse'll git another break at Woodfords, a nice stop afore ya follow tha Carson River through tha canyon."

"Whar ya endin' up?" Lucky asked.

"Takin' my family ta Sacramento. Wantin' ta establish a blacksmith shop thar. If ya git out that way, stop in. Name's Bellows." The man extended his hand.

"Lucky, an' Sam. We're wantin' ta do some prospectin'. We've heard tha strikes are 'bout done whar we're headed, but we wanna see how things are for ourselves."

"I'm not one ta keep another from pursurin' thar dream. Many have told me that I couldn't carry my blacksmithin' stuff on tha trail, but we've made it this far."

Sam saw a look of concern on the man's face. "We were with a wagon train on our way across. Seen how tha extra weight can be a challenge."

"I've split tha load amongst several wagons. I wouldn't want ta overexert my beasts. They have it hard enough. They like tha rest stops as much as yar horses."

"Gotta take care of 'em. Thar tha ones that'll git us through," Sam acknowledged.

"My last *test* for 'em will be gittin' over tha passes in tha Sierra Mountains. I'll be home free from thar."

Lucky reached the counter. "Good luck ta ya. Maybe we'll git out yar way."

The boys left Ragtown early the next morning. They followed the Carson River, but had to cross the waterway multiple times. The route was rugged and rocky in sections, with dry deserts between the meandering bends in the river. They stopped at the settlement of Woodfords, where they got hay and grain for their horses.

"On ta Hope Valley," Lucky said as they left the comfort of the station.

"Gotta git through tha canyon first," Sam reminded his little brother.

The ride through the canyon was steep and rocky. The climbing was slow.

"Ornery section," Lucky noted after they had passed a precipitous drop in the trail.

"Reckon we'll have more like 'em as we go. Uh-oh! Looks like thars trouble ahead."

When they approached the chaotic scene, they heard a frustrated pair of men trying to lift their wagon. It was full of freight.

"Ya need some help?" Lucky asked.

"Reckon we could," one of the men replied. "Can't seem ta keep tha wood from crackin' in this bone-dry air. I've been soakin' tha wheels in water as much as I could, but this un's just plumb stoved in."

"Be obliged if ya could help unload some of tha supplies, so we can git tha wagon light enough ta lift. Got a spare wheel ready ta put on. By tha way, he's Jim, an' I'm George."

"Sam, an' my brother, Lucky."

George elaborated. "We've got supplies fer a store in Sacramento. Tha wagon's full, so it'll be a mighty big chore, if'n ya wanta help."

It took a while to remove the cargo. When they were done, Jim outlined the plan of attack. "Lucky, we'll lift tha axle. Sam, if ya can help

George git tha wheel on, then we'll finish from there."

Jim and Lucky lifted the wagon and held it level. Just as Sam and George inserted the wheel, Jim's foot slipped, and he lost his grip. The brunt of the weight fell on Lucky. He tried to hold on, but the jolt caused him to fall. The wheel took on the additional force, but it wasn't fully inserted. It tilted and, for a brief moment, held the wagon in place.

The men had instinctively backed away, but Lucky couldn't react as fast as the others. He was lying face up, and his legs were under the wagon. He started to back crawl just as the wagon came crashing down.

CHAPTER 16

Sam rushed toward Lucky. He grabbed his arm and pulled hard. The wagon made a strange, creaky sound when it hit the ground. Sam cringed, thinking it was the cry of his brother.

"That was close," Lucky said when the dust lifted.

Sam exhaled. "Yar not *crushed*!"

"Reckon not. Yar pullin' got me out in time." Lucky looked over his outstretched legs. He took off his boot and inspected his foot. "Tha wagon did nip my big toe. It may be broken."

Sam saw the dark blue that had started to form under Lucky's toenails. "Got that *turkey toe* too."

"Reckon I may be feelin' some pain thar," Lucky reluctantly agreed. He had been teased since childhood about his longer second toe.

"Ya all right, boy?" George asked. "Jim feels really bad. His foot hit 'em rocks wrong an' just gave way."

"Yeah," Jim admitted. "I'm real sorry."

"May be hobblin' for a while, otherwise, no harm done," Lucky assured him.

Jim offered a bottle of whiskey that he had retrieved from the supplies. "Glad yar not hurt to bad. *This* may ease tha pain."

"Inside an' out." Lucky took a swig, then he

poured some of the contents over his aching toes. His bruises had started to show red.

"We'll git back ta tha wheel later. Gittin' late. Why don't ya stay an' sup with us? Tha least we can do fer yar trouble," George kindly offered. "As ya can see, we have plenty."

The supplies were still laid out, so it was easy to find what they needed for a fine-tasting meal. The stew was ladened with fresh vegetables, meat, and potatoes. They topped off the dinner with some preserved fruit that the men had put aside for themselves.

Jim served the dessert. "Keepin' these fer special occasions. Reckon yar helpin' qualifies."

After they finished eating, they found a spot around the campfire. A fresh pot of coffee sat above the flames.

"Whar ya boys headed?" Jim asked.

"Placerville." Lucky told them about their plans to visit the original goldfields.

"Watch yarselves when ya git thar," George warned. "Was called *Hangtown*. And with good reason."

"Why tha nickname?" Sam asked.

"Haven't ya heard 'bout thar necktie parties? Just recently, three men were hung. They never even got a trial. Lynch justice." George snarled. "Thar group tried ta git me once. Jim convinced 'em otherwise."

"Not expectin' ta cause any trouble. Just checkin' things out," Sam assured him.

"Any stranger could be suspect. Keep that in mind is all I'm suggestin'."

"Ya sound like ya know yar way 'round. We were thinkin' of goin' by way of tha Carson Pass.

Is that how ya figure ta cross tha mountains?" Lucky asked.

"That ol' pass is hardly used nowadays. A man named Luther found a better way ta git through. Ya boys should use that route. It's a newer wagon road just up from here. It's easier, if ya can call goin' over any pass *easy*, that is," Jim laughed.

George pulled out a map. "Have a look." He pointed out the route. "You'll miss tha steepness of tha Devil's Ladder an' end up on tha Johnson Cutoff Trail. Once ya git on it, it'll take ya all tha way ta Placerville."

"Is that tha same route as tha Lake Tahoe Trail?" Lucky asked.

"Yep," George replied. "It's also called tha Placerville Route or tha Day Route."

"Should be called tha Hard Day Route." Jim scowled. "Still have tha steep climb up tha pass, then ya got tha rugged downhill descent."

After a few days of riding, Lucky had to agree with the men's assessment of the Luther Trail. "Jim was right. Tha climb is tough. I wonder how much rougher tha other trail woulda been."

"If'n tha words *devil* an' *ladder* are used in a name, I can only imagine. Sure glad I checked Lindy's shoes in Carson City. She'll need ta have good footin' goin' up this."

"Tha down side will be just as challengin', if'n not more so." Lucky rubbed Bullet's neck. He knew his horse would bear the brunt of the work.

When they reached the high point of the pass, they didn't stop except to give the horses a chance to catch their breath. They were told to go a short distance more, so they rode on to Grass Lake. As the horses grazed, the boys sat against a fallen tree trunk.

"Sure can feel tha elevation gain," Sam noted.

"Yeah. Wonder if'n tha horses can too?"

"Hard ta know. Gittin' thar footin' with tha rocks givin' on tha steep part's enough ta cause thar strugglin'."

"Reckon so." Lucky looked at the patches of unmelted white left in the shadow of the trees. "Snow musta fallen recently."

"No worries. We'll be over tha mountain soon. One stop at a time. Next one, Lake Valley."

Hills were mounted, and rock outcroppings were passed. The boys met each new venture without incident. Their daily challenge was to tackle the tough terrain.

"Johnson Pass should be our last major crossin' afore reachin' Placerville," Sam said as they approached the base of the saddle and started to climb. Other users ahead of them had kicked up dust, and they had to watch for falling rocks. "Lots of people on this section of tha trail."

"Yeah. Didn't expect all tha freight wagons."

"Most seem ta be headin' ta tha Comstock area. Somethin' ta think 'bout, huh?"

The question was left unanswered. Lucky was focused on finding gold nuggets. He was not interested in the silver ores.

They reached the top of a lower pass. "Time ta stop again. Gotta take advantage of tha flatter land," Lucky said more to his horse than to his brother.

The steep, rocky terrain had taken Bullet's

full strength and concentration. He threw his head high and gave a welcoming snort when they reached level ground.

When the boys headed down, they kept riding and only stopped to give their horses a rest. They didn't have to worry about food or drink. The rivers provided water, and there were stations selling supplies. They eventually reached the Slippery Ford Bridge. The granite rock on the riverbed was slick at this crossing, so they decided to use the man-made overpass. Since they had to wait on other travelers, they decided to get some refreshments. There was a store near the wooden structure.

"Popular place," Sam said as they made their way through the crowd.

"How much farther ta tha next restin' spot?" Lucky asked when they reached the counter.

"Yar not far from Register Rock. Ya can add yar names, if'n ya a mind ta. Then, you'll follow tha trail ta Strawberry Flat House, but don't expect ta eat any. Tha season's over."

After they ate, they were able to get over the bridge, but the trail was still busy. When they got to the meadow where the Flat House was located, they decided to stop for the night.

"Wish they still had tha wild strawberries, especially if'n thar as big an' sweet as tha owner bragged." Lucky licked his lips, thinking of the juicy berries.

"Next time." Sam got his blanket and laid it out on the ground. He positioned his saddle so it would act as a headrest, then he lay on top of his bedding. He laid his hat to the side. "Sure feels good ta git outta tha saddle."

"Ya still gittin' sore?" Lucky saw a snake crawling toward Sam's hat. "Don't move!" He grabbed a stick, scooped the serpent up, and threw it into the brush.

"Good eye! Wouldn't want ta share my hair with that hitchhiker."

"Remember when I did?"

"I'd forgotten, but now that ya bring it up... yeah." Sam grinned. "It all started because ya had insisted on wearin' my hand-me-downs, even though they were way too big for ya."

Lucky defended his childhood behavior. "Ta prove I was a big boy too."

"It was just another of yar antics. Anyway, as I recall, ya was watchin' Mum an' me hang up clothes an' didn't know ya was standin' on an anthill. After ya felt thar sting, ya saw 'em crawlin' up yar legs, so ya ran ta tha pond ta git 'em off. Tha baggy clothes caused ya ta stumble, an' yar hat fell ahead of ya."

"I do remember yar clothes trippin' me up."

"Watchin' ya swattin' at tha ants an' tryin' ta stand with tha loose fittin' clothes was a trip... had my sides splitting."

"It was all downhill from thar."

"A garter snake had crawled inside your hat, and when ya put it on, tha snake slid down yar back. Ya felt it 'bout tha time ya jumped into tha water. We didn't know why ya was shriekin' 'til ya tore off yar clothes an' we saw tha snake swimmin' in tha water with ya." Sam, knowing what came next, was laughing so hard he could hardly continue.

Lucky was laughing, too. "What would *you* do if'n a snake slithered under *yar* shirt?"

Sam chuckled as he finished the story. "Ya came out of tha water buck naked, only ta see our neighbors had ridden up. They had thar young daughter with 'em."

"Patricia was in my class!"

"Thar ya stood, in yar birthday suit, so ya jumped back into tha pond, only ta find tha snake was still thar. Yar squealin' an' splashin' had everyone in stitches. I never saw Mum laugh so hard."

"Glad I could be yar entertainment."

Sam was still giggling when he got up the next day. "You sure were a sight ta watch."

"Next time, I'll let tha snake git in yar hat."

The childhood memory had them inwardly laughing as they hit the trail for another day of riding. A few hours later, they faced another noted rise, Peavine Hill.

"Granite Springs shouldn't be too far away," Lucky said after they had been descending the slope for a while. It'll be a good place ta stop afore tacklin' tha Peavine Ridge."

"Yeah. It's likely tha red dust that we've been warned 'bout'll git kicked up since it's so dry. It may be too early for tha ice haulin', but tha route will be busy."

"Placerville is just ahead. Now, *I* feel like tha horse goin' ta tha barn," Lucky sang.

They could see the dust before they reached the ridge. They rode about four miles through the fine powder, then dropped down to cross the American River.

Sam read the sign. "Tha Brockliss Bridge."

"Thars a tradin' post."

"Reckon we should stop an' see why thar's

a bridge here."

"It's tough if'n ya decide ta ford tha river. Ya have ta ride through thick brush, an' tha rocks can trip yar horses when yar forgin' through tha water. Yar likely ta falter an' take a swim. Cost ya fifty cents each. Covers you an' yar horse," a merchant informed them.

"Should we pay tha fare?" Lucky asked Sam after they heard the man's account.

"Lindy'll be squealin' tha whole time."

"Bullet won't like it either. He doesn't like surprises an' has that strange way of blowin' air through his nose ta let me know when he's unhappy."

Tha boys thought of their horses. They paid the fare. After crossing the river, they traveled to the recommended camping area, Fresh Pond. Several wagons had also stopped for the night.

"That was *some* descent," Lucky said to a neighboring camper.

The man nodded. "Aye. Junction Hill is *tough* ...an' long."

Sam scanned the horizon. "You'd think we'd git used ta all tha ups an' downs, but each one is a new challenge."

"Ya boys headed ta Hangtown? Hope things have changed thar. Tha place has some nasty sidewinders, so-called vigilantes, an' others who wanna follow thar own law," the man warned.

"We'll keep our heads," Sam assured him.

The man stared at the boys. "Yar young. Sum will try ta take advantage of that."

"So we've been told. Thanks for yar concern." Lucky kept his tone civil. The reference to their young age was getting tiresome. "We heard tha cutoff is just down tha way.”

“It is. When ya git ta Johnson’s Ranch, yar less than an hour away. Yar almost thar.”

They reached Placerville the next day.

“We’re here!” Lucky cheered.

“Looks just like another town. Don’t know why I thought it’d be different.”

They rode by the muddy potholes that filled the street. There was the usual pick of shops. Brick buildings had replaced ones burned in a fire. They passed the livery and a smithy before reaching the post office.

Sam’s face beamed when he read Sally’s letter. Lucky could see it was good news. “They found a nice town.” The firing of guns caused Sam to stop and look at his brother. “Get down!” They ducked behind the railing.

Several riders raced past them.

“Robbers. Stop them!” someone yelled.

Lucky and Sam instinctively jumped on their horses and pursued the outlaws. After some hard riding, they were within firing range of the fleeing fugitives and started shooting. One of them dropped.

“I’ll go on. You attend ta ’im,” Lucky said when they reached the fallen man.

Sam got off his horse to see if the bandit was dead. When he got close to the body, the smell was overwhelming. The stench made him gag, so he stopped and started to back away. The man took advantage, and in a snap, he rolled over and pointed his gun at Sam.

CHAPTER 17

"Drop it," the robber instructed. He had blood seeping out of his shirt. The bullet had pierced just above his hip.

Sam instantly recognized the outlaw, Fighting Sam Brown. Though he had never seen the desperado, this man fit the description. He was a big man: heavy, broad, tall, and unkempt. His refusal to wash explained the obnoxious odor. The man was loathsome.

The repulsive robber rubbed his shaggy, red beard. "Yar gonna regret this!"

Brown's reputation as a gunman was well known. Sam had heard how the drunken bully purposely provoked misunderstandings so he could show off his shooting skills. Sam knew he was in the presence of a dangerous man, so he threw his gun down. He waited for the villain to make the next move.

Instead of ending Sam's life instantly, Brown wanted to make the boy pay for knocking him down. His vicious nature took over. "Take off yar belt." After Sam complied, Brown grabbed it. "Hold out yar hands." He strapped Sam's hands tightly together. "Git down. On yar back."

The man's playing a cat and mouse game, Sam thought. If I don't think of something fast, my time's limited, and I'll be another notch on his pistol. Sam tried to figure a way out of this dilemma. Before he could come up with a plan, Brown brought over a knotted rope. He placed the noose over Sam's head, then tied the other end to the horn of his saddle. He mounted his horse.

"Giddy up." Brown's horse started to move forward.

Sam could feel the rope tighten around his neck. He grabbed the noose and was able to keep the loops from crushing his throat, but he knew it would not be enough to stop the pressure when the horse started to gallop.

"Want ya ta *feel* tha *fear* first," Brown taunted.

The horse slowly pulled the helpless boy across the field. Though Sam was able to keep the rope from tightening around his neck, the dragging caused him to wince with pain as the gravel tore his shirt and cut into his back.

Lucky lost the outlaws' trail. He decided to go back to town, expecting to meet Sam at the sheriff's office. On his return, he met up with the posse.

"Lost 'em 'bout a mile up. One of 'em was shot an' fell off his horse. My brother should've brought 'im in."

"We just came from town. Got no one behind bars," the sheriff informed him.

"Fell 'bout here." Lucky looked around. In the distance, he could see a lone horse and, just farther on, dust. He felt his neck crawl. "Lindy! Hyah!" he yelled to get Bullet moving. When he was close enough to see what the outlaw was doing to Sam, he stopped and got out his rifle. He took a deep breath to steady his nerves, aimed, and fired.

Fighting Sam looked back at his prey. He laughed, then turned forward. He poked the horse with his spurs and broke into a full gallop. Sam could feel the noose tighten, then it suddenly loosened. Lucky had shot the rope, causing it to fray. When Brown's horse started to run, the force caused the fibers of the rope to give. Brown stopped and turned to see why his beast had moved so easily. He saw Sam struggling to get the noose off and a rider coming up from behind. The posse was close on his heels, so he decided to make a break for it.

Sam Brown escaped justice that day but was a menace throughout the west, especially in Virginia City, Nevada. He enjoyed killing, seeing it as a sport. His vindictiveness was his downfall. After shooting at and missing a saloon owner, Henry Van Sickle, a pursuit followed. Eventually, Van Sickle was the victor, killing the outlaw on his 30th birthday.

"We got what we need ta start prospectin'," Lucky said after they had loaded their horses with supplies. "Did ya git yar letter off ta Sally?"

"Early this mornin'."

The boys left Placerville and headed up the mountain. They could see where the previous strikes had taken place. Water ditches had been abandoned. The banks along the river were devoid of vegetation. The removal of timber had left the hillsides barren. They followed a streambed that flowed through a wide ravine. After they had ridden a while, they came upon a lone man stooped along the edge of a creek.

At first, they thought he was filling his water pouch, but when they saw his pan, they knew he was after gold.

"Thought these waters were tapped out," Lucky said as they approached the miner.

The stranger reached for a rifle that was lying on the ground beside him. He quickly got up and pointed it at Sam, who happened to be the closest. "Stay right where ya are!"

"Hold it, mister. Mean no harm." Sam raised his hands to show that he was not holding a weapon. "Just passin' by."

The man took in the boy's tone and his young appearance. He lowered his gun. "Sorry. Have ta be sure."

"Understand." Sam sighed with relief.

"Prospectors?" The man had a friendlier tone.

"Reckon we *will* be," Lucky answered. "Just startin' out. Thought we'd git tha hang of it up here first. That's why we're surprised ta see ya. Figured everyone's moved on."

"Most of 'em have. Like it better that way. Don't like puttin' up with others' behaviors nor lookin' over my shoulder so much."

"Anythin' left?" Sam wondered why the man was spending time on deserted diggings.

"If'n yar expectin' big nuggets...*no*, but if'n ya stay at it, ya can git a pinch here an' thar. Not gittin' anythin' at this spot, though. Will be movin' on soon."

Lucky gave Sam a nod to head out. "We'll leave ya to it then."

The novice placer miners spent long days in the Sierras along the edge of the waterways. They filled pan after pan with the bed's gravel and tried to figure out what method worked best when swirling the mixture. Though they didn't find the golden flakes, they did improve their panning technique.

"Sure is backbreakin' work." Lucky stood and stretched.

"Know it's tirin', but tha repetition hasn't gotten old...not yet anyway."

"Maybe we should look elsewhere. This spot's a dud," Lucky suggested after a time.

"We could move on, but remember, that old prospector said these places are still productive. Our time will come."

Lucky decided to move to another part of the streambed. "Gold!"

"Let me see." Sam was skeptical. "Fool's gold ...ya *fool*." He laughed. "Look closely."

"Let me test it." Lucky crushed the mineral. It shattered. "*Shucks*."

"Gold would have dented. No go...*this time*." Sam tried to cheer up his brother. "At least, ya got yar hopes up."

Lucky scoffed. "Would like ta git some *flakes*, though...even git some *flour*."

Sam stood up and went to his supply bag. He took out a pinch of baking flour. "Here, now yar huntin' hasn't been in vain."

Lucky couldn't help but smile. "Ha-ha. Yar a *laugh* a minute."

Though they were unsuccessful at finding gold, the boys never had financial worries. Both were good with a rifle, and they traded the meat they killed with the miners and shop owners for food and supplies. They rarely paid for lodging because they enjoyed sleeping outside, under the stars.

The boys followed all the waterways: rivers, streams, creeks, and even the dry beds, but the ore remained elusive. They saw that others, who were also panning for scraps, had devised wooden rockers or cradles so they could process pails of gravel at a time.

"Wonder what those boys are doin' over thar," Sam said when they came upon some men who were spraying water onto a steep slope.

"Whoa!" Lucky exclaimed when a significant chunk of the hillside fell.

Bullet halted when he heard the command.

"Wasn't talkin' ta *you*." Lucky laughed and patted his horse.

"Hydraulic minin'. So *that's* how it works." Sam had also stopped. "Scary how they can take down tha whole bluff. Tha pressure must be strong ta demolish it so quickly."

"Doesn't seem right. So much of tha debris washes into tha creek," Lucky observed as they rode downstream from the site.

"Be a ways afore tha water'll be clean enough ta git a decent drink."

They rode until the stream was clear, then they stopped to water their horses.

"Finally, water worth drinkin'. It's gittin' late. Why don't we call it a day?" Sam suggested. "I'll git some wood."

"Fine with me. I'll see what meat I can rustle up for dinner."

"Bet I know what you'll bring."

When Lucky returned, he held up his catch. "Rabbit stew."

"Knew that's what you'd git. Already got tha

potatoes an' onions cookin'."

It didn't take long for them to finish off the meal. "Good eatin's." Lucky scraped the bottom of the pot.

"Yar turn ta do tha cleanin'," Sam informed his brother as he got up to fill his cup with some fresh-made coffee.

"Riders." Lucky put his hand over his gun.

The three horsemen quickly approached the campsite. "Howdy," one of the men said in a friendly manner. "Saw yar horses, an' thought ya might be someun we're lookin' fer."

"We must be a disappointment then. Name's Lucky. This is my brother, Sam."

"Arthuro. These two are Clay an' Simon. Have ya seen two men in passin'?"

"We've been followin' tha creek all day," Sam replied. "Only passed some miners blastin' tha hillside with water."

Arthuro looked troubled. "Reckon we'll meet up with 'em tomorrow. Too late now."

"Ya seem sorry ta have missed 'em. Are they someone we should be on tha lookout for?" Sam pressed.

The man was lost in thought. "No, no. We're all *family*...gonna work a claim together. Reckon they may still be thar."

Lucky realized the miners weren't bandits. "Tha food's all gone, but tha coffee's hot. Yar welcome ta share tha fire."

"Thank ya kindly. Know tha water's gonna be tainted if'n thars hydraulic minin' ahead." The man dismounted. Clay and Simon followed his lead.

"It's been a long day." Clay reached into his

saddlebag and retrieved a bag of beans. "Mind if'n I heat these up?"

"Fire's yars. If'n ya want, ya can use our pot. May have stew scrappin's ta give ya some extra flavor." Lucky hoped the man, being the last user, would volunteer to clean the pot.

"Ya out here lookin' fer gold, too?" Clay asked after the men had settled around the fire.

"Yeah. Wanted ta start out from Sutter's Mill ...whar it all started," Lucky added.

Clay remembered the deserted site. "Yeah. Tha 49ers sure messed up his land."

"Have ta say, it wasn't what we expected," Lucky admitted.

Simon got up to get more coffee. "Not much left of tha place or tha gold, but thars still sum out thar. Ya just gotta work harder ta git at it."

"Yar claim far from here?" Sam asked.

"'Bout a day's ride," Arthuro answered. "All we know is that tha shaft's started. Simon won it playin' cards. Hope it's gonna pay out."

Simon was confident the mine would yield a profit. "It's located 'round others we've heard have done well."

"Wouldn't be followin' ya this far if'n I didn't have hopes," Arthuro assured his kin.

Clay was skeptical. "We've heard too many tall tales ta take this ta heart just yet."

Sam poked the fire. "Makes tha journey more excitin' though, hearin' tha stories that have been circulatin' since tha rush started."

"Yep. Ya know tha one 'bout Marshall...how he's gotten all tha headlines?" Simon asked. "Our uncle were in Hangtown at tha time tha gold was discovered. Told us sumthin' different.

He'd heard it from a man named Wimmer."

"Marshall found tha nugget," Clay confirmed. "He an' this Wimmer fellow, one of his mill workers, were walkin' 'long whar tha water from tha mill had run. Uncle Bruce said that Marshall saw a rock that was tha shape of a bear, so he picked it up."

"California had recently won independence from Mexico. Sum men from Sutter's Fort had helped, an' Marshall was one of 'em. They made a victory flag, an' tha bear was an emblem they used," Simon clarified, then continued with the story. "He gave tha rock ta Wimmer. He was tha one who thought it could be gold, so he took it home whar it were tested by his wife. Others had been curious 'bout tha shiny rocks they'd seen 'round tha site, Wimmer's wife bein' one of 'em. She'd been sayin' they were gold, but many scoffed an' teased her. She had a kettle of lye prepared for makin' soap, so she put tha rock in. Lye's known ta bring out tha color. Jokes were made, but tha next mornin', tha ore came out shiny."

"Still, they were doubtful. Of course, when Sutter had it tested, it were gold." Arthuro added with a grin. "They tried ta keep it a secret, but word always gits out."

Lucky smiled. "An' we know tha rest of tha story."

"Without tha Wimmers' help, thar may not have been a rush at all," Simon pointed out.

"Then *where* would we be?" Sam yawned. "On that note, we can all go ta bed an' dream 'bout findin' our own bear nugget."

The next morning, Lucky asked Arthuro about

his kin. "Ya sounded worried last night. Do ya think somethin' has happened?"

"They'd been prospectin' out here, an' when I wrote of tha mine, they went ta check it out. They were ta meet us back a ways. Show us how ta git thar or save us ridin' further if'n it proved ta be worthless."

"Maybe yar claim's good, an' thar protectin' it 'til ya arrive. We'll hope that's tha case."

"Yeah. Won't know 'til we git thar."

"Well, good luck ta ya."

"Hope yar efforts pay off," Sam added.

"Yars too." Arthuro's party got ready to ride.

Clay waved. "Thanks fer yar hospitality."

The two groups of prospectors headed out in opposite directions.

"Think we should invest in some pickaxes an' do some diggin'?" Lucky asked Sam after they had ridden a while.

"Wouldn't know whar ta look."

"Gold's found in rocks like granite or quartz."

"Yeah, but granite an' quartz are everywhere. How do we know which has tha rich stuff?"

"Just a thought. Seems hard rock mining's tha way ta go now."

The boys continued to search the Sierra Mountains for gold. They were still optimistic about their chances of success, even though they had yet to eye the color.

✠✦✠✦✠

One day, fate worked in their favor. They were exploring a waterway that flowed out of a gully. They had seen evidence that others had been panning the downstream section, but the rocky ravine above seemed to be untouched.

143

"Let's check it out," Lucky suggested. "Tha bed's been awfully disturbed, so thar musta been a reason. Maybe we should go higher up tha hillside."

"Know what yar thinkin'. If'n they found somethin' downstream, then whar did it come from an' how hard will it be ta find? It's worth investigatin'."

"Looks like tha willows aren't too thick over thar. Let's try goin' up that way."

They rode until the slope steepened, then they decided to tie the horses to some branches near the water and to climb on foot. As they got higher, the slope got steeper, and the ground became less stable. The water only trickled through the rocks.

Sam stepped on a loose pile of debris. "Rock!"

Lucky barely had time to dodge the cascading stones and avoid being hit. "Wait! Let me git closer, so I don't git clobbered on tha head," he shouted from below.

"See why no one came this way." They had maneuvered through another thicket of willows. "I'm hungry," Sam realized. "All these *bushes* have left me *bushed*."

"*Funny*." Lucky laughed. "I have ta agree with ya, though. Let's eat, then we can decide if'n we should go on."

"See those two large boulders up ahead? Looks like thar flat. Would be a great place ta sit an' eat lunch."

Within minutes, they reached the tantalizing spot. The tops of the rocks were easily gained. They got comfortable, then grabbed some jerky, eggs, and hardtack. As they ate, they enjoyed the surrounding view. The boys saw how high they had hiked, yet they were still far from the top of the ravine. They weren't above tree line, but the vegetation was sparse. There was enough room on the rocks to lie down, so they placed their hats over their eyes and relaxed. The warmth from the sun lured them into an easy sleep.

Lucky sat up and yawned. "You awake?" Sam's snoring told him the answer. He decided to explore. When he hopped off the rock, his foot hit the ground at an angle, causing his ankle to give. As he stood there and massaged the tender joint, he heard moving water. Once his foot felt better, he went to investigate.

The flow runs under this talus, he realized, and then he followed the sound. Must be coming from a spring up the way, he deduced.

The water became visible near some brush that grew amongst the rocks. Lucky was able to follow the flow until he came to a small pool where it had collected before sinking back under the surface. His heart skipped a beat.

"Can't be!"

CHAPTER 18

He saw something glow. Could it really be gold? Not pyrite? I don't want to make that mistake again. Lucky picked up a small shiny nugget. This looks different, though. It feels different, too, he realized.

"It *has* ta be!" He rushed to get his pan. He didn't want to wake Sam until he was sure, so he went back and filled the container with the sand from the bottom of the pool. Lucky swirled the contents around. When the lighter material floated away, he saw the shine of gold. He held the pan in awe.

"Sam!" he cried when he was sure. "*Gold!*" He ran to show his brother his find. Particles of varying sizes flashed with color inside his pan.

Sam was dreaming about panning for gold. He was reaching for a huge nugget when he heard Lucky's cry. The transition to the real world was disheartening. "Thought ya was part of my dream. I'd just found tha mother lode." Sam yawned himself awake.

"Yeah. Well, this one's *real*. Look what I got! Here, take it. See for yarself." Lucky shoved his pan toward his brother.

Sam looked inside. His face lit up with the same joy that Lucky felt. "*Gold!*" Sam grabbed his pan, then they raced back to the site and sifted through the gravelly bed.

They gathered all the treasure the small pool had to give, then they dug up the larger, loose rocks along the water's edge and sifted through the sediments that were trapped underneath.

After a while, Sam got up to stretch and to get a drink of water. "The sun's startin' ta set behind tha ridge. Reckon we've cleaned out all tha reachable spots."

"How'd it git so late? Doesn't seem like we've been at it that long."

"Feels like it, though." Sam felt the tightness in his body. "Startin' ta stiffen up, bendin' down so much."

"Come ta think 'bout it, my back does ache, an' my knees are a bit sore."

Sam filled another pan and came up empty. "If'n thars more, it must be embedded in tha rocks. We followed tha waterway up an' down. Tha pool had tha biggest bonanza."

"Seems we've gotten what we could. I was hopin' ta find a strike big enough ta file a claim, but I reckon thars no need ta come back. Not complainin', though."

"I agree. We did all right."

"To our first taste of gold!" Lucky held up his bulging pouch. Sam raised his sac and knocked it against Lucky's.

Supper turned into a fine festive feast, even though they were camping and had a limited supply of food.

"Why don't we name our unclaimed claim?" Lucky mulled over what to call their find.

"How 'bout Rainbow's End? Irish Luck?" Sam was thinking of their heritage and his brother's well-earned name.

"Maybe, but it should also reflect our efforts here, too. Be related ta today somehow. Got it— *Fool's Pool!*" Lucky beamed when he found the perfect name. "A play on me bein' fooled earlier. What do ya think?"

"I like it."

"Reckon we shouldn't let it show that we have any gold on us."

"I agree. We need ta be discreet an' act as if nothin' was found. I don't trust those men who were pannin' with us tha other day. They saw us head up tha ravine, an' may be watchin' ta see if we come out with happy faces."

"Once we make tha exchange, we'll have ta be even more careful. As many have warned, thieves are lurkin' everywhere."

They knew the mining camp mentality and saw how easily a reckless man and his money were soon parted as gamblers, highwaymen, and saloon gals waited like spiders after a fly. Though the boys had tired of the warnings about their youthful appearance, they knew the words rang true.

"Reckon we do look gullible," Sam confessed. "Especially you, with yar *boyish* manner."

"Yar cherub face doesn't exactly *scare 'em off*," Lucky countered.

"OK. So thar right. We do look young, but we're smart. Banks an' his crew taught us well. Now we're more experienced...an' aware. That's what's important."

"Plus, we're pretty good with a gun, if'n we have ta defend ourselves."

"An' I've got a brother who can 'bout talk his way out of anythin'." Sam now appreciated his brother's skill.

Lucky recalled the times Sam had told on him. "Ya used ta use that against me."

"It was fun ta git ya in trouble. Now, it works in our favor."

"We've got nothin' ta worry 'bout, then. We just don't want ta follow in Argent's footsteps. Do ya remember 'im? He's tha miner ya saved in Independence."

"I'm sure tha bartender helped 'im git soused an' had his girls flaunt thar attention upon 'im 'til they got all his earnin's."

"Probably made 'im feel important. Bet tha card sharks took advantage of his state, too." Lucky remembered Tincup's teachings. "He was lucky that he wasn't ambushed."

"Tha bushwhackers probably watched as tha others siphoned it all away."

"Maybe our boyish looks can work in our favor. No one thinks we have but tha shirts on our backs."

"Shirts with a substantial amount of gold hidden inside. An' mum's gold coins. We haven't spent 'em yet." Sam took his out of his pocket.

"Haven't had an emergency. We've taken care of our finances." Lucky got out his Double Eagle, and it flashed with the flame of the fire.

They left for town early the next day.

"Let's go ta tha saloon afore goin' ta tha assay office so we can git tha lay of tha land."

"Thar sayin' that gold dust's goin' for 'bout $20 an ounce," Lucky whispered. Even though they sat at a table in the corner of the tavern, they didn't want to be heard.

"When we're finished here, let's head down

tha street an' git supplies. Then we'll git tha gold exchanged an' make a quick getaway."

Before they approached the front of the assay office, they made sure no one was watching from the street. When they felt it was safe, they went inside the building. The clerk took their pouches and poured their contents onto the scale. He added weights until the two sides were balanced. He took a larger nugget from the pile and ran it over his touchstone. The mark left on the piece of schist indicated a high-grade ore. Once the purity was determined, a price was offered.

"Watch yourselves when you leave. Lots of shady characters hang around my place."

"Thanks for tha heads-up." Lucky turned away from the man and hid the majority of his money in the pocket his mom had sewn in his shirt. He saw Sam do the same.

Lucky went out first. He didn't see anyone who looked threatening, so he waved for Sam to follow. "Tha assayer may tell someone 'bout how much he paid us. We should circle 'round an' git somethin' ta eat at tha next town."

"Agree. That'll keep 'em off our trail. By tha way, sups on me. After all, yar tha one who found our fortune."

"We're partners. Remember *that* big brother. Now an' forever." Lucky's serious expression softened. "Let's git outta here an' find a suitable place ta git some food, then we'll figure out whar ta go next."

The boys decided to go south and check out other areas where gold had been discovered in the Sierra region. They rode until they reached

Sonora, another mining town in California with an established post office. It was given as a mail drop in their earlier correspondences. Since it was late when they arrived, and the shops were closed, they got a room for the night.

"Why don't we send some money home?" Lucky suggested after they had taken care of their horses.

"We can send 'em double thar grubstakin' money an' they'll see we weren't *so foolhardy*."

"Yeah, an' show 'em that our journey's been profitable as well as adventuresome."

"I'll tell 'em 'bout Sally." Sam knew this was long overdue.

"'Bout time!" Lucky hadn't pushed Sam on the matter, but he wondered when his brother was going to share his news.

The first thing they did the next morning was to arrange for the money transfer, and then they headed for the post office.

"Letter for Doyle?" Sam asked the clerk when they entered the building. He handed the man two letters to mail.

"Let me look." The clerk took Sam's posts, then he bent down and brought up a box from under the counter. He inwardly whistled as he read the names. "Doyle. Sam an' Lucky?"

"That's *us*," the boys said in unison. Lucky grabbed the letter.

"Looks like thars also a *sweet-smellin'* one... addressed to just Sam Doyle."

"That's *me!*" Sam snatched Sally's post from the clerk.

They went outside and sat on the bench in front of the building to read the letters.

Lucky shared what he had read first. "Papa's enlisted."

"Wearin' tha blue?"

"Of course. Otherwise, tha family is doin' well. Mum didn't say, but I know she's worried 'bout Papa leavin'. Connor'll be tha man of tha house once he's gone."

"He'll step up." Sam felt guilty because he, the oldest, wasn't there to support the family.

"Just as *you* would have." Lucky knew his brother was concerned. "Don't forget, Mum has Jacob an' Jamie ta help, too." Lucky changed the subject. "How's Sally?"

"Fine. Her family's moved outta tha valley. They've moved ta tha Rocky Mountains. They'll be settlin' in tha Colorado Territory."

"Whar'd she say ta send yar next postin'?"

"Denver."

Lucky watched as Sam reread Sally's words. "*Sure* ya not wantin' ta go an' see her?"

"Yep. I'm *eager* ta be with her again, but I wanna spend more time explorin' with ya. Git tha fever outta my system, *too*, I reckon." Sam was still young, not ready for a commitment, and he believed love would wait.

"Whar did ya tell Sally ta write ya next?"

"Santa Fe."

"*Santa Fe*?"

"Meant ta see what ya thought. Heard some temptin' tales 'bout gold in tha Ortiz Mountains. It seems placer minin' is still profitable. We said we wanted ta do some explorin' while we were out here. Right?"

"True. Not objectin'. You've been followin' my whims...glad ta follow yars."

They went south to the Territory of New Mexico and started their search for gold in Birchville (later Pinos Altos), along the banks of Bear Creek in the Pinos Altos Mountains.

"These beds are awful *stingy*," Lucky said after a day of panning. "Thar not sharin' thar riches. Seems they've nothin' ta give."

"Reckon it depends on what kind of *riches* yar talkin' 'bout," Sam replied as if in a dream. He had been thinking of Sally. "Tha *treasure* is tha *pleasure* of bein' in tha mountains."

Lucky looked at his brother and laughed. He knew why Sam was being so poetic. "Yar *woolgathering* again. No doubt, ya got Sally on yar mind. Let's head on up ta Santa Fe."

"Yar readin' my mind." Sam emptied his pan. "I'll get Lindy an' Bullet. They look like they're ready ta leave, too."

"We can pan as we go. Maybe we'll even find enough ta pay our expenses."

The boys made their way northeast and only stopped to rest along the waterways that had potential for panning. So far, none produced. When the Ortiz Mountains loomed ahead, they decided to check out the southern slopes, then work their way to the eastern side.

"Was told tha first western gold rush began here, back in the '30s," Sam announced when they reached Dolores Gulch.

"Seems tha historical district *still* has gold ta give. Pay dirt!" Lucky had swirled most of the sand out of his pan when he saw the color in the remaining particles. "It's only a few flakes, but it's a start."

"I got some too. Thought my suggestion ta

come here was gonna leave us empty-handed."

"It wouldn't have been tha first time. An' remember, 'tha *treasure* is tha *pleasure* of bein' in tha mountains,'" Lucky teased.

They arrived in Santa Fe a few days later. Before they headed to the nearest hotel, they stopped at the post office. They had mail.

"You read yar's from Sally while I read tha one from home."

Sam sat on the railing, deeply engrossed in Sally's words. He didn't see Lucky's letter drop to the ground.

CHAPTER 19

Lucky waited for his brother to finish. When Sam brought his paper down and stood up, the expression on Lucky's face showed the sorrow he felt.

"Thar dead," Lucky choked out.

"What?" Sam almost buckled.

"Typhoid fever."

"But...how?" Sam stammered. "They don't live in tha city...'round tha crowds. Tha farm's fairly isolated."

"They'd been invited ta a picnic at tha Hales. Thar new cook came from tha city. She didn't have symptoms...was what they call a *carrier*. She spread it through tha foods she prepared."

Sam could barely speak. "All of 'em?"

"Jamie went first, then tha boys. Mum was soon afterwards. Few of our neighbors as well. Then Papa passed."

"Papa?"

"He was wounded an' came home. His knee was shot up, but he still had limited use of his leg. He was gittin' 'round with a cane. Ben saw 'im ride up an' told 'im 'bout tha family. A few days later, Papa went ta town. He was steppin' off tha boardwalk when his leg gave out. He stumbled in front of an oncomin' horse. Was trampled."

"No!" Sam cried.

"Ben found our last letter on tha kitchen table. He was tha one who wrote us back."

"Let me see." Sam saw the paper lying on the ground. He picked it up and read it word for word. "Ben said he'd take care of tha property 'til we return. Why don't we give it to 'im?"

"I agree. Can't see either of us goin' back."

Both brothers went to their horses and pretended to adjust their saddles while they released the sadness that they felt for the loss of their family. Lindy turned to show that she understood Sam's distress. She snorted to comfort him. Bullet added a consoling whinny of his own.

❦ ❦ ❦

Sam picked up an old newspaper that was lying along the side of the road. It was a few months old, but one story grabbed his attention.

"We've pushed tha talk of silver behind us, but maybe we should rethink it. Tha Comstock Mines are still producing. Thars more silver than gold at Sun Peak (Mt. Davidson)."

"Thar rush still goin' on?"

"Yeah, but it's well underway."

"Reckon we should go an' see what all tha fuss is 'bout, then."

To get to Virginia City, the boys had to head west through the desert before going north. They would stay east of the Sierra Mountains. By the time they reached Genoa, in the Nevada Territory, the boys were ready to get a room for the night. They stopped off at the local eatery first. The Comstock mines were still the talk of the town.

"Sure are goin' on 'bout Comstock's loss."

156

Sam defended the miner. "Can't blame 'im for sellin'. Even if he knew that tha troublesome mud that hindered thar pannin' turned out ta be silver, it takes a lot of money ta git tha equipment ta process tha ores."

The following day, they arrived in Virginia City. The sound of hammering greeted them when they got to the town. The construction boom had already lined the streets with an ample number of businesses, but the building frenzy was still in full swing. They passed a number of shops, restaurants, and hotels, some three stories high. The boys walked into one of the more prosperous-looking saloons. The inside was filled with an assortment of miners who were either working in the pits or were winging it on their own. Their clothes, like their beards, were worn and shabby.

A fancily-dressed man was talking to a group at the bar. "I admit. I expected the silver to be lying about, waiting to be scooped up. An exaggerated notion, but it kept me feverishly hopeful, so when I saw the yellowish sparkles in a rivulet, I was overly optimistic. Though not the silver I was hunting, I gathered the shiny scales with visions of wealth. I hesitantly showed my find to my companions, fearing they'd want to know from whence they came, only to find my dreams were colors on drifting puffs of clouds. The shine was only mica. All that glitters is not gold, I learned."

"Had a similar experience," Lucky told the man. "Except mine was pyrite. Learnt ta look for tha dull yellow color after that."

"Mining wasn't for me. I swapped my pick for

a pen. I'm a writer...for the *Territorial Enterprise.*
Name's Samuel Clemens."

"Lucky, an' my brother Sam."

"You make a strike yet?"

"Just got here," Lucky replied. "Heard many
of tha early prospectors lost out 'cause tha
sand boggin' down thar gold minin' operation
was silver."

"There's gold and silver in the rock. But it's
the veins that keep drawing the crowd. You'll
see once you get out." A man who had pushed
his way through the crowd handed him a note.
"Must go. I have a story to write. Look for my
articles...under the name of Mark Twain."

The boys decided to spend the night in town.
The horses were curried and fed. By morning,
they were all well rested. Sam went to the livery
to get his horse saddled. Lucky was waiting in
the street. They were going to Gold Hill to pan
for gold.

"*Whoa,* girl!" Sam said when Lindy started
to act skittish. "What's got ya so jumpy?"

A man, hiding behind a hay pile, decided to
show himself. "*Hold it* right there, mister!" He
pointed his gun at Sam.

"*Drop it!*" Lucky countered. He had come back
to see what was keeping his brother.

The stranger hesitated. "Seems we've got us
a stalemate."

"We're not lookin' for any trouble. I'll just git
my horse saddled, an' we'll be on our way." Sam
directed his words to the man and to Lucky.

The man scoffed and then headed out. As
he passed by Lucky, a bloodstain was visible
on his shirt.

"Probably caught tryin' ta ambush someone else. Reckon he'll wind up in Boot Hill."

"Just glad I have ya ta watch my back."

Lucky remembered all the times Sam had come to his rescue. "Reckon we both help each other when things git rough."

As they rode out of town, they looked to see if the man was lurking about. When they were sure he wasn't following them, they headed toward the hill. They had decided to stay out until they were either buried in gold dust or the sun was high in the sky.

"It's past noon. Tha sun won. Reckon I won't be leavin' a golden footprint. Ready ta head into town?" Lucky asked.

"Haven't even been teased. Yeah, let's go."

They stopped at the post office but came up empty there, too.

"Not my best day," Sam growled. "It hasn't improved any since tha ambush attempt."

Lucky addressed all of Sam's frustrations. "On a positive note, yar still alive. An', we knew tha place was pretty much panned out. Knowin' how slow news travels, I'm sure Sally's letter's on tha way."

"Thought with everyone goin' after tha silver, they'd leave some of tha gold behind."

"They did. It's just underground."

When they reached town, they dismounted and tied their horses to the hitching post in front of the saloon.

"First round's on me," Sam announced. "Ya got me feelin' better after yar speech."

They found a spot at the bar. "We could work in one of tha mines," Lucky suggested after the bartender slid a drink his way.

A man standing next to Sam joined in their conversation. "If ya wanta die."

"What?" Sam looked at the stranger. He knew it was hot and dark inside the shafts, and there were risks, but this man seemed to have strong convictions.

"It's tha mountain. Tha ground's not stable, so tha shafts don't hold. Thar 'bout done gittin' tha minerals that are easy ta reach. Can't safely git at tha rest."

Only a portion of the ores in the Comstock area could be collected by open pit mining. They had to dig deep to follow the veins, but because of the nature of the unstable land, the wooden support beams weren't holding up, and cave-ins were common. Many lives had already been lost.

"Heard an engineer has designed a new shaft system," Lucky interjected. "A newfangled way of supportin' tha mine levels."

"He did. Thar fittin' box-like frames together ta form a honeycomb...like a beehive."

Sam didn't understand the man's concern. "So, workin' in a mine should be fairly safe."

"Bein' new, not all of tha mine owners are convinced that they need it, or they don't wanna spend tha money. Takes a lot of timber. Tha Ophir's been installin' tha square sets. I been cuttin' trees for 'em. Work for a big operation. We could use sum help...if'n yar after work away from tha mines, that is."

Lucky looked at Sam and got his look of approval. "When do we start?"

"Drink up boys, then I'll take ya ta meet tha

boss. By tha way, name's Paul."

"I'm Sam, an' he's my brother, Lucky."

They rode until they were at the outskirts of the forest, where the headquarters of the timber operation was located.

"Tha boss should be in here."

They entered a small room that was built off the side of a large wooden building. A man was staring out the window. He turned when they entered.

"Mike. Got some fellows lookin' for work, if'n ya wanna hire 'em."

"You cut trees before?"

"Helped our Papa clear land for our farm," Lucky answered.

"We've got more work than we can handle. You seem like a teachable lot. You're hired. You can start tomorrow. What do you go by?"

"I'm Lucky. This is my brother, Sam."

"You look strong. You'll need to be. Expect long days. Paul'll show you to your bunks."

"Ya git a clean place ta overnight. Tha rest of yar time, you'll be workin'." Paul led them inside the dormitory. The stench in the air—a mixture of unbathed bodies and old, heavily worn boots—was overwhelming. "It's not so bad once ya git used ta it."

A latern sat on a table in the middle of the room. Its illumination was just strong enough to help them see the interior space. Some of the men were seated around the table playing cards. Others were lying on the bunks that were lined up against the walls. A large fireplace along the far wall helped to keep the room heated.

A man playing poker taunted Paul. "Ya inta

babysittin' now?"

Lucky quickly retorted in a cocky tone. "We may look young, but we'll carry our weight an' likely'll put ya in yar place soon enough."

"We'll take any challenge ya offer us, startin' tomorrow. We'll see who needs tha *babysittin'* then." Sam knew that the snide remark was made to show the newcomers that they had to prove themselves or the crew would not stop badgering them.

"*Enough*, Brutus!" Paul knew the man was a bully and wanted to keep the peace. He faced the boys. "Take those two beds. We're ta keep things tidy, but after tha last rain, gittin' our garments dry has been a chore in itself."

Lucky untied the clothesline that blocked his cot and tied it to another post. Once it was out of his way, he tested the comfort of his mattress. "This will do fine."

Sam's bed was above his brother's bunk. Room with a view, he thought when he saw a small window in the wall near where his head would lay.

The next day, Sam got his chance to back up his words. He was helping to cut through a thick tree trunk when the man on the other end of the saw put him to the test. The seasoned sawyer pushed and pulled so quickly and with such force that Sam knew it was to see if he could tire out the young boy. Sam kept up the pace. He heard the man talking with his cronies later that day. He had passed muster. They never challenged him again.

Within the same week, an incident allowed Lucky to prove his worth. He was loading the cut branches onto a wagon. His co-worker had been complaining about the heavy work.

"My back's actin' up. Goin' ta git my elixir." The man left, so Lucky had to finish the job.

Lucky knew what the man was after. He had a reputation as a heavy drinker. After the wagon was filled, he went to see Sam. "Help ya?" Lucky asked as he approached his brother, who was felling a tree with Paul. They had just finished making the notch in the trunk. "Janks's at it again, so I'm waitin' for 'im ta git back."

"Not surprised," Paul replied as he worked on the back cut.

"Hold it!" Lucky shouted. "It's Janks. He's not payin' attention an' he's headin' whar yar tree's suppose ta fall."

"Too late," Sam warned. "Paul's too far into tha cut."

"Janks...watch out!" Lucky ran to help the tipsy man.

Janks stopped in his tracks. What's that irksome boy shoutin' 'bout an' why is he running toward me? His loopy state left him in a fog.

"Timber!" Paul yelled.

Lucky grabbed Janks's vest and pulled him out of the way.

"Wha...what? Let me go!" Janks shook until he was free of Lucky's hold. The boy's trying to make me look like a fool, he thought. In his anger, he pushed Lucky down, back under the falling tree.

CHAPTER 20

Lucky sprang up and dove headfirst toward the outer perimeter of the expansive tree. The swooshing sound made as the branches moved through the air was followed by a loud, explosive blast when the thick trunk came to rest against the ground.

Sam watched as the tree covered his brother. "Lucky?" When there was no answer, he pressed on. "Ya all right?"

Although the main part of the tree missed Lucky, the widespread network of branches had him pinned down. The uprising dust caused him to choke.

"Lucky?" Sam asked again.

Lucky recognized his brother's concerned voice. He coughed. "Can't move...stuck...under this limb."

"Workin' on it." Sam was busy cutting a path toward his brother. "Ya almost made it out, but this part of tha tree has ya surrounded."

"Took ya long enough," Lucky kidded when Sam finally reached him. "Don't think anythin' is broken, but I got a few good cuts." He sat up, removed his bandana, and wiped the blood that was running down the side of his face.

"A temple bleed, just a scratch. Ya got blood comin' through tha back of yar shirt, an' looks like yar leg got punched too. Can ya walk?"

"Ya need ta ask?" Lucky slowly stood up and put pressure on his hurt leg. "Seems ta wanta work." He took a few steps.

"I know. It'll take more'n a tree ta keep ya down." Sam watched as his brother struggled.

The sawyers waited. When Lucky limped out of the confines of the tree, they whistled and cheered to show their support.

Janks sauntered over to offer a half-hearted apology. "Sorry, *kid.*"

The demand for wood kept the outfit busy. A massive amount of timber was needed to brace the walls of the Comstock Mines, and as they proved their worth, the town continued to grow. Before long, the surrounding woodlands were cleared, so trees were taken from either the forests surrounding Lake Tahoe or the Sierra Mountains.

Chutes and flumes were built to carry the logs down the hillsides. To keep the wood from breaking up, the slides ended at a lake or other waterway. The floating logs were then loaded onto wagons and transported to the sawmills.

"Janks ask ya ta grubstake 'im yet?" Sam asked Lucky as they drove a load of timber to the mill.

"Be *his* partner? Ya know tha answer ta *that.* Heard he's tried everyone else, though."

"Me included. No one's interested 'cause no one trusts 'im. His drinkin' doesn't help."

"Shame he didn't try ta change when tha tree nearly kilt 'im."

"I kinda feel sorry for 'im. Maybe he's on ta somethin', an' this'll git 'im outta his rut."

"He made his choices." Lucky shrugged. "I reckon thars no turnin' back for 'im."

Janks, thinking he had staked a good claim, needed a partner who could help pay for the mining equipment. Since no one backed him, he felt his coworkers had let him down. One night, after the crew had been paid and everyone had gone to sleep, he slipped over to a mate's saddlebag with the intent of stealing his wages. Lucky happened to roll over and awaken. He saw Janks and called out. The noise woke the intended victim, who drew his gun and shot the thief. The wound was not life-threatening, but Janks was run out of town.

"Once again, tha boy's made me look like a fool. I'll git ya yet," Janks promised as he made his hasty retreat.

✦ ✦ ✦

Lucky poured the rest of the gravel out of his pan. "Know why no one's out here."

Sam heard the frustration in his brother's voice. "Ya ready ta quit for tha day?"

"Maybe so. Was hoping this spot had been overlooked, but again, nothin'."

"More likely yar mood is 'cause it's time ta move on?"

"I reckon. Thought tha prospectin' done on our days off woulda been more productive."

Sam emptied his pan. "Got what we could."

"A paltry amount. Kinda sad, when ya think of tha big operations makin' so much money."

"We coulda worked for 'em. Heard all kinds of ways tha miners are gittin' some of tha gold for themselves."

"We already have a secret pocket. We could

166

chip off some small pieces from tha gold veins an' fill 'em up," Lucky joked.

"Think they've gotten wise ta *that* trick."

"Heard some officers of tha mines are in it with assayers. They stash ores ta be picked up later or substitute low-quality rocks when lode values are determined."

"Lots of schemin' goin' on."

"I think that bartender, Bull, may be one of thar go-betweens. He's always slippin' money into someone's hand when he thinks no one's watchin'."

Sam looked at his empty pan. "Reckon I'll stick ta makin' it on my own—*honestly*."

"More rewardin' that way. What would we do with all 'em fancy things, anyway?"

"Less ta worry 'bout."

"Yar right." Lucky was feeling restless. "Got that *itch* ta go somewhere new. Know yar ready ta move on, too."

"Yeah. Been thinkin' tha same thing. Should we wait an' leave next week after we git paid? I can let Paul know. It'll give 'im plenty of time ta git replacements."

"An' time ta git a letter off tellin' 'bout our new plans." Lucky could sense a change in his brother's behavior. He had not received a letter recently, and he knew that Sam was worried about his relationship with Sally.

Before they left, the boys moved out of the bunkhouse so they could spend their last night in town. They met a few of their coworkers at a fancy restaurant to celebrate.

"Ya know," Lucky started. "We're a part of tha history here, supplyin' tha wood for tha new type of minin' shaft."

"Ta tha Comstock Lode," Paul toasted, "an' all tha jobs it's provided."

"An' ta Virginia City," Gristy saluted. "We've watched 'em both boom usin' our lumber."

Lucky held up his mug. "An' ta all tha *fun* we had."

"Ya referrin' ta tha time ya 'bout gave me a heart attack, ridin' tha log down tha chute." Sam scoffed after remembering the daring act.

"Only dangerous at tha end, when I had ta leap over tha other timber ta git into tha lake."

"Ya had ta clear 20 or 30 feet ta do so."

"Well, I made it, didn't I?"

Sam laughed. "Yar a lucky one, all right. Ya'd think I'd be used ta yar antics by now."

"Couldn't resist after Gristy flew tha chute first. Knew if'n he could do it, so could I. Had ta try." Lucky remembered how close he came to hitting the logs at the end.

"Now, leave me outta this. I was gettin' my own rush."

Sam shook his head. "Yar both daredevils."

"Reckon we do what we feel we have ta do. Kinda like how we stripped tha land of its trees." Lucky knew their work came with a cost.

"Goes hand in hand with tha boom. But at some point, tha Comstock will peter out," Paul predicted. "Then, like tha other busts, people will move on."

"Reckon Virginia City could become another ghost town," Gus proposed.

"Many of 'em have." Sam was optimistic. "If'n it does, then maybe tha forests will grow back."

They all pondered the thought.

The brothers had spent over a year working in the lumber industry. They saw the erosion brought on by the exposed land and how the nearby waterways were polluted by the runoff. But, as Sam foretold, by the 1890s, after the Comstock boom was over, the area's population declined. The demand for lumber decreased, and the land was able to revegetate.

"So, what's next?" Lucky asked Sam after they had returned to their room.

"I've done enough prospectin'. Time ta *settle down*, I reckon."

"Missin' Sally?" Lucky asked even though he knew the answer.

"Yeah. I think I'm ready ta start my life with her. I just hope she hasn't met someone else."

"I'm sure she's *moonin'* after ya, too."

"Hope so."

"We still have most of our Fool's Pool money," Lucky reminded Sam. "What are ya goin' ta do with yar share?"

"Maybe git into tha trade business. Seems tha stores sellin' supplies are doin' well...with tha miners an' thar followers needin' so much. I won't jack up tha prices or take advantage like many of tha others have done."

"A good profession ta be in. Sally would be a great help, too."

"What about you?"

"Don't know. I'll keep driftin'. Reckon it's not time for me ta settle just yet."

PART THREE

Crossing Paths

1863-1870

CHAPTER 21

Janks drifted from one gold camp to another, but each was a blurred memory of drinking and brawling. He had resorted to robbery to get money, which was mostly used to buy more booze.

"Nobody said life was easy," a prospector at a bar told him once. "Ya gotta take what ya want …grab it by tha horns…make it yars."

"Ya sound like my dad."

His troubles were mostly of his own making. He taunted other downtrodden drunks, hoping for a gunfight. After another tavern tussle over something he couldn't even remember, Janks found himself lying in the alley behind the bar. He was surrounded by darkness. When he tried to pick himself up, he fell back onto the filthy trash that rested behind him.

"I'm nothin' but a bum, a saddle tramp," he vocalized before passing out.

When Janks woke, the sky had brightened with the light of the early sun. He sat amongst the muddy muck and reflected on his life. How long have I been passing through one no-name camp after another? Life has a way of gnawing at you, he realized. If only I had someone I could have counted on, who wouldn't of let me down. Maybe they would have helped me to find the good in life. Regardless of the reason, I'm tired of being one step away from the hoosegow.

He thought about how it all began. It wasn't something that happened overnight, he knew. It stemmed from years of disappointments and missed opportunities. As he sat in the shadows of the alley, the memories came flooding back.

"Janks the Jinx." He vocalized the hurtful name-calling. Being born on Friday the 13th did not help, but it was his dad's actions that led to his cowering nature and left him vulnerable to being teased by the kids at school. Their families would avoid his because Broak, his dad, was a mean-spirited drunk that drove everyone away with his abrasive personality. Janks found some relief when he was with his mom, but she was just as beaten down.

Broak left when his son was still a young child. Then, one day, he came back, and the stable home life that Janks had finally found disappeared. His dad couldn't keep a job, so he became even more abusive. He would take his anger out on anyone who happened to be nearby. His parents constantly bickered, and oftentimes, their arguments had violent endings.

Janks grabbed his head. "No," he cried as the bitter memories swirled in his cluttered mind. He heard the heated arguments, the crunch of fist against jawbone, and the cries his mom tried to suppress. At first, the beatings were behind closed doors, but as time passed, it didn't seem to matter where, or even who, his dad attacked, including his frail son.

One night, his father came home late—drunk as usual. Janks had already fallen asleep, but he woke up when his parents started to argue.

He heard his mother cry, so he jumped out of bed and hurried into their room.

"Stop!" He ran to shield his mom, who had collapsed against the far wall.

"Get outta my way!" Broak approached the pair and threw a fist at Janks, who dodged the drunken hurl and threw a punch of his own. His landed. Broak flew across the room, hit the frame of the bed, and landed with a loud thud. He was out cold.

His mother saw that Broak was not moving. "He's unconscious. We must go afore he wakes up, or he'll kill us!" She grabbed a small bag and started to pack. "Go on. Hurry! Git only what yar horse can carry."

"But..." Janks looked at his dad. He felt he should help him somehow. He hesitated for a few seconds, but he knew they had to go, so he ran to his room and gathered his things.

"Come on...now!" His mother grabbed some food from the kitchen and took money that had been hidden behind an old wood panel in the wall.

"What 'bout Lobo?"

"If'n yar dog follows, he's welcome ta come with us; elseways, he'll have ta make it on his own."

They got their horses saddled and left. The dog tagged along behind them. He didn't need any encouragement. He, too, had been beaten by Broak and was happy to leave.

They left Missouri and headed west.

"Are we gonna stay with Aunt Linda?"

"That'll be tha first place yar father'll go ta hunt us down. I'll git in touch with her after things have settled down a bit."

Janks had never been away from home and was still dependent on his mom, but he was old enough to know that they were vulnerable to the outside world. "Where're we goin' then?"

"I've heard 'bout places...where thar buildin' new towns...'cause of tha gold strikes. They'll have businesses that'll be needin' someone ta provide services. I'll find work at a diner or clean clothes. I can sew, too. 'Til we land somewhere, we'll find jobs ta pay for things 'long tha way. We'll just keep goin'...may even go as far as California."

They didn't make it to the Golden State. When they reached Virginia City, in the Nevada Territory, the Comstock Lode was proving to be a long-term source of wealth. The town was growing and had yet to become one of the richest in the nation. Janks's mom found employment cleaning rooms at an older, wooden two-story hotel. The job was demanding, and she often came home weary from the hard work, but she made enough to pay for a room in a nearby boarding house.

"Yar dog can sleep under tha roof by tha back door," the proprietor assured Janks. He fixed a soft bed for Lobo to sleep on, but once the dog became a favored friend in town, he had many spots to call home.

Janks eventually found work at the livery, cleaning up after the stock. His employer was a dour man, a drunk who treated Janks harshly, but the young boy endured. Living with his dad had taught him well.

Janks and his mother adapted to their new

routine. They worked long, hard hours. Too tired to make changes, the days passed. Then, one night, while they were eating supper, his mom, without preamble, made an announcement.

"We'll be movin' in with a man livin' in Tent City."

When she didn't elaborate, Janks questioned her further. "When? Why? Someone I know?" He couldn't believe his mom was proposing such an abrupt change.

"Gittin' outta here tomorrow. Hauer'll come an' git our things afore we're off ta work."

"What 'bout Dad?" Janks knew what their new living situation implied.

"Didn't tell ya, but I'd heard that Broak was stoved in. He'd gone back ta tha saloon that night we left an' git hisself inta a brawl. Was his last."

"All this time, I didn't know if'n I did 'im in, or not. Ya didn't *think* I'd wanna be relieved of *that* burden of guilt?"

"Didn't wanta upset ya."

"Well, good riddance!" Janks was relieved. "I'd feared he'd show up one day an' be even meaner than before. Now I can sleep in peace. When's tha ceremony?"

"Got hitched last night after my shift was over. It's all 'bove board."

"Ya didn't *think* I'd wanna be thar?"

"Ya was still workin'. Ya know how Stiles is. Didn't want ta cause ya any trouble."

"Just hope he's a good man an' treats ya right." Janks abruptly rose from the table and went out.

"I hope so *too*." Sarah knew her decision was

made more for her protection than out of love. She sat there a moment and contemplated her marriage, then she got up and cleared the table. While she washed the dishes, she thought about the times she had been harassed by visitors at the hotel. She was still a pretty woman and needed a man to protect her, and her new husband, Hauer, had come to her rescue on more than one occasion. He was a miner, a strong, beefy fellow who had taken her under his wing. Though he drank, she knew he was kindhearted and wouldn't beat her like Broak had done.

Hauer spent long hours working deep inside the mine, where the temperature easily reached over 100 degrees. After a hard day of pounding rock, he and his coworkers would unwind by drinking and gambling. He often came home bloodied from a fight, usually from a dispute in his card playing.

"Janks," Hauer started one day. "Yar not bein' treated right at tha stable, an' I think ya may wanta find better work."

"Ya know someone who's lookin' for help?" Janks knew where the conversation was headed and that Hauer had something in mind.

"Heard Jon's expandin', an' needs an extra hand at tha store. He has a small room in tha back...with a cot fer sleepin'. Had a talk with 'im, an' he's willin' ta give ya a try. That's if'n ya want it." He didn't say that he felt the boy was old enough to be making it on his own. "It's not that I don't like havin' ya 'round, but tha tent can git cramped. Yar mom thought it would be good fer ya, too."

“An’ Lobo?”

“Jon said it’d be OK ta let ’im sleep by yar bed.”

“Seein’ how he is with his help, I reckon he’s a decent fellow ta work for.” Janks was ready to leave, and this proposition was his way out. “When do I start?”

“Tomorrow.”

CHAPTER 22

Janks was like many of the young of his time. He grew into his manhood in a town that lacked a decent moral compass. His inept learning came from witnessing the corruption that was commonplace. The mines that kept the town in prosperity also brought in other entrepreneurs, legal or not. A proper code of conduct was hard to enforce, allowing lawless behavior to rule the day.

A few months after he had started to work at the mercantile, Janks was told of the brutal killing of his mother. She was cleaning one of the rooms at the hotel when a man came in and accosted her. She had fought her attacker but, ultimately, lost the battle.

"I'm sorry I weren't thar ta help her," Hauer told Janks after the ceremony was over.

"I know ya woulda stopped 'im if'n ya could. Thar was skin under her nails, so someun is wearin' her marks. Gives us a chance ta identify tha murderer, an' when we know who it is, I'll git 'im," Janks promised his stepfather.

"If'n I don't git ta 'im first."

It wasn't long before they had their chance to get their revenge. Hauer had finished a hard day at work and had stopped at the gaming house to drink and play poker. A stranger asked to join in the game and sat on Hauer's right.

The man had several scars on his left cheek that appeared to be of recent origin. Hauer signaled to Francie, the barmaid, to keep the drinks coming. He knew he'd start the game by dealing the man poor cards. Then, when it was his turn to deal again, he would lay his trap.

"Ya new in town?" he asked when he was ready to make his move.

"Been 'round."

Hauer talked as he dealt the cards. He made sure the stranger got a good hand. Loosens the tongue, he inwardly sneered.

"Chard, what's Emily got ya doin' now?" he asked the man who was sitting across from him. He knew that Chard was a lazy man with a meddling wife who constantly nagged him to do work around the house.

"Fixin' tha roof...again!"

"Annie's been on me too. I had ta put her in her place just this mornin'. Ya'd think she'd be obedient by now." Hauer gave Chard the wink, hoping he would figure things out and would go along with his made-up story.

"What—" Chard started, then he saw Hauer's signal. "What...*does* it take ta git these women in line?" Though bewildered, he went along with Hauer's playacting.

"Yar wife musta had *her say*...by tha looks of those marks on yar cheek." Hauer gave the stranger a malicious grin to drive home his point.

"Not married."

"Musta been sum feisty tart, then," Hauer pushed. He was trying to get the man to tell him about the origins of the scars.

"She be too uppity, but she got her due," the man bragged after seeing the three aces he had just been dealt.

Hauer turned the conversation to the usual card talk. In time, the man's money ran out, but not before he was well on his way to a hangover. When the stranger got up to leave, he staggered and knocked a couple of chairs over. Hauer excused himself from the table and followed him out. He saw Janks sweeping the walkway outside the store. He pointed to the stranger. "Think he's our man." He followed him down the street.

Janks knew what Hauer meant. He went inside and grabbed his gun. "Be back," he told Jon on his way out of the shop. Janks saw the two men heading into the shadow of a nearby alley. By the time he caught up with Hauer, the stranger was down and had his arms shielding his face. His nose was bleeding, and his left eye was swollen. Hauer was getting ready to give him another blow.

"Stop!" the man cried. "I don't know *who* yar talkin' 'bout. 'Twern't a gal 'round here."

"*Whar*, then?" Hauer slammed his fist into the man's stomach.

The man was in too much pain to come up with a lie. He didn't know why the gambler was asking about the maid. She wasn't wearing any jewelry, so he figured she was some wanton woman up for grabs. He wanted the man to stop punching him, and the alcohol was acting like a truth serum, so he decided to spill his guts before Hauer did it for him.

"Stop! All right. I *was* with sum cheeky gal...

a housemaid in town. So what?"

Hauer had his fist ready. "*Whar?*"

"Tha hotel...tha one by tha livery." The man's admission confirmed his guilt.

"You *scum*. She was my wife, an' she was a respectable woman." Hauer spat as he backed away from the man.

"An' she was a good mom...*my mom*" Janks fired a shot to end the man's miserable life.

Hauer confirmed that the man was dead. "Ya shouldn't of done that. Yar a *wanted man* now." He looked around to see if anyone was lurking nearby.

"Don't care. He deserved it."

"Ya *should*...but ya may git away with it. I don't see anyun. If'n he's a stranger, maybe no one'll come lookin' for 'im."

"He's just a shiftless drifter...no different from any of tha others that pass through."

"No matter...but he can be linked ta me, so we need ta bury 'im. Go an' git yar horse."

When Janks returned, they put the body over the animal's back and walked him out of town. They came upon an old miner's claim and looked for signs of recent activity.

"Seems ta be deserted. Let's dump 'im here." Hauer pulled the man off the horse.

"I see an old shovel over thar. I'll go an' git it." Janks brought back the rusted tool.

After they buried the corpse, they gathered some large rocks and placed them over the grave. When Hauer was satisfied that the body would not be found, he took the shovel and threw it into the brush.

"Ride yar horse on back ta town. I'll walk. I

don't want anyun ta see us together. I'm gonna finish playin' cards."

As Janks rode back to town, the adrenaline rush caused by his rash behavior replaced any feeling of guilt. He had never killed a man. "I just kilt someone," he said aloud. Not sorry, though, he realized. Janks didn't have time to reflect. Lobo came to greet him. He got off his horse and gave the dog a rub. Lobo followed him into the stable. Once the horse was taken care of, he returned to work.

The stranger's disappearance went unnoticed. Janks had gotten away with murder, but his behavior started to change. His drinking was getting out of hand, and he was getting into fights. He became reckless and cocky, traits he didn't have before. Hauer tried to become the father the young boy needed, but his words fell on deaf ears.

"What's goin' on with yar young'un?" Hauer was often asked.

"Gotta grow up an' make 'is own choices. Tried talkin' with 'im, but..."

Hauer knew Janks's behavior was linked to the killing. The boy's been following an evil path rather than seeking forgiveness. I feel I've let his mother down, but I had ta avenge her murder. The boy needs a firm hand, he decided.

"What're ya doin', hangin' 'round with that motley crew?" he asked Janks one day.

"Ya mean Bart an' his gang, don't ya? Thar helpin' me out. We're gonna be partners...gittin' our own mine."

"He'll just git ya inta trouble." Hauer tried to warn the errant boy, but he knew that it was useless. Janks was on a slippery slope, and there was nothing he could do to stop his downhill slide.

Not long after they had that conversation, Janks's future was forged. He got word that Hauer had been killed in a mining accident. There was a cave-in, and by the time they got to him, he was gone.

Janks had no one to keep him in line. He spent more time with Bart, whose influence only made his behavior worse. Bart encouraged him to steal from the store. He was caught, then fired, so he moved into the old shack that Bart shared with his gang.

"Movin' on," Bart told Janks a few days later.

"When do we leave?"

"Not we, *us*," Bart curtly replied. "You'll have ta go yar own way."

"What 'bout tha rest—"

Bart cut him off in a voice that left no doubt that he didn't want to be bothered. "Don't want ta fool with ya anymore, now *git!*"

Janks tried one more time. "But Bart, why..."

"*Enough!*" Bart had tired of the boy, and now that he wasn't at the store, he was of no use. "I don't want no *tag-along kid* botherin' me," he snapped, then he drew his gun and fired. "What'd ya make me do that for?" Bart saw the boy's pleading eyes, but his sympathy didn't last. His partners were waiting. He left the cabin and rode off with the gang.

Janks grabbed at his belly. Blood instantly coated his hands. He collapsed.

A man passing by heard the shot. He saw a group of men ride off in a hurry, so he went inside the shack to investigate. He found Janks unconscious. After inspecting the wound, he went to get a bottle of whiskey from his saddle. He soaked a bandana with the alcohol and cleaned the infected area.

The man chatted while he tended to Janks's injury. "Looks like ya got off...this time. Tha bullet went straight through. Doesn't seem ta have affected any of yar innards." He waited until Janks gained consciousness. "Tha shot was clean. If ya rest, ya should be fine."

Janks's mind was in a fog. When his head cleared, he remembered what had happened. He scoffed. "Bart!"

"If that's tha man that shot ya, he's long gone. Saw tha lot of 'em ride off when I come up, an' they were kickin' dust."

Janks reached for his gut. He felt where the bandage had been placed. He realized the man had dressed his wound. "Much obliged."

"Coulda been worse. How ya feelin'?"

"Fine...now."

"I'll be on my way, then. You can have tha rest of tha whiskey...for yar pain."

With the help of the liquor, Janks spent the next few days in and out of sleep. Bart's gang didn't take all the food, so he didn't have to leave the comforts of the cabin until he was better. When he was able to venture out, his first stop was the saloon. A man was there, looking for workers to cut trees for the mill. Janks got a job with the timber crew. He was able to curtail his drinking, and the team had accepted him, but after a while, he fell back into his old routine.

CHAPTER 23

It was a new year—1864. Lucky and Sam had gone their separate ways a few months earlier. Lucky had yet to receive word from his brother, but he knew that he was headed to the Colorado Territory. Lucky had decided to stop for the night and was lying under the night sky, remembering their words before they parted.

"Ya got yar lucky nature ta git ya by, but keep in mind, ya won't have yar big brother ta *watch* yar back."

"Reckon, I'll have *ta see* how I do without ya." Lucky held back tears. "Now *go on* an' find yar gal!" He gave Sam one last hug before mounting his horse. They looked at each other for a while. "Take care." Lucky turned his horse and rode off.

At first, he missed his brother, but as time passed, his feeling of kinship was placed on the back burner as his imminent needs demanded his attention. The mining camps were full of men looking for trouble. His youthful appearance had led to several confrontations, but so far, he had managed to talk his way out of these conflicts. His quickness saved him when he had been drawn into a few gunfights. He realized that many liked to wreak havoc for the fun of it, so he didn't stay in the camps long enough to be picked as someone's next target.

"What's a boy yar age doin' out here alone?"

he was once asked by an old prospector.

"Same as you." Lucky was tired of the pesky question.

"Ya know what yar doin'?"

"Same as most." Lucky studied the seasoned miner. His worn and torn clothing spoke of the man's luck, so Lucky decided not to ask about the prospecting in the area. He left for the next camp. After riding for several hours, he decided to stop for the night.

Lucky threw the last of his coffee into the fire. When he heard a strange clopping sound, he stood up and grabbed his gun. He saw a man weaving as if in a drunken state. A burro was following. Lucky could see that the man was hurting. His face was bruised and swollen.

"Looks like ya could use some help."

"Had a claim, up tha way." The man doubled up in pain.

"Come. Sit over by this rock." Lucky went to assist the man.

"When I refused to sign over my mine, they got rough. They took my claim paper an' made it thar own. Said they'd be back an' if'n I was still thar...well, I loaded ol' Mary Margaret an' took off." He groped for the rock and sat down.

"Just finished tha coffee, but I can git another pot goin'."

"Might...y grate...ful." The man groaned and grabbed his stomach.

Lucky helped him to lie on his back. He got his rolled-up blanket and placed it under the man's head. "Yar pretty stoved in. Ya may be bleedin' inside."

"They took a piece of timber ta me." The man

struggled to breathe. "*Please*...take care of Mary Margaret. She's been a good..." The man gasped, and then he passed out. A few minutes later, he was dead.

Lucky dug a grave and left a marker.

"Reckon I own a mule," he said, using the common misnomer for the animal. "Now, what do I do with ya?"

The next morning, after he had packed up, Lucky brought Bullet over to meet their new companion. The horse sniffed. The burro sniffed. They seemed to accept each other, so Lucky tied Mary Margaret's rope to his saddle. When Bullet moved, the cord tightened and tugged on Mary Margaret, but she would not budge.

"What's wrong?" Lucky asked the animal. He got off his horse and rubbed Mary Margaret's face, then he scratched between her ears. He pulled the rope forward, and she hesitantly followed. "All right." He quickly mounted Bullet. This time, when they moved, the burro kept pace.

Before long, they approached a creek with swift-moving water. Though Bullet had been through similar scenarios, Lucky was unsure of the burro, so he slowly entered the stream. As expected, Mary Margaret refused entry.

"Yar stubborn as a *mule!*" Lucky repeated his earlier petting technique to get the burro to trust him again.

Lucky got back on Bullet, and they pulled the temperamental beast into the water. The rocky bottom proved to be more of a challenge than expected. Bullet stumbled but recovered and kept his footing. Lucky was relieved when they were on the final stretch until he saw the churning, white-crested waves that he knew hid the strong current beneath them. Bullet stepped into the deeper water and was pulled by the faster flow. As he worked to regain his footing, Mary Margaret turned to head back. The jerk on the rope caused the horse to lose his balance. Lucky felt the opposing forces, and he knew what was coming.

"Mary Margaret...*you*—" he started, but his scolding was cut short.

CHAPTER 24

ullet went down and pulled Mary Margaret into the current. Lucky fell to the side and hit his head on the pack of ore that the burro was still carrying. Though he was knocked out, the creek's cold water quickly revived him. When he moved, he realized that he was caught in the rope and was being pulled under the water. He grabbed the burro's pack to stay afloat. The three toiled and moiled until they reached the shore.

"Ya *low-down, no-good, two-bit, useless—*" Lucky cursed when they finally made it to the water's edge. "If'n it weren't for yar hemmin' an' hawin', none of this would have happened," he yelled as he cut through a tangled piece of rope.

"*Hee-haw.*" Mary Margaret's bray sounded like a sneer.

Like Lucky, she didn't like confrontation, and the tone of his voice told of his anger. It wasn't her fault that Lucky's foot got caught. She was tied up and had to make do the best she could. She decided that she didn't want to stick around. When she felt the rope loosen, she sprinted forward.

"*Ow!*" Lucky screamed when Mary Margaret stepped on his foot. "Ya *cantankerous clot.* Go on, then!" He looked at Bullet, who was patiently waiting by the side of the creek. "Don't let her git outta yar sight."

Lucky removed his boot, then peeled off his sock. He saw blood-filled bruises where the burro had stomped on his foot.

"Tha same toes that got it under tha supply wagon." As he dipped his foot into the creek, Lucky remembered the times Sam had teased him about his turkey toe. "Sure miss ya, big brother!"

The cold water relieved the pain. His spare clothing was still dry, so he changed out of his wet ones. When he finished taking care of his needs, he went to check on Bullet. He ran his hand down the horse's legs to check for signs of injury.

Bullet snorted. Mary Margaret had left him on edge.

"Whoa, boy." Lucky rubbed Bullet's face and offered him a clump of grass. "I'm just seein' if'n ya have any soreness." Lucky walked the horse in a circle to see if his gait had changed. "Everythin' looks good."

After Bullet passed inspection, they started to search for Mary Margaret. Lucky scanned both sides as he slowly rode up the road, but there was no sign of the missing burro.

"What's that?" Lucky saw something lying on the branches of a willow. "A miner's pick. Kinda strange it bein' here *unless* she went this way."

Other items had also fallen out of the burro's packs, and like breadcrumbs, they were leading them to Mary Margaret's whereabouts.

"She has ta be out here, *somewhere*." They approached an entrance to a box canyon. "We'll stop here. You can graze while I look for her." He grabbed his rifle and went on foot to search through the thick brush cover, but the burro was nowhere to be found. Lucky felt that he couldn't leave the animal, as her care was the dying man's last request. He came back alone. "Did all that I could." He hesitated, then he mounted Bullet and turned to go back. To his surprise, in front of some boulders, stood Mary Margaret. Her big, brown eyes showed a hint of laughter.

"Shucks," Bullet snorted.

"Lo an' behold, tha prodigal gal has shown herself." Lucky joked, but he was relieved. "Yar ta be tha death of me yet!" He rode up to her and scooped up the dragging rope so he could tie it to his saddle.

After the caravan was secured, they headed back to the road. Their progress was slow, as the stubborn burro was never in a hurry. Lucky sang a song to relieve the tension he felt. Mary Margaret walked up to his side so he had Bullet move faster. The burro kept the pace as long as he kept singing, so like a pied piper, he would hum, whistle, or voice musical tunes to keep their small train moving.

A few days later, the threesome reached the mountain that had been looming in the far distance. An old wagon road led to the top of the pass. At first, it was fairly straight, but as they gained elevation, it started to snake its way around the steep, rocky cliffs.

"Stop all that hemmin' an' hawin'!" Lucky yelled at the agitated burro. "I can see what we're headed into."

Bullet snorted. He was just as uneasy.

The fall warmth that had prevailed in the foothills was becoming more wintry as they worked their way to the top, and the animals had sensed the coming of a storm, but Lucky didn't need them to tell him what he already knew. The clouds ahead were dark and thick. The last rays of the afternoon sun had already been blocked, and the air had started to chill.

"Horse ta tha barn," Lucky sang as Bullet picked up his pace. "An' burro, too," he added so Mary Margaret wouldn't feel left out.

When the storm finally hit, the snowfall quickly coated everything with white powder. Before long, the weary travelers stumbled upon a welcomed sight. The animals declared the building "the barn." They stopped in front of what appeared to be a trading post.

"Is that a stable over thar? Looks like ya got yar *barn* after all. Lucky led his entourage inside the enclosure, found feed and water, and got them secured for the night. He went inside the establishment and approached a tall, stocky man who looked like the owner.

"Got a room ta spare? Be needin' ta board my horse, an' burro too."

"Space in thar." The proprietor pointed toward the dining area. "Tha tables'll be moved after a spell. See 'bout yar animals, then we'll settle up."

"Thar already stabled. Reckon I'm ready ta order somethin' ta eat."

"Sit anywhar."

The room was filled with men finishing their meals or gambling. Lucky went to a table where two others had already been served. The men ate in silence. When they were done, they got up and went to join a group playing poker. By the time Lucky finished eating, it was time to move the chairs and tables. The games stopped. As the space opened up, the travelers claimed their spots and laid out their bedding. Before long, the lights were put out, and the fire was stoked. The sound of snoring soon followed.

It snowed through the night, but the morning light revealed a clear, blue sky. The supply station stayed in the shadows until the sun crested the eastern hills. As the light moved over the frozen ground, the rays reflected off the powder and sparkled like miniature prisms. It was still below freezing, but as the energy of the sun was absorbed, the snow slowly started to melt.

"Git up! Breakfast's a comin'," the proprietor shouted to get the patrons moving.

The rustle of people waking and packing their bedding replaced the sound of snoring. Lucky rose with a yawn and looked around. The room had filled after a late-night stage had deposited its passengers. Now the sojourners were ready for something to eat before they continued with their travels.

"Sure was some storm," a man beside Lucky said as he rolled up his blanket.

"Yeah. Wasn't plannin' on stoppin', but glad I did."

"Whar ya headin'?" the man asked to make polite conversation. He didn't really care, but the closeness seemed to warrant talking.

"Bannack. An' you?"

"Goin' down ta tha New Mexico Territory. I heard thars still gold 'round tha Gila River, so

I thought I might try my luck thar."

"Hope it *pans* out," Lucky joked.

The prospector laughed at Lucky's wordplay. "Me too!"

Another man slowly rose from the sleeping spot on Lucky's other side. He was ready to make small talk with the stranger, but the man rolled up his bedding and left without speaking.

"Pleasant fellow," Lucky sarcastically stated.

"Man by tha name of Catfish...nothin' ta do with fishin', either, 'cept he's a *bottom scraper*, skimmin' off of others. Waits 'long tha creeks, an' when tha panners find gold, he *bullies 'em* 'til they move away. A claim jumper, too. Thar scared ta challenge 'im if tha law's brought in, so his story stands. Since he never seems to get much, he's tolerated."

"He is a *big man*...see why most people leave 'im alone. One day—"

Lucky didn't have a chance to finish. Two men were bringing a table their way. Others followed with the chairs. The room was quickly transitioning back into a diner. Breakfast was already being served to travelers eager to get on their way.

Lucky and the prospector shared a table. When they finished breakfast, they went to get their stock. Lucky had Bullet saddled and was ready to ride out, but Mary Margaret would not budge.

"Looks like I'll be delayed. Godspeed," Lucky said to bid the man safe traveling.

"Pops."

"Huh?

"Call me Pops," the man clarified.

"Thought ya were *punnin'* with me," Lucky laughed. "Yar voice...tha way yar name came out. I heard POP. Sounded like somethin' had exploded or a gunshot."

"Why, who said *silence is golden*? I've enjoyed talkin' with ya an' hearin' yar take on things."

The man waved goodbye and walked his horse out of the stable. He had one foot in his stirrup and started to mount. Before he could swing his leg over, Catfish came up from behind a tree and knocked him out with the butt of his gun.

CHAPTER 25

Catfish grabbed Pops as he fell. He heaved the miner over his horse, belly side down, and went to grab the reins.

"Hee-haw." Mary Margaret brayed to protest Lucky's tugging.

The burro's cry startled Catfish, causing him to slip on the icy surface. Before he could regain his footing, the miner's horse had hightailed it back to the stable.

Lucky got Pops down and laid him on a pile of hay. "Do ya know who did it?" he asked when Pops came to.

"Got me from behind." Pops felt for his money pouch. "How long was I out?"

"You'd just left, then yar horse brought ya right back. Was still tryin' ta git Mary Margaret ta go, but she was havin' a poutin' fit."

"Yar burro may have saved my life...an' she probably stopped an attempted robbery." Pops showed his gold pouch.

"Her brayin' *is* loud enough." And annoying, Lucky wanted to add.

"Ya got a good burro thar." Pops scratched around Mary Margaret's ears. She instantly warmed up to him.

When Lucky saw the bond between the two, he got an idea. "Ya seem ta know somethin' 'bout burros."

"Just lost one. Was a loyal friend."

"I've only had Mary Margaret a short while. Her owner had a mishap, an' he asked me ta take care of her. Seein' as ya git 'long so well, an' she saved yar life...reckon ya two belong together."

"I couldn't—"

"You'd be doin' me a *real big* favor. She's been buckin' me ever since I got her, but she seems ta like you."

"Reckon I'm in tha market for a replacement for Bessy."

"She's yars, packs an' all." Lucky held out Mary Margaret's rope.

Pops could see that Mary Margaret was a fine burro. "OK." He grabbed his pouch. He wanted to compensate Lucky for the gift.

Lucky held up his hand. "No need for that. I'm just glad ta know that Mary Margaret's in good hands. Just promise that you'll take good care of her."

"Ya got it."

"After I got ya settled, I heard a horse gallopin' away, so I went out ta look. I couldn't be sure, but it may have been that man ya was talkin' 'bout—Catfish."

"Been usin' dust ta pay. I should've been more careful. I'll keep a lookout." Pops led Mary Margaret away.

Lucky watched the burro go. He was relieved, yet sad. I was getting used to her ornery ways, he realized. "Take care." He went back inside the stable to get his horse. He saw a gleam in Bullet's eyes. "Ya happy *now*?"

Bullet pulled his lips into a big horse smile.

Lucky worked his way north through the Idaho Territory. He passed land where the water was hot enough to shoot out from vents in the ground. Other places had pots of boiling mud. He saw a group of Indians sitting around one of the geysers. They watched as it erupted. They were waiting for that to happen, he realized as he passed. He found plenty of game, as bison and elk shared the grasslands with rabbits and squirrels. The wildflowers had lost their colors and had turned into fluffy seeds. Old Man Winter was marking his time.

"Thars ta be a hangin'," a stranger said when Lucky joined the crowd that had gathered in front of a primitive gallows. He had just arrived in Bannack, a town along Willard's Creek (later Grasshopper Creek) that had been built after gold was found a couple of years earlier.

Some men were brought forward. "What'd they do?"

"Thievin' murderers who've been robbin' stages outta Virginia City. Tha gang's been led by tha sheriff hisself. That's 'im." The stranger pointed to a man with dark hair and a heavy beard. "Tha vigilantes have been gittin' his lot, one by one. Thar not even givin' 'em a trial."

Lucky knew about the self-imposed Safety Committees. "Seen 'em in action at tha minin' camps. I reckon someone has ta take on tha burden of enforcin' tha law ta settle disputes."

"They can do good, if'n thars no formal justice system, but when they take ta killin', without usin' tha courts, well then...thar no better."

"Makes it harder when it's tha sheriff that turns." Lucky watched as the outlaws faced their final journey.

"Sheriff Plummer's a man of questionable character...why thar anxious ta git rid of 'im. He's done some good an' has influence. It's how he's avoided punishment of tha law afore."

"Sometimes, tha vigilantes are needed, but many have been wronged by thar dark justice." Lucky knew a man who was hung for stealing horses by a similar group. He was with Lucky when the act had supposedly happened, but no one believed his story.

"Hard knowin' what side's right, or who ta trust. Learnt ta mind my own business." The man cringed as he watched the executions.

Lucky learned more about the infamous sheriff. Plummer had led a controversial life. While some thought he helped the people in his jurisdiction, others had witnessed his lawless behavior. He had killed several people without justification and had been identified at several stage holdups. Once his gang was eliminated, the robberies stopped. Plummer was buried as an outlaw, not a lawman, in Hangman's Gulch outside of Bannack in 1864.

Lucky stayed in town overnight. He found Bullet a place to rest and fattened him up on oats and other grains. Winter had moved in, and Lucky was still days away from his final destination. He was headed to another town called Virginia City, which was much farther north than the place with the same name that he had left months ago in the Nevada Territory.

"The mountains may be white with snow, but tha creeks are still golden," an old-timer told Lucky at the saloon. "Tha winter storms can stir up tha rock, so more gold is carried down."

"What I'm wantin' ta hear!"

When Lucky reached Virginia City, he stopped and mailed a letter to his brother. Once this was done, he looked for a spot to settle on the hillside. He was eager to put up a one-pole tent that he had made. He had seen a miner using one with a similar design.

"Ya git ya a piece of canvas," the old man explained. "Ya punch out holes along tha edge, like I did here." He pointed to where some rope was looped through the slots. "Ya use a branch as a pole, center yar canvas over it, and stake tha bottoms down. All thar is to it."

Lucky had his materials ready and went to put up his temporary home. "Huh. How do I hold tha branch up an' git ta stakin'?"

He tried several methods, but his efforts fell short, and he had yet to get his tent standing.

After another try, Bullet snorted.

"So ya think this is funny, do ya? Be a lot easier if'n you could help, ya know."

A man who was riding past was amused as he watched the boy fight to get his tent properly staked. As he neared the spectacle, he thought the young man looked familiar.

"Lucky?"

The tent collapsed as the boy tried to tighten a stake. He was ready to give up when he heard someone call his name.

"Lucky?" the man repeated.

CHAPTER 26

This time, Janks was able to stand. It took a moment for him to think, but as his head cleared, he was able to remember his plight.

"Virginia City," he vocalized. "That's where I am, but in tha Montana Territory, not Nevada." Janks headed for the nearest saloon. When he entered, he faced a familiar foe.

"*Bart*?" The man had aged since they had parted company. His hair had started to thin, and he had a mean scar on his cheek.

"Janks? Thought I'd *kilt* ya."

"I survived."

"Seems so."

Janks remembered how Bart had treated him in the past. "See ya 'round." He turned to leave.

"*Wait*," Bart pleaded. He walked up and put his arm around Jank's shoulders, acting as if they were old friends. "Tha boys had me tied up in knots, an' you was just a *kid*, gittin' in tha way. Didn't wanta shoot ya." He tried to sound apologetic.

"Reckon you can understand my *reluctance* ta renew old acquaintances, then."

"Things are different. Yar older now. Let me buy ya a drink."

Janks hesitated, but he recognized that he needed help. He knew it was just a ruse to use him, but he couldn't refuse. He was vulnerable.

He had no money, no place to go, and he was hungry. "Sure." He felt like he was going from the frying pan into the fire. He allowed Bart to lead him to a table at the back of the saloon.

Bart went to the counter and came back with two pints. He watched as Janks gulped his drink. "What ya been up ta since...?"

Janks answered the unfinished question. He decided to reply honestly. "*Since* I last saw ya, I haven't made much of my life. I've drifted ...become tha town drunk. Been outta money for a while now."

Bart waved a barmaid over and ordered food. When the biscuits and beans arrived, the smell made Janks nauseous. Bart wondered why the man wasn't ravenously devouring the meal. "It's fer *you.*"

Janks looked at the plate and started to eat. He only took small bites until his stomach could tolerate the food. When he had eaten about half of what was on the plate, Bart waved for the saloon gal to bring another round, and then he got to the point.

"If'n ya want work, I got a job. I'm in with a *new* crowd now...a better bunch of guys. Thar smarter too."

Janks could only stare. It was as if he was floating above the table, looking down at the two of them, drinking together, almost like old times. But he knew better. Bart wouldn't have bothered with him unless he was needed for something. The question was—what? He waited until Bart stopped talking. "*What* do ya want me ta do?"

"I want ya ta meet tha boys. Can ya ride with

me *now*?" Bart was beginning to wonder what had happened to the boy. He seemed to be daff, but he needed someone quickly. The job was happening soon.

"Lost my horse somewhar 'long tha way. Do ya have one for me?"

"I'll git ya one."

They rode until they came to a run-down cabin. Two other men were seated inside the dirty dwelling. They were introduced as Tick and Sting.

Once everyone was seated, Sting gave a rundown of his plan. "We're gonna holdup tha stage outta Virginia City. A prospector who did well will be ridin' it tomorrow mornin'. I got tha tip-off from a banker I know. He exchanged tha gold for currency. Tha miner's *beggin'* fer someun *like us* ta take it off 'im."

"*How much* ya talkin' 'bout?" Bart asked.

"He's got $50,000...cash. Should be $10,000 each...includin' tha banker's cut."

When Janks heard the numbers, his interest was piqued. "That's a lot of money. What's he carryin' it in?"

"He took it outta tha bank in saddlebags."

Tick sneered. "'Ems our *target*."

"Tha road passes through sum rocks 'bout two hours outta town. That's whar we'll strike. Bart, you an' Janks will come out from tha front an' start shootin' at tha driver an' anyone else ridin' up front. At tha same time, me an' Tick will come out an' shoot from tha sides. With tha driver down, Bart, you'll go an' git control of tha horses. Tha rest of us will take care of tha passengers. Any questions?"

Tick was the first to respond. "Got it."

Bart lit a smoke. "With ya."

"Nah." Janks assumed the meeting was over, so he went outside and sat in the rocker on the porch. He grabbed a dried-up biscuit that he had stowed in his pocket. His appetite was starting to come back.

The following morning, the four highwaymen rode out, hid behind the rocks, and waited. The stagecoach was on schedule and moving fast. There were two men sitting up front and several passengers were inside.

"*Now!*" Bart ordered. He charged forward, and Janks followed. They started shooting. The driver went down, but not before he got a shot off. Janks was wounded and fell from his horse. He was able to run behind a boulder before the man riding shotgun was able to get off a round. Bart kept shooting, but he missed his target. A bullet grazed his shoulder. A second one dug into his leg.

Sting and Tick had rushed the stage, but the passengers inside were fighting back. Each window sported a gun, and shots were coming from both directions. The miner, having the most to lose, leaned out of the window and fired at an oncoming bandit. Tick fell from his horse. Sting got the man on his side, then went to stop the man who was still firing from the front.

Sting recognized the infamous man who was riding shotgun on the Overland stage. "Slade!"

When Slade heard his name called, he turned and fired. His shot ran true. A slow trickle of blood fell out of a hole in Sting's forehead. He slumped and was carried away on his horse.

Bart, having watched his partners go down, turned to run. Slade wasn't going to let that happen. He quickly rotated forward and pulled the trigger, but the click of his gun told him that he was out of bullets. Bart hightailed it back to the cabin.

The stagecoach stopped.

"Ya need any help *up thar*?" the prospector shouted as he clutched his saddlebags.

"Got it *covered*," Slade yelled back.

The driver moaned. Slade helped him to sit upright. "Jack, look *what* I got ya inta."

"Nothin' I didn't take *pleasure* in doin'. I'm always ready ta fight for tha stage line."

Jack Slade was a notorious gunslinger who thrived on shoot-outs. His success as a stage driver on the Central Overland route led to an appointment as a division superintendent. He developed many of the routes used by the stage lines and helped to establish the Pony Express. Alcohol was his downfall. When he was drunk, he would become a violent and dangerous man. After one of his rampages, vigilantes captured and hung him on March 10, 1864.

Janks waited behind the rocks, hoping that he had been forgotten. The passengers of the stage stepped out so they could tend to the wounded man. Janks gasped when he thought he recognized an old adversary.

"Likely *yar bullet* that winged me," he spat, knowing full well that it came from the driver, not the young man that looked like Lucky.

The stage eventually rolled on, giving Janks a chance to work his way back—to where? he wondered. His horse had run off, leaving him to flee on foot. After walking for several miles, he saw a horse, but it was still far down the road. When he got close to the animal, he saw that it was Sting's horse. Sting had fallen off, but his boot was stuck in the stirrup. The horse was dragging his limp corpse as it moved to graze.

"*Whoa, boy.*" Janks got the leg untangled and let the limb drop. He mounted the horse and started to ride toward the old cabin, but he decided to do an about-face and rode in the opposite direction.

CHAPTER 27

Lucky saw a familiar face. "*Banks*! What tha ...*where* did...what're ya doin' *here*?" he stuttered with excitement. "Yar sure a *sight for sore eyes!*"

"You look like you could use some help."

"Reckon tha tent's gittin' tha best of me."

"You by yourself?" Banks saw that the boy was alone. He hoped that his brother hadn't run into trouble.

Lucky knew the meaning behind Banks's question. "Sam's doin' fine...at least tha last I know'd. He left a while back...ta find Sally. He's gonna marry her."

Banks sighed with relief. "Glad to hear."

"Give up bein' a wagon master?"

"It was time. Brought my last train through last summer. Kept hearing about all the others getting gold, so I'm giving prospecting a go, too."

"Ya havin' any luck? As you can see, I'm just settlin' in."

"I've got a sluice box up the canyon. Could use another hand, if you're interested. I'll have to check with my partners first, but I don't think they'll mind. Come out and have a look. It would be a better fit for your skills than *home building*," Banks joked. "I can help you get your stuff loaded."

"Tempted ta *leave* tha tent behind. I've done

well enough under tha stars 'til now, anyway."

"Best to bring it along. May yet have its use."

Banks led him toward the other side of the gulch. They approached the claim from a high point that was upstream from the setup. Banks wanted to present a birds-eye view.

Lucky whistled. "Impressive. Ya got quite an operation goin'."

"We get enough to draw attention. Have to keep a regular watch out."

"Lots of scum out thar, tryin' ta git what others have earned. Came into town when tha sheriff of Bannack met his maker. Strung 'im up on his own gallows."

"Plummer? The vigilantes did the town a favor. He used his position to get information on the freight being shipped out of Virginia City. His highwaymen knew which stage had the gold and payroll money…and when they rode. Too bad, too. He was elected to protect the shipments, not rob them. We're hoping that once the Montana Territory is established, law and order will be more organized."

"*Montana* Territory?"

"We'll be our own territory soon. The Idaho's too big, so we're splitting off," Banks clarified. "It's a necessary solution."

"I reckon governin' will be easier with smaller regions. Especially as more'n more people come ta mine."

"Towns, like us, that are on the eastern side of the Rockies are far away from Lewiston, the capital. Crossing the mountain is tough enough. Then there's hundreds of miles left to go if you have business to do over there."

"Have been out that way. Not an easy feat. Afore ya know it, Montana will be petitionin' for statehood."

The Montana Territory was created later that year, May 26, 1864. It would be another 25 years before the territory would become a state. Montana was admitted to the Union on November 8, 1889.

"You'll be glad to meet my two partners. You *might* recognize them," Banks said with a tone of mystery as they headed toward the camp.

They tied their horses to the hitching post in front of the cabin and walked down to the sluice box. Two men were sifting through the trapped material. One looked up as Banks and Lucky approached. His face lit up when he saw Lucky. They shook hands.

"Well, *I'll be*! Lucky!"

"Should have known. Where Banks goes, yar sure ta follow. How ya doin', Davis?"

"Fine. Just fine."

The other man stopped working, too. "Holy cow! How ya been?"

"Tincup! Good seein' ya. So, they brought ya with 'em, huh? Musta needed someone ta do tha cookin' an' tha *housework*," Lucky teased.

"See ya haven't changed a bit. Always *jokin'*." Tincup laughed as they exchanged greetings.

"Ya here ta prospect?" Davis asked. "Wouldn't mind havin' another hand helpin' us."

"We could use ya, if'n ya want a *piece* of our pie," the cook quipped.

"Ya sure?" Lucky saw how much work they had already done.

The partners looked at each other, and all

nodded their heads in agreement.

Lucky was grateful to these men once more. "I look forward ta workin' with ya again!"

Banks spoke for the group. "You're now a part of *Trains To Claims*. We'll go into town and do the paperwork tomorrow."

"Thanks guys. Sure is good ta be among friends. So, fill me in. I'm a *quick* learner." Lucky grinned after saying the last statement.

"You said that when I first hired you on. Your words *rang true* then," Banks recalled. "Working a sluice is a bit more complex than just sitting by a stream and panning. We did some of that when we started."

"We had ta figure things out 'long tha way. Took a lot of trial an' error." Davis explained how they constructed the sluice. "We fitted tha wooden troughs together, tha upper one ta bring in water from tha small pool above ya, an' tha lower one ta sift tha gravel. Tha tight curve in tha creek allowed us ta angle our sluice so tha water'd go right back into tha stream."

"Keeps tha place from muddin' up. That was *my* suggestion," Tincup boasted.

"A good one," Lucky assured the cook. "I can see ya thought things through."

Davis lowered a hinged section at the end of the upper trough. "We can stop tha flow here if'n we need ta." The water splashed onto the ground. A channel had been dug to guide the runoff toward the stream. He put the panel in place, and the water ran back into the lower sluice.

"Ya picked a nice spot here." Lucky looked around and saw that where the cabin sat, the ground had formed a flat floor above the stream. "Ever have any floodin' problems?"

"Got close once," Banks answered. "I think the diversion at the pool helped to disperse the flow. As a rule, the stream stays fairly consistent through most storms. Also means all the gold's not pushed on down, too."

"How long did it take afore ya found some color?" Lucky asked.

"We'd been at it for a while, randomly pickin' spots 'long tha main creek an' gittin' nothin'. Then, it happened." Tincup easily remembered the details. "It was a cold an' wet day. Most of tha others that had been pannin' with us earlier had decided ta stay away. Thar was only a few out, an' afore long, it was only tha three of us. While we waited for tha rain ta ease up, we noticed that a side creek up tha gulch had swelled, so we thought we'd go an' try our luck on it. Davis was tha first ta find flakes, then we got sum in our pans, too."

"The rain must've washed out a new source," Banks clarified. "The three of us made sure we claimed as goodly a portion as was allowed, knowing that we'd be expanding our operation. As you've noted, this was an ideal location to build on. Once we collected enough gold to pay our costs, we built the sluice."

Lucky watched as the water flowed over the gravel that was still in the trough. "How does it *actually* work? I mean, how does it separate out tha gold particles?"

"Another thing we had to figure out—how to sift through the gravel without losing any of the gold, especially the smaller pieces." Banks pointed to strips of wood running from side to side on the bottom of the sluice box. "These bars are called riffles. Placing them at the right angle was the tricky part."

Davis explained further. "Look what happens when tha water passes over 'em? Forms eddies. Tha idea is ta slow tha water down enough so tha heavier stuff can drop out."

"The gold, being the *heavier stuff,* is caught behind the riffle bars. It stays there 'til we pick them out, either while the sluice is running or when we empty it at the end of the day. We'll show you." Banks handed Tincup a bucket that he had brought over from the creek. Tincup dumped the mixture into the first segment of the lower trough.

"Tha hope is that tha sediment has sum gold chunks." Davis laughed. "We got 'em at first, but now we're mostly gittin' tha smaller stuff."

As the water carried the rocky substance down the box, the riffles collected their shares. The heavier particles fell out, while the lighter ones were drawn down with the flowing water. A larger flake of gold had become wedged in a riffle near the beginning of the sluice.

"Ya got *somethin'!*" Lucky pointed to a shiny flake that was reflected by the sun.

"Yep." Tincup picked the piece out of the gravel and handed it to Lucky. "Have a look."

"'Bout a bit's worth?" Lucky guessed before he handed the chip back to Tincup.

"More or less." Tincup deposited the sliver of gold inside a small pouch called a poke.

Banks stashed the sack behind some rocks. "Larger than what we usually find. We're mostly catching the finer flakes now...some are too light to settle. That's why we have the blanket at the end...to trap them."

Lucky laughed. "Tha dust. Flour gold. Mostly what I got in my pannin'."

"It adds up," Davis assured him. "So much so that we keep a guard through tha night. A few have already tested our shootin' skills."

"Bandits, looters, good-for-nothin's...we can't take chances," Tincup added. "Thar all out thar, lurkin' 'bout, an' they don't care if'n they leave ya dead or alive."

Banks expounded on the situation. "It wasn't like that at first...we were all getting something. Now that the good claims have been staked, the rest of the pickings are poor. People are getting desperate. And more keep coming. Usually, by the time they get to camp, their money's run out, so they're turning to thieving."

"Been thar...only gittin' tha scraps. Never found enough ta do any stakin'. I was close once." Lucky told them about Fool's Pool. "We got enough ta put some away for a rainy day. It's sad...what tha greed an' tha desperation has brought out in some men. Not in me ta be that way, though."

"Only our sharp shootin' has kept tha scum away. But ta be honest, ya came at a good time. We need another man good with an iron, someone we can *trust*," Davis emphasized.

"I've been lookin' over my shoulder for most of my journey. Lawlessness is rampant in tha camps." Lucky looked at the three men. "I know that honest men are hard ta find these days, an' I'm glad ta be of help...for whatever share ya decide. You've done tha hard part, gittin' tha claim up an' runnin'." Lucky looked at the cabin. "You've even built yarselves a nice lookin' home."

"Kind of been made into a fortress." Banks smiled as he added, "Got an extra cot for you, or you can sleep in that *fine* tent you have."

Lucky grinned. "I'll take tha *cot*. But I'll git tha *testy* thing up yet. Ya never know. It may come in handy."

Banks thought of a practical use. "Might be a good shelter for the night patrol when it rains."

"Reckon so," Lucky admitted. "Been wantin' ta try sluicin'. Maybe if'n Sam stayed, he'd have liked it too."

"I've been wonderin' 'bout 'im. How *is* he?" Davis asked.

"Doin' fine."

"Whar is he? How come yar not together?" Tincup wondered.

"Gone ta Colorado...*ta git married*."

"*Knew it*! Ta that gal, Sally. Didn't I tell ya they would end up together?"

"You were right," Banks acknowledged.

"Let's go into town an' celebrate. To our *new partner*!" Davis waved an imaginary glass, then added, "an' ta *love*," to honor Sam's news.

"Whose night is it to stay and keep watch?" Banks hadn't forgotten the lurking danger.

"Wouldn't ya know, it's *mine*." Tincup was disappointed. "Y'all go an' whoop it up. I'll git with ya later," he directed to Lucky.

"While we're in town, we can get Lucky added to our claim," Banks pointed out before they left for the celebration.

Lucky quickly picked up sluicing. It was just as mundane as panning with long days of gathering and sifting through gravel. Though the sluice box allowed them to filter more, faster, they still had to pick out the fine particles. But this was different, he realized. He was working with a fine group of men, men he knew he could trust. Plus, they got gold daily. Though most of it was the fine powder, it was enough to keep him content.

After a spell, they got into a routine. The chores to keep the sluice running were divided and switched on a regular basis. Finding the shiny remnants kept the gold fever alive, and their long-standing friendship kept the partners going. A few strangers had wandered onto their property, only to be rebuffed by the competent gun handlers.

Banks had gone to Virginia City one day to get supplies. It was April 1865. The town was abuzz as people shared the long-awaited news. He quickly finished his errands and came back shouting. "Lee surrendered at Appomattox!"

"How're folks takin' it?" Tincup asked.

"Cheered. Course, the pro-union supporters were hooting the loudest. While the rest of us are thankful, we inwardly groan at what the loss will mean to the South." Banks remembered his days in the army and how relieved he was when his war was over. "Regardless, everyone's glad for it to have ended."

Lucky sympathized with both sides. "I know *all* tha soldiers are ready ta return home."

Loyalties to the cause were divided in many of the western territories. The two factions had lived and worked together during the war years, but many disagreements had stemmed from the strong feelings that were held by each side. Though the fighting had ended, the emotional healing was far from over.

Five days later, Banks topped off his poke with the gold dust that he had collected from the sluice. "Got another full pouch!"

"I think that's a reason ta celebrate," Davis declared. "Why don't we quit a little early? Could do with a change of scenery. I've been lettin' you boys do all tha shoppin' lately."

"It'd do us all good ta git away from this an' relax a bit. We could splurge on a juicy steak an' a cold beer." Tincups mouth watered with the thought.

"I'll stay," Lucky volunteered. "But, can ya see if'n we got any mail?"

"You *sure*?" Banks asked.

"My turn ta clean out tha box, anyways. After I'm done, I might git at one of tha bottles we've stashed in tha creek."

"*What* are we *waitin' for*? Let's saddle up tha horses!" Tincup was eager to leave and wanted the group to get moving.

"We better clean up first," Davis suggested. "I don't think anyone would wanna be 'round us, tha way we are now."

"Don't put tha wagon afore tha horse." Lucky repeated the phrase Davis often used when they were on the Oregon Trail, and he got ahead of himself.

"First things first. See, I taught ya well."

Lucky smiled. "Some things ya never forget."

As the miners prepared to leave, a lone figure

approached the hillside. He was hidden by the shade of a large rock. After a while, three others came and joined him.

"Three of 'em rode off a while ago. Tha one by tha creek is drinkin' whiskey. Should be an easy target." The man spit out a wad of chewing tobacco.

"Ya see whar they stashed thar gold?" one of the arrivals asked.

"Got somethin' when he cleaned tha sluice. Took it inside. Must be whar they keep it."

"Well, Bruin, let's go an' find out. What're we *waitin'* fer." The young man was impatient. He watched as Lucky put the bottle back in the water and walked toward the cabin.

"*Patience*, Lance. Gotta have a plan," Bruin, their leader, cautiously urged. He then outlined how he wanted to do the job.

The four bandits started down the hill. Lucky had finished putting on his fresh clothes and happened to look out the window. He saw the men emerge from the shadows and watched as they came his way. He knew they meant trouble, so he locked the door. By the time the strangers stepped onto the property, he was ready. He had strapped on his gun, found extra ammunition, and grabbed his rifle. He waited by the window, ready to take action.

"Yar *trespassin'*!"

"Says *who*?" Bruin spat back.

Lucky shot at the ground, just to the right of the man's boot. The four men scattered, but only to seek shelter under the trough.

"OK. Let loose, boys," Lucky heard someone shout.

The bandits started firing. A barrage of lead came at the cabin. One hit the window where Lucky was stationed. The shattering glass hit him in the face. He dropped to the floor and reached for his bandana. He sat under the window and wiped the shards from his face. The blitz continued. He could hear the rat-a-tat sound as the slugs bombarded the outer walls, then the breaking of more glass. He popped up to get a quick look outside and thought he saw a moving target, so he fired a shot.

"Got ya!"

The firing stopped.

CHAPTER 28

At first, Lucky thought he might have a chance. "Maybe they're rethinkin', now that one is down. Tha cabin *is* hard ta git into." His grounds for being optimistic quickly faded.

Their leader shouted an ultimatum. "Yar *gold*! Throw it out, or we come *git it*!"

"Thars *nothin'* here. My partners took it all when they went into town." Lucky hoped this would encourage them to give up.

This time, the gunfire was less intense. He knew that was because the others were circling the cabin. Since the only way in was through the front door, he wasn't worried about them, so he kept shooting to keep the others at bay.

Two of the men headed to the rear of the cabin. "Here." One of the ruffians handed his partner a burning torch. Though the window was too high for the bandits to see into the room, it was open. The man managed to get the fire stick between the bars and pushed it inside. It dropped, landed on a table, and ignited some newspaper that was lying on top. His partner went to the side window and tossed another blazing weapon inside.

"*Smoke!*" Lucky realized what the men had in mind. He had to abandon his post and put out the fire or die from inhaling the smoke, or worse. He grabbed a blanket off a cot, doused it with water, and started to beat out the flames. The outlaws took advantage and rushed the front of the cabin. Bruin found an ax and started to work on the door.

While Lucky fought the bandits, his partners made their way into town. When they got there, they heard the news that had been spreading across the nation like a prairie fire.

"Lincoln assassinated!"

The men looked at each other, speechless. They, like others around the country, went about their business feeling the loss of their President.

Banks picked up a few supplies, and then he went to the post office. A letter was waiting for Lucky. After he pocketed the piece of mail, he headed to the bar. A filled mug sat in front of the only empty seat. He sat and started to grab the brew. "*What the—*" Banks hollered when his chair gave way.

Davis got up and went to help. "*Sorry.* We knew tha table was wobbly, but we didn't know tha legs on yar chair were bad."

"Kinda *funny* ta see ya go down, though," Tincup laughed. "At least yar drink was spared."

Banks sneered. "Next time I'll make sure *you* get the dribble glass."

Davis brought over a better chair. "What took ya so long? Yar drink's been sittin' for a while."

"We're 'bout ready ta start our second round an' yar just in time ta *buy*," Tincup hinted.

Banks gave the cook a crooked smile. He got out the letter. "It's from *Sam*. I think we should finish up and deliver it."

"Lucky'll be excited ta git *that*. Kinda like ta

know what he's up ta *myself,*" Tincup admitted.

"Agree." Davis went back to his seat. "Tincup, you've had enough, anyway."

"Party pooper."

"After hearing the news about Lincoln, I'm not in the mood for partying." Banks picked up his warm brew and raised his glass. "To a man who kept the country united."

Davis joined in the toast. "An' for *his service* durin' such tryin' times."

Tincup stopped his fooling. "May tha country heal after bein' split for so long."

The three men talked about the death of their president. Then, in a somber mood, they drank in silence. Banks gave his drink a few more sips and stood up. The others followed his lead.

"Tha celebratin' kinda went sour," Tincup noted as they rode out of town.

"Maybe Sam's news will cheer us up." Davis changed the gait of his horse to a full gallop.

When they topped the rise that led to their property, Banks thought he heard gunfire. He stopped. "*Listen.*"

"*Shots*," Davis confirmed.

They hurried down the hill. When they were in sight of the cabin, they could see a man with an ax pounding on the door.

"*Footpads!*" Banks charged forward. Davis and Tincup were right behind him.

The robbers were so focused on getting into the cabin that they were unaware of Lucky's incoming recruits, who got off a few rounds before being detected.

"Take cover!" Bruin yelled after dodging a bullet. He dropped the ax and ran toward the sluice. Lance was just ahead of him.

"*Agh*," Lance choked out when a stray bullet hit him. As he fell, he grabbed the frame of the flume and pulled the hinge that controlled the water's flow.

Bruin arrived just as the water was released. The unexpected dousing caused him to drop. He fell on top of Lance. "Move," he cried before he realized that the man was dying. The shot had pierced Lance's carotid artery, causing him to bleed to death. Bruin rolled off the body, only to land in a bloodied mud pit. Before he could gain his composure, a slug got him, too.

The other two sidewinders, still a force to be reckoned with, kept the shoot-out going. Each side fired off multiple rounds to show their strength, but the freely flying ammunition missed their intended targets. The men were in a standoff.

Lucky had put out the fires and was ready to join in the fight. He cautiously worked his way back to the front window. When he looked out, he saw Davis and Tincup and knew that Banks was nearby. He waited for them to flush out the robbers for the final showdown.

The tent had become useful after all, Banks was thinking as he ran to hide behind it. When he saw the two outlaws up ahead, he gave his best rebel yell and charged. His bullets missed, but they caused the outlaws to hit the ground. Though they wormed their way out of Banks's gunfire, the bandits faced a new front. Davis and Tincup had moved in to finish what Banks had started. The outlaws didn't even have a chance to fire back.

Lucky came out when the firing ceased. "I wasn't expectin' yar help, but *sure* am glad ya came back early."

"Had a *letter* to deliver." Banks pulled out the piece of mail from an inside pocket.

"Yeah. We wanted ta hear what Sam had ta say." Davis watched as Lucky took the envelope and tore the seal open.

"My big brother's *still* watchin' over me, even from afar. Thank you, *Sam*!" Lucky scanned the script, then he summarized for the group.

"He went an' *done it*. He was wantin' ta wait 'til he got his store up an' runnin', but tha business was boomin', so they decided ta go ahead an' tie tha knot. He wanted me ta come an' be tha best man, but when he finally saw Sally again, they realized they'd already wasted enough time. Wants us ta come an' visit. His property's on main street. Tha front of tha buildin' will serve as his store, an' they'll live in tha back for now. Wants a bigger place when tha children come."

"They *expectin'*?" Tincup asked.

"Thar ya go puttin' tha cart afore tha horse," Davis teased the cook.

"Just wonderin'."

"Thars no mention of young'uns, *just yet*," Lucky clarified.

CHAPTER 29

"**Z**ero! *Again!*" Banks moaned. He had just finished panning through another load of gravel that he had collected from the sluice.

"Can't always be a winner." Davis tried to be optimistic, though he, too, had noticed that the gold was petering out.

"It's hot enough ta cook an egg on that rock over thar." Tincup had his own complaint.

It was a blistering day. There was no shade to give the prospectors relief. The heat from the sun penetrated through their hats. Clothes didn't seem to offer any protection either.

"My *back* is burnin'." Davis pulled on the backside of his sweat-soaked shirt.

Lucky groaned. "Been pourin' water over my head, an' still don't git relief."

"We're all starting to be miserable. Isn't that telling us something?" Banks asked. "Maybe it's time to think about folding up this operation."

Tincup frowned. "All good things must end. Tha gold had ta dry up at sum point."

"We had a *good run*. Hard ta believe, but I've been with ya for more'n a year," Lucky realized.

Tincup reflected on their carefree mining days. "A lot has happened while we whiled away tha hours. A president was sadly kilt."

"The war's come and gone," Banks noted.

"Nevada became a state," Davis added.

Lucky thought of his brother. "Sam went an' got hisself hitched."

"*Time sure flies*," Tincup observed. "Lookin' back, though, tha days weren't hard at all."

"Because our stash steadily grew," Banks justified.

"But *now*, it's beginnin' ta be monotonous." Davis said what they all were thinking. "Reckon it may be time ta move on."

They sold out to a prospector who had been working the neighboring claim. It didn't bring much, but they had already reaped the rewards.

"Best to not use the assayers in Nevada City when we cash out," Banks advised before they vacated the property.

Davis had also heard stories. "Nor Virginia City. Miners have been ambushed thar recently, too. We should head ta Bannack instead. I'm hopin' that since tha death of Sheriff Plummer, tha town's more law abidin'."

They packed up the rest of their belongings and left the following day. They decided to take the stage to Bannack, then return to get their horses.

"Did you get your letter finished?" Banks asked Lucky before they boarded the coach. They were carrying carpetbags filled with their clothes and toiletries. Hidden amongst these items were pouches bulging with gold. Each would be paid a handsome sum once they were exchanged for currency.

Lucky opened the door. "Dropped it off."

Two other passengers, their partners, were already seated inside the stage. "Neither of ya was followed," Tincup informed them.

Davis had watched the other side of the street. "Didn't see anyone suspicious, either."

"Well, we've faced many trials together and find ourselves at the end of another journey," Banks began when the coach started to roll. "I'm too old to start on another. I think I'm ready to find a place to call home."

Lucky offered a suggestion. "Sam likes tha Colorado Territory. Says tha mountains are a wonder ta look at every day."

"Ya took ta that place in Kansas," Tincup reminded Banks. "Do ya remember tha town that was by tha river?"

"Or ya could go back South, ta Tennessee," Davis proposed.

"All good suggestions," Banks confirmed. "I want to go somewhere new. Reckon I'll drift a bit...'til the right place comes along."

Tincup looked at Davis. "How 'bout you?"

"I'm of tha same mind as Banks. I'm going ta wander, but I'd like ta stay out West. There'll be lots of changes, especially once tha railroad comes through."

"Well, I'm gonna find another wagon train ta cook for. I kinda like tha bumpy ridin' an' seein' tha country, an' all," Tincup confessed.

Banks wasn't surprised when Tincup made his revelation. "The way won't be as rough... compared to the early days, that is. We saw the changes with each trip. Roads had improved as easier passages were found, and more places had popped up to offer all kinds of supplies."

"You'll probably experience tha last of tha great *wagon train* adventures." Davis knew that once the transcontinental train service was up and running, the cross-country wagon trains would become obsolete.

"Probably won't be tha same…maybe even less challengin', but for now, when someone says *train* out here, thar still talkin' 'bout a *wagon* train. Think I'll be headin' for St. Joe," Tincup confirmed.

Banks looked at Lucky. "That leaves you."

"I'll keep driftin'. Don't know what I'll do. Reckon I got most of tha gold fever outta me, but not all. Wanna see what tha next adventure holds for me, too."

Lucky slowly made his way eastward. When he reached the controversial Bozeman Trail, he was hesitant to use the route. It ran southeast through the Dakota Territory, land held by the Indians. He had heard about Red Cloud's War, but a group of soldiers was heading back to Fort Reno, so he tagged along with them. He stayed there overnight and then left for Fort Laramie. He had not ridden far when a blinding windstorm struck, obstructing his view of the Black Hills. Without this valuable landmark, he could only wander through the wide-open plains without direction. He chanced upon a rock outcropping that offered protection, so he dismounted and worked his way out of the wind. When he rounded the corner, he saw a boy sharing a fur blanket with a young woman. Behind them, a coiled rattlesnake was ready to strike. Lucky ran and kicked it away, but in the act, he was struck. The girl, who was wearing a deerskin dress adorned with intricately woven beadwork, rushed to his aid.

CHAPTER 30

"**K**imimela, what are we to do?" the young boy asked his sister. At first, he thought the man was going to harm them, then he saw the snake.

"I'll tend to him until we can get a travois."

Lucky passed out before they reached the village. Kimimela had him placed in her teepee so she could use her medicines to tend to his bite. Lucky briefly opened his eyes, and in his dreamlike state, he thought he was in heaven because the buffalo hide that surrounded the pine poles diffused the light and gave an angelic aura to the pretty girl.

During the next week, Lucky was in and out of consciousness. The site of the bite was painful, but the powders she had given him were slowly taking effect. When he was able to stay lucid, he tried, without success, to get out of bed.

"You stay," the woman ordered.

"Speak English?"

"Little."

"Thought ya was an angel. What's yar name?"

"Kimimela."

"Lovely…like you. Wanta thank ya. Whar am I?" Lucky was still woozy and lightheaded.

"Village of the Lakota Sioux."

"My horse?"

"Here. Followed us."

Lucky was too tired to continue talking. When he woke again, he found he was able to sit up. He slowly rose from the bed and walked to the door. An Indian brave stopped him.

"Stay," he commanded. "Kimimela come."

"Tha young woman who helped me?"

The man didn't talk further but indicated that Lucky wasn't to leave the confines of the teepee. Lucky went back inside and noticed that his belongings were lying by the wall. His guns were missing. He got some water from his canteen and waited.

Kimimela came back later that day. "Come." She stood with the door open and gestured for Lucky to follow her.

They walked to the far side of the village. The others in the tribe stared as he passed. Lucky smiled, hoping they would see he was friendly, and he meant them no harm. They came to a group of men who were sitting on a blanket that was spread out on the ground. No introductions were given.

"Sit," the man in the middle directed. His black hair was predominantly white, and his skin was tanned and wrinkled. The elder was a man of importance, but Lucky didn't know how much. He was too concerned about saving his own skin to worry about the hierarchy of the tribe.

Lucky sat where the man had directed and faced the panel that was to determine his fate. They sat in silence, staring, then the face-off was broken.

"You on *our land*," the elder started.

Lucky tried to explain. "Got lost—windstorm. Didn't know."

The man prodded. "Why you *here*?"

"Tha dust. Thick. Couldn't see whar I was goin'. Tryin' ta git ta Fort Laramie."

The man held up Lucky's pan. "You *look* for gold? You bring *others*?"

"*No.*" Lucky held his ground. "Headin' ta tha fort. Got lost in tha windstorm."

At the time, Lucky didn't know why the man questioned him so. He would soon learn the reason. The Lakotas had already been displaced by other warring tribes, so they were determined to hold on to their existing lands. They had seen the consequences of the gold rush, especially for the Indians. They knew the gold in the Black Hills would bring the miners; some had already tried to get at it. The Bozeman Trail, which had opened in '63 for emigrant travel, brought many unwanted visitors. They knew what was coming and had been fighting ever since.

"*Go.* Kimimela, take away." The elder waved to indicate the meeting was over.

Lucky stood. He wanted to explain further, but Kimimela's expression warned him against further talk.

Lucky was allowed to stay in the village until he recuperated. He knew he was in danger, but he didn't have the strength to leave. When his pan was returned, he felt some relief, at least for the time being. Most in the village ignored him and went about their business as if he wasn't there. Some of the braves who could speak his language would come and talk, but it was the younger ones, those who had never been around a "white" man before, who sought his company. With Kimimela's help, he taught them how to play hide-and-seek and tug-of-war, which soon became popular with the older kids as well.

"Yar an angel...*my* guardian angel," Lucky told Kimimela one day.

"No understand."

He felt that the young woman influenced the others, so they tolerated his presence in their camp. "It's 'cause of you that yar tribe accepts me an' lets me stay. But I've yet ta gain thar trust."

"You kept snake away. We are grateful."

A few days later, Lucky was called back for another counsel. The same group was waiting as before.

"More of you come," the same elder told him. "Want gold."

"Thar not with me. I've been travelin' alone."

"They come. Look. Braves scare away."

"If'n they find gold, they won't be stopped. They will be followed by many others," Lucky warned. "They will take what is yours."

"You go, you tell?"

"No. Friend."

Lucky was dismissed. He was worried, so he went to find Kimimela. She was teaching him the Lakota language, and he felt that he had her confidence. He spotted her with others, cooking over an open fire. He got her to follow him to a quiet place by the stream.

"Why does yar elder think my people come for gold?" He had not heard of any finds in the Black Hills.

She hesitated. She didn't want to reveal the truth. "They take our land. We protect."

"Tha gold brings 'em. Thar not interested if'n thars none ta be had."

Kimimela looked at him, then shook her head up and down.

"Tell no one 'bout..." Lucky stopped. Several warriors ran into camp to gather their weapons. One of them was someone Lucky had spent time with, so he knew the brave's name. "Akecheta. What's up?"

"Your people come."

"Not *mine*. Show ya. Give me a weapon." The brave threw him one. Lucky smiled at Akecheta. "My rifle."

"*Show* me!"

Lucky followed the warriors to the edge of their camp. He could see white men hiding behind some rocks not too far away. One of them fired at a Lakota brave. He missed, but the counterfiring began. Soon, bullets and arrows were ricocheting off the trees and rocks. It was a standoff, so the miners backed away, and the skirmish was over.

When they returned to the village, Akecheta slapped Lucky on the back. "Brother."

Lucky was allowed to keep his rifle. He had finally gained their trust.

The prospectors were not deterred. Later that night, they returned and headed into the hills. A brave out hunting the next morning saw them panning in a stream. He was spotted. One miner grabbed his rifle and shot. The brave was hit. The noise alerted the village, and the Lakotas were once again engaged in a fight to protect their land.

The warriors organized their forces. The miners, knowing the Indians were sure to come, had strategically placed themselves so they could fire from different heights and angles. The first braves to arrive were instantly shot down. The others backed off and found cover.

Lucky stuck with Akecheta, who was heading up and around the hill to the other side of the stream, where the prospectors had chosen to pan. They got behind the intruders. Akecheta fired at an exposed head but missed. As the miner turned to shoot in return, Lucky fired. The man fell but was not dead. Akecheta finished him off.

The other two prospectors knew that they were outnumbered and decided to fight to the finish. As the Lakotas moved in, one of the men stood so he could shoot at an approaching Indian brave. The elder that had spoken with Lucky had the man in his sight. He had his arrow nocked and drawn. After he launched his weapon, the man's companion popped his rifle out from behind a large boulder and aimed it at the bowman. Lucky saw the exchange and got a shot off first. Though his bullet ricocheted off the rock, the cracking sound caused the shooter to jerk his rifle when he fired. His bullet went astray, and he missed the elder. Lucky's second shot took the miner down. Before the exposed prospector got off his shot, the elder's arrow pierced through his chest. The battle was over, but, like Lucky, the braves knew there would be more to follow.

They brought the dead warriors back to the

village. Lucky didn't know their burial traditions, so he went back to his quarters. Kimimela came by to commend him for his bravery.

"I feel conflicted. They were miners with tha gold fever...same as me."

"They were warned. You only fight to help."

"I know. It's just...well, it's somethin' I can't explain."

Killing the prospectors didn't sit well with Lucky. Though Kimimela had saved his life and the others had allowed him to stay and recover, he knew he could not be part of the Indian wars that were forthcoming. He had seen the ways his country was changing, and he had no idea how it could be stopped, especially once the railroad was completed. Lucky knew it was time to leave.

The following day, a large group gathered to see Lucky off. Kimimela brought Bullet to his owner. "Your horse."

"Thank you." Lucky threw his saddle over the horse's back and started to cinch it into place.

"Takoda, you come back." The elder handed Lucky a cedar box.

Lucky had a puzzled look on his face.

"Our chief give you name. Means friend to all," Akecheta clarified. "Take offering."

Lucky was shocked. He didn't know the rank of the elder. "Tha *Chief*? I thought he was one of yar wise ones. Didn't know he was tha *Chief*."

Akecheta laughed at his friend's ignorance.

"Why didn't ya tell me?"

"You never asked."

Lucky opened the offered gift and found a stunning trinket inside. It was made of gold, a bigger nugget than any he had seen panning. Inserted throughout the soft, malleable chunk of ore were colorful stones and crystals. The back had been flattened so it could be worn as a necklace. He was so enamored with the gold piece that he almost missed seeing the finely engraved pictures that lined the inside of the box. The images were filled with gold and silver. Kimimela told him the meaning of the artwork.

"I don't know what ta say." Lucky was at a loss for words. He knew that the Lakotas were nomadic. They traveled lightly, so parting with this gift showed genuine gratitude for his help with the miners. "Wopila." Lucky remembered their word for thank you.

"You saved my father's life. For that, we offer our *thanks*," Kimimela replied.

Again, Lucky was dumbfounded. "Yar tha chief's *daughter*? Why didn't ya tell me?"

Kimimela laughed and repeated Akecheta's response. "You never asked."

When Lucky mounted Bullet, Akecheta made a request. "Don't tell the others where the gold came from."

"Yar secret is safe," Lucky assured them. "I'll keep yar gift hidden." Now that he knew that he was in the presence of a chief, he didn't know how to act. He was honored.

"Tókša," he heard as he rode away. The Lakota didn't have a word that was equivalent to his goodbye; instead, they used a word that meant later.

Lucky looked back. "Wowahwa." He wished them peace.

CHAPTER 31

Lucky left the Lakota camp and headed to Fort Laramie. He followed the North Platte River, a sight that lightened his mood because he remembered the familiar waterway from his days on the wagon train. His experience with the Lakota people had given him hope. Maybe there can be a peaceful coexistence between the emigrants and the Indians, he thought. His optimism didn't last long. While at the fort, he heard about more skirmishes. The Bozeman Trail crossed sacred hunting grounds, and its use violated the Fort Laramie Treaty of 1851. Red Cloud's War was well underway.

The news did not sit well, so Lucky decided to shorten his stay. He left the fort after Bullet was watered and fed.

"Tha Oregon Trail!" Lucky had reached the sign that marked the infamous road. "An' here comes tha railroad." He looked east and saw the frontline of the Union Pacific's crew. He rode over and watched as the workers paved the way for the upcoming track laying. Sad how quickly the landscape is altered, he thought as he watched the line move forward. The flurry of activity and the accompanying frenzy helped Lucky decide which direction to take. He went west. "I wanta see tha country one last time... afore it's altered forever."

As Lucky followed the tracks, not those of the forthcoming railroad but those made by the outgoing wagon trains, he thought of his time with Banks and his crew. "It seems like forever since we came this way." Lucky rubbed Bullet. He did not respond. "Why aren't ya snortin' ta tell me you agree?" Bullet didn't react, so he focused on the horse's stride. "Yar strugglin' a bit...seem ta be less light-footed." Lucky knew that something was wrong.

There were numerous opportunities to stop along the way. Places had sprung up since the wagons had passed in '59, but Lucky was in need of a good liveryman. Eventually, he found someone who seemed to know about horses.

The stableman ran his hand down Bullet's leg and felt the swollen joint. "Fetlock's startin' ta droop."

"Thought that might be it. I noticed he wasn't ridin' tha same. He's gittin' on."

"With his age an' all, ya might think 'bout puttin' 'im out ta pasture. We have a nice field outside of town. Lots of grass, an' thars already a herd runnin' wild out thar."

Lucky hung around the station for several days, trying to decide what was best for Bullet. He had been a reliable horse. They had traveled many miles together. The horse was a friend that he hated to lose.

"Reckon, ya earned tha right ta end yar days as nature sees fit." Lucky released his longtime companion. He hadn't felt such a hurt since he had learned of the passing of his family.

Without a horse to ride, Lucky took the next stage west. The route followed the same part of the Oregon Trail that he had traversed with Banks's train. Sure has changed, he thought. The gold rush had initially started the boom. Now, the railroads spurred new life into the heartland of America.

"Stage stop!" the driver shouted when they approached a small outpost along the dusty road. "Got time ta git somethin' ta eat an' ta stretch yar legs."

The passengers took his advice and entered the structure. The food was simple: ham and biscuits. Lucky downed his with a brew that brought back memories of the rank, alkali water of the plains. He went outside and got a few strides in before it was time to board the stage. When he got on, he saw that he was alone. He lay across the seat and tried to sleep.

The coach had not gone far when a man wearing a cavalry uniform waved it down.

"My horse went lame," he said to the driver. Mind if I ride to the next station?"

"No problem. Tie 'im up ta tha back, then git in," the driver instructed.

Lucky sat up when the stranger entered the carriage. The man settled without talking. He looks young, about my age, he thought. After another jerk from the wagon, Lucky broke the silence. "Tha driver seems ta be aimin' for tha bumps."

The soldier grinned. "Seems so. Rather be on my horse."

"Me too." Lucky remembered his parting with Bullet. The pain resurfaced. It was too soon, but he added, "I recently put mine out ta pasture."

The soldier could see the man's distress. He

had ridden multiple horses while scouting and regretted the hardships imposed on the animals who had served him so well. "My horse went lame, but I think I caught it in time. Once I got off, he seemed to do much better. It may only be a loose shoe."

"Mine was gittin' on in years. Seemed ta be tha best option," Lucky admitted.

"Better than riding the horse to death."

"Agree. Name's Lucky."

"Creede."

"By tha looks of yar uniform, ya must be in tha army. I haven't heard 'bout any Indian trouble 'round here. Not even with tha railroad comin' through."

"I reckon our presence has helped."

"I've managed ta avoid confrontations with tha Indians. Even stayed with tha Lakotas for a spell."

Creede didn't mention that he had spent time with the Pawnee hunting down the Sioux, a common enemy. Instead, he acknowledged the alliance. "They usually don't take too kindly to outsiders."

"Sort of happened. Was in need of healin' an', I was brought ta thar village. Was treated fairly. Shame what's goin' on now."

"It's part of tha expansion." Creede believed that uprisings needed to be contained. It was his livelihood.

"Reckon it's ta be expected, with all tha minin' bringin' in so many newcomers. Been all over, lookin' for gold, myself."

"Oh yeah? Prospecting might be something I'd like to try. Any luck?"

"Did OK. Started pannin' in California, then was a partner in a sluice box operation, but it was peterin' out, so we sold it. Back ta pannin' now...an' wanderin'. I want ta explore more... afore tha country changes."

"I understand. Thought tha prairie was tha place for me, but after spending time in tha mountains, I'm not so sure."

During the ride, the two men became well acquainted. They shared similar views on the status of the expanding country and what that growth would bring. Creede was especially interested in Lucky's prospecting tales. After a cordial goodbye, Creede got off and untied his horse. Lucky saw the kind attention he gave the animal as he took him to the livery stable.

A passenger entered the coach and sat facing Lucky. "Howdy. Name's George."

The fellow was middle-aged, well-dressed, and looked like a man of importance. He's a friendly, chatty type of person, Lucky noted before giving his response. "Lucky."

"I saw the cavalry man getting out of the coach. Have any trouble?"

"No. His horse went lame."

"Good. I'm glad to hear the Indians aren't causing delays. Where are you headed?"

"Not rightly sure. Reckon I'll know when I git thar. How 'bout you?"

"Sacramento...to check on the progress of our tracklaying. We're still blasting through the Sierra Mountains."

"Ya work for tha railroad? Saw 'em gittin' tha ground ready just east of here."

George smirked. "The UP...Union Pacific. I'm

with their competitor, the CP...Central Pacific.”

“Tha ones layin’ track headin’ eastward.”

“Started out of Sacramento in ’63, and we’re hoping to conquer the Sierra Mountains soon. I did some of the early surveying while I was an engineer in the Army. They decided to follow the tract that I was assigned to cover.”

“Heard tha route’ll follow tha California Trail. I came over with a wagon train in ’59.”

“The route’s very similar. Did you take the Truckee Route to Sacramento?”

“No. Followed tha Luther Trail ta tha Johnson Cutoff. We were headin’ ta Placerville.”

“I see. You were too late to make much of the goldfields.”

“We knew. Even though we were only placer pannin’, we wanted ta be whar it all started. Found some gold in a hidden pool...gave us a generous return. We cleaned it out, so we didn’t stake a claim.”

“At least your efforts paid off. You say *we*. What happened to your partner?”

“My brother. He went an’ married a gal he’d met on tha wagon train we joined when we came west. Has a young’un now.”

“You seem to be doing fine on your own.”

“So far.” Lucky knew the man was referring to his boyish look. “I’m curious. Tha terrain was challengin’ enough for tha wagons. How’re ya gittin’ yar train through tha Sierra range?”

“Dynamite! Son, we have ways to make the earth tremble. We’re blasting our way through the best of what the old mountain has to offer. You ought to come and see. Better yet, we can always use another hand.”

Lucky was caught off guard. "Work for tha railroad...layin' track?"

"It's incredible what we're accomplishing. It's a laborious job. I won't deny that. I already have a strong force of Chinese workers getting it done, though. You may be young, but I sense you're also tough."

Lucky sighed. "I'm older than I look. Anyway, how can I git on with yar outfit?"

"I'm to meet one of our agents in Sacramento. He's to give me a progress report. I know they're still boring, and I'm sure they'll need more help getting through the mountain. I'll introduce you to the man. If you work out, you can ride to the site with us."

"Reckon I'll give railroad work a try."

CHAPTER 32

"**G**eorge has spoken well of you," the agent said after the introductions were made. "We have a reliable group of Chinese workers, but the others that work with them seem to come and go. How do you feel about working with people from other countries?"

"I judge a man by his actions, not his looks. I've been taunted a time or two 'cause of my Irish background an' lookin' so young."

"I see. Tell me about yourself...*something* that lets me know you'll *stick it out.*"

"I made my way 'cross tha country with my brother. That's noteworthy in itself. Then I've worked a variety of jobs ta have money for my needs, an' those of my horse."

"You'll be swinging heavy tools and be inside tunnels that are dark and confining. Do you think that's an *environment* you can handle?"

"Did some lumberin' 'round tha Comstock area. I went into tha mines a few times. Didn't seem ta bother me."

The agent looked the boy over. "You're young, but strong. Reckon I'll give you a chance."

Before leaving the city, Lucky wanted to post a letter to his brother. Unless their situation had changed, Sam and Sally were living in a small mining town outside of Denver, in the Colorado Territory.

Sam,

Back in California. Goin' ta work for tha CP buildin' tha railroad line. At first, I'll be with a crew blastin' rock, makin' tunnels through tha Sierra Mountains. Reckon I'll keep tha work 'til we meet up with tha UP. Thar kinda racin' ta see who lays track tha fastest, braggin' rights, but tha railroads are after more—funding an' property rights. Thars lots of questionable money an' land grabbin' already goin' on. Lookin' forward ta ridin' tha train outta Sacramento. Tha town's full of activity with all tha minin' an' railroadin' that's goin' on.

My regards ta Sally an' tha young'un. Glad yar store's doin' so well. Knew my grubstakin' ya would pay off.

In endin', left ol' Bullet behind. Age caught up with 'im. He's grazin' in pastureland off tha Oregon Trail, near whar we passed in '59. Just left tha Lakota Sioux village after bein' taken in by a beautiful Indian woman. She took care of me after havin' been bitten by a rattlesnake—saved my life. Will hold that tale for another day.

Yar devoted brother, Lucky

Lucky met George the next morning. Not long after they boarded the train, the steam-powered engines hissed, and the cars moved forward.

Lucky watched the changing scenery as they left the station. "Never ridden a train afore."

"Soon, it'll be commonplace…even out here. In '64, we connected with the California Central at Junction (later Roseville), and we're expanding services to Lincoln. But to be fully operational, we need to be linked to the rest of the country. We need to get the transcontinental finished."

"A tall order."

"Yeah. But think what it'll mean. People will be able to cross the continent in days instead of months, and along with them, all the supplies and merchandise they'll need to carry out their businesses. People will have access to places ...places they never thought they could go to before," George orated with pride.

✠•✠•✠

Lucky was dropped off at the entrance of the Summit Tunnel, the Donner Pass detour. His first job was to haul off the rock and debris that came after blasting. When a worker left, he was assigned to help the crew that drilled the holes for the dynamite.

Mr. Lee showed Lucky how to chisel through the tough granite. "No need to go as deep now. Nitro *more powerful* than gunpowder."

"How do they git tha nitro here? I heard it exploded easily, makin' it *tricky* ta haul."

"Bring the glycerin and acids separate. Then mix it here. Wong knows what doing. He *very careful*. Now we get work done *much faster*."

When they finished making the hole, they headed toward the entrance of the tunnel. The nitro was added, then ignited. The blasting crew waited until a path was cleared through the rubble before heading back.

"I started with this bunch...cleanin' up," Lucky told Mr. Lee as they walked past a cart that was being loaded with the debris. "Have ya always prepped for tha blastin' or did ya work elsewhere?"

"Was moved around. Learn different work. Go where needed. Only workers like Wong stay on one job."

A man grabbed Lucky. "*Hey kid*."

Lucky gave him a blank stare.

"*Rocky*. Remember? We worked together on

247

tha cleanup crew."

"Oh yeah. Didn't recognize ya without all tha *dust* on yar face," Lucky joked. "Ya on tha drillin' team, too?"

"Yep. Just after they pulled ya. They've been shiftin' us 'round more after tha losses this past winter."

"What happened?"

"Just be glad ya weren't here." Rocky started to drill another hole in the tough rock. "I'd only been workin' a few weeks when tha blizzards came. Non-stop. Tha snow buried *everythin'*. Couldn't keep tha tracks clear, so tha train couldn't git supplies ta us. Had ta ration our food. Even so, they had us workin'. We dug a tunnel through tha snow just ta git ta tha tunnel ta blast."

"As steep as it is up here, did ya have ta worry 'bout avalanches?"

"*All tha time*. One almost took me. Got some that were comin' up from behind. Took out one of tha barracks an' all that were inside, too. Never knew from day ta day who just up an' left or was caught up in 'em."

"This winter shouldn't be as bad. By then, we should be off tha mountain."

When the Summit Tunnel was completed in August 1867, Lucky was reassigned to help a group of Chinese graders in the Truckee Valley. Here, he prepared the path prior to the lying of the ties and rails. It was backbreaking work, and just as he got into a routine, he was moved to the back of the line. This crew was made up of Irish workers who took him under their wings. He was taught how to use a maul to strike the spikes that secured the rails.

The tracklaying process was well-planned. As soon as the surveyors chose the best path to follow, the graders, guided by the engineers, cleared and leveled the land. When the ground was ready, ties were laid, evenly spaced apart. The rails, brought on horse-drawn carts, were placed over the ties. The last group staked them together. Lucky and his fellow Irishmen had this honor. Men behind them placed more ballast between the rails. A continuous clanking sound filled the air as the work cycled throughout the day.

Once on flatter ground, the teams moved much faster, and the work became routine. If bridges were necessary, they were hastily built with the assurance that improvements would come later. Trains that were able to follow the completed tracks brought in materials. Wagons supplemented as needed.

The days passed, and the line moved forward.

As they laid track through the Great Basin, Lucky remembered the dry, desolate land that he and Sam had ridden through. Since then, new settlements had sprung up to service the needs of the railroad workers. By May 1868, the tracklayers had reached Lake's Crossing. The shantytown, soon to be named Reno, had passenger service by June.

The days passed, and the line moved forward.

They entered the Humboldt Valley. A number of small tent towns had arisen since Lucky's last visit. Before the year had come to a close, they were in Elko, a small construction camp that had sprung up along the Humboldt River. Lucky recalled how humbug this section was.

The days passed, and the line moved forward.

Lucky was pounding in another stake when he noticed a wagon train coming up the trail. Tincup was driving the lead wagon. He had a coworker take over his job, and then he ran up to say hello.

Lucky surprised the cook. "Ya *did it*. You've hooked up with another wagon train."

Tincup grinned when he saw Lucky. "What are ya doin' *out here*? Ya pop up in tha most unexpected places."

"*Layin' track*, this time."

"Yar lookin' fit. Must be *harder work* than haulin' gravel."

"Much more, but like sluicin', ya git into a routine. Banks wouldn't be tha wagon master, now would he?" Lucky hoped to see his former boss, too.

"Nah. I joined up with tha Bond group. Ya *remember*, his was tha one we bought tha rafts from...on tha North Platte."

"We *lost two* that day. Who could forget?"

"Thars a bridge now. Travelin's easier."

"Reckon so. Tha tracks are followin' much of tha ol' route. Been *comparin'* how things were then ta now."

"*Me too*, with every trip. This is my second since our gold minin' days."

"Doyle," someone called.

"I'll tell Sam I seen ya. He still has his shop in Golden. They should have two young'uns by now. Stop in if'n yar out that way. Heard from Banks or Davis?"

"Once. They both wound up in California but had yet ta settle."

"Doyle," Lucky heard again.

"Best be gittin' back ta work."

"Good seein' ya again. Ya *take care* of yarself." Tincup bid a fond farewell, then got his wagon moving.

"*You too.*"

The days passed, and the line moved forward.

Nevada was left behind. Another tent town, Terrace, in the Utah Territory, was reached. It was April 1869. The tracklayers were only days away from Promontory, the place where the opposing companies were to meet and complete the railway line. Though Lucky's team was there with days to spare, they lost the competition. The Union Pacific had laid the most track, over 1,000 miles. The Central Pacific had put down less than 700 miles.

May 10 was chosen as the day to celebrate the great achievement. Both sides made brief speeches. Special spikes, two of them made of gold and silver, were driven into the track by the railroad presidents to signify this momentous meeting. When the gold spike was hit, the strike of the maul was to send a signal, via telegraph, telling of the final linkage of the new rail line that now ran from Sacramento, California, to Omaha, Nebraska, with connections East.

"Reminds me of when tha transcontinental telegraph was completed," a coworker standing beside Lucky commented.

"Ya work for 'em too?" Lucky asked.

"Yep. Fer tha Overland."

"Didn't Western Union git tha credit? Back

in '61, wasn't it?"

"Uh-huh. In October. They hired tha Pacific an' tha Overland Telegraph Companies ta do tha actual work."

"Tha stakes weren't quite as high as with tha construction of tha railroad."

"Yeah, but there was a race, just tha same... ta see who could git ta tha end point first. Salt Lake City was our destination. Tha Pacific laid line westward from Omaha, an' we started at Carson City."

"Who was tha winner?"

"The Pacific got tha *braggin' rights*."

Similar to the railroad's system of laying track, the telegraph companies had surveyors mark the route. Another group followed to dig the holes before a team came to put up the poles. Once they were in place, the wire was strung. Supplies were brought in by wagon. Much of the route also followed established wagon trails.

As he was leaving the ceremony, Lucky ran into George. "We did it!"

"*Good job*, son! You kept with it and stayed for the finish, I see. I knew you had the right stuff when I had you sign on."

"Was tough but worth it. Tha railroads are puttin' on a great celebration."

George frowned. "Barring a *few* hiccups. Our esteemed railroad presidents couldn't hit the side of a barn...*both* missed the spike."

"Spent some time with a maul. I'll admit, it took me a while ta git tha hang of tha swing."

"Yeah, but your pings weren't to be *historic*. The gold spike had a telegraph line attached.

When it was hit, a signal was to be transmitted across the country telling of this great feat.”

“Oh, yeah. Well, I reckon words relayed tha same message.”

“The city boys heard. The operator took it upon himself to send tha signal out anyway.”

“*Sounds* like he saved tha day.”

George commended the man’s action. “That kind of *quick thinking* has made our country great.” In a less serious tone, he asked Lucky about his future plans. “Are you going to stay on with the railroads? There will be lots of work, just keeping the tracks maintained.”

“Reckon it’s time for me ta move on. Leave tha rest of ya ta figure out what’s next for yar iron horses.”

“Son. We’ve only just begun!”

❦❖❦❖❦

The sun’s rays caused the gold to glitter as it sat on the bottom of the sparkling stream. Lucky pushed his pan under and collected the ore. He was swirling the gold-laden gravel when the sound of gunshots caused him to drop his pan and reach for his rifle.

He woke up and quickly came out of the haze brought on by deep sleep. The stage suddenly jerked forward as the driver got his team to move faster. Bandits, firing from behind, gave chase. The coach was moving so fast it almost careened out of control, but even with the jolts from the bouncy ride, Lucky was able to get into position and join in the fight.

CHAPTER 33

"**G**et down," someone calmly commanded.

Lucky didn't take the advice. Instead, he stuck his head out farther and searched for a target.

"You'll get yourself killed."

"If'n they stop us, won't likely matter." Lucky fired a shot.

The stage slowed, then stopped. When the door opened, everyone inside anticipated the worst. Lucky had his pistol pointed.

"Ya can put that away," the driver informed him. "Thar gone. Is everyone all right?"

A woman spoke for all of them. "We're fine, now that we know you're not a bandit."

"Happened upon a cavalry troop. Thar in pursuit of 'em now."

"Well, they couldn't have come along at a better time."

"Ditto that, Miss Anthony. We'll be gittin' on our way. Wouldn't want ya ta miss yar *meetin'*," the driver smirked.

"How kind of you." She ignored his sneer. She was used to men treating her that way.

"Did ya recognize any of 'em?" Lucky asked.

"Too busy tryin' ta keep tha coach rollin'," the stage driver admitted. "Up ta tha troops ta tell." He closed the door and went to get the stagecoach underway.

Mrs. Stanton, the other woman in the coach, spoke for the first time. "You're *invited*." She handed Lucky a brochure containing material on women's rights. "We could use you as our bouncer. Your courage and shooting skills would help to keep some of the riffraff under control."

Lucky scanned the brochure. "Well, *ma'am*, I'm 'fraid, I won't be gittin' off thar. I'll be goin' on with tha stage."

Lucky didn't know it, but he was riding with two well-known advocates of the equal rights, suffrage, and temperance movements. Susan B. Anthony was honored in 1920 when the 19th Amendment, ensuring women's right to vote, was named after her. The other passenger, who often traveled with Miss Anthony, was Elizabeth Cady Stanton, also a well-known activist and abolitionist. They were working their way to Virginia City, Nevada, giving speeches at the various mining camps along the way.

When they stopped, Lucky wished the ladies well. Though the stagecoach was only staying to change horses, Lucky figured he had time to get a quick drink and something to eat. The small saloon was filled, but he found a spot at the bar.

"What can I git ya?" the bartender asked.

"Beer an' a couple of yar eggs."

The proprietor handed them over. "Dollar."

Lucky didn't even argue about the high price. He had gotten used to price gouging, which was commonplace. I know Sam wouldn't be chargin' like this, he thought. He quickly drank the beer that was room temperature, then threw some coins on the countertop. He took the hard-boiled eggs with him and headed to the carriage. The driver had already taken his place. Lucky found a seat just before the horses were given the command to go. He was surprised to see another passenger in the coach.

"*You!*" the man spat.

"*Janks!* Still up ta yar tricks?" Lucky kept his eyes on the vindictive man, knowing he would probably try something.

Janks didn't disappoint him. He pulled out his gun, but before he could fire, Lucky sent a bullet his way. It entered his right leg, causing him to wince in pain. He passed out.

"Ya all right in thar?" the driver yelled.

"We're fine. Just a friendly exchange between ol' acquaintances."

Lucky untied Jank's bandana and wrapped it around the wound. He saw a stain below the scarf. "Looks like ya got another piece of lead 'fore mine...an' fairly recent. Wonder if ya was part of tha gang tryin' ta rob us?" He tied Janks hands behind his back. "Good thing you're out. Makes it easy ta use yar belt ta tie up yar ankles." Lucky sat back in his seat. "That should hold ya."

"*Doyle,*" Janks snarled when he regained consciousness.

Lucky gave Janks a scornful look. "Thought I'd seen tha *last* of ya in Virginia City."

Janks instinctively reached for his pistol, only to find his hands were tied.

"Ya lookin' for *this*?" Lucky waved the man's gun to emphasize who was in control.

Janks squirmed. "You'll be sorry. *One day...* I'm *not* finished with *you,*" he threatened.

If Janks was part of the group and got away, then it's possible that the other highwaymen were also nearby, Lucky thought. He hoped to get some information. "Funny how this stage was just attacked an' yar sittin' thar with a fresh bullet wound. Ya wouldn't know anythin' 'bout *that*, now would ya?"

"Yar barkin' up tha wrong tree. You'll get a bellyful of *nothin'* from me!"

They rode on in silence. Lucky had to be on his guard in case Janks tried to get the upper hand. When they got to the next stage stop, Lucky explained his suspicions to a lawman and turned Janks over.

"My men'll escort 'im ta town. Tha sheriff'll be more'n happy ta have a go at 'im," the man assured Lucky.

Lucky watched as Janks was taken away. "Hope this *truly* is tha last I see of ya."

PART FOUR

Colorado

1870-1877

CHAPTER 34

ucky had heard about the uniqueness of the Great Salt Lake and decided to test the waters, so he got the next stage heading in that direction. As he made his way across, he decided it was time to own his own horse again. When he stepped out of the carriage in Salt Lake City, Utah Territory, he headed straight for the livery. A man was leading a mare inside a corral that was full of horses.

"All of 'em for sale?" Lucky asked.

"Most."

"Mind if'n I take a look?"

"Reckon not, but don't take a fancy ta that Appaloosa stallion. He's spoken for."

"Beautiful animal. How 'bout tha gray colt over thar?" Lucky pointed to a large horse with a light mane and tail. His face sported a wide blaze that ran up to his ears. The equine pointed its ears forward and let out a happy sounding neigh when Lucky approached. *Hey boy.* He rubbed the colt's neck.

"He's one of my better uns. Gonna cost ya. I'll let 'im go...for $100."

"Give ya $85 if'n ya also include a saddle an' gear," Lucky countered.

The man paused as he internally figured out the costs and his profit. "Yar a hard un ta strike a bargain with, but ya got yarself *a deal.* It'll cost ya a dollar extra if'n ya plan ta board 'im overnight."

"Fine. I'll pick 'im up in tha mornin'." Lucky paid the man his money. "Gonna try tha lake. Are 'em stories true? Do ya really *float* in tha water?"

"Like tha *bobber* on a fisherman's line."

Lucky found a saloon that served food and ordered the day's special. He spent the night playing poker and was lucky to have left the table with only a small loss. The competition was stiff. He headed out to the lake the following morning. As he was riding, he realized that his horse had not been given a name.

"Reckon I need ta call ya somethin'. You've a hard act ta follow. Ol' Bullet, well, he was..." Lucky nudged the colt so he'd go faster. The horse darted. "Why, yar a real *sharpshooter*! That's it, I'll call ya *Shooter*!"

By the time they reached the shoreline, the outside temperature had risen above 80°. When Lucky tested the water with his toes, the 72° felt cold, but he continued to walk out into the lake until he was able to make a shallow dive. He surfaced and faced upwards.

"I'm *floatin'*," he yelled to his horse.

Shooter whinnied.

"Ya sounded just like ol' Bullet." Lucky was beginning to like his new companion.

As Lucky relaxed in the water, he thought of Sam and how much fun it would have been to share this experience with his brother. He decided to make a surprise visit. Lucky stood up and made his way to shore. When his skin dried, the salty coating felt worse than the dust he had washed off. He headed to the river that he had crossed earlier and rinsed his body with the fresh water. After cleaning up, he headed back to Salt Lake City and got advice on the best route to take east.

"Tha other paths through tha mountains are shorter but thar rougher. Best ta follow tha railroad. Tha gradin' makes for an easier ride," the clerk explained. "Ya just follow tha wagon road ta Junction City (later Ogden), then go east an' follow tha transcontinental line."

Lucky agreed with the man's assessment. The ride was not too difficult, and he got to watch as the powerful trains huffed their steam in passing. Before heading south, he decided to stop in Cheyenne, Wyoming Territory. After getting a room at the inn, he sought the saloon, hoping to get in a game. He enjoyed playing poker, but he knew his limits and when to walk away, especially if he thought that others were cheating. Accusations often turned into shoot-outs, something he wanted to avoid.

It was his night. Lucky was on a winning streak. He was currently holding two threes, but he knew other hands could easily beat his pair. Lucky decided to stay in the game and added his raise to the others. Two players dropped out of the game.

"Don't have any money ta raise ya...but I'll put up my place...got a house an' some land," the remaining player offered. "Blain thar, will vouch for me."

"Thar not much...tha house is standin', but it's *his*." Blain confirmed.

Lucky knew the man was drunk. "Ya *sure*

ya don't want out?" He tried to reason with the gambler, but the man was adamant, so Lucky relented. "OK, then."

The final cards were dealt. Lucky got his third three. The man, holding two black aces and two black eights, conceded when he was left with the two pairs. This combination would later be called the "dead man's hand" because Wild Bill Hickok held these cards when he was shot in the head in '76 while playing poker. This time, though, the man holding the jinxed hand only lost his property and not his life.

Lucky tried to give the man his deed back, but he refused. Since he now had a place to call home, he decided to postpone his brotherly visit and check out his new abode. Based on the man's description, it was about a mile east of a place called LaPorte that was in the Colorado Territory. When he found the town, he decided to stop at the general store so he could get better directions.

The proprietor looked at the deed. "Reckon ya got Curry's place. Not much ta speak of, but tha roof's still on. Ya follow tha road outta town, then follow tha path east. You'll go 'bout a mile. Can't miss it."

Lucky laughed when he arrived at the site. *"Home Sweet Home."*

Shooter's whinny sounded like a snicker.

Lucky's initial reaction was to keep on going and visit Sam. *We're in the same territory now, so you probably aren't too far away,* he thought. "Reckon I ought ta at least see what tha inside looks like." He dismounted and headed to the cabin. He pulled on the old, weathered leather handle, but the door was stuck. After a few more attempts, it started to move, and with a loud creak, it opened.

"Probably hasn't been used for a long time." Shooter snorted.

Lucky started to walk into the dark interior, but before his foot went over the threshold, he was under attack.

CHAPTER 35

"**B**ees!" Lucky screamed. At some point, a swarm had made its way into the cabin and established a colony. When he opened the door, it jarred the nest loose, and the startled insects quickly reacted. Lucky could hear the drone as the first round struck in full force. His initial reaction was to duck and swat at the unforgiving insects, but he quickly moved backward, out the door. He ran to find his horse. Shooter had found a patch of grass behind the house and was peacefully eating when Lucky climbed onto his saddle, bringing the angry mob with him.

Shooter gave a loud snort when the first one gave him a sting. Lucky didn't have to spur the horse on. Shooter bolted and headed toward town. Lucky rubbed the stings that had already started to swell. His adrenaline was running high, so he had yet to experience the full consequence of the attack.

"They kept after me for nearly a quarter of a mile," Lucky told the clerk after he explained his dilemma. "How do I git *rid* of 'em?"

"Best way I know is ta *smoke 'em out*. If'n thar tha right ones, ya may git some honey outta it all."

"Thanks..." Lucky paused.

"Jared," the man filled in.

"Thanks, Jared."

When Lucky returned to the cabin, he saw activity around the nest that was now lying on the floor by the door. He gathered some wood, gauged the wind direction, and built a fire. As the smoke filled the shack, the insects filed out. He waited until he thought they were all gone, then he grabbed a pine branch full of needles and slowly made his way to the entrance. The nest appeared to be empty, so he whacked it with the improvised broom. It flew out the door, leaving a trail of paper-like confetti.

"*Wasps*. Means ya offer nothin' in exchange for puttin' up with all yar stingin'." Lucky was disappointed that it wasn't the honey-producing bees. He picked up the smashed nest and threw it over the burning flames.

Lucky went inside and scanned the room for other invaders. Even with the door open, his eyes had to adjust to the darkness. The two windows that would have brought in the afternoon light were covered with dirty blankets. He pulled them off and instantly saw that the cabin needed a lot of work. Light came through the holes in the roof and the walls, as neither were well sealed.

The following months found Lucky doing the housework that had been neglected by the previous owner. He patched the leaky structure, then put in wood floors. He fixed the furniture and made some of his own.

Jared introduced him to others in town, and they occasionally came around to help or give advice. One visitor, Argent, was someone that Lucky knew, but neither of them made the connection right away. After a night of drinking and playing cards, Lucky followed Argent out of the saloon. When the inebriated man walked down the street, his drunken swagger triggered Lucky's memory.

"Argent!"

The man stopped and turned.

"I *remember* now. It was in Independence… in '59. I was 'bout ta sign on with a wagon train, an' ya was 'bout ta git run over by a buggy."

"Reckon my brain was pretty addled then. Had sum trouble with my drinkin'."

"I went ta turn tha horses while my brother drug ya away from tha oncomin' wagon."

"Seems I can recall sumthin' 'bout meetin' up with sum red-headed boys."

Lucky rubbed his red mane. "That was us!"

Argent's mouth fell open. "Well, *I'll be*! Sure wanta *thank ya* for yar concern at tha time. Still in yar debt."

"Yar hair's silvered since then. Reckon that's why it took so long ta recognize ya."

"Livin' up ta my name." The older man pulled on his silvery-white beard.

Once Lucky's house was put in order, he went to the nearby Cache La Poudre River to pan for gold. Like the earlier prospectors, he quickly discovered that the river only had a scant amount to give. When another day of panning left him empty, he decided it was time to visit his older brother.

"Tha roads are improvin' between tha gold camps. Should take ya two, maybe three days ride," Jared told Lucky before he left.

The reunion was long overdue. When Lucky

walked into Sam's store, he thought his brother was going to faint. After they whooped around some, Sam closed the store and took him into the back area that served as his home. Sally, who was surrounded by their two kids, gave him a big kiss.

"Meet yar Uncle Lucky," she said to the shy youngsters. "Lucky, I present Miss Melanie an' Mr. Mason."

"Pleased ta make yar acquaintance." Lucky poked them in a ticklish fashion. He got heaps of laughter. His niece and nephew warmed to him instantly. Sam led them into the parlor so they could talk before dinner.

"Tha minin' was endin' 'round Golden City when we got here, but tha town was needin' more businesses ta sell supplies." Sally called them in for dinner before Sam could finish. He waited until they were seated and had started to eat before he continued with his story. "Tha prospectors were still after gold in tha nearby mountains. Several mills an' smelters had been built, an' farmers were fillin' tha valley."

"Ya picked tha right time ta settle," Lucky confirmed.

"We couldn't keep tha store stocked." Sally got up to put the children to bed.

"Within tha first six months, I coulda paid back yar Fool's Pool money if'n I knew whar ya was." Sam pulled out a Double Eagle gold coin from a hidden shirt pocket. "I have Sally sew me a pocket like Ma did. Do ya still have yars?"

Lucky withdrew a similar coin. "I had tha secret pocket added ta my shirts too. Never had that emergency that Mum worried 'bout either."

"Neither of us did, thanks ta yar *luck.*"

"An' ya savin' me when *that* wasn't enough."

"Ya know yar welcome ta come an' help with tha store, anytime."

"I like bein' yar *silent partner.*"

"So, how ya settlin' in, bein' a homeowner an' all?"

"Reckon I should be doin' somethin' with tha land. It's dry an' rocky. I'd need ta dig an irrigation ditch."

"You...*farmin'*...can't see it." Sam shook his head. "Remember *why* ya came west?"

"Ta *not* be planted like tha potatoes!"

Sam laughed. "Yep. No *roots* for you."

"Reckon so. Still, havin' a home is comfortin'."

Sally came back and sat by Sam. "Must be. It took ya *long enough* ta come an' visit."

"Took a while ta git tha place fixed up. Afore that, well, ya know what it's like. *Something's* always comin' up."

"Speakin' of, Shooter looks like a good steed. Know how well Bullet served ya." Sam wanted to affirm Lucky's loss. He knew there was a strong bond between Lucky and Bullet. Both of their horses had endured a lot to get them across the country.

"Reckon Bullet's enjoyin' tha easy life. How's Lindy holdin' up?"

"Gittin' up in years, but still a good mare."

"Reminds me, I've something ta *show ya.*" Lucky went to his saddlebag and took out the box that the Lakota Chief had given him. He pulled the trinket out of his secret pocket and placed it inside.

"Wow! How'd ya lay yar hands on this?" Sam

inspected the gift, then passed it on to Sally.

She picked up the gold pendant, but it was the inside of the box that grabbed her attention. She examined the intricate carving that lined the interior panels. "Someone sure spent a lot of time with tha artwork."

"Given ta me by tha Chief hisself. I carry tha nugget with me. It's my good luck charm. Let me tell ya tha story portrayed by tha pictures." Lucky repeated what Kimimela had told him, then gave a detailed account of the time he spent living with the Lakota tribe.

"Mum didn't call ya *Lucky* for nothin'. How many times have I said that?"

Lucky's visit ended all too soon. As he made his way back to his cabin, he thought about his brother and his family. Mason reminded him of Sam, and Melanie was growing into a feisty toddler. Sally was a busy homemaker who still managed to find time to help her husband run the store. They were the quintessential modern family. For the first time, Lucky felt lonely.

Shooter's increased speed brought him out of his reverie. His home was in sight. Lucky saw the chaotic terrain that surrounded his cabin, and he knew he had no interest in cultivating the land. It's too late in the season, anyway, he justified.

Winter came early that year. The cold kept Lucky close to the fire. He was starting to feel the confinement brought on by solitary living. The snow, which had been falling off and on for weeks, had stopped by late evening, so when Lucky woke up to a sky that was filled with more blue than gray, he knew he had to get out. He decided to take a hunting trip.

"Tired of bein' holed up here." Lucky put the saddle on Shooter. "Reckon I've been driftin' for so long that it's hard adjustin' ta settlin' down." He mounted his horse. "Listen ta me, with only you ta talk to."

Lucky rode around the hills and looked for signs of game. The sun melted the snow that had covered the rocky terrain, so tracks were erased. He saw scat and tree markings that told of the passage of the animals, but each led to a dead end. After a few days in the cold, Lucky decided to return home.

"Just one more night," he promised Shooter when they had stopped to set up camp beside a large pile of rocks. After feeding his horse, Lucky ate supper. By the time he fell asleep, clouds had started to mask the star-filled sky.

Lucky woke and saw the white dusting on the ground. "Snow." He shook the flakes off the wood and started a fire. When he picked up his bedding, a tiny mouse, who had sought his bodily warmth during the night, ran out and disappeared under the brush. "I'm not after vermin like *you*." He made coffee and ate biscuits, then he packed and got ready for the ride back.

Shooter snorted his readiness.

"Tracks," Lucky announced. He had Shooter follow the animal's trail. He saw movement in the distance and dismounted. "Looks ta be a *big* buck," he whispered as he tied Shooter to a tree. He found cover and waited for the stag to show itself. Before long, he had his chance to fire. The deer went down.

Lucky made sure the kill was clean, then he went to get his horse. He prepared the buck, loaded him on Shooter's back, and headed home. Lucky rode to the front of the cabin and dropped the deer on the ground. He started to relieve Shooter of the saddle when a huge mountain lion came out from behind the door. Shooter dashed off and took Lucky's rifle with him. Lucky stood there, face-to-face with the oncoming beast.

"Shoo!"

The cat stopped for a brief moment and stared at his prey. He bared his teeth and let out an intimidating hiss that turned into an menacing growl, and then he charged.

CHAPTER 36

Lucky ran behind a nearby tree. He grabbed his knife and stood ready to fight.

The cougar rushed past him, sunk his teeth into the fresh kill, and dragged the buck into the woods.

"Phew!" As his adrenaline began to subside, Lucky started to shake and fell to his knees, laughing. "Didn't even notice that tha door was open." He got up and went inside the cabin. It was trashed. Even his bedding was thrashed. He rummaged through the mess to see what he could salvage. "Looks like a bear got here first," he vocalized to the now departed feline. "Probably how tha door got unlatched. Reckon I happened upon yar *scavangin'*."

Lucky did what he could to tidy up the cabin while he waited for Shooter to return. Most of the food was gone or scattered on the floor. When the horse didn't come back, he started to walk into town. He came upon his old friend along the road. He saw the loaded burro.

"Howdy Argent. Ya look like yar movin' on."

"Yep. Reckon tha Poudre's given me all she's gonna. Me an' Jenny Jo are headin' out."

"Whar ya goin'?"

"Crossin' tha mountains...ta Lake County. Gonna check out tha California Gulch an' settle in a place called Oro City. Hear thar still gittin' gold outta thar."

"Been restless myself. If'n I git thar, I'll look ya up."

"Ya do that. Come, Jenny Jo." Argent tugged on the animal's lead rope. After a few pulls, the burro brayed and started to move.

Jared saw Lucky walk into his store. "Yar *OK*! When yar horse come inta town all saddled up, we was worried. He's in tha livery."

"Came home ta a mountain lion greetin'."

"Ta tell tha tale, ya musta done sum quick shootin'."

"*No chance*. Wasn't wearin' my gun. Shooter took off with it an' my rifle."

"Now that ya mention it, I did hear yar rifle was still with yar horse."

"Tha cat went for tha buck I'd brought back. Reckon it favored its taste. Last I saw, it was draggin' tha carcass through tha trees."

"Good thin' ya got a kill."

"Reckon so. Regardless, thar was a *fine* party in my cabin."

"Trashed?"

"Yep. Way I see it, a bear opened tha way an' took his share, then tha cat came upon tha mess an' was prowlin' 'round when I rode up."

"Maybe ya can stay at Argent's place. He came in earlier. He's goin' west."

"Saw 'im comin' in. Thinkin' I might git out that way, but not 'til tha snow's done for tha season. Reckon Argent knows what he's doin', leavin' *now*."

"No worries. He's a mountain man. Nothin' fazes him. Why, he told me a story once…he was out in a *mighty mean* snowstorm, as he put it, an' was runnin' low on food. He stumbled onta a small cave...checked fer other users afore he claimed it. He built hisself a large fire an' waited fer tha weather ta calm. When it did, he went ta tha creek whar he had seen a beaver dam. He walked ta whar he thought tha den was an' dove inta tha icy cold water. While under, he pulled out his knife an' *stabbed* one of 'em. He brought it back ta tha cave, removed tha pelt, cut tha meat inta strips, an' cooked 'em over tha fire. Used tha fur ta make a *new hat* afore he took off."

"I'll be! Thought he was just an ol' prospector driftin' 'round, like me."

"Now he is, but only after tha fur tradin' had died out."

"Ya never know 'bout people 'til ya hear thar stories." Lucky knew Argent was tough, but he never knew why. Like many of his generation, he didn't realize how easy he had it compared to the harsh living conditions the early explorers had to endure. "If'n our paths cross again, I'll see what other stories he has ta tell."

"Reckon ya got a *few* of yar own, countin' yar escapin' a mountain lion attack."

Lucky waited until late spring before he sold his property in LaPorte and headed to Oro City. Though the two towns were not too far apart, he had to cross the mountains to get there. He was starting up another pass when a bright flash of lightning, accompanied by the cracking sound of a struck tree, caused him to cringe and Shooter to whisk his tail and snort. The loud thunder that followed only added to their discomfort.

"It's OK, boy." Lucky tried to soothe the jittery

animal. "Take it easy."

The skies let loose with a light and sound show. The rain soon followed.

"Best ta keep goin'." Lucky pushed the horse harder. "Tha *sooner* we git this over with, tha *better.*"

The rutted wagon road, already riddled with potholes of varying sizes, was turning into a slick, muddy slide. Lucky stuck to the side, where the vegetation still supported the topsoil. The water formed tiny streams that cut paths through the mud and filled the tracks that were made as the horse found his tread. Eventually, the lightning stopped, but the rain continued to fall. Lucky decided to wait out the worst of storm, so he pulled off the road and stopped under a stand of ponderosa pine.

"We'll be alright," Lucky informed Shooter. "Tha lightning has passed."

A freight wagon, following in Lucky's wake, appeared through the haze. His mules were struggling in the mud, and the wagon started to slide. When the rear wheels slipped into a large pothole, the rig came to a stop. The man driving the rig yelled and jerked his whip, but to no avail. They were stuck.

CHAPTER 37

The driver jumped down from the wagon and went to inspect the wheels. Lucky came out of the trees and offered assistance.

"If'n ya git tha horses ta go, I'll push from behind," the man suggested.

They cajoled and coaxed. They pushed and pulled. The wagon would not budge.

"Got shovels or minin' tools in yar load?"

"Maybe I can find a pick under here." The wagoner untied the canvas cover. Lucky held the tarp while the man shuffled through his supplies. "*Ah-ha.* Here it is."

"I'll hold tha team while ya dig. Give me a shout when yar ready, an' we'll see if'n we can git tha wagon movin'."

After the man finished cutting trenches out of the holes, he went to the back of the wagon and got into position. "*Now,*" he yelled over the falling rain.

The horses pulled, the man pushed, and the wheels rolled. "Way station up ahead. Let me buy ya a drink," the driver offered when the wagon was on solid ground again.

"Much obliged. I'll git my horse."

By the time Lucky reached the relay stop, the rain had turned into a light drizzle. He left Shooter tied to the hitching post in front of the building and went inside.

The teamster was close behind. "Some ale fer me an' my friend," the man shouted as they discarded their wet slickers.

The man handed Lucky a drink. "Thanks. Feels good ta be outta tha rain."

"Yeah. Wanna *thank ya* fer helpin' me out thar. Don't know how long I woulda had ta wait afore someun come 'long."

"Glad I was thar ta help."

"Ta *safe* journeys!"

"*Cheers!*"

"Name's Joshua."

"Lucky."

"Reckon I'm tha lucky un. Whar ya goin'?"

"Oro City."

"Not much of a camp now. Most of tha miners have moved on. Those that stayed are settlin' lower down. Strange lookin' place. Thar callin' it Slabtown 'cause tha structures were hastily built with pieces of slab. Tha black sand that's coverin' tha area doesn't help. Ya hear how ol' Lee tried ta claim tha whole gulch fer hisself when he first found tha gold?"

"What stopped 'im?"

"Ta make things fair, sum bylaws were put in place. Don't know 'em all, just that limits were set on tha number an' size of claims...ta give others a chance ta git sum of tha spoils."

"A fair practice. I know of similar laws that were passed at other minin' operations. Did it work out here?"

"Reckon so, but don't rightly matter now. They took it all an' left."

"Well, I'm hopin' ta find what they missed, or didn't wanna work over enough ta git."

"Tha place's gittin' rough, more'n usual fer a minin' camp. Keep a watch out thar," Joshua advised before he left.

When Lucky walked outside, he could see the sun trying to peek out from under the clouds. He untied Shooter and made his way down the road. The rain returned in the late afternoon, so he found another rest stop and decided to spend the night indoors.

The next day, he reached Slabtown. The skies, still dark and gray, along with the rough-looking buildings, presented a cheerless picture. He stopped to get supplies. After a man outside the general store gave him directions to the mining camp, he headed up the hill.

"Somethin' 'bout that man," Lucky was telling Shooter when a rider came up from behind.

"Hands up! Now, *slowly* drop yar weapons."

Lucky took his gun out of his holster and let it fall to the ground.

"Tha rifle, too."

Lucky dropped his rifle on top of his gun.

"Git down an' move away from yar horse."

Lucky dismounted and faced the crook. He recognized him as the man he had talked to earlier. The bandit rode up and gave Shooter a good whack. The horse laid his ears back, let out a startled groan, and took off.

"Empty yar pockets."

Lucky took out the change he had received from the clerk.

"Hand it over!" The man got off his horse and walked toward Lucky. Before he could get the payoff, a voice stopped him.

"Hold it, mister! Drop yar gun!"

The man turned to shoot at the interloper but was not fast enough. He fell, clutching his chest. Lucky pocketed his money, then rushed to get the gun that had fallen from the wounded man's hand. He didn't have to worry. The thief had already cashed in his chips.

Lucky looked at his rescuer. He was sitting on top of a black Clydesdale. "Ya probably saved my life. Wanna thank ya."

"Saw Crusty leavin' after ya. Knew he would be up ta no good, so I followed. He steered ya in tha wrong direction, likely ta git ya out alone. World's better off without 'im." He pointed up the hill. "Saw yar horse go off that way. Should find 'im at tha ol' camp."

"Just thinkin' thar was somethin' *fishy* 'bout tha guy, then he showed up."

"Keep yar wits. Thars nothin' invitin' 'bout tha place these days. Many of tha men that are still here are tha kind who take pleasure in thar menacin'. Troublemakers...wherever they go."

"Was told ta be on my guard. Reckon I need ta do a better job."

"If'n yar here ta mine, you'll wanna head ta tha newer camp. Tha town has moved ta whar thar was better prospectin'." He pointed toward another spot on the hill. "Oro City's now over thar."

"Much obliged. Name's Lucky."

"Sam." The man turned the stocky horse and rode in the direction from whence he came.

Lucky smiled. "Sam. Yar still watchin' over me ...even if in name only." He grabbed his shooters and headed up the hill to find his horse. He felt the effects of the altitude as he made the long hike. Eventually, he reached an area where a few old-timers lived in makeshift shanties. He saw a scraggly-looking man who was sitting by a fire.

"Howdy. Lookin' for my horse. Ya seen 'im?"

The man sneered. "Nope."

Lucky heard a familiar whinny. He drew his gun. "Don't move!"

"Got no iron on me."

Lucky saw him reach for a knife. "Toss it ta tha ground." After the man complied, he had him walk behind the dwelling. Shooter was tied to a tree, hidden from sight. His saddlebags were still there, but his supplies were missing.

"Reckon ya haven't seen tha sacks that tha horse was carryin', *either*."

"Ya got yar animal. Tha rest is inside."

"Grab my horse an' follow me." He had the old-timer lead the way into the shack. When he saw the empty supply bags, Lucky had the man gather his items and refill his sacks. "Now, load 'em back onto my horse." Before they left the dwelling, he took the man's weapons and threw them into the brush. "If'n ya ever cross me again, I'll not be so lenient," Lucky threatened before he rode away.

He made his way toward the newer camp that Sam had spoken of earlier. After passing a mishmash of living quarters, Lucky came upon some shops that were still operating. Though this second Oro City was still a viable camp, there were telltale signs of its decline. The first man he spotted was standing beside a familiar burro in front of a small general store.

"Argent!"

"Ya made it!" the trapper, turned prospector, responded when he recognized the caller.

"Yeah. I thought it was 'bout time ta move on myself. Ya on yar way in or out?"

"Takin' Jenny Jo back up tha hill."

"Whar ya stayin'?"

"Up thar." Argent pointed to a canvas tent that was sitting on a wood base. "Ya can pick most any spot an' call it home. Use tha scraps ya see lyin' 'round. Tha place was thrivin' a few years back, but once tha gold ran dry...well, ya can see what's left."

"Looks like they're startin' a new town down tha way a bit. Seems they took thar buildin's with 'em—wood an' all."

"Tha lower camp has gamblin' an' drinkin' houses. When tha Tabors go, they run tha store here, tha last of us will likely have ta follow on thar heels."

"Reckon I'll do some explorin' afore settlin' in. Havin' any luck with pannin'? A man I ran into said this is whar tha better minin' was."

"Gittin' sum here'n thar. Tha first strike was over that way." Argent pointed to the area where Lucky had just left.

"Been thar. A man below steered me wrong, then later tried ta rob me."

"Yar lucky ya weren't kilt. Thars sum ornery characters livin' thar."

"Probably so, but a man named Sam came up ridin' a Clydesdale...a black one. Tha thief drew on 'im but was worsted."

"That was Sam Turner...good guy...lived here when tha ol' city was started. He did well, but fer sum reason, he stayed. He said he bought that horse from sum drifter a few years back. It's sumthin' ta see, all right."

"*Leastways*, he helped me ta git here an' ta find Shooter…who'd been taken by someone at tha ol' camp, 'long with my supplies. Had ta convince 'im ta give 'em back."

"Tha town's full of mischiefin', but tha worse of tha lot has stayed on thar."

"I was prepared. I've seen how those camps operate, especially after tha gold runs out."

"An' this town's been no exception."

"Tha way it seems ta go 'til everyone leaves or somethin' bigger comes 'long."

"Tha saloon's located in tha store." Argent retied Jenny Jo to the hitching post. "Augusta's a friendly woman who'll take care of our thirst."

"Lead tha way."

After they left the drinking establishment, Argent got Jenny Jo and headed home. Lucky scouted around the camp. He found enough scrap wood to construct a small shelter.

The next day, Argent gave Lucky a tour of the old mines. They panned the offshoot waterways and got some flakes, but the prospecting was slow. The black sand was everywhere.

"Let me help ya build a trough ya can carry," Argent suggested after watching Lucky's futile and time-consuming attempts at panning.

"Yar portable one seems ta be more efficient."

"Thar easy ta make."

With his new sluice, Lucky worked up and down the nearby streambeds. If Argent or Sam Turner joined in, they would steer him toward the more profitable areas. The leftover gold kept the fever fed, but working through the black sand to get to the small flakes was proving to be more trouble than it was worth.

"Somethin' 'bout this stuff reminds me of tha Comstock mud," Lucky mentioned to Argent one day. "Thars turned out ta be silver."

"Was pannin' thar after that."

"If'n it's true of *this*, it'd be worth findin' out."

"Yeah. Those miners sold short 'cause they didn't know tha stuff was silver or they didn't have tha money ta process it."

"Be nice ta be tha one ta reap tha rewards."

"Could happen. Who knows?"

"Better happen *soon*. With winter comin', I been thinkin' of gittin' off tha mountain...afore tha snows come."

"Reckon I'll stay."

A week later, Lucky took his leave. As Argent watched him go, he thought of their earlier conversation. He wondered if the black sand in his backyard was worth consideration. He decided to stake some claims and went to file the paperwork. Remembering his debt to the Doyle brothers, he put several in their names, too.

"Granite," Lucky read the welcoming sign.

The lively town was full of activity. A stage had stopped, and the passengers went to an inviting eatery. It was lunchtime, but Lucky was weary from the sleepless nights he had while living in the mining camp. He headed toward a building identified as Willard's Hotel, got a room, and took a rare nap. He woke up when a couple in the hallway started to argue. Their anger soon turned into laughter, then he heard the sound of a door closing. He noticed that it had turned dark, and he was hungry, so he washed up and headed out to get some food. He got a table at a busy restaurant. A nice-looking gal came to take his order. She introduced herself, then asked what he wanted to order.

Lucky caught himself staring at the lovely girl. He was tongue-tied. "Uh...yar special... *Lily*." Saying her name was like smelling the flower's sweet scent on a clear summer day, Lucky thought. Oh no! I'm sounding like Sam, he inwardly laughed.

Lucky watched Lily as she moved around the room. She had a pleasant way about her, one that he found attractive. He realized that he wanted to get to know her better. To extend his stay, he ordered more to drink. When she brought the beverage to his table, he tried to say something charming, but the words got stuck in his throat.

"Ya have a very...a nice...*way* 'bout ya," he finally choked out.

"What *way* may that be?" Lily curtly replied. She was used to customers leering at her. She had been accosted on several occasions.

"I didn't...I *mean*...I was tryin' ta say that ya have a *nice way* with yar customers." This conversation is not going well, Lucky thought. I need to make myself clear. "Yar very pleasin'."

"If yar lookin' for somethin' more'n food, tha *saloon's* down tha street."

"No. No. *I'm sorry*." Lucky realized how his words had been misinterpreted. "That's *not* what I meant."

"Ya have a strange way of expressin' yarself then," Lily countered.

"I was tryin' ta say yar good at yar job." I wasn't tryin' ta make ya feel uncomfortable." Lucky wanted to explain further, but he knew he was losing ground.

"Reckon yar tha one who's *uncomfortable*." Lily slapped Lucky's bill on top of the table and stomped off without giving him a second glance.

When Lucky left the restaurant, he took a last look at Lily. She passed without turning his way. He had never felt so shy and clumsy around a girl before, and he was feeling rather defeated. I'll come back and try to make amends, he promised himself before he left.

The next morning, Lucky went to the café to confront Lily. The dining hall was busy, so he decided to wait for a better time. He wanted to talk with her properly. He got food from Curtis's General Store and headed up the hill to explore. Broken-down flumes, used to mine gold in the early '60s, still littered the slopes. When Lucky reached Cache Creek, he saw several men with pans in the water. One of them gave him an ugly stare, so he rode until he found a secluded spot of his own. Lucky tried to pan for gold, but his mind was elsewhere. He couldn't stop thinking of Lily. After a few futile attempts, he decided to head back to town. Once again, the restaurant was crowded, but Lucky didn't want to wait, so he went inside.

A man saw Lucky standing alone. "Got an empty chair here. Yar welcome ta sit with us."

Lucky took him up on his offer and sat down. "Much obliged. Name's Lucky."

"I'm Harry, this here's Laird, an' sittin' on

yar other side is Bob.”

Harry studied the stranger’s appearance. “Ya been huntin’ for gold up north?”

“Wanted ta git out afore tha cold weather set in.”

“Gits bad up thar. Much worse than here,” Bob pointed out. “Ya made a good choice.”

“Thar still gittin’ gold in tha hills outside of town,” Laird told Lucky.

“Did some pannin’ this mornin’. Looks like tha area’s already been worked over.”

“It’s been more’n ten years,” Laird confirmed. “But thar tryin’ different techniques…an’ some are still gittin’ gold.”

“Saw remnants of hydraulic minin’. Was it productive?”

“Maybe, at first,” Bob answered. “But, luckily, it wasn’t profitable. They really messed up tha waterways.”

“That’s a destructive way ta git tha gold. I’ve seen tha results. I’m happy ta just use a pan.”

“Yar chasin’ *rainbows*,” Harry interjected. “I prefer tha ranchin’ life myself. But I figure ta each his own, so I watch as ya come an’ go, lookin’ for yar pots of gold. It seems that those makin’ it now have ta have tha luck of tha Irish ta find tha big strike.”

“Reckon so, but tha *journey’s* part of it…for me at least,” Lucky justified.

“Go n-éirí an bóthar leat.” Laird shared the Irish wish, then explained for the others. “May ya have a successful journey.”

“An’ yars young man. Have yar journeys been successful?” Harry asked Lucky.

“Gittin’ ’long all right, I reckon. Learnin’ as

I go.”

"If ya git tired of movin' 'round an' wanta settle down, ya could git sum cattle an' start a nice ranch here," Bob suggested. "Tha grass is good an' tha soil's fertile...ya could raise crops. This is a nice area ta call home."

As they were talking, a man rushed into the bar and spoke to some of his friends. The low murmuring quickly intensified as they spread the disturbing news. Harry rose and went to one of the groups to find out what the fuss was all about.

CHAPTER 38

The year was 1874. Colorado was still a territory, just a couple of years shy of becoming the 33rd state in the union. The gold rush had given the country a reason to invest in the West, and though many Colorado towns had come and gone, there was enough stability for some to prosper. With growth came competition, which ultimately led to conflict as the populace fought to retain their rights to the resources. To resolve these issues, law and order had to be maintained.

Until a proper legal system was established, the towns formed Vigilante or Safety Committees to curtail criminal behavior. Even though these groups provided a needed service, they often overstepped their authority and broke the law. When this happened, the outcome was likely to be worse than the initial quarrel, causing small disagreements to turn into large-scale conflicts.

The residents of Lake County, in the Colorado Territory, found themselves in such a situation. The dispute started innocently enough. The use of a water ditch was under discussion by two neighbors. They disagreed, and in the heat of the moment, a shot was fired. No one was hurt, but without an agreeable solution, the issue festered, and dissension grew.

The Lake County War had begun.

Harry came back to the table and reported what he had heard. "Been a skirmish between Harrington an' Gibbs. Neighbors livin' here," he clarified for Lucky. "Gibbs shot at Harrington but missed. Whether intentional or not is up for debate."

"What was it 'bout this time?" Bob asked.

"Water." Harry looked at Lucky. "It's mostly 'bout water 'round here...or cattle. They've been arguin' 'bout boundaries an' fencin' for a while now. Ya see, tha first ta settle has tha rights ta tha water 'round thar land. Harrington's been here longer, so it should be his say."

"People're always wantin' more'n they've a right ta," Laird observed.

Lucky had seen the same trouble before. "Tha gold fever has brought out similar traits. Has made men into an odd lot of characters."

"Sounds like ya have a good head on yar shoulders, boy," Harry noted. "It usually takes years of livin' ta realize that."

The crowd thinned as people left to spread the news of the dispute. Lily worked her way to their table. She was surprised to see Lucky sitting there.

Lucky smiled. "Hello."

Harry made the introduction. "Lily, this is Lucky, a miner who's passin' through."

Lily sneered. Lucky was the last person she expected to see sitting with her father. "We met last night."

"I'm afraid we didn't git off ta a good start," Lucky acknowledged. "I was meanin' ta give Lily a *compliment*, but it came out wrong."

"Implied I was *a tart!*"

"Seems this is somethin' *you two* need ta work out." Harry stood and looked at Lilly. "Add his meal ta my tab. See ya at home." He turned and addressed Lucky. "Hope ta see ya 'round."

The other two men followed Harry's lead. They nodded at Lily. Lucky didn't miss the grins they gave him before they left.

"So yar buddyin' up with my father."

"Reckon I'm gonna be misunderstood, *again*," Lucky protested. "Ta set things straight, thar was an empty chair, an' with tha room bein' full an' all, I was offered a seat. I had no idea who Harry was 'til ya came up."

Lily pondered his words. It could have been a coincidence, she thought, then she asked him what he wanted to order.

"I'll have yar steak, done medium-well, an' potatoes." Lucky added, "I'll run my own tab."

"If my father wants ta pay for ya, then let him." Lily grinned. "He's used ta havin' his own way."

Lucky returned her smile. "Whatever ya say, *ma'am*."

Lily was more cordial when she brought Lucky his food. They kept their exchanges to polite conversation. By the time he was ready to leave, he felt he had made headway, but to where? he asked himself. This time, when he left the restaurant and looked back, he saw Lily watching him. She smiled, then turned away.

Lucky decided to stay in Granite, at least for the time being. When he reached his hotel, he extended his stay. "Another week," he told the clerk.

Lucky slept well, so he woke up late. He sang

as he dressed, and with a spring in his step, he headed to the diner. He was looking forward to seeing Lily again. When he entered the café, there was a crowd, and an agitated hum of conversation permeated the air. Lily came to his table to get his order.

"What's all tha fuss 'bout?"

"There was a shootin' late last night. George Harrington was *murdered.* He was one of tha men that had been arguin' yesterday. People think that Elijah Gibbs is responsible."

"Wasn't thar gunfire already?"

"By Gibbs. He probably pulled tha trigger last night too."

"How did it happen?"

"Strangely, a fire had started on Harrington's property, an' when he was puttin' it out, he was shot. *In tha back.*"

"Tha law will be on it. Whoever is responsible will be taken care of," Lucky assured her.

Supper proved to be more amiable, and when Lily's shift ended, she even joined Lucky for dessert. He told her about his adventures with his brother, which led to Sam meeting and marrying Sally. Lily, in turn, told of her life on her dad's ranch, living with two other sisters, each named for a flower. This time, when he left, Lucky tipped his hat to Lily, and she waved.

The next few weeks flew by as Lucky got to know Lily better. He found work, cowboying on a ranch that was nearby so he could easily ride into town and visit with Lily. He finally got the nerve to ask her out, and she accepted. They set a date when they could get the same day off from work. Lily had a special place in mind for a picnic, so the night before, Lucky paid for the best basket of food the café had to offer.

Lucky met Lily at the diner. She was dressed in a blue pastel dress trimmed with white lace.

"You look lovely!" Lucky blushed. He wasn't used to giving out compliments.

"Thank you. You look nice when yar all cleaned up, yarself."

"Not when I'm *cowboyin'*?" Lucky joked.

Lily laughed. "Yar different lookin' *then*. It's like comparin' apples an' oranges."

They went out the back, where Lily had her family's buckboard waiting. Her older sister, Rose, who was to act as the chaperone, was already seated. She was dressed more conservatively, wearing a plain, green cotton blouse and a long skirt. She held a basket in her lap. Lily introduced the two, then Lucky helped her onto the cart. He took the driver's seat. He was told to follow the road north, as they were going to a town with a beautiful lake. It was late morning when they reached Dayton. Though the air still held the morning chill, the wind was calm, so they rented a boat. As Lucky rowed, Lily and Rose told him stories about the area.

"There're actually two lakes. Why tha name— Twin Lakes," Lily told Lucky as they cruised along the shoreline.

"Strange creatures live under tha water."

"Now, Rose. Don't share those silly stories 'bout monsters," Lily scolded.

Lucky didn't want Rose to feel left out. He wanted to include her in their conversations, so he encouraged her to continue with the tale. "Oh? I'd like ta hear more."

"Grotesque lookin' heads just mysteriously pop up. Ya never know when or whar."

Lucky pointed toward the middle of the lake. "Ya mean like tha one over thar?"

Rose and Lily looked, but they didn't see anything. "Whar?" they both asked.

"Too late. Ya missed it. It's gone back under," Lucky teased.

"Ya had me fooled," Rose admitted.

Lily concurred. "Me too."

Lucky smiled. "Perhaps these curious heads belong ta those bigfooted creatures I've heard roam 'round these parts."

"Or they're figments of people's imagination," Lily countered.

"Campfire stories," Lucky joked.

The rest of the day went by all to fast. Lucky and Lily laughed and shared stories. Rose joined in the fun and never felt as if she was a third wheel. By the time they were ready to go, the picnic basket was empty.

"I hate ta call it a day, but we need ta git back ta Granite...afore sunset," Lucky told the girls.

Lily gathered the picnic items and put them in the wagon. "I forgot how much fun tha lake can be."

Rose looked at her sister and grinned. "Maybe it's tha *company* yar with."

When they returned to town, Lucky gave Lily the reins. When their hands touched, he looked deeply into her eyes and silently told of his love. Lily also shared this sentiment, so she spontaneously kissed his cheek.

"Thank you for a *lovely* day."

Lucky stepped down from the buckboard. He looked directly at Lily and smiled. "My pleasure." He turned his attention to her sister. "Rose... enjoyed yar company." He tipped his hat. "Have a good night, ladies."

"Bye," he heard as the wagon rolled away.

As soon as they were out of earshot, Rose berated her sister for her boldness.

"I'm gonna *marry* him," Lily emphasized to end the discussion.

CHAPTER 39

No one could link Gibbs with Harrington's murder. He did go to trial, but he was acquitted. Harrington's friends felt that justice was not served, so a Vigilante Committee was formed with the purpose of enforcing what they thought was fair justice, but they took matters too far. They went to Gibbs's house and tried to force him out. When he refused their request, they threatened to burn his home. Gibbs fired into the crowd, and in the mayhem, three men died. Gibbs escaped.

The vigilantes didn't let up. They harassed anyone who disagreed with their views. People were threatened or forced to leave. Some had mysteriously disappeared or were found dead.

"If'n ya support tha antics of tha vigilantes, yar not supportin' law an' order. Me...I believe in followin' tha rule of tha law," Lucky said to Lily one day.

"Mob rule is winnin' out." Lily felt a sense of trepidation. She knew her father favored the group. "Loyalties are divided. Thars dissension between friends an' neighbors in Lake County. Everyone has taken sides, wanta or not."

"Ya have ta keep yar viewpoint ta yarself, or someone'll give ya tha *evil eye*. I'm tryin' ta keep ta myself so I don't offend anybody."

"Or be judged by yar associations. Since yar

boss spoke in favor of Gibbs, Dad hasn't spoken well of ya."

When Lucky walked Lily to her door, Harry came out, toting a rifle.

"Anyone workin' on Giebfried's Ranch is no longer welcome at my house. My daughter is now *forbidden* ta see ya." Harry raised his rifle and pointed it at Lucky.

Lucky squeezed Lily's hand and gave her a loving look. He knew that Harry wouldn't back down, so to keep the peace, he left.

Harry's wishes didn't stop Lucky from seeing Lily. He had Giebfried's cook pass on times and places for their rendezvouses, so the young couple could continue to meet.

Shortly after Harry delivered his ultimatum, Lucky went to visit Argent. "I haven't even taken sides. It's *not* right."

"Heard tha stories, but yar vigilante troubles haven't really affected folks up here."

"It's like livin' in a war zone...neighbor 'gainst neighbor. Lily an' I are *right* in tha middle. We're strugglin', but I'm *not* givin' up."

"Ya keep after yar lassie. Missed my chance 'cause of tha War, an' have been regretin' it ever since. Don't ya let *that* happen ta ya."

Lucky stopped in town on his return from Oro City. He had to look twice, but he thought the woman loading a wagon looked familiar.

"Mrs. Loback?"

She had to stare at him for a few seconds before she recognized his familiar face. "Lucky! My, you've filled out. Yar not tha lanky, young boy on tha train, but yar still a fine-lookin' fellow. How are ya?"

"Doin' good. Did ya git yar bakery goin'?"

"We did. Our first stop was at a place called Jackson's Diggin's."

"Wasn't that tha place whar tha *second* gold rush started? I read 'bout it, an' how some wrote 'Pikes Peak or Bust' on thar wagons. What got me an' Sam ta come west. Funny how Pikes Peak isn't even near where tha gold was found, though."

"It was a beacon for those comin' across, an' they had gone many miles by then. They knew they were much closer ta thar destination when they saw tha mountain."

"Yar town musta been fairly new when we crossed tha Kansas Territory in '59."

"It was. By year's end, tha town's name changed ta Idaho Springs an' tha Jefferson Territory was established. Since it was only a provisional division, it only lasted 'til '61, we weren't surprised when tha Colorado Territory was officially named. I think we'll stay under this jurisdiction 'til Colorado becomes a state."

"With all tha regulatin' needed for tha mines, smaller divisions make sense. I was in Alder Gulch when tha Montana Territory was formed."

"Tha madness of tha rushes has kept things pretty much in a state of change, but we never had ta worry. Business has always been good, no matter whar we set up."

"Sounds like you've moved more'n once."

"We sold out an' went south. Wound up in Colorado City. Now, we're hopin' that this area will work for us. Tha view of tha mountains is tha best we've seen."

"I've been takin' 'em for granted, but I can

see what ya mean. They are scenic."

"What 'bout yar brother? Did he finally git hitched ta Sally?"

"He *did*. Got two young'uns keepin' 'em busy. Thar runnin' a general store in Golden. How's Bion...an' tha Bakers? Are they still with ya?"

"Everyone's fine. Bion's out gittin' supplies. We've had two children of our own, Randy an' Bion, Jr. Tha Bakers are still with us. Her two have become beautiful young adults. Besides helpin' at tha shop, thar a big help with tha raisin' of tha kids."

"Whar ya located? I haven't seen yar store in town."

"We're just gittin' settled...in an area thar callin' Cottonwood (early Buena Vista). Tha place seems ta have promise. We're wantin' ta live somewhar that's quiet an' peaceful. We were *too* busy. Now, with tha children, we don't want ta spend so much time at tha shop. This place has tha potential ta grow, so when tha children are old enough, tha business will be established, an' they can take over an' raise young'uns of thar own."

"If'n tha sign says *Loback's Bakery*, you'll have no problem gittin' customers. I remember some of tha bakin' ya shared with tha folks on tha wagon train. Even with tha bad tastin' water an' tha limitations of wagon livin', yar breads an' sweets were always tha tastiest."

"You an' yar brother were my favorites. Ya always appreciated tha treats we shared...both of ya were easy ta please."

"I'm stayin' at Giebfried's Ranch. If'n ya need help buildin' yar store, look me up."

"Tha Baker's would love ta see ya. Come by anytime. Ya can't miss our place. Thars only a few of us around. Not enough ta make up a town. Not yet, anyway."

"Sure good ta run into ya again. Promise. I'll stop in an' visit with all of ya sometime soon."

After his encounter with Mrs. Loback, Lucky stopped in the saloon for a quick drink. As he listened to the conversation around the bar, he realized that the tense atmosphere in town had only grown worse. When he tried to contact Lily, he was told that Harry knew about their meetings. Someone had seen them together.

Since Harry had his friends watching Lily at work, she had to sneak out at night to meet Lucky. "I *don't* understand 'em," Lily declared when she was finally able to see Lucky again.

"Tha best I can figure is that it's some kind of domino effect. Once tha committee members got this bee in thar bonnet, they couldn't back down. An' they've created this chain reaction of violent acts. People are scared *not* ta take up with 'em."

"I think some of 'em are usin' this dispute as an *excuse* ta break tha law. Thar chasin' people out ta take over thar property...even committin' murder ta git what they want. An' worse yet, thar *gittin' away* with it!"

"Reckon thars some truth in that. But what I *hate* tha most...this feudin's makin' our meetin's harder ta arrange...an' thar way too *few an' far between!*"

CHAPTER 40

atfish was lying in the creek. He had mud on his face, and his clothes were wet. He remembered trying to take over a miner's claim, but this time, he failed. The man's partner must of come up from behind and clubbed me, he realized. He moaned when he tried to move. It feels like they kicked me some, too.

He looked around. The sun was setting, so he figured he had been out for about half of the day. The horse that he had stolen was gone. When two men rode up, he reached for his gun. It was also missing.

"Looks like ya been up ta no good," one of the men goaded when he saw the bruises that had distorted Catfish's face.

"Do ya think he's tha one we've been hearin' 'bout?" the other man asked. He didn't mention that he had seen the man's wanted poster.

"Now don't git a pricklin'. We got a business that could use someun of yar caliper, but I reckon yar not interested."

Catfish stared at the intruders. His pursed lips and furrowed brow spoke volumes. Neither of them deserved a response, he realized, so he kept his thoughts to himself. He could hear them laughing as they rode away. After they were out of sight, he stood up and fought the pain as he walked to the nearest mining camp.

His swollen face kept people at bay, even the town's troublemakers. Before he left the ambit of the encampment, a naïve, young miner was left lying behind the tent that housed the saloon. He rode the boy's horse hard until he reached the next camp. He went straight for the bar.

"Shot of yar *best* whiskey." He offered the boy's bag of dust for payment.

The barkeep took a pinch. When he went for a second, Catfish jerked the bag away.

"*Two pinches* fer tha drink, mister! Read tha sign." The man pointed to the wall.

"Yar *long* nails give ya a much bigger take. 'Sides, tha drink's not worth four bits," Catfish protested.

The bartender was insistent. "Hand it back or *no* service!"

"Wouldn't do that, mister," a man wearing a badge warned when he saw Catfish go for his gun. The lawman already had his drawn.

Catfish realized he was beat. He shoved his pouch back at the barman so he could get the rest of his fare. "Not lookin' ta cause trouble." He retracted his pouch and grabbed the drink, then he went to a table in the corner of the room to cool down. He had only taken a couple of sips when two men came up and sat in the seats next to his.

"Almost didn't recognize ya," a familiar voice said. "Yar mendin' well."

"Out with it. What's yar business?" Catfish recognized the men who had been at the creek after his beating.

The older man replied. "My brother an' me are in tha cattle business. We're always lookin' fer help ta keep our stock a healthy size.”

Catfish spoke directly to the intrusive men. “*Stop* beatin’ ’round tha bush. Ya want me ta *rustle* with ya.”

“*Cowpunchin’*,” the younger man amended.

“What’s *my* cut?”

The older man sat down and lowered his voice. “Yar paid when tha beeves are sold... *equal* splits.”

“Why *me*?”

“Yar *reputation*,” he replied. “Know ya don’t mind gittin’ yar hands dirty.”

“How do I know ya aren’t after tha reward?”

The old man grinned. “We coulda taken ya in when ya was lying in tha creek if’n that was our purpose.”

❦ ❦ ❦

The Giebfried Ranch had only been up and running for a few years but was growing fast. Giebfried owned over 500 acres of land and maintained, on average, 200 cattle. Lucky and Buster were branding calves when two other hands rode up.

“Tha counts down,” Theo informed them.

“Ya check tha draw?” Buster asked.

“An’ tha brush ’long tha canyon, too,” Theo confirmed.

Buster stuck the iron in the fire. “Help us finish up here, then we’ll take a look ’round.”

They broke into two groups and rode the perimeter of the ranch. The hills offered views of the valley below, but nothing looked out of place. They were about to call it quits when Lucky spotted tracks.

“Over here,” he called to Theo. “Looks like

they may have passed this way.”

“Whar would they go from here?” Theo looked around. “Down thar.” He pointed to an opening in the trees.

They rode down the hill and through a grove of pines and firs until they reached the entrance to a small ravine.

Lucky could see that there was no easy way to ride out. “Looks like a box canyon.”

“More tracks. Thars been recent activity.” Theo got off his horse. “Let’s go on foot. Bet thars somethin’ ahead, an’ I wouldn’t wanta ride inta a trap.”

They didn’t have to go far before they spotted a corral full of cows. Two men were building a fire. Branding irons were close at hand.

“Suspect some of ’em are ours.” Theo drew his gun, anticipating a confrontation.

“I recognize one of ’em,” Lucky whispered. “Goes by tha name of Catfish.”

“Seen a poster on ’im. Rewards up ta $500.”

They heard a stick break behind them. Before they had a chance to react, a man came up with his gun pointed.

“Drop yar irons.”

CHAPTER 41

Alarge man was walking toward them. He aimed his gun their way. "Hey, boys!" he yelled out to his brother and Catfish. Before he could add more, a bullet brought him down.

Buster came out of the brush. Lucky and Theo picked up their guns, then followed him to the camp.

The thieves had the branding iron in the fire and were getting ready to bring out the first cow. When they heard the call, followed by a shot, they went for their weapons. Before they could take the offensive, two cowboys from Giebfried's ranch came at them with their rifles cocked. The other wranglers joined them.

Buster cut the rustlers' rope into pieces. Theo grabbed a strand and tied one of the thief's hands behind his back. Lucky got the man's feet bound.

Buster tied Catfish's ankles together. "Hey, I *recognize* this one. Saw his wanted poster in town."

"Had tha pleasure of sharin' space with 'im a while back. He showed his true colors *mighty* quick." Lucky explained how Catfish tried to ambush Pops.

"Yar *burro* botched it for me. Caused me ta lose my footin'," Catfish spat.

"Ta Mary Margaret's credit. She only foiled

yar *thievin'*. Probably saved Pops life, as well."

Even though he was in the wrong, Catfish would never admit it. He only sought revenge. "Ya better *watch* yar back. I never *forgit a face* or *let go* of a grudge." He glared at Buster. "Goes fer *all of ya.*"

Lucky ignored Catfish's remarks. "Sure glad ya showed up when ya did. How'd ya come upon us?"

"Was headin' back when tha boys came up. Said they'd seen tracks, so we went ta figure out whar they led. Saw ya in tha distance. We had just caught up with ya, an' was 'bout ta holler when we saw tha old man comin' toward ya," Buster explained.

"Haven't had a chance ta brand over ours yet," Theo broke in. He had been inspecting the corralled cows. "Not sure of tha others, though. That'll be for tha sheriff ta work out."

"Got all of 'em with tha Giebfried brand," one of the other cowboys informed Buster.

Buster addressed Theo. "You an' tha boys can start tha drive. I'll take Lucky with me an' git these two inta town. Like ta git 'em off our hands. We'll tie tha dead guy ta 'is horse an' bring 'im in, too."

"Yar entitled ta a reward," the deputy said when they brought in the three rustlers. "Tha ranchers'll be relieved now that this bunch is behind bars."

Buster watched as the men were led to the jail cells. "Someun'll be by ta collect. Just make sure these no-goods git what they deserve."

"I reckon yar boss an' tha other cattlemen'll ensure they do," the deputy confirmed, knowing the consequences of cattle rustling.

"Yar *dead* men!" Catfish threatened before the cowhands left.

❦ ❦ ❦

A sound caused the young girls to turn. When the man riding a horse came over the rise, they stopped. His ruggedly handsome face caused them to stare. Red hair protruded from the brim of his hat. His face was hardened and strong. His expression revealed little. He rode as if he were on an important mission. His gray horse was breathing heavily and looked as if he had been ridden hard.

The girls quickly moved to the side of the road. The man passed without looking their way. He headed to town and stopped in front of Doyle N Doyle General Store. The rider dismounted and tied his horse to the hitching post. After he looked around, he walked through the open entryway.

"What tha...*Lucky*!" the shop owner happily shouted with recognition. He hadn't seen his younger brother in quite some time. "Well... what brings ya here?"

"Sam. I *need* ta stay with ya awhile." Lucky brusquely announced before he embraced his brother in greeting. "How 'bout goin' with me ta tha saloon, so I can explain. Can Sally watch tha store?"

"No problem. I'll go in tha back an' git her. She'll be excited ta see ya, *too*."

Lucky anxiously waited by the door, but from time to time, he would peek outside. It was too soon, but they could have tracked me here, he thought. Do they know I know? he questioned.

"Lucky! It's *so good* ta see ya!" Sally gave her brother-in-law a strangling hug.

"An' you *too*." Lucky broke the embrace. "Do ya mind if I buy yar husband a drink an' discuss old times?"

"Of course not." Sally scanned Lucky's face. Sam had warned her, but even so, she could see that something was wrong.

"Thanks. Won't keep 'im long, I promise," Lucky assured her as they headed out the door.

"What's up?" Sam asked as they crossed the street. "Ya seem a bit on edge."

"Wait 'til we git seated at tha bar."

"Two beers," Sam ordered. When the glasses were filled, Lucky directed him toward a table in the back. He sat where he could watch the door.

"I told ya of tha *trouble* in Lake County."

The expression on his brother's face told Sam that this was important. "Yeah, you *did* mention it in yar last letter."

"Well, it's gittin' worse. Ever since Gibbs was acquitted, Harrington's friends have grouped together. They formed what they call a Safety Committee, but they are only a bunch of wild vigilantes that are out of control."

"Heard how they've overstepped tha law."

"Ya know I've been workin' with Giebfried, on his ranch in tha valley just outside of town?"

"Yeah. Yar last letter said you'd been doin' some cowboyin'."

"Well, he's friendly with this Alfred fellow who's been vocal 'bout how tha law's not been followed. Tha committee members are curtailin' all of tha opposition. People have been beaten, chased out of town, an' some have even been killed 'cause they won't be intimidated by these thugs."

"Sounds like things are gittin' rough."

"I've managed ta git in tha middle somehow. Was waylaid. I was headin' ta tha ranch when I was jumped…a man flew at me from tha rocks an' took me off my horse. They got a sack over my head afore I could react an' tied my hands. We rode for a few miles afore stoppin' at some run-down shanty. I was questioned…asked if'n I knew anythin' 'bout some of thar antics. I said that I knew nothin', but they didn't believe me. This fellow, I'd seen 'im around town but don't know his name, started toward me with a raised fist. He'd placed hisself between me an' his buddy, who'd been pointin' my gun at me, so I took tha chance an' bulldozed 'im. He was pushed backwards, right into tha other guy. When I gave 'im a solid kick, I felt tha rope loosen 'round my wrists. I grabbed my gun, which had been dropped in tha scuffle. Havin' tha upper hand, I tied tha two of 'em up. I went ta tha ranch ta warn Giebfried, grabbed my stuff, an' came straight here."

"Yar guilty by association." Sam was worried. He knew that vigilante committees knowingly convicted innocent people.

"Ta make it worse, Lily, tha gal I wrote ya 'bout…her family has turned against me. Her dad is one of tha committee members. He may have arranged tha setup. I'd just heard that he knows that I'm still seein' Lily. He's already forbidden me ta see her, but we've been meetin' in secret."

"Well, yar welcome ta stay here as long as ya want. You can help 'round tha store."

"Thanks, but I don't know if'n it will be safe for ya. Reckon thar spies are everywhere. I don't know who ta trust, an' I *do* know somethin'... names of tha committee members who've been breakin' tha law, but as I said, I don't wanna be involved."

"I'm not worried 'bout those hooligans. I've got friends here. They'll support us if'n there's trouble."

"Thanks. But Lily, well, she's important ta me. I wanna marry her...woulda by now if'n not for all of this. I'll be goin' back. Just needin' ta lay low for a while."

Sam stood and took tha last sip of his beer. He turned the conversation around to a more lighthearted topic. "Sally's closed tha shop by now an' will have a good stew cookin'. Let's move this discussion ta my place. 'Sides, you've yet ta see our new house."

They got Shooter and led him to the barn. After taking care of the animal's needs, Sam gave Lucky a tour of his property.

"Sally has her garden over here." They saw tomatoes and lettuce ready to pick. "I help when I can, but tha store demands most of my extra time."

"Ya sure tha store's not an excuse?" Lucky goaded. Neither of them had wanted jobs that involved working the soil.

"Nah. I kinda enjoy it. I reckon it's different when yar workin' with someone ya care 'bout... someone who makes it fun."

They walked around the two-story wooden

structure. They passed a bay window before reaching the door. "Did ya buy a house that was already here, or pay someone ta build it for ya?"

"Got one that was vacated. We had ta spend a bit of time an' money fixin' it up."

"A white picket fence an' all. Sure is a nice place. Ya did good, big brother." Lucky patted Sam on the back.

They went inside. Sally had decorated the cabin with lace curtains and porcelain lamps. The furniture that sat around the fire presented a comfortable, homey environment.

"Supper's almost ready," Sally informed them when they entered the house.

Sam walked over to his wife and gave her a kiss. "I'm starved," he said with affection.

"Sure smells good," Lucky was saying when Mason came runnin' into the room. Melanie followed. "Look who's grown up."

"Uncle Lucky," they chimed.

"How are my monkeys doin'?" Lucky picked them up one by one and gave each a great big hug. "Missed ya. Come sit with me." He led them to the couch.

As they sat around the parlor, Lucky gave a summary of his recent exploits. Sally was not surprised to hear about the vigilantes. She had heard how the committees in some of the newer towns had overstepped their bounds. Lucky then explained how the violence was affecting his relationship with Lily.

Sally got up to check on dinner. When she returned, the group retired to the dining room, where she had set a stunning table that was adorned with linen, sterling cutlery, and crystal glasses.

"Looks like Christmas!" Lucky pulled out Sally's chair.

"Yar visitin' is a special occasion, too," Sally justified. "Gives me a chance ta use our finery."

"I see tha stew has been replaced with roast beef an' all tha trimmings. I reckon that means our finest wine." Sam went to the cabinet and pulled out an imported red.

"Never guess who I ran into." Lucky looked first at his brother, then at Sally.

Sam tried to read Lucky's expression. "Way yar actin', I gather we both knew 'em?"

"Yep. Tha Lobacks...an' tha Bakers."

"How are they?" Sally asked. "I've thought 'bout 'em from time ta time, an' wondered how they'd made out."

"Tha Lobacks built thar bakery business up real well. They got two young'uns of thar own. Mrs. Baker stayed on with 'em. Her crew's now grown into fine young adults."

"Whar they livin' now?" Sam asked.

"Place outside whar I'm at. Not a town yet, just some families livin' in tha area. Seems a good tradin' center for now."

"We should go an' see 'em," Sally proposed.

Lucky shook his head. "I'd wait 'til things calm down. So far thar outta it, but I don't know 'bout thar neighbors."

The home-cooked meal with his brother's family made Lucky miss Lily even more. One day, he hoped to have all this with her. When he finally dozed off, Lucky slept peacefully and dreamt of Lily.

CHAPTER 42

Lucky decided to stay a few days with his brother. Since he hadn't been followed, he was able to relax and enjoy his visit with Sam and his family.

"Remember how *green* we were at first...when we started prospectin'?" Sam said one evening.

"Yeah. We'd swirl our pans so hard, all tha gravel would come out," Lucky laughed.

"What 'bout tha time ya screamed *gold* an' it was *pyrite*?" Sam teased.

"Mason jumped on Lucky's lap. "I wanna hear tha Fool's Pool story."

Though the children had heard the tale many times, they wanted to hear Lucky tell it again, so he retold how he and their dad had been prospecting and stumbled on the find.

"OK. *Bedtime*," Sally announced when Lucky finished his narrative.

"Oh, *Ma*," they protested. "Can't we stay up a little longer?"

"I'll come up an' tuck ya in," Lucky promised as Sally led them upstairs.

"I still have *all* yar money in tha safe," Sam reminded his brother when Lucky came back from reading a story to the kids.

"Reckon I'll git ta it when I settle with Lily." Lucky thought about his prospecting days. "Got more from sluicin' than Fool's Pool."

"No word from tha boys, huh?"

"Just when I saw Tincup while layin' track. He hadn't changed a bit. Reckon they're livin' out thar lives, same as us."

Sam thought about his family. "Yeah."

"Reckon it's time ta face mine. I'll be leavin' tomorrow mornin'."

"Ready ta git back ta see Lily?" Sally asked.

"How'd ya guess?"

"Woman's intuition."

Sam laughed. "*Hogwash.* You've been wearin' that moony look since ya got here."

"Ya mean tha one you wore 'til ya came back ta Sally?" Lucky retorted.

"Reckon we both got bit," Sam confessed.

"'Bout time, too," Sally cut in. "It was bound ta happen sooner or later."

"On that note, I think I'll retire for tha night."

"*Sweet* dreams," Sam teased. He remembered all the times Lucky poked fun at him because of how he felt about Sally.

"I *deserved* that." Lucky laughed as he, too, thought of the times he had kidded Sam.

Lucky was saddled up and ready to ride by sunrise.

"Let us know when yar safe an' sound." Sam gave his brother a final hug.

Sally waved goodbye. "Bring Lily by sometime soon. We're lookin' forward ta meetin' her."

Lucky would have immediately gone to the café to see Lily when he got back, but he knew that her family would be watching. The livery on the edge of town was the location for their next rendezvous. He entered through a back door and left Shooter in a stall. He was the first to arrive. He recognized Lily's silhouette when she came through the door.

"Why are ya so nervous?" he asked when she approached. "Has anythin' happened?"

"Don't know if ya heard. Judge Dyer was shot an' killed," Lily reported.

"Tha vigilantes?"

"He was in court, tryin' tha ones that had been issued warrants. No one would testify against 'em. Tha charges were dismissed, yet they *still* murdered him."

"Do they know who did it?"

"Thar rumors of men leavin' tha courthouse right after shots were heard, but no one's sayin' who they were."

"Do ya think yar papa was one of 'em?"

"No...I hope not," Lily stuttered. "Pa's in with 'em, real deep, but I don't think he'd go that far."

"Reckon he won't be comin' 'round 'bout us anytime soon."

"Tha town's not been tha same since this started. Seems people are either ignorin' each other or are arguin'."

"Yeah. I'm afraid it's too dangerous for me ta stay. But...I don't wanna go without ya."

"Nor would I like ta be left behind."

Lucky's throat became dry. The words he was ready to say seemed to get stuck, but he choked them out without a pause.

"I was savin' this for a better time an' place, but..." he started, then he fell on one knee, "Lily, *will ya marry me*?" Before she could answer, he continued. "I know it won't be like we were hopin', with yar papa's blessin' an' all, but he'd been happy with me afore all tha fightin' started, so ya know that otherwise he would of—"

Lily put her finger to his lips and stopped his narration. "*Yes, yes, yes*," she repeated to express her joy. "I know yar worried that my family won't be there an' we can't do it properly, but yar my family now, an' hopefully, when all this dies down, Ma an' Pa will come ta love ya as much as I do. 'Til then, it's *you* that I need an' wanna be with."

Lucky was prepared. He pulled a ring from his pocket. When Lily saw it, she held out her hand, and Lucky slipped the precious stone onto her finger. They both looked up at the same time and sealed their feelings with a kiss.

"*I love you*," they said in unison.

Their next meeting place was at an old cabin outside of town. Lucky tied his horse to a tree behind a group of aspens and approached the building from the back. He saw a gap in the logs where the clay filling had fallen out. He looked through the peephole to make sure that the place was empty. He went inside and waited for Lily.

"Ya beat me *again*," Lily announced when she finally arrived. "I had ta be careful. Pa was still home an' in a foul mood."

"Ya think he knows yar gone?"

"If he did, he woulda had me followed. I kept lookin' ta be sure. I didn't see anyone."

"How'd we git in this *mess*, anyway?"

"Just *lucky*." Lily smiled, then she gave him a reassuring kiss.

"Reckon so. Ya got everythin'?"

"Yes. I got *everythin'* I need. I'm ready. Did ya git word back from yar brother?"

"He's got a nice place all picked out, an' tha preacher who'll tie tha knot."

"What are we waitin' for? *Let's git married!*"

CHAPTER 43

"I now pronounce you man and wife," the minister proclaimed.

The organ sang while Lucky and Lily sealed their marriage with a kiss. They headed down the aisle, followed by Sam's family and a few others who attended the ceremony.

They went to Sam's house for the reception. "My little brother finally got hitched." Sam gave a short toast. He held up his glass. "May thar union bring 'em many future blessin's."

"Wish I could have been yar best man, but I understand why ya didn't wait," Lucky said after he heard Sam's tribute.

"You were there in spirit," Sally assured him. "Sam even made yar toast for ya."

"Oh yeah. What did I say?"

Sam had to think a moment. "I remember. You said, 'May tha pot at tha end of tha rainbow be filled with love...an' *lots of gold,* too!'"

"I did pretty good, huh?"

When the ceremony was over, the bride and groom walked to the house that Sam and Sally had picked out for them. Lucky carried Lily over the threshold.

"Feels like my life has just begun!" Lucky pulled his wife near him.

"Mine too!" Lily replied as she fell into his loving embrace.

Though the cabin was in good shape when Lucky and Lily moved in, they wanted to make it their own. Lily freshened up the inside while Lucky made changes to the outside of the building. They frequented the Doyle N Doyle General Store to get the materials needed for their upgrades.

"Been keepin' yar name on tha sign," Sam said when Lucky came in one day.

"Still hopin' we'll work side by side?"

"Too much ta wish for?"

"Ya know me. I'd feel cooped up. I need ta be doin' somethin' outside."

"Thought ya might be closer ta settlin' down now that yar startin' yar family."

"Found a compromise. Got a job heavin' 'em barrels for tha brewery."

"With tha Schueler & Coors Golden Brewery, huh? They just opened in '73. Good stuff."

"Was told they're usin' a Czech recipe ta make thar Pilsner beer. I'll load tha draughts, then haul 'em ta thar distributors."

"Leastways, I'll see ya when ya make my deliveries. How 'bout you, Lily? Are ya goin' ta work, too?"

"I like servin' food. I got a job workin' at tha diner 'cross tha street from ya."

"Reckon I'll have ta be content just havin' ya in town, an' seein' ya when ya stop by. I'll be right back." Sam went to help a customer.

Lucky watched his brother go. "All tha time."

"Ya still got an interest in prospectin'?" Lily asked. She had seen Lucky talking with an old miner who had come into the store.

"Reckon so," Lucky realized.

Sally came out of the back storeroom. "Lily. We got this cloth yesterday. Ya might like ta use it for yar new curtains."

"It's beautiful. I'll take tha whole bolt." Lily went with Sally to find matching thread and lace trimming.

"Ya ever have prospectors ask ya for help in exchange for a share of thar findin's?" Lucky asked Sam.

"Grubstake 'em? Git offers most every day. On occasion, I've given away some tools, but no one's ever come back...unless thar passin' by on thar way home."

Before Lucky left, a man approached Sam and asked for a loan on some equipment that he needed to work his mine. When Sam refused to back the miner, Lucky pulled the man aside and arranged a deal. The man's hard-luck story reminded him of many he had heard while he was prospecting.

"Yar throwin' yar money away," Sam said after the man left.

"Maybe I won't git anythin' in return, but it makes me feel good, helpin' someone out. I saw tha ugly side of minin'. Sometimes, all ya need is a break. Had some of my own 'long tha way."

Sam exhaled. "It's yar gamblin' nature."

Sally and Lily walked up and heard the end of their conversation.

"It's my brother-in-law's kindheartedness. That's why he does such things."

"Maybe it's a way ta quench tha gold fever that's still in him," Lily countered.

"Lily, are you defendin' 'im? Yar OK for 'im ta spend yar money this way?" Sam asked.

"As long as it doesn't become an obsession. I kinda understand." Lily smiled at her husband.

"It was only some extra money that we could spare," Lucky assured everyone.

His brother was free to manage his money as he saw fit. It's none of my business, Sam realized. He deflected the conservation. "I read 'bout 'em goin' after gold in tha Black Hills. Thar stakin' claims, even though tha government hasn't officially opened up tha land."

"Yeah. Saw tha story in tha *Globe*. It'll mean trouble for Kimimela an' her people," Lucky confirmed.

"Ya still have tha box with tha gold piece?" Sally asked Lucky.

"It's safely stored away. I carry tha ornament with me. My *lucky charm*."

"Ya already got enough of that," Sam joked. "Lily, did he tell ya tha story?"

"Before we were married. Put it 'round my neck. Said he was a miner stakin' his claim." Lily remembered the day he gave her the trinket. "He wanted me ta keep it, but it's so valuable, I feared others would wanna do some claim jumpin' of their own, so I gave it back."

Sam laughed. "It's an impressive nugget."

"I told him ta keep it someplace safe. He gave me his Double Eagle instead."

"Since I had two good luck charms, I wanted her ta have one of 'em ta carry."

A few days later, Sam was approached by a miner who was looking for Lucky. He sent the desperate man on his way.

Sam berated his brother later that day. "Tha word's out. You'll be hounded by all tha grifters."

"Don't worry, big brother, I'll handle 'em. I got a way of sizin' 'em up."

"Reckon ya can," Sam submitted. "Looks like yar in tha business of grubstakin'."

"Got any wood for makin' a bassinet?" Lucky asked his brother after they had settled his charity business.

"Yar startin' yar family! I'm ta be an *uncle*?" Sam found a box of cigars under the counter and lit up two.

"Yep. Lily told me last night." Lucky took a deep puff and exhaled. "Gonna be a boy."

"An' if'n it's a Melanie?"

"Won't be."

Before long, young Harry was born. They named him after Lily's father, hoping that he would soften and accept the union. Lily had written to tell of their marriage, but she had posted the letter from Denver when they were on a shopping spree. The vigilantes were still active, so they continued to keep their whereabouts a secret.

"I want tha family ta know 'bout little Harry," Lily informed Lucky one day.

"Why don't ya try communicatin' with Rose?"

"Yeah. She always liked ya. I will try ta git a note ta her. I won't give out whar we're livin', but I do wanta have a way of hearin' back."

"I know just tha right person ta deliver yar message an' bring one back. Let me know when ya git something scribbled out, an' I'll make sure she gits it."

CHAPTER 44

ose missed her younger sister. Though never confirmed, she suspected that Lily had left with Lucky. Her family refused to talk about Lily's disappearance, and since Violet, the oldest sister, had married and moved to the Kansas Territory, she had no one in whom to confide her suspicions. When it was obvious that Lily was gone for good, Rose asked to fill her sister's position at the diner, and she was given the job. She had been serving meals for over a year when a stranger entered the eatery and asked after her.

"Yar name Rose?" the man inquired when she approached his table. He saw the strong resemblance between the two siblings.

Since the man looked like another two-bit miner, Rose held back. "Why're ya askin'?"

"Heard that a young gal by that name worked here."

"Why would that be of interest ta ya?"

"Know a friend of hers who told me if'n I was ta come this way ta look her up."

"Who would *that friend* be?"

"Her sister."

"Which one?"

"Lily," the man whispered.

Rose was so delighted she let her guard down. "Oh! You know Lily? Please. Tell me 'bout her. Is she well?"

"Reckon ya be *Rose* then." He handed her the note. "Told if'n ya wanta reply, I was ta carry it back."

"Yes! Ya wantin' ta order somethin'? It's on me!"

"Yar special will do me fine."

"I'll git it for ya. Afore yar ready ta go, I'll have a letter for ya ta take back."

The courier was a miner that Lucky had agreed to grubstake. He returned with Rose's response. Lily instantly broke the seal and read the words aloud.

Lily,

Ya don't know how happy I was ta git yar note. No one would tell me 'bout yar leavin', but ya hinted enough, so I figured that it had ta do with Lucky. Ya did as ya said an' married him, an' now ya have a sweet, young boy! When tha time's right, I'll tell Ma an' Pa, but thars still some unrest goin' on. 'Til then, I'll keep yar secret an' hope you'll keep correspondin'.

News from this end. Violet met an' married a farmer from Nebraska, an' they bought land tha railroad was sellin' out thar for a good price. They are expectin' thar first one soon.

I took over yar job at tha diner an' have been savin' for my trousseau. I've been seein' a young man from a family who came out ta ranch after ya left. His name is Charles, an' he's tha one "I'm gonna marry". Remember when ya said that ta me?

I have ta keep this short, as yar messenger found me at tha diner, an' I've gotta git back ta workin'. Please keep in touch.

Yar lovin' sister, Rose

Lucky watched the tears flow down Lily's cheeks as she read Rose's words. "Glad we could pass on our good news, an' we're gittin' ta hear hers."

"Didn't realize how much I missed her, all of 'em, 'til now. How long will tha silly feudin' go on? Tha die's been long cast, mistakes made. Isn't it time ta move on?"

Lucky held Lily tight. "Things will eventually calm down. Yar folks'll come 'round."

❦ ❦ ❦

Rose had married and moved out of her childhood home. She still lived near Granite, but she was no longer subject to the authority of her parents. After she had settled into her new role, she decided it was time to visit her sister.

"Thars still an undertone of distrust, but Ma has softened, so I told her 'bout little Harry. She was happy for ya an' wanted me ta tell ya so. I told her I was comin' ta see ya."

"I'm glad she knows. If only Pa..."

"I think tha worst is over for now. Give Pa a little more time."

"With tha new one comin', Lucky's talkin' of movin'."

"Ya got a cute cabin here, but I can see why."

"Too small for our growin' family."

"Have ya found a bigger place yet?"

"We're not stayin' here. Lucky wants ta settle somewhere 'long tha Arkansas River, farther south than Granite."

"Yar not worried 'bout tha—"

Lily cut Rose off. "Ya said so yarself...things are quietin' down. Now that Colorado's gained statehood, Lucky's convinced tha vigilantes'll

326

have ta become more law abidin'."

"What's he gonna do down thar?"

"He's takin' 'bout bein' a huntin' an' fishin' guide. Says enough are passin' through who'll want someone ta show 'em whar ta go. He'll supply meat for tha groceries when he's not on a trip. Says huntin' provided enough ta pay for his an' Sam's needs when they first came west."

"I'm so glad ta hear that yar movin' *closer* ta us! Then we can raise our young'uns together." Rose happily shared her news. "I just found out that I'm to be a mother, too!"

Lily got up and gave her sister a hug. She was equally excited. "I'm goin' ta be an *aunt*?"

"For tha *second* time. Violet's girl's got mine beat."

"How's she doin'?"

"Fine. Takin' a while for thar farm ta git goin'. Had trouble with tha drought, then locusts, but they've replanted, an' thar crops are lookin' good …at least, for now."

"Georgianna's growin' up an' I haven't seen her. Wish they weren't so far away. Maybe when we git settled, I'll write Violet a letter."

"Know she'll be glad ta hear from ya directly instead of through me."

❦❖❦❖❦

The South Arkansas River was running high when Lucky and Lily took a trip south to locate their new property. They found a piece of land by the waterway where the terrain was level and the channel was not too deep. The flatter ground caused the flow to slow and to form a small pool along the edge of the bank.

"What do ya think?" Lucky asked. "See that rock over there? It'll make a great fishin' spot."

Lily scanned the surrounding scenery. "Tha whole area's beautiful."

Lively cottonwoods lined the sides of the rippling waterway. As their leaves fluttered in the wind, the air filled with their fluffy, white seeds that fell to the ground and covered the surface like a fresh layer of snow. Lily turned to the northwest and saw the white-topped mountains that majestically rose until they met the cloudless, blue sky.

"A wonderful place to raise our family!" Lucky took their new daughter from Lily and rocked her in his arms. The baby laughed.

"Heather gives her approval." Harry walked up and gave Lily a flower. "Harry too."

"I'll go into town an' purchase tha deed."

"We can camp here 'til tha cabin's ready."

"Shouldn't take too long. Argent said he'd help, an' Sam's hopin' ta come after he finds someone ta watch tha store."

"Sally's been after him ta hire an assistant. Since tha children have grown, she's had her hands full. He'll have ta hire someone afore he comes."

"He's been talkin' of expandin' for a while. Business hasn't dropped since he opened up. Givin' up some of tha responsibilities will be hard for 'im, though."

"When he has more time ta spend with his family, he'll be glad ta have gotten tha help."

Sam was sad to hear that Lucky had found a place so quickly. "Gonna miss ya, little brother."

"Same here, big brother."

"We'll visit often," each promised the other before the loaded wagon took the younger Doyle and his family away.

Lucky had the ground ready, and the logs stacked when Argent arrived. They had finished the fireplace and chimney and had started to size the logs for the windows and the door when Sam got there.

When Sam met Argent again, it was under much better circumstances. "Howdy Argent. I'm glad Lucky ran into ya. Seems ya did live ta see another day."

Argent gave Sam a funny look.

"What Lucky said as we watched ya walk away in Independence."

"Thanks ta ya both, I got more'n *one*. I told yar brother, an' I wanna say ta ya...I'm *mighty appreciative* of yar help that day. Had a good run with tha prospectin' an' had taken ta tha drinkin' an' gamblin'. Lost all of my earnin's."

"Saw a lot of that goin' on. Yar lucky ta have seen tha light an' ta have made tha necessary changes," Sam acknowledged.

"You an' yar brother had a *lot* ta do with *that*."

Lily brought lemonade for the reunion. The brothers gave quick accounts of their homelife. Argent had waited for Sam's arrival to tell about the claims he took out in their names.

"Don't know if'n ya heard, thar keepin' it low, but sumun had tha black sand analyzed."

Lucky knew the answer. "Silver?"

"After ya compared tha black sand with tha Comstock mud, I had a *feelin'* myself. On a whim, I went an' took out sum claims. They may bring us a pretty penny. Tha discovery's been kinda hush-hush, but news like that tends ta leak out. Been gittin' a lot of interest an' each time thar offerin' more."

Sam had already heard the rumors. "Reckon we've an obligation ta you now...if'n it plays out like we're all thinkin'."

"Yar friendship's enough."

"Don't know if'n it's 'cause of tha fever that's still in ya...you with yar silver claims," Sam said, looking at Argent, "an' you with yar grubstakin'," he added, looking at Lucky, "but yar both very generous people."

Lucky remembered times his brother had gone out of his way to help others. "Yar just as bighearted. I've seen ya hand out food an' not charge."

"Only if'n thar in need."

"Same thing!" Lucky looked at the men sitting at the table. "I know ya both got other things ta be doin', so yar help *really* means a lot."

"Got nothin' goin' on that can't wait," Argent responded. "An' with tha three of us puttin' up tha cabin, it should be done in no time."

The men worked well together, so it didn't take long for them to get the home built. Once they finished laying the foundation, they started on the walls.

Lucky looked at their progress. "See why this is called a *house-raisin'*. Once ya start puttin' on tha logs, in no time, ya got yarself a place ta live."

Argent finished securing the last wall log. "If'n tha door an' window fittin's weren't so troublesum, we woulda started tha roof."

"No worries. I gotta git more tin, anyway."

To get extra space for a loft, Lucky decided

to use a vaulted rooftop that would be covered with tin. Before doing this step, they filled the wall spaces with a clay mortar mixed with ash.

"We'll be startin' on tha inside tomorrow," Lucky told Lily a few days later. "Whar do ya want our room ta go?"

"Over thar?" Lily pointed to the left corner of the house.

"Done. An' when we're finished, ya git ta fix tha inside anyway ya like."

It was a clear, sunny day. The cabin was almost finished, and the barn was standing. Lucky and Lily went outside to admire their new home. Sam and Argent walked up.

"Tha town's startin' ta boom again. Got a few friends watchin' tha claims, but I can't take tha chance of claim jumpers tryin' ta move in," Argent told the group.

"Hate ta leave ya, too, little brother. Though Mike's workin' out, I need ta be at tha store."

Lily gave each of the helpers a hug. "We're thankful for tha time ya both have given. It's been wonderful havin' ya this long."

"Can't thank ya enough for all yar help," Lucky added. "Tha cabin's 'bout done, an' we've made a lot of progress on tha barn. I'm able ta do tha rest."

The following morning, Lucky's helpers were mounted and ready to leave.

"Come an' settle yar claims, whenever. I'll work 'em 'til then," Argent said before he left.

"My turn ta visit next," Lucky yelled as Sam rode off.

Lily tried to console her husband. "I can see ya miss him already."

Lucky went to the barn and saw that the two men had finished Shooter's stall. I have space for two more, he thought as he scanned the open area. There would also be room for the buckboard and hay storage.

"Can ya go ta tha store?" Lily asked Lucky when he came in for lunch later that week. "We're in need of some staples."

"I'll go after I finish eatin'."

Lily handed him a list. "An' don't forget tha licorice...like ya did tha last time."

Now that he had a growing family, Lucky found himself going into town more often. Lily usually stayed with the children and left him to do the shopping.

"Be back afore tha sun sets," Lucky assured her as he went to saddle his horse.

When he got to the store, John, the owner, was in the backroom, stocking supplies that had just arrived.

"Be with ya in a minute," he called out.

Another man came into the shop while Lucky waited. They started conversing, so he thought he would promote his guiding business. "Ya new in town? If'n yar interested in huntin' or fishin' while yar in tha area, I'm a guide. Name's Lucky."

"Grady. Keep you in mind, but I'm headed up the way."

"Prospectin'?"

"Got some claims staked."

"Gold or silver?"

"Neither."

John came out from the back. "OK. What can I git for ya?"

Lucky handed him Lily's list. While John got supplies from the back, Lucky collected items that were on the shelves in the front. Before Lucky had his purchase loaded in the wagon, Grady came out with two bags full of food and supplies. They exchanged a few more words, then Grady left. Lucky was about to go on his way, then he remembered something he had forgotten. He went back inside the store, but the room was empty.

"John?"

The clerk returned to the front. "What'd ya forgit this time?"

"Licorice. Harry's favorite."

"I haven't seen Grady in a while," John said as he packaged the candy.

"Ya know 'im? Didn't know if'n he saw my postin' on yar wall, so I told 'im 'bout my guide business."

"Met 'im when I was in Colorado City. He was scoutin' for tha military. Lookin' for some mineral with an odd name...what did he call it? Oh yeah, beryllium, I think it was."

"Never heard of it. What's it used for?"

"Don't know. Tha project was dropped, but Grady put his name on some claims up on tha mountain anyway."

"Reckon he saw somethin'."

"Sure did. Precious *gemstones*, like topaz an' aquamarine. Some high-quality stuff. He came back an' staked out a good portion 'round tha Mount Antero area."

"I remember hearin' 'bout some conflict a miner was havin' 'round thar."

"He's tha one. Tha big mining conglomerates

were interested in buyin' 'im out. Grady told 'em he wasn't interested in sellin'. They sent some roughriders ta help 'im change his mind, but Grady held his own 'gainst 'em. More'n once, shots were fired. Grady never confessed ta any killin', but he did say that some who went up tha mountain never came back down."

"You mean—" Lucky didn't have to finish his thought. He figured the man had done more than scare some of the people away. They never returned for a reason.

"Howdy, gentlemen," John said as some men came into the store. A couple of others followed them. Lucky saw a familiar face and went to greet the man while the remaining customers browsed the shelves. The day was going to be a busy one for the shopkeeper.

❦◆❦◆❦

Lucky had returned from another shopping spree. Lily helped him with the groceries. "Tha town's name's changed."

"Oh yeah. What's it ta be called now?"

"Poncho Springs. After tha hot springs that Kit Carson liked so much."

"Should we stop usin' South Arkansas on our letters, then?"

"Reckon tha post office will take 'em both for a while." (changed to Poncha Springs in 1924)

"Did ya hear anything more 'bout tha new general store?"

"Should open soon. Towns growin' now that it's been plotted. Ran into an old acquaintance. A man named Creede. I met 'im years ago on tha stage. His horse had gone lame, so he got a ride 'til we got ta tha next stop. Was a scout for

334

tha army back then...now he's prospectin'."

"Let me guess; yar gonna grubstake him?"

"Maybe. He looks like he could use some help. I'm ta meet with 'im later. Talked with a couple of boys who also came into tha store. Wanna show me thar diggin's. They're green, but reckon I may go up tha mountain an' see what they got. Sounds like it's located in that area I've been meanin' ta scout, anyway," he said to justify the trip.

Lucky got up early the next morning and helped Lily with breakfast. Once Harry and Heather finished eating, he gave each a big kiss, then went out to saddle his horse. He came back to the cabin to give Lily a goodbye kiss.

"Should be back by supper."

CHAPTER 45

A group of ponderosa pines surrounded a small wooden cabin. It was the only structure around for miles. The A-frame roof was covered with freshly fallen snow. There was a lone window to let in the light. The wood supporting the porch floor was loose and had cracked in places. Steps led down to a creek that flowed into a nearby river. The place didn't look like much, but it did provide an escape from the harsh, cold environment.

Large cliffs towered to the west, blocking the late afternoon sun. The ensuing shadow they cast created a bleak and eerie loneliness. A man was panning in the creek below the steps. He threw out the contents, then knelt down to refill his pan. Up the hill, another prospector, who was working an open-pit mine, swung his pick a few more times, then gave up. He dropped his tool and headed down. He met up with his partner.

"Gittin' cold, now tha sun's gone. Goin' in. Ya havin' any luck?"

"Nah. Reckon it's why tha cabin's deserted. Thars no gold here."

"Musta been somethin' once...ta have built tha structure."

"Probably a shelter, ta keep 'em protected durin' tha winter."

"Thars that pit inside. Reckon they worked it 'til tha ground froze."

"Tha cabin did seem ta be a mirage after all tha work it took ta git up an' over tha pass. Thought we'd found somethin'."

"Uh-huh, but when Mister Reality crept in, he blew smoke in our faces."

"Time ta move on?"

There was a light dusting of snow on the ground when the two men left the following morning. The precipitation had stopped, but the clouds kept the sun's rays at bay. It was a gloomy start to the day. They followed the river, randomly stopping to pan the waterway. Their efforts were futile, and each disappointment caused them to become more and more cross. By the time they reached Poncho Springs, they had decided to go their separate ways.

"Headin' east," the man informed his partner. He continued down the road.

The other prospector stopped at the general store. He was hungry, though he couldn't afford more than a strip of jerky. He was browsing the stocked shelves when he noticed a posting on the wall.

Lucky Doyle's Hunting and Fishing
Guide Service. Ask at counter.

After the man read the name, he forgot about his hunger. He waited for a young lady buying cloth to leave, then he approached the counter.

"Interested in findin' tha fishin' guide."

"His house's by tha river, 'bout a mile down tha way."

"Much obliged." The miner left with a new

sense of purpose. "Now, I've tha upper hand," Janks spat. His antagonism toward Lucky had resurfaced, and he started to think of ways to get even with his old adversary.

Lily responded to his knock on the door. "Pardon me. I saw a notice at tha store. I'm lookin' for tha huntin' guide."

"Sorry, but he's out."

"Someplace I can catch up with 'im?"

"He's with some miners on tha mountain." A toddler's cry caught Lily's attention. "I must go an' see what tha trouble is." Lily closed the door.

"So, ya got yarself a family." Janks sneered, thinking how lonely his life had been. Musta just missed crossin' yar path, he thought.

❦ ❦ ❦

Lucky met the young prospectors in town before they headed up the mountain. It took most of the morning to reach the claim. They followed the main road for quite a ways, then took a right into the thick forest and headed up a steep incline. The boys had dug into the side of a rocky slope. When they reached the entrance, it looked more like a cave.

"Usin' picks is slow. We need ta blast ta git deeper," Hugh, the older boy, explained.

"Ya can see tha color." Gene, the other miner, lit a lamp and held it inside the cavity.

"Can't see anythin'. Can ya cut a sample?"

Hugh went inside with a pick and broke off a piece of rock. He brought it outside and handed it to Lucky.

Lucky examined the specimen. "It's pyrite. Called fool's gold."

"Ya sure?" Gene asked.

"*Sorry boys*. Why tha nickname. It can look like gold, but it's not...has no value." Lucky saw their defeated expressions. "Don't feel bad. When I started out, I was fooled by it too. An easy mistake ta make 'til ya git a trained eye."

"What should we *do*?" Hugh sounded lost.

Lucky could see his disappointment. "Ya can stay an' dig deeper, or ya can move on. If'n it was me, I'd do tha *latter*."

"Reckon it don't make sense ta keep diggin'." The young miners gathered up their equipment and prepared to leave.

"I'm gonna look 'round an' see if'n this area is suitable for my guidin' service. I'm thinkin' I might bring clients up here ta hunt." Lucky took off to inspect the hillside.

Janks spotted the dejected miners coming down the mountain. He just knew they had been with Lucky. He rode up and started a casual conversation. "Howdy boys. Ya look like ya lost yar best friend. Anythin' I can do?"

Hugh was too despondent to converse with the stranger, so Gene did the talking. "Not 'less ya have a gold mine ta share."

"Ya sound defeated."

"Hopin' ta have our claim grubstaked, but tha gold turned out ta be that fool's stuff."

"How do ya know?"

"Reckon tha man knew what he was talkin' 'bout."

"Wouldn't be a man named *Doyle*, would it? Is he still up thar?"

"Ya *know* 'im? Would he be *certain*?"

"Depends. Ya want me ta see? Couldn't hurt

ta have a second opinion."

Hugh felt hopeful again. "Would ya, mister? Make us feel better if'n we know'd fer sure."

"Take me ta yar mine. I'll tell ya what ya got."

When they reached the dig, Hugh picked up the sample. "Here."

"Yep. Yar outta luck. It's pyrite, all right."

The boys left their mine for a second and last time that day. Janks started out with them, then parted when they turned to head west. As soon as they were out of sight, he went back to the mine. He knew Lucky was up there, and he intended to find him.

Lucky had been wandering for about an hour, then he decided to head back. The area had potential, but there were steep places that made the traverse tricky. The view from the ridgetop revealed some impressive lakes and ponds lying far below. He thought that they were worth checking out further, but at another time. He was thinking of his family and was ready to go home, so he retraced his steps to avoid the steep terrain. As he passed by the mine, he decided to stop and eat the food Lily had prepared. The cavity would offer protection from the wind, he thought. He had just bitten into an apple when he heard trotting hooves. He got up and stood outside the opening. When he saw the rider, he instantly regretted leaving his rifle with Shooter.

"You!"

"We meet again." Janks drew his gun and pointed it at Lucky. He saw Lucky turn to look at his horse. "Wouldn't try anythin'. I'm eager ta use this. I happened upon yar postin'. Yar wife led me yar way," Janks taunted.

"You hurt my family...I'll hunt ya down."

"Maybe I'll stop by an' visit with 'em...after I'm finished with ya," Janks threatened.

Lucky knew he was at a disadvantage. When Janks dismounted, he took advantage of the distraction and picked up the large rock sample that was lying at his foot. He threw it at Janks and ran toward Shooter. He grabbed the rifle and got a shot off. Janks was just as quick. He fired, and the second bullet hit. Lucky fell to the ground. The slug cut through his stomach. He put his hand over the wound in hopes of stopping the flow of blood, but the red that oozed between his fingers showed the extent of his injury.

"Told ya I was anxious ta git a shot off," Janks bragged before realizing that he had been hit too. He still held his gun and kept it pointed at Lucky.

"Go ahead an' finish me off. Ya been waitin' ta git yar revenge, though I never did nothin' but try ta stop yar meanness."

"You were always thar ta thwart my plans." Janks grabbed his shoulder and sat down in pain.

"Yar so-called *plans* were ta harm others," Lucky was saying when a strange weakness overtook him. "Ya placed yar guilt onto me... instead of acceptin' that it's *on you*...yar tha one ta blame..." Lucky struggled to get the words out. He faltered and then passed out.

Janks approached the body. "Ya dead? Like ya, ta git in tha last word." He noticed that Lucky was still breathing. He looked around to make sure they were alone. Janks grabbed Lucky's wrists and dragged him into the cave. "Leave ya ta bleed out in here." As he stared at Lucky's inert body, he noticed the glow of his wedding band. "Maybe yar wife'll want ta see this." He pocketed the ring.

Janks left the mine feeling a sense of loss. His hate had been his guiding force. Without that, he felt empty, and the void made him feel even worse than the burden brought on by his desire for revenge. "Yar not gonna win over me." Janks knew that Lucky's last words had hit their mark. He started to mount his horse, then stopped as the loathing took over. His nature, or maybe it was his instinct to blame, had overwhelmed him once again. "Knowin' yar luck, you'll crawl back out an' haunt me yet."

Janks went to the discarded debris pile that the boys had created when they cleared out their mine. He got the largest rocks and stacked them in front of the cavity until they formed a barrier that covered the entrance. His obsession would not allow him to let it end there. In his stuporous state, he continued to close up the entrance while ignoring the cry of his wounded shoulder. He kept at it, lifting and filling, until there was no space left between the rocks. Janks wasn't finished yet. He dug up the gravelly sand and added it to an old bucket that still had water inside. The muddy mixture drizzled down the stones and oozed into the last of the open pores.

"That should seal yar fate!" he exclaimed before realizing the toll the work had taken on his own injury.

He had been bleeding, and his shirt had turned a sticky red. With the lifting of each stone, blood was pumped from his wound. He didn't feel the pain or notice that his blood pressure was dropping, but now that he had stopped, he began to feel tired and nauseous, early signs of hemorrhagic shock. By the time Janks was ready to ride, he was getting too weak to move. After a drunken-like struggle, he mounted his horse. As he rode, his organs, without the life-sustaining nutrients provided by his blood, struggled to perform their duties. They eventually gave up, and he died before he got off the mountain. His horse threw him and wandered off. Janks's remains, like the other animals before him, became fodder for the forest. A destitute prospector, who had been out scouring the hillside without success, was thrilled to take the horse that had suddenly appeared out of the trees.

Shooter made it back to the cabin. After weeks of inquiry, Lily had to accept that the worst had happened. She was feeling a little melancholy one evening and went out to gaze at the night sky. Argent had just told her about the money they had made on their silver claims.

"Just when ya struck it big. Reckon yar luck finally ran out," Lily cried.

As she stared up at the stars, she had this overwhelming sense that Lucky was gone, so she gave up even the faintest hope of his ever coming back.

PART FIVE

Revelations

2024

CHAPTER 46

April was overdue. At first, Lacy thought that her daughter was held up in traffic, as the snow-covered highway out from the ski area could be bumper-to-bumper. But when three o'clock rolled around, and she had not heard from April, she knew something was wrong. She called the ski area.

"April would have called," Lacy explained to her friend, Carol, the Executive Assistant who had answered the call.

"Hold on," Carol said after her attempts to calm Lacy had failed. "BL, I have Lacy on the line. April came to ski and was supposed to be back hours ago. She's worried that something has happened." BL was the VP of Guest Services and would be involved if there was trouble at the resort.

"Nothing has been reported, but I'll definitely look into it."

Randy, the resort's General Manager, came out of his office. "April's a good skier. If she's missing, then we need to follow up."

BL agreed. "I'll radio Ski Patrol."

Dan, the VP of Marketing, had also heard the conversation. "I'll get her license plate number and pass it on to Base Area Services. Let's see if we can find her car."

Cara, VP of Sales and Marketing, and Bryce,

her husband who worked in Food and Beverage, joined in. "Bryce might be able to help."

"Mark came to get food from Gunbarrel. He mentioned seeing her on his way in today."

"I'll see if Mark can narrow down the car's location." Cara went into the ticket hub.

"I met her in the parking lot. I was just about to climb the steps. She could have come up from anywhere in the lower lot," Mark remembered.

"Lower lot," Cara relayed.

"Great. I'll get on it." Dan headed back into his office.

Randy looked at Carol. He knew that Lacy was anxiously awaiting their response. "Tell Lacy we'll check it out and call her back. I don't want to keep her waiting on the line."

"Lacy? Let us see what we can do here. We'll give you a call as soon as we know anything."

"Thanks so much. Cory will be home soon. If I haven't heard from you, we'll be heading up."

Most of the employees at the resort knew the Doyles. They had a history with Monarch. Cory's granddad had pushed to get the ski area established. Since then, their family has been involved in one capacity or another.

Scott, VP of Operations, came through the door that led to the administrative offices. He saw the group that had formed around Carol's desk. "Looks like an impromptu meeting. Have I missed anything?"

"We may have a situation," Randy replied.

"Lacy called. April came up here today. She was expected back hours ago," Carol explained.

"April Doyle? She's a competent skier. Maybe she went up to the Crest," Scott suggested.

Dan came out with some news. "They found it. Car's still here."

"She could've left with a friend, but we need to investigate anyway." BL updated Ski Patrol.

"Why don't we start asking around? She's well-known. Maybe we can retrace her day," Randy suggested. "Try to keep the questioning low-keyed. We don't want to sound any alarms just yet."

"I'll get with the lifties," Scott volunteered. "Surely one of them saw her."

Carol hung up the phone. "The Doyles are on their way. Let's hope April is located before they arrive."

The ski patrol followed standard search and rescue procedures. The resort was divided into grids, and teams were assigned to check each section until the whole mountain was covered. After a preliminary check, April had yet to be found. The heavy snow had subsided but had not stopped, and the wind was still blowing. Nightfall was not far away.

Though the managers were discreet, word of April's disappearance spread fast.

"Jules and I saw her from the lift. She was on Upper Hall's Alley," Kelly told Jeremy, the Senior Director of Sales and Ticketing, when he asked his employees at Reservations if they had seen April.

"What time?"

"During our ride break, between eleven and eleven thirty," Kelly estimated.

Jeremy relayed this information to the ski patrol. Billy responded to the call.

"Pedro, Tom. This is Billy. Head to Breezeway.

Two employees reported seeing her on Upper Hall's Alley during the late morning hours."

"Ten-Four. Affirmative," they each replied. They had just finished searching Gunbarrel and other runs accessed by the Garfield Lift on the other side of the mountain. There was no sign of April.

The snow continued to fall. When the sun moved behind the hills, it cast its ominous shadow over the frosty slopes, causing the temperature to drop. The wind lessened, but the white powder continued to fall and cover the ground. If someone had come by earlier, April's skis would have been a beacon. Now that they were coated in white, they blended into the background.

The information search had given the staff a timeline of April's whereabouts since she had entered the resort. Pat remembered seeing her pull into the parking lot. Mark's information confirmed where her car was parked. Matt, Shayna, and Sydney had seen her at Java Stop, then she later talked with Jack by the fireplace in the lodge. Tristen verified that she had skied runs off the Garfield Lift. Kelly and Jules, the two Monarch Experience Specialists, had called out to April from the Breezeway lift. Skyler, another liftie, and Julianna, who worked at Guest Services, were snowboarding on their ride break. They saw her on Geno Meadows. Though these reports had helped to establish her whereabouts, April was still missing.

The shuttles that took the skiers and the snowboarders back to their cars in the Paradise Parking Lot had made their final run of the day.

They were loading employees who were headed back to Salida and Buena Vista. Before it was time to leave, Jeremy stepped into the BV bus. After he sat down, he heard Banny and Teresa talking about a missing skier.

"You know April, don't you?" Banny asked.

"April?" the liftie questioned.

"April Doyle?" Teresa clarified.

"I saw her earlier today. Why do you ask?"

"She's disappeared," Banny relayed.

"She was headed to Mirkwood when I last spoke with her," Jeremy recalled.

"Did you talk to Scott?" Teresa asked. "He was questioning anyone who saw her."

"No. I got off early and skinned the rest of the day. I didn't know." Jeremy immediately went to the front of the shuttle.

"Don't worry. I won't leave you," Don, the shuttle driver, assured him. He opened the door. "Hope your information helps."

Jeremy rushed to the administrative offices and found Scott in the hallway. "I just found out about April. "I saw her earlier at Breezeway. She said she was headed to Mirkwood."

"When did you see her?"

"Probably around twelve o'clock. It was just before I got off for the day. Sorry I didn't tell you earlier, but I've been skinning."

"Thanks for letting us know. You may have been the last to see her." Scott got on his radio and passed on the information.

"Blythe and I are headed up there now," Billy reported when he heard the news.

He dismounted when they reached the ridge and followed the coordinates he was given to search. The basin's 130 acres, Billy thought as he skied down the slope looking for signs of April's passage. He headed toward a stand of evergreens, found an open passageway, and weaved through the pines. When he saw a group of newly downed trees, he decided to investigate. Hope she's not under these, he thought as he worked his way over. When he reached the disarray, he saw a strange configuration—some roots were perfectly cut protrusions. He was questioning this illusion when he realized that they were skis. As he reached to wipe the snow off, he saw what he thought was a dark shadow. He walked around the root system and peered into the cavity. He caught his breath.

"I found her!" Billy reported. He wanted to add that it didn't look good, but he kept this thought to himself. He knew that many were listening, including April's parents, who were at the lodge, anxiously awaiting news. "She fell into...a...it looks like a *cave*. I'm on my way down now." He relayed his coordinates.

CHAPTER 47

"**Wh**...*whoa!*" Billy gasped when he saw April up close. She had landed on top of a pile of bones—a skeleton. He saw the hand resting on her hip. "*That's* interesting."

After a quick evaluation of April's condition, Billy transmitted his preliminary report. "I'm with April. She's unconscious but breathing... has a strong pulse. You *may* want to get the sheriff involved, though."

"*What?*" The relief Randy felt collapsed after Billy's last statement.

"The cave...you have to see! This must be an old gold digging, but it's also a *tomb*. Believe it or not, there's a *corpse* here. An old one. She's actually lying on top of a *skeleton*."

This revelation left everyone speechless.

Billy's first concern was April, so he carefully checked her over. Since she was still breathing, he checked for signs of broken bones. He didn't want to move her in case she had trauma to her neck or back. A cut on her head had stopped bleeding, but he cleaned it up and applied a bandage. She would need to be checked after they got her out, he knew.

"She's got a nasty cut, but it's not bleeding, and her breathing is normal. I don't see any signs of broken bones or other trauma," Billy relayed after he finished his examination.

Pedro got on the radio after hearing Billy's report. "I'm about there. Tom and Blythe went down to bring up a stretcher."

"Roger," Billy replied.

Billy decided to explore the inside of the cavity. I should leave things untouched in case this becomes a crime scene, he thought. Since it didn't interfere with his examination, he left the skeleton's hand in place. He took several pictures of April lying on the bones with his cell phone, then he looked around the cave. He saw a few wood pieces embedded in the soil. His phone's light reflected off the rock.

"Something's shiny, but I don't think it's gold. You had to be a prospector. That's probably why you're here. So how did you die?" He heard a motor. Pedro had arrived. When he saw him peering down, Billy called out a warning. "Be prepared—" He didn't have to say more. Pedro's reaction was the same as his. "This is how I found her."

Pedro took a few pictures, then he worked his way down. Maybe it was the flash or just the right time, but April opened her eyes.

"Uhh...what...?" she stuttered, then slowly sat up. The skeleton's hand fell flat.

"Hello. You may want to sit for a moment," she heard. "You hit your head."

Once her brain refocused and she was able to think clearly, April started to remember. "The blizzard...I lost my way. How did I get here?" The musty smell seemed familiar. She took in the scenery around her. "The *bones*!" She was too stunned to move.

"You fell on top of them. The skeleton's old

and looks like one you'd see in your science class. Probably a prospector from the gold era," Billy speculated. "We're in an old miner's dig, I think. The remains have been *hiding here* all these years...until the tree uprooted."

April carefully rose and sat away from the skeletal remains.

"We'll need to make it easier for you to climb out," Pedro realized. "Let me see if I can make a ladder out of some of the roots."

"Are you feeling up to drinking or eating something?" Billy saw that April's color was coming back.

"I might. Maybe." April took the offered drink and energy bar.

"Are you feeling any pain?" Billy inquired.

"Just my head. My back feels a little sore, but I think I can move OK. Nothing else feels out of place."

Pedro finished making his makeshift steps. "Sit for a moment and see how you do. Then, when you're ready, we'll get you out of here."

"Your parents are waiting at the lodge," Billy told her. "They'll be relieved to see you."

"Ditto that. I think I'm ready to get out now." April started to stand.

"Wait. Let us help." Pedro grabbed under her arm while Billy provided support on her other side. When April was on her feet, they stayed as spotters in case she needed assistance. "Are you still feeling OK? Can you walk?" Pedro asked.

"Yes. I'm good, *really*."

Billy went up first and made sure the steps were stable. When he gave the OK, Pedro had April climb up the stairway. He followed in case she stumbled. When April grabbed Billy's hand for the final step out, she marveled at the sight. The skies had cleared. The white snow gleamed in the light of the moon. After they went a short distance through the trees, they reached the snowmobile. Pedro got April seated.

Tom and Blythe arrived with the stretcher.

"Won't need that," Pedro affirmed.

"Great! How're you doing, April?" Tom asked.

"Fine, thanks. Sorry to put everyone to so much trouble. I'm rather embarrassed."

"You've no need to be. It wasn't your fault," Blythe assured her.

"Pedro. We'll follow you down," Tom said as they prepared to leave. "Billy. BL's coming to get you."

"Are you ready?" Pedro asked April. When she nodded, Pedro started the engine. The full moon's light illuminated the snowy world around them. "A moonlight traverse."

April turned to look back. She saw bright colors through the snow. "Look! It's Chomi, the gnome. Someone's into the Game of Gnar! Have you heard of it? You put mints in the gnome's mouth for points."

"Does that bring you good luck?"

"Not sure. If it did, I wish I'd seen it earlier."

The white slope showed the way down. Two snowmobiles were coming their way. Randy, Scott, and BL were heading up the hill. Once they confirmed that April was doing well, they went to inspect the mine. Billy showed them the steps that Pedro had made.

"Follow me down. It's quite roomy inside."

"I don't see anything that shows this mine

was productive," Randy observed.

"No one found gold or silver in the ski area," Scott emphasized.

BL stared at the skeleton. It seemed to be looking back at him. "We know that prospectors were up here. They left piles of old cans, but I've never seen any evidence of digs, except for some depressions."

"We better not touch or disturb anything," Randy advised. "Leave it for forensics."

"Could this be a prehistoric cave?" BL asked. "The Game Drive is just over the rise."

"That's for the experts to figure out," Randy concluded.

"Wonder what happened to the...I want to say, *old guy*?" Scott said what all were thinking.

"He's certainly one *now*," BL joked.

"No sign of a bullet hole to the head," Billy informed them.

"He may have been hit by a falling rock," Randy speculated. "*Caved in* by his own *cave*," he grinned.

Scott imitated the talk on the old western shows that he had watched as a boy. "Reckon tha *down'n* out *digger* had *double trouble*."

They all laughed, more from the relief that the search and rescue had not turned into a recovery, at least not for April, than from their silly humor.

CHAPTER 48

When Cory and Lacy arrived at the ski resort, April had yet to be found. Carol took them to the Sidewinder Saloon to await news. Cara and Bryce joined them. Dan came after getting an update from Ski Patrol. Kristin, the Head Bartender, served them a round of drinks. By the time Todd, the Head Chef, had brought out a plate of appetizers, April had been located. Once the tense atmosphere had lifted, it was only natural to reminisce and talk about the old days.

"Hard to believe so much time has passed since we were the young guns on the slopes," Dan started. "I remember when we first met."

Lacy laughed. "I was showing off and lost control on Gunbarrel."

"When Cory pulled you out of the creek at the bottom, I saw how you two connected."

"Love at *first sight*," Lacy confessed.

"You played the damsel-in-distress act *really* well." The memory made Cory smile.

"The following year, the culvert was put in place to channel the water. If you had met later, the creek wouldn't have been there to act as a catalyst," Dan teased.

"We were ski instructors after that. Maybe something else would have brought us together." Lacy speculated. "Luckily, a moot point."

"Those were fun times," Cory admitted. "We did help a lot of people learn how to ski, too."

"There were many times when your mom had to keep us in line," Dan reminded Cory.

"She was the one who inspired my passion for the sport. She loved to ski. Dad told stories about how he'd be using an old snow packer that was nothing more than a bicycle tire with wood slabs to pack the snow down, and Mom would come racing by and try to cover him with snow."

"That old equipment was time-consuming, but it got the job done," Dan laughed. "We sure have come a long way since those days."

"Took a while. When the ski area first opened in '39, there was a lot of enthusiasm. Granddad was one of those who pushed to get it going. He helped to clear the trail for Gunbarrel and Snowflake. After they opened, the ski area had a couple of good seasons, then World War II came along. Like others in the club, Granddad left to serve. When they came back, the place had been neglected. They sought funding for improvements, but the city, which owned the ski area at the time, saw it as an unwanted liability." Cory recalled.

"The original agreement was for the city—Salida—to apply for the permit, and the ski club would handle the rest. The town didn't take much of an interest while the members were gone," Dan informed the group.

"Good thing Berry wanted to take on the responsibilities and took them up on their offer to buy them out for a whopping $100," Cara added. She had read about the history of the resort and knew some of the facts.

"Seems he got a good deal until you look at what he had to invest to bring things up to par," Dan reminded everyone.

"He got the resort moving...built a better lodge, improved the lifts, and opened more runs." Cory remembered hearing his dad tell the stories. "By the time Bevington took over in '68, Monarch was becoming popular and was ready to grow even more. And with each change of ownership, the resort continued to grow. Now, the experience is a far cry from what the club members who started it all had to deal with."

"As different as the ski equipment they used back then. Remember those long, wooden skis? Imagine trying to turn or veer away from a tree in those *clunkers*." Dan laughed. "No wonder the Salida Winter Sports Club fought so hard to get a resort started."

Lacy had heard many of the ski club stories. "It's hard to believe the group took a train up to Marshall Pass and skied five miles through the forest to that railroad stop."

"The Shavano Switch. Once they got there, they'd wait in a club car until the train returned to Salida," Cory recalled. "Must have been a long day."

Cara shrugged. "Seems crazy to us now."

"There were a lot of takers until the train stopped running." Dan knew he would have been one of them, too.

"The D&RGW...the Denver & Rio Grande Western." Bryce had an interest in the railroads that had once served the area.

"When the new highway was constructed over Monarch Pass—" Dan started.

Cory cut in. "To replace the *Old* Monarch Pass road."

"Which had replaced the *Old Old* Monarch Pass road," Lacy comically added.

Dan jumped in so he could finish what he was going to say before the joking about the road names had started. "They found a new place to recreate."

"Just think," Cara reflected, "when the ski area opened, there was only the one run. Now there are over fifty...and more are yet to come."

"What's the latest on the expansion?" Cory asked.

"We have all the permits. Hope to open by the 25-26 Season," Dan confirmed.

"I've heard a lot about Monarch's background from Cara, but hearing your stories has really brought the history to light," Bryce was saying when the rescue team came into the room.

April's parents immediately stood, rushed to their daughter, and smothered her with hugs. After she had assured them that she was fine, they joined the others around the table. April told them about her resting spot. Pedro's pictures helped to show the incredible details. They all gasped when they saw how the skeletal hand had embraced April.

"We've checked the hillsides all around here ...multiple times. We've never seen signs of a dig this intense," Dan informed the group.

"Guess it was hidden by the rocks, and when the tree grew over it, it stayed well hidden," Cory noted. "After all, it was nearly 150 years ago."

"The hole left the tree more susceptible to falling," Pedro added. "The gusts out there were pretty intense."

"April was in the wrong place at the wrong time," Lacy confirmed.

"Or maybe she was *meant* to be there." Billy had just come back from the mine. The rest of the group was close behind. He looked at April and arched his eyebrows. "Seems you found a *friend*...I mean by the way the skeleton's hand was placed."

"It *was* rather odd." April didn't say more. She couldn't tell them that while she was out, she had dreamed of the dark abyss, and when she had finally reached the light, ready to face whatever lay beyond, she was awakened. It was the same dream, but this one made her feel that she was closer to finding its hidden truth. She was sure that somebody was trying to tell her something. Maybe the purpose of the dreams, she decided.

"Ready to go? We're stopping by the hospital, just as a precaution," Cory informed April.

"But I feel fine," April protested.

Randy backed her dad. "Wouldn't hurt to have a medical professional clear you."

"Guess I'm outvoted," April sighed, knowing they were probably right.

CHAPTER 49

"*It can't be!" April exclaimed. "Not in the middle of a whiteout." She took off her skis and slowly worked her way toward the exposed rocks. She still couldn't believe it. What secret are you trying to tell me? She was now more interested in her find than she was in getting out of the blizzard. Human? She touched the protrusion. While she held the bony hand, she felt like she was comforting an old friend. She was so mesmerized that she couldn't let go. It was as if it had power over her, and she wanted to find out why. She released the limb and started to scrape out the soil that held it in place. A warm, musty odor permeated the air. Is there a mine? Did it cave in, and the person tried to dig out? How long has he been here? Was he prospecting? Was it an accident, or worse, was he murdered? Her analytical mind kept asking questions. She couldn't wait to get back down and tell of her find. She put on her skis and prepared to leave.*

"April?" the nurse said to awaken her. "Time to take your vitals," she heard as she was lifted from her dream.

April came out of a deep sleep. She had to remember where she was. I'm in the hospital for observation, she recalled. "Huh? Oh. I just had the strangest dream."

The nurse checked the monitors. "I could tell. Your face was twitching."

April's mother came to visit her early that morning. "How are you feeling?"

"I *really* don't need to be here." April held up a fork full of mushy eggs. "Your breakfast would've tasted better."

"You had a nasty fall."

"I guess so. You know, I can't help thinking about the skeleton. How long do you think they will wait before they remove it?"

"Not long. I'm sure the area is secure, but the curious will probably want to go and see it. Word does get out."

April decided to open up to her mother. "I've had *strange* dreams related to what happened yesterday." She told her mom about the one she had that night. "I've had similar dreams...more than once...since I was a kid. Had one while I was in the cave, too."

"That's probably because you've heard us tell the tales about your Greats Granddad Lucky. Since we talked about him yesterday, I'm not surprised that it'd be fresh on your mind."

"How often did you talk about him when I was little?"

"Enough. We usually told his story when company came. They must have stuck with you, causing you to have those dreams. Yesterday's ordeal certainly didn't help."

"You're probably right. But what if..."

The nurse who woke April during the night came to relay good news. "You're free to leave anytime you want. You just need to sign some forms." She handed April the paperwork.

The first call April made when she got home was to Judy so she could explain why she had missed her birthday celebration.

"Gosh!" Judy exclaimed after April told her about the accident. "When your mom called to cancel, I was really concerned. She was pretty vague about why. I didn't stop worrying until she called back and told me that you were all right."

"Sorry they had to leave you hanging. There were other factors to consider."

"I'm glad everything turned out OK. That's the *main* thing."

"You know, while I was out, then again at the hospital, I had strange dreams." April decided to run her thoughts by her best friend to see her reaction. She told Judy about the dream she had had while she was in the cave and how it was similar to ones she had since she was a kid. Then she told of the mysterious hand reaching up through the rocks. Wait until you see how I landed. "Let me send you pictures that the ski patrol guys took."

Judy looked at the bony hand resting on April. "Strange! I don't know what to tell you. Do you think there's a *connection*?"

April shared her mother's interpretation.

"That makes sense."

"This last dream was different, though. It was as if the skeleton's hand was reaching out to me. As if it wanted, no *needed*, me."

"A sign?"

"To tell me something"

"Or, for you to find something?"

"What *if*?" April started. This time, she was

able to finish her thought. "What if it's some kind of *message*? Billy joked that I was meant to find *my friend* in the cave. Suppose *my friend* is trying to communicate with me because *my friend...*"

"Is your *Greats Granddad*," Judy finished for her.

"Yeah. I know it sounds crazy."

"But this is a pretty mysterious conundrum you seemed to have been drawn into, too."

"Should I suggest that I get a DNA test and see if there's a match? Somehow, I *just know* it's my ancestor. Would people think I'm being melodramatic?"

"Maybe, but what if you're *right*? Wouldn't that be worth it? Just knowing one way or the other?"

CHAPTER 50

"Quite the story!" Marshall, the sheriff of Chaffee County, affirmed when he heard about the unusual discovery at the ski resort.

"I know!" Randy agreed. "Not something we thought we'd be dealing with."

"There may be cultural implications, but let's not get ahead of ourselves. The bones need to be tested. Did you reach Perry?"

"Said the same thing. From what I saw, it's more likely a prospector, though."

The next day was quite eventful for the ski resort. Since Monarch was located on Forest Service property, they followed the guidelines that were set by the agency. Perry, the Salida District Ranger, and Ashley, the Salida Ranger District Archeologist, came up to document the find. Marshall rode up with the Chaffee County Coroner. They would inspect and remove the skeletal remains. Billy and Pedro drove the two teams to the site, then they helped to clear the snow and roots from around the mine's opening.

Pedro watched as Ashley and Perry carefully mapped and photographed the area above the cave. "What are you looking for? I don't see any obvious artifacts, like pottery, left behind."

"I'm looking for earthworks or changes in the level of the surrounding land. Unfortunately, there are too many trees to get a true picture.

If the terrain was better, I'd look to see if the soil was covering something below the surface," Ashley told him.

"We're also looking for soil marks, like color differences, that show if something unusual has changed the composition in some way," Perry added. "Of course, the uprooting of the tree has made this tricky to evaluate."

"Wouldn't the Forest Service have scoured this area before allowing the ski area to be developed?" Billy wondered.

"Yeah, but as you can see, new discoveries are always a possibility. Have you been to the Monarch Pass Game Drive?" Perry asked.

Billy had read the signs. "Yes. It was really clever, the way the prehistoric people herded the animals to their rock walls while they waited nearby."

"And killed them using only spears and their bows and arrows," Ashley emphasized. "So you can see why something that seems insignificant, like the uprooting of a tree, can open a new door and show us what wasn't so obvious before."

"If it's either an archeological find or just an old miner's dig, what will you look for inside the cave?" Pedro asked Perry.

"Any evidence that's been left behind. As was mentioned earlier, pottery. Or tools. Even jewelry or clothing that may have been preserved."

Billy couldn't resist adding, "Or *gold!*"

"We want to find and protect *any* artifact," Ashley pointed out. "We have acts in place to ensure that this happens. The Archaeological Resources Protection Act (ARPA) protects items that are over 100 years old, and the NHPA, the

National Historic Preservation Act, covers those that are over 50 years old. Each protects any valuable article that is found on our public lands."

Inside the mine, the coroner examined the skeleton. He, too, made notes and took pictures. Marshall helped him move the delicate body onto a stretcher. They wanted to keep the bones intact.

"Okay for us to come down?" Perry asked after they had finished their topside work.

"We're just about ready for the removal," the coroner relayed.

They carefully lifted the stretcher out of the pit and attached it to the snowmobile. Billy had the honor of driving it back to the lodge. From there, it was loaded into a van that had been fitted with a cot.

"We'll do a forensic analysis and get you the results ASAP," Marshall told Randy after the skeleton was secure. "Perry and Ashley will be down shortly. They were finishing up when I left. They found an old ledger that may give us some information. The pages were too fragile to attempt a reading there."

The rest of the crew took longer to return than Randy had anticipated. When he finally saw the snowmobiles coming down the hill, his curiosity was piqued.

"*Well,* what'd you find?" he asked the group when they dismounted.

"More than we expected. Seems the cavity was sealed enough to keep things dry. A few items were preserved," Perry answered.

"We almost missed some stuff." Pedro's face

revealed the importance of their find.

Ashley produced the brittle ledger, which had been placed in a clear plastic bag. "Looks like a journal. It may give us some information before the person passed. I'm pretty sure the writing on the cover is English. I didn't want to damage it, so I left it closed. There's a curator at the museum who's had experience working with old books. She should be able to open it without destroying the pages."

"We also found *this*!" Perry held up another plastic bag. It contained a large gold nugget.

"*Gold*?" Randy couldn't believe his eyes. "But this area—"

"*Jewelry*," Perry jumped in. He turned the bag around. The nugget had several colorful crystals and stones embedded in it.

"We found it where the skeleton had been lying. Almost missed it. It was covered by a layer of dirt. May have been the reason for the man's demise," Ashley speculated.

"If the guy was waylaid, his pockets would have been checked for anything of value," Randy noted. "So why wasn't it taken? Did you find any rings or other jewelry?"

"No. Marshall said the bones didn't have any adornments," Perry verified. "Even the teeth were clean."

"The soil was pretty loose, so we were able to explore the mine in detail. I'm confident we've uncovered everything that's important." Ashley held up the journal. "We'll wait and see what we learn from *this*, then proceed from there. In the meantime, try to keep the curious away from the opening."

"I'll have someone on watch until you give us the OK to cover it up," Randy assured them.

As everyone patiently awaited the results, the ski resort ran as usual. Billy, Pedro, Tom, and Blythe took turns watching the restricted area. On more than one occasion, they had to divert a curious guest.

April called Judy after she heard what was taken out of the mine. "They found a ledger. I can't wait to see what *that* says. It will answer a lot of questions. They also found a piece of jewelry. I'm sure it goes with the box that I was given on my birthday. I just know it's my Greats Granddad's lucky charm."

"Are they convinced it belongs to your family?"

"Dad's told the story so many times that others can verify it fits the description. And I went ahead and did the DNA test since I had already scheduled it."

"Hopefully you'll get all the answers soon."

"I'm sure the people at Monarch will be glad when this is over."

"They'll need to remove the trees that fell and secure the digging."

"I know that zipping through the trees is fun, but I think falling into a cave would not be a desirable way for any skier or boarder to end up," April laughed.

"You should know!"

The results from the DNA report came first. April was a match. "I knew it! I haven't had the dream since the night at the hospital. It's like this was all meant to happen."

Cory exhaled. "I don't know what to say. It's so unreal, but I'm glad we have answers."

Lacy agreed. "Lucky had an eventful life. It was only a matter of time before something caught up with him."

"Now we *finally* know. Fruition after years of long-standing speculations," Cory sighed.

"Perry said we should get results regarding the ledger later today. The pages were harder to separate than they thought," Lacy reported.

"Will we get to keep it now that we know who it belongs to?" April asked her dad.

"Probably, but I would like to donate it to the museum. It would make a great exhibit."

"I concur. What about the gold trinket?"

"Fits the description of the one we've been talking about," Lacy confirmed. "We know he called it his *lucky charm* and that he carried it with him."

"Not sure if we'll get it back. We'll have to wait until everything has been checked and cleared," Cory reminded them.

Lacy was impatient. She called the museum to get an update.

"We've yet to separate all the pages, but I can tell you what we've discovered so far. The ledger is a record of your ancestor's grubstaking and lists clients of his guiding business. There were names, dates, places, and the amounts he paid the prospectors or received as a guide," the curator informed her.

"Do any of the names stand out?"

"One. Nicholas Creede's name was entered with a date, nothing else. It was before Creede discovered the Monarch Mine. Your ancestor obviously talked with the prospector, but it's unclear if he actually backed him."

"I *knew* he had to have known the man!" Cory exclaimed when Lacy told him the news. "He was grubstaking miners at the time, and Creede would have been out this way."

"The last entry showed the names of two men. The money column showed $0, and the description could be the place where he was found. The date looks to be around the time he disappeared," Lacy recapped. "That's all we've got for now. There are a few more pages that need to be separated before we can make a final analysis."

"The two men may have killed him when he refused to help them out," Cory theorized.

"No good deed goes unpunished," April said with sarcasm. "After all these years, we now know the sad ending to Lucky's story."

EPILOGUE

There was one more chapter in Lucky's tale. The last pages chronicled his final words. The paper was bloodstained, and the writing was shaky, but the scribbled text was legible. He wrote as if scripting a letter to be mailed the next time he passed the post office.

My family,

Don't blame tha boys—they had gone. I stayed ta see if'n tha area would be good for huntin'. Stopped back at tha mine ta eat, an' thar was Janks, a man full of hate. He'd seen my postin' an' found me here. Tha man had it in for me since I caught him stealin'—when Sam an' I were lumberin'. Ran into him a time or two 'long tha way an' had ta deal with his lawlessness, but seems he managed ta escape tha jails. When he appeared at tha mine, thar was a shoot-out. Got hit in tha gut. Woke up in tha mine, only ta find that he'd sealed me in real good. Luckily, tha boys left matches an' candles.

Reckon my lucky charm'll have ta be real strong since I don't have Sam ta git me outta this one.

My love ta ya Lily, Harry, an' Heather, an' Sam an' yar family. I'm thinkin' of ya 'til my last breath.

I'll be yar's forever, Lucky Doyle

"His message in a bottle," April sighed after the letter was read.

"Seems that Janks fellow did us *one* favor," Cory noted. "He sealed the cave tight enough to preserve Lucky's last words."

"Do you think he would have been able to escape?" April asked.

"If he had, he probably wouldn't have made it back to town. Sounds like his wound was pretty bad," her dad speculated.

Lacy had questions of her own. "Why didn't they find a bullet in the cave? If that man, Janks, didn't take his lucky charm, what happened to his wedding ring?"

Cory could only theorize. "The bullet may have gone through him. He said he woke up in the mine. He could have been shot outside and dragged inside. And to answer your second question, I guess the gold piece was hidden, whereas the ring would be exposed and easy to take."

"Shame that Lily and Sam never got to read his last sentiments," April noted.

"I'm sure they knew what they would have been," Lacy assured her.

April was pleasantly surprised when she woke up the following week and remembered her dream. She was back in the all-consuming darkness, and she could smell the cave-like odor. This time, she made it to the light and saw beyond its brightness. There was a mine. The same one I fell into, she realized. A red-headed man had his arms around the woman sitting beside him. She could only see their backs. A small girl picked up and then dropped rocks, while a young boy, also red-headed, threw her discarded stones into the cavity of the mine. Eventually, the people gathered and then walked down the hill. The figures shrank as they moved farther away. Before they were out of sight, the man turned and waved.

April knew that this dream was to be her grand finale. The pieces of the puzzle were in place. Lucky's lucky charm was back in its box, and the mystery of his disappearance was solved. Now we know how your story really ended and that you are able to rest in peace.

"Goodbye, Greats Granddad."

It was another Monarch Monday, and April was meeting friends to go skiing. It was a perfect bluebird day.

"Who could ask for anything more?" she exclaimed aloud and headed for the slopes.

Author's Notes

The Wimmer story came from *California Gold Book: First Nugget: Its Discovery And Discoverers And Some Of The Results Proceeding Therefrom,* by W. W. Allen and R. B. Avery, Donohue & Henneberry, 1893.

In *The Silver Queen: The Prospector. Story Of The Life Of Nicholas C. Creede,* by Cy Warman, The Great Divide Publishing Company, 1894, p. 21, Warman writes of Creede, "...he was forced to fancy himself the "merry monarch of the hay-mow," or a shepherd guarding his father's flocks..."

In *Roughing It,* by Mark Twain, The Reader's Digest Association, Inc., 1994 (from the 1872 version), Chapter 28, pp. 127-130, Twain writes about his adventures while hunting for silver. On p. 130 he says "Moralizing, I observed, then, that "all that glitters is not gold." See summary and quote on p. 157.

About the Author

Pam Carothers grew up in South Carolina, but the lure of the Rocky Mountains kept her in the West. While working at the Monarch Ski Area, she decided to write a book about the "Old West," and the ski resort made a timely backdrop. She felt it was a challenge to use real people in a real place, and as it happened, like Mark Twain, she, too, discovered that "all that glitters is not gold." She enjoys skiing and feels she is not an "old dog" yet, as she is attempting to master snowboarding. Maybe this will be the year!